The Black Tower

The Eleven Episode Serial

David R. Beshears

"The Black Tower Serial"
the complete series

Greybeard Publishing
Washington State

ISBN: 978-0-9914327-6-9

The eleven episodes in this collection have been previously
published individually in novella ebook format.
Copyright 2013 / 2014

Greybeard Publishing
P.O. Box 480
McCleary, WA 98557-0480

The Black Tower

Contents...

Episode One
The First Floor

Prolog

The Quonset hut sat in the predawn shadow of the black obelisk-like skyscraper towering eighty stories high, surrounded by the dark silhouette of the city skyline. Everything gleamed from an overnight rain.

Staff Sergeant Miller stepped out of the hut and held the door open for the civilian. SSG Miller, in his early twenties, clean-cut and dressed in starched army fatigues, moved with a smooth self-assuredness.

In sharp contrast to Peter Asher; Asher was in his late thirties, wore loose, casual dress, untrimmed and unruly hair, and had a quiet, preoccupied look.

Miller moved out ahead and opened the rear door of the black sedan. Asher mumbled an unintelligible thank you before climbing in.

Asher watched from the back seat as they approached the massive, windowless tower. The jet-black walls of the structure, and the asphalt from which it rose, were wet from the rain. At the base, a lone door was illuminated by an industrial strength light mounted on a tall tripod set a short distance away.

The sedan came to a stop. Asher climbed out before Miller could get out and open the door for him. He took two steps and stopped, let his gaze rise slowly up the side of the awesome structure reaching up to the sky, just beginning to take on some early dawn color.

Miller pulled a small canvas knapsack from the trunk of the car and stepped up beside his charge. He indicated the door set into the side of the building.

"Sir?" he urged, then led Asher to the door. It opened as they approached, and Corporal Ramos stood in the opening.

Ramos' face showed more experience than his twenty three years would suggest. His fatigues weren't nearly as crisp as that of Miller's; no starch and a bit haggard.

He gave Miller a curt nod, who handed him Asher's bag.

Asher looked uncertainly at Ramos, then back to Miller.

"Thank you for everything, Sergeant," said Asher.

"My pleasure, Professor. Good luck to you."

Ramos slipped one strap of Asher's knapsack over his shoulder. "Professor Asher? We should get inside."

"Yes," said Asher. He looked again to the sergeant. "Well... thank you again."

Asher moved to the door and disappeared inside.

Miller gave Ramos a sharp look. "Take care of him, Ramos."

"Do my best, Sarge."

Miller watched the door ease closed, turned at the sound of another vehicle pulling up. It looked just like one he had used to bring his professor over.

A young man climbed out of the front passenger side, a young woman out of the rear passenger side.

The driver, another army sergeant, slid from behind the wheel and opened the left rear door. Elizabeth Owen slowly glided out, seemingly accustomed to be waited on. Once she was clear, the driver closed the door and moved to the rear of the sedan, opened the trunk.

Elizabeth Owen was in her mid-fifties. There was an in-charge bearing in her manner. She was calm in her direction, and fully expected every order to be carried out without question.

She waved a hand to her staff without taking her eyes off the building in front of her. "Get the bags," she stated.

Ray Do and Lisa Powell both moved to help the driver. Both were in their early thirties. They were clean, neat, sharp and intelligent. They were science wizards who found themselves spending as much time doing menial labor for their boss as they did working in their field.

Inside the tower, Ramos squeezed past Asher and led the way down the long, brightly lit corridor. As they walked, Asher took notice of his guide for the first time. The young soldier's manner appeared as tired as his clothes.

That didn't bode well.

They stepped out of the corridor onto a wide landing. It was enclosed on three sides, with the side directly opposite opening out onto a large, sunny expanse. The sky was an unfamiliar shade of red. Thick vegetation, twisted and alien, covered the landscape.

The landing was little more than a balcony positioned thirty feet above the rest of the first floor of the building. Amongst a small collection of cardboard boxes and an assortment of canvas bags and packs were four other soldiers.

Lt. Gordon Quinn was in his late twenties, medium height, a slim build but strong. He had the manner of a military man without the severe gung-ho cliché. He kept his hair trimmed but not close-cropped, his face clean-shaven, his uniform sharp but not necessarily crisp.

Sgt. Sara Costa, also in her late twenties, would rather use her brain than her brawn, yet still came across as fully capable of taking care of herself. She was strong willed, knew what she was doing and didn't need to prove herself to anyone.

PFC Raso and PFC Carmody each had the college-kid look about them, as if their plan was to quietly do their three years in the army, then get out and go back to school. They wore the military uniform, but it wasn't enough to make them look all that military.

At the moment, they were using machetes on vines that clung to the walls of the landing and were threatening to move down the access corridor that Asher and Ramos had just come through.

Several M4 Carbines were leaning against the wall, and beside these two holsters with side-arms. One of the demands had been no weapons, but they had brought them in anyway. Wasted effort, as it turned out. Firearms wouldn't fire in the tower. There was no logical reason for it, but such was the case; leave it to illogic to sort out.

Lt. Quinn and Sgt. Costa were standing at the edge of the landing. Costa gave a sharp nod and turned away as Asher approached. She followed a narrow trail down to the forested floor below.

Quinn waited until Asher was standing beside him before speaking, and then he kept his attention on the alien forest that was spread out before them.

"Professor Asher," he said calmly. "Welcome to the First Floor."

Episode One / Chapter One

The clearing was twenty feet in diameter, with four trailheads opening to narrow paths leading away from it. It was encircled by alien vegetation that reached high and loomed menacing overhead; brush and twisted trees and vines of thick rope and triangular leaves, all threatening to push in and swallow up the clearing. The few streaks of light that managed to stream in had a reddish tint.

Wes Banister knelt over the lifeless body of Captain Carver, lying face up on the floor of thick mulch. Nearby, Susan Bautista tended to Nathaniel Church's injured arm. The three scientists were visibly worn down, with the much older Banister and Church in particular having seen better days.

Wes Banister was in his late sixties. Long gray hair encircled a balding top and a face with sharp features and crystal clear eyes.

Nathaniel Church was a black man a couple of years younger, graying at the temples and wrinkling about the eyes.

Susan Bautista was Wes Banister's assistant. She was thirty years old, average height and a couple of pounds overweight. Her hair and makeup were worn efficient. She had a quiet confidence that showed itself in her manner.

She did her job and left the bantering to the professors.

Banister sat back, rubbed his pale face with both hands and looked again at the body of Captain Carver.

"He's dead, Nate," he said, glanced for the hundredth time at the vegetation that surrounded the clearing.

Susan Bautista finished bandaging Church's arm, stood and looked at Banister and the dead man.

Church, glancing at the bandaging, mumbled almost incoherently.

"Thank you, Susan."

Susan nodded without looking back, turned away from the others and found a level spot to sit down.

Banister avoided looking at the dead military man. "So, then. What do we do now?"

"We keep moving," said Church.

"I'm not keen on continuing down that trail."

"Neither am I," said Church. "But we really have little choice. We're in as much danger here as on the trail."

Banister looked again at the surrounding vegetation.

"Perhaps so," he grumbled. "It seems quieter here, though... d'you notice?"

"Quite peaceful," Church said with more than a hint of quiet sarcasm.

They both looked questioningly at Susan.

"The only safe place is back at the landing," she said.

"She's right, of course," said Banister.

"She usually is." Church positioned himself to stand, and Susan scrambled to her feet and started towards him.

"Let me help you, Doctor." She held onto his uninjured arm and helped him to his feet.

"Thank you, Susan."

"Yes," Banister said snidely. "Do bring the old man along, Susan." He picked up the machete that was lying alongside the captain and started toward the trailhead. He paused then, looked back at the body. "I'm not comfortable leaving Captain Carver like this."

Church gave a low grunt. "We certainly can't take him with us."

"No. No, of course not."

"We'll send someone back for him, Doctor," said Susan.

"Yes, of course." Banister turned back to the trailhead. "I'll take the lead for a while."

Asher stood at the edge of landing, mesmerized by the scene. From the landing, the terrain fell quickly away, the floor taking the shape of a large bowl. To all appearances, there were no walls and there was no ceiling.

There was a faint shimmer where walls and ceiling should have been.

Something was there. And yet, there wasn't.

He could hear Sgt. Costa behind him, at the back of the landing, directing the two privates, Raso and Carmody. She had them once again hacking away at the vines. They were complaining, again, but it was little more than background noise to Asher.

He saw movement below, and a moment later Lt. Quinn appeared from one of the side trails. He stepped past a small, thick mass of short brush and started down what Asher had been told was the main trail.

He was startled at the sound of a woman's voice, turned to see Elizabeth Owen following Corporal Ramos out of the access tunnel. He missed what she had said, but it had the sound of an order to her staff. Asher recognized the young man as her assistant, though he couldn't remember his name. The young woman with them must have been a fairly recent addition.

Ramos set down a bag he was carrying, looked quickly about the landing, and started in Asher's direction.

"Corporal," said Asher, turning back towards the floor.

"Professor." Ramos looked down at the trailheads. "The lieutenant out on the floor?"

"Said he'd be back in a few minutes."

Ramos nodded, scanned the floor again. "Extraordinary, isn't it?"

"It certainly is."

"Nothing can quite prepare you for it."

Asher glanced up at what should have been the ceiling. "Eighty floors."

"So the experts say." Ramos' gaze continually returned to the main trail. "The lieutenant is starting to worry. They should have been back by now."

Asher only nodded in reply.

"Do you know them, Professor?"

"Only by reputation." Asher indicated the floor. "How long have they been gone?"

"Almost a day. Captain Carver took them out."

Lt. Quinn appeared at the trailhead, walked steadily up to the base and climbed the rise toward the landing.

Ramos patiently waited, and Lt. Quinn spoke up just as he reached the landing.

"Yes, Corporal?"

"The last of 'em sir," he said, indicating the group he had just brought in. There were no salutes. This was a conscious decision. No sense putting a big sign over Lt. Quinn's head reading 'shoot me first'.

"Thank you." Quinn looked briefly at the people scattered about the landing, then back behind him at the floor. "Take Carmody and Raso down the main trail. Listen up for the Captain."

Ramos gave a terse nod and went to get the privates. Lt. Quinn waited until they were starting back across the landing before stepping towards the rest of the group.

"Folks?" he urged, moving into the center of the landing. "Gather 'round, please."

Elizabeth Owen sat on one of the boxes, warily eyeing the military man. Her assistants, Ray Do and Lisa Powell, stood behind her. They quietly watched and waited, looking to Quinn more like servants than assistants.

At least Professor Asher appeared to have an agreeable way. He moved to another box and sat down.

"My name is Lieutenant Quinn," the lieutenant started. "Captain Carver is out on the floor with the rest of the scientific staff assigned to this project. We expect them back at any time."

"Is the military to be in charge, Lieutenant?" Owen asked, somewhat accusingly.

"You have all been thoroughly briefed on the protocols, Dr. Owen. Captain Carver will be in overall command, but he will not be encroaching into the scientific aspects of the project."

"I should hope not."

"However, you will remain within the project parameters established by General Wong and Dr. Church. Captain Carver will step in should civilian activities endanger team personnel or threaten the goals of the mission."

"As was explained to us, Lieutenant," said Asher.

Owen looked from Quinn to Asher. "And what is your role here, Peter?" she asked. "Your name came up rather sketchily in the briefing that I was forced to endure."

"Professor Asher is an anthropologist, Dr. Owen," Quinn offered.

"I am fully aware of his credentials, Lieutenant," Owen said tersely. She looked back again at Asher, continued to speak to Quinn. "Our paths have crossed from time to time over the years. Peter is quite the respected figure in his field. Several fields in fact."

"Of course," said Quinn.

Owen turned then to look directly at Asher. "Of late, however, your activities have been, shall we say, hidden in the government shadow?"

"A few obscure projects, Elizabeth," said Asher. "Nothing mysterious. Nothing very important, really."

"Did those projects have anything to do with what you are doing here?"

"I have absolutely no idea what I'm doing here. I can only assume that it was believed my areas of expertise might prove useful."

"And well they might," said Lt. Quinn, jumping back in, eager to get the conversation back on track. "We have eighty floors to traverse, and, to be honest, we have no idea what we might find."

Owen turned her attention fully to Quinn. "And you, Lieutenant? What is it that you bring to the expedition?"

"Have no delusions, Dr. Owen," Quinn said curtly. "Your function here is to assist us in getting to the top floor. Anything that you learn along the way, other than what helps you in getting us there, is secondary. I'll be pleased as punch for you, but beyond that it won't mean a thing to me. I hope that I am clear on this."

"In typical grunt fashion, Lieutenant."

"As may be, ma'am. Now, if I might, I would like to get the preliminaries out of the way. Best we be prepared upon Captain Carver's return."

Elizabeth Owen didn't give Lt. Quinn the benefit of a response, leaving Asher to step back in.

"Please, Lt. Quinn," he stated quietly.

"Thank you, Professor," Quinn nodded to Asher, then spoke again to the group. "This landing will serve as our first floor base camp. It is from here that we will conduct our search for an access to the second floor."

Lisa Powell spoke up for the first time. "The floor can't be that large."

"Miss Powell," Quinn gave her a nod. "Welcome. As you have no doubt noticed, the inside dimensions of the tower do not appear to correspond to the outside dimensions."

"I assumed that was just illusion."

"As yet, we don't know how it is being done. The fact is, we have traveled much further than the exterior dimensions would suggest without reaching a wall."

"Will we be coming back to base camp each night?" asked Asher.

"Each--?" Elizabeth Owen looked from Asher to Quinn. "Surely you don't expect it to take that long to find the second floor?"

"It could, ma'am."

"Or..." Asher calmly urged, "we would have people on the second floor by now."

Quinn slowly nodded in agreement before continuing. "Each floor's base camp will serve as the one permanent location that you can count on. If we become separated, you return to base."

He indicated a row of olive-drab knapsacks that were lined up along one wall.

"We've prepared a small backpack for each of you containing basic supplies. There should be enough room remaining to accommodate what additional personal gear and equipment you may have brought with you."

"No, not nearly enough," said Owen. She could see that the pack was already nearly full.

"You were advised to bring in only what you considered absolutely necessary."

"I did."

"Yes, well, I am very sorry, but you may have to leave one or two things behind. Given the opportunity, once on the next floor, we'll return to the landing, retrieve what we can."

Corporal Ramos led Carmody and Raso along the main trail. It was just wide enough for them to travel without having to push brush aside.

"More of 'em," said Raso. "How many lab coats we gotta babysit on this op?"

"As many as they send in," said Carmody. "What's your problem?"

"Doesn't feel right."

Carmody smirked. "Of course it doesn't feel right. It's alien. It's gonna feel alien."

"I don't like it. I don't like any of it."

Ramos spoke over his shoulder without looking back. "It's not our place to like or not like it. Not the situation, or the civilians." He stopped then, having arrived at their first watch post. He turned stiffly about. "It doesn't matter to me one way or the other. I do my job, you do your job."

Raso frowned and grumbled under his breath.

"We do our job," said Ramos. He pointed sharply at a spot alongside the trail. "Plant it."

Raso took a long step and straightened.

"Plant it... oh, that's funny." He grimaced at Carmody. "Isn't it? I mean—" he indicated the vegetation around them. "Ya know..."

"No," she answered. "Not so much."

Raso called out to the retreating corporal. "Hey, what're we supposed to do if we see something? Throw a stick at it?"

Ramos spoke over his shoulder.

"Cry like a little girl. I'll hear ya' and come running." Ramos did feel a bit naked without a big, bad gun, but he wasn't going to let on to these guys. Firearms were useless in here, so they would have to make do. Deal with it.

To all appearances, it looked like dusk out on the floor. The reddish tint had turned to gray. Asher and Owen sat on the edge of the landing, feet hanging over the lip.

Animal sounds came from somewhere in the distance, crow-like yet more predatory, more menacing.

Asher could see Sgt. Costa standing watch along the left side trail. Looking directly ahead toward the main trail, he saw Lee

Raso. The young private looked restless. He looked up toward the landing, in Asher's direction. He lifted a hand wiggled his fingers jovially.

Asher smiled good-naturedly, waved back. He continued watching the man as he spoke to Owen.

"According to Quinn, this is about as dark as it gets." He glanced up at the ceiling, which had now taken on the appearance of an early evening sky. "It lasts about eight hours, then daylight... or... whatever. The full cycle is about twenty four hours."

"Hmm."

"That might mean something."

"The man is a Neanderthal."

"Oh, Elizabeth," Asher smiled. "You've dealt with a lot worse."

"Hmm."

"Quinn's a pussycat."

"Well," she said, grudgingly. "Perhaps."

The animal sounds, which had been distant and very much in the background, were suddenly very near. Down below, Lee Raso was at full alert.

Asher spoke as calmly as he could. "The recon teams reported finding no animal life."

"They were mistaken."

"Apparently."

The world calmed, grew quiet again. Down below, it took Lee Raso a few more seconds to let the tension subside. Over at the side trail, Sgt. Costa seemed unconcerned, her focus on being ready in case the away team needed help.

Hearing the sound of metal plates and spoons clattering together, Asher looked back over his shoulder. Elizabeth's assistants were near the back of the landing.

He remembered the young man's name then.

"I'd have thought Ray would be out on his own by now."

"My magnetic personality," said Owen, not bothering to turn around. If something made an appearance out on the floor, she didn't want to miss it.

Asher gave a polite chuckle. "I can see that. Really." He turned back around. "He's been with you... ten years? The Janus Project?"

"Don't recall," she stated flatly. "He's doing all right for himself."

"I know you manage to get the plum projects, but I'm surprised that's enough for him. Let's be honest, Liz... working in your professional shadow can't be easy."

"As you said, I do find the little gems that keep us all interested."

Asher accepted that. He gave a nod back over his shoulder. "What about her?"

"Lisa is bright enough, or I wouldn't keep her around. And she frees Ray from some of the more mundane tasks."

"Which in turn helps keep him around," said Asher. "How long will she be willing to do the grunt work?"

"That is what research assistants are for, Peter. It's what they do."

Ray Do came up to them carrying a plate of food. He handed it to Owen.

"Your dinner, Doctor," he said.

Owen gave Asher a conspiratorial grin and took the plate.

"Why thank you, Ray," she said, oozing sweetness. "So kind of you."

Ray wasn't quite able to completely hide his surprise, turned quickly to Asher.

"Would you like me to bring you something, Professor?"

Asher groaned loudly as he slowly climbed to his feet. "No... thank you, Ray. That's quite all right. I think I'll burn the two or three calories that it takes to fetch it for myself.

Susan Bautista led the way along the trail through the vegetation, Church and Banister following closely behind. She had the machete in hand, had to use it occasionally to clear the path. Alien, crow-like sounds pushed in from the vegetation.

One of the vines suddenly reached out to Susan. She hacked at it with the machete and the vine pulled back, screeching.

Banister placed a hand on Church's shoulder.

Church pushed it away in irritation. "Stop babying me, Banister."

"Well then keep up, you old fart."

The trail ended abruptly.

Susan stopped in her tracks, Church and Banister came up short behind her.

Susan looked back over her shoulder at them. "But... this is the trail. This is the main trail."

"Yes, my dear," said Banister. "It should have taken us all the way to the landing."

Church nodded irritably. "Yes, yes. It may well have been the main trail earlier, but now they have closed it off." He growled under his breath. "We'll just have to hack our way through."

"With no trail?" asked Banister.

"We have to."

"What about finding another way?"

"Oh, come on, Wes," Church said impatiently. "If they're blocking our path here, do you think they'll leave a way open somewhere else?"

"It's bad enough traveling an open trail. I dread the thought of tromping through the brush."

"Same here," said Susan.

"Yes, well," Church sighed. "We are all in total agreement on that point. However," he looked anxiously about them. "I for one do not intend to stay here to await their pleasure."

Banister took a few moments before offering grudging agreement.

"There really is no choice, is there?"

Church gave a curt nod and turned to Susan. "Susan? If you please?"

In answer, Susan Bautista turned and lifted up her machete, brought it down decisively and sliced through the alien vines.

The animal sounds grew suddenly very loud.

Episode One / Chapter Two

Asher and Owen stood at the edge of the landing, from where they could watch as Sgt. Costa led Susan Bautista up from the overgrown left trail. Church and Banister were stumbling along right behind.

Lt. Quinn scrambled down from the landing to the floor, hurrying to help... and to find out why Captain Carver wasn't with them.

From the main trail came Raso, Carmody and Corporal Ramos.

As they came up nearer the landing, Asher could hear Susan speaking low to Costa, repeating herself and shaking her head from side to side. "Turned around somehow."

Once on the landing, Susan, Banister and Church were guided to a row of boxes serving double-duty as a bench. Someone shoved coffee cups into their hands as everyone gathered around to hear what had happened; all but Corporal Ramos, who hurried over to the radio to let those in the command center outside know that the team had returned, minus the captain.

The two elder scientists told of an attack by the very plants that made up the forests, of vines reaching in and twisting themselves about them, tightening themselves around their torsos and arms and legs.

And of strange dark shadows that flew about the clearing in which they fought.

Church set his coffee cup down on the ground between his feet, looked up at Lt. Quinn.

"I have no intention of letting Captain Carver's sacrifice go for naught," he stated flatly. "I'm going back out in the morning."

"That is not your decision to make, Doctor Church," said Quinn.

Church glanced in Ramos' direction. The corporal was speaking into the radio.

"General Wong understands the importance of this project," he said. "And the urgency."

"We all do, Doctor. You must also understand the importance of being properly prepared to take on this mission." At a signal from Ramos, Lt. Quinn excused himself and went to the radio.

Church turned to the others in the group, most of whom had arrived in the tower during the recent foray onto the floor. He acknowledged Professor Asher.

"Asher, isn't it?" he asked.

"Hello, Doctor Church."

Church indicated Banister. "That's my sidekick. Wes Banister. Nice enough fella, I guess."

Banister gave Asher a tired wave. Church then gave Elizabeth Owen a smile.

"It's been a while, Liz. How have you been?"

"Have I ever been less than magnificent?"

"Not that I can recall."

Owen took a step closer and sat beside Church. "Nate, tell me true. What are we facing out there?"

Banister snickered, and Church smiled thinly, looked at the group as a whole.

"On that subject," Church sighed, "There is a bit of disagreement."

"A bit," grumbled Banister.

Church slowly shook his head. "And as of now, I have to admit that I just don't know."

"Whoa..." Banister straightened. "Someone get my diary."

Church ignored his partner in crime. "There are entities out there. Shadows... with a physical presence."

Banister cut in. "The vegetation itself seems to exist with a purpose, whether its own, or that of some controlling force..." His words trailed off.

"The Adversary," Asher stated.

"That would appear to be the case," Church shrugged. "Or... it may all be the Adversary. Not controlled by, but actually be this... being."

Banister stared down into his half-empty coffee cup. "Whether of its own accord, or at the specific direction of this entity, the vegetation is at the very least acting at the behest of the Adversary."

"And these shadows?" asked Owen.

"I have no doubt they are creatures of the Adversary."

"Or," Church urged, "are manifestations of this being. As the vegetation itself may well be."

Asher was struggling with the whole idea. He scratched at an imaginary itch in his scalp. "But, either way, why bother going through all this—" he indicated the floor beyond the landing, "all this, just to kill a few helpless individuals?"

"I don't believe the intent is to kill us," said Banister.

"Could he be trying to prevent us from getting to top the floor?" Asher had been given to understand that this 'Adversary' had specifically directed them to go to the top floor. "I was told that he asked us to come."

Church agreed. "He was very insistent about it."

"This is a test," Banister said sharply.

Church waved a dismissive hand at Banister, but said nothing.

"For what purpose, I cannot fathom," Banister went on. "But we are very definitely being tested."

"Melodramatic anthropomorphizing of an extraterrestrial whose thought processes we cannot begin to understand."

Banister struggled to not look flustered, attempted to put himself into a lecturing mode.

"A being arrives in our midst in the most dramatic fashion and asks that we meet with it, and yet insists that we first traverse a series of obstacles before we are allowed an audience. Sir... we can safely postulate that we are being tested."

Church looked thoughtfully at his partner for several very long seconds, the others in the group looking on as silent observers.

Church finally, grudgingly, nodded in agreement. "Very well," he said softly. "As sensationalistic as you insist on making what should be a straightforward presentation, I will –concede- to your argument."

"I am humbled."

"As you should be."

Banister snorted. "It is also quite evident that this individual, by stating its name as 'Adversary', is intentionally establishing a confrontational tone to this test."

"This being is an alien," said Church. "The thought processes behind these requests are alien. Therefore, the reasoning behind the requests cannot be accurately determined."

Just when that was starting to sink in, everyone's attention shifted to Lt. Quinn as he returned from the radio.

"Okay, folks," he said firmly. "I suggest that you get what rest you can. We have a go for the expedition, despite recent events. We move out at true dawn."

Banister approached the landing's edge, half lost in thought. The world beyond the landing held what this bizarre landscape took for predawn. The night was never fully dark, the day never fully clear.

At hearing Asher's approach from behind him, he spoke without turning from the view. "Professor Asher... trouble sleeping?"

There was a flicker of reddish light across what should have been the east wall of the first floor.

"I've never needed much sleep," said Asher. "Not sure if that's a blessing or a curse."

"Savor every minute of your waking hours, my dear Professor. When you reach my age, you will come to realize they are the only things of any real value."

"I'm not so sure about that, Doctor Banister."

Banister raised a brow and looked askance at Asher, but said nothing. Asher grinned apologetically.

"Please, don't get me wrong," he said. "I do place a high value on what time I have in this life. But none of it would mean much without what I believe to be the one item of real worth."

"Oh? And what would that be, my young friend?"

"The pursuit of knowledge."

"Ah, yes... I have heard of your idealism."

"Idealism be damned. The thought of reaching the end of my life and realizing much too late that I had squandered what years I had been given... that is downright terrifying."

Banister nodded approvingly, spoke as if offering a toast.

"May you have many hours of life yet before you, Professor, all of which to be dedicated to seeking out wondrous truths and the discovery of great and profound knowledge."

"Thank you, Doctor." Asher's brow wrinkled. "I think."

They stood in silence for a few moments. From behind them came the soft sounds of people sleeping: steady breathing, shifting and turning bodies, and someone's light snoring.

From the floor came the hint of a breeze, its source unknown.

"And what of you and Doctor Church?" asked Asher. "Haven't you spent your lives seeking knowledge?"

"Knowledge be damned, sir. We seek fun."

"Ah... fun. I believe I've heard of it."

"The secret to our success is our dogged desire to enjoy whatever it is that we are doing at the moment. If we are bored, or if whatever we are working on just doesn't do it for us anymore, we drop it and find something else, something that keeps the life in our lives."

Asher indicated the scene before them. "I would say that you have certainly found that here."

"If we survive it," agreed Banister. "But that just adds a little kick and spice to the project, eh?"

"Is that where the fun comes in?"

Banister gave a noncommittal shrug, and after a few moments grew more thoughtful. "So, where were you when we plucked you out of your earthly existence and dropped you in here?"

"A little college in New Mexico. Research mostly, and doing a little teaching." He gave Banister a side-glance and subtle smile.

"But you must know that. You did select the members of this expedition."

Banister gave a shrewd grin in return. "I may know a little of your background. And yes, I've read a few of your published papers." There was a polite pause, then. "I liked the voice that I heard calling out to me from behind the printed word."

Behind them, the sounds of sleep slowly morphed to the subtle sounds of waking. Banister gave a glance back over his shoulder, turned again to the floor covered in alien jungle. "Our fellow travelers awaken," Banister said with a hint of resignation. "I believe it is time to get ready."

The group marched slowly along the same trail that Banister, Church and Susan Bautista had traveled the day before. Each had an olive-drab backpack, several of them overstuffed, particularly those on the backs of Lt. Owen's assistants.

The military contingent led the way, with Carmody and Raso out in front, Lt. Quinn a few yards behind them.

An uneasy, eerie quiet lay over the group. Even Church and Banister's bantering had fallen to silence. What sounds there were seemed muffled.

Carmody and Raso reached a fork in the trail and stopped. Lt. Quinn looked questioningly back at Church, who looked about them uncertainly before turning to Susan.

Susan nodded to the left fork, looked about again, nodded again to the left. She finally shrugged, waved a hand to the left.

Good enough, thought Lt. Quinn, who turned back to Carmody and Raso, pointed to the left fork. *Civilians. Gotta love 'em.*

Two hours later they came into the clearing where they had left the body of Captain Carver. The body wasn't there.

Susan moved well into the clearing, noted the disturbed ground from the earlier conflict, and the spot where she had worked on Dr. Church's injury. She saw the few traces of blood where the body of Captain Carver had lain.

She gave the lieutenant an affirmative nod. Lt. Quinn in turn gave Carmody and Raso a silent order and they moved quickly to stand at two of the four trailheads.

Sgt. Costa and Cpl. Ramos came into the clearing behind the rest of the group. At seeing the situation, Costa pointed to the far trailhead and Ramos moved to position, leaving Costa to remain at the trailhead where they had entered.

"But why take the body?" asked Asher.

"Why any of this, Professor?" Lt. Quinn was at a loss.

Church and Banister joined them as Elizabeth Owen found a place to rest, her assistants beside her. Church spoke as he watched Susan kneel down near where Captain Carver's body had been.

"This is most definitely where—"

"Yes," stated Banister.

Asher shifted uncomfortably. "I would as soon not stay here."

"Yes," Banister repeated. He gave Church an inquisitive glance before indicating the far trailhead. "That way, wasn't it, Nate?" he asked.

"I believe so."

"That way, what?" asked Asher.

Church appeared embarrassed to bring it up, and Lt. Quinn finally answered.

"The captain thought he saw something," he said, looked to the elder scientists for verification. "Perhaps a ladder."

"Only for a moment, then it was gone," said Church. "Several hundred yards distant. I'm afraid no one else saw it."

"But something was there," said Banister.

"Yes," sighed Church. "The captain said that he saw two ladder rungs hanging in the open air. We looked for it, but it never reappeared."

Real or illusion, thought Asher. *As if either has any meaning in here...*

After a long, uncomfortable silence, Lt. Quinn indicated the trailhead that Church had pointed out. "Shall we?"

An empty trail winding its way through the alien forest...

The sound of muted voices in the distance.

The vines on either side of the trail trembled. Tendrils began to move. The vines began to slide.

Slowly at first, then in a sudden flash, the vegetation rushed in from either side.

The trail was closed.

Carmody and Raso came into view. They stopped. They turned to face the rest of the group as it closed in on them.

"Oh, great," said Elizabeth Owen.

"Everyone stay alert," said Lt. Quinn. This didn't feel right. He pointed sharply at Raso. "Keep an eye forward."

He studied their immediate surroundings. The trail here was fairly wide right up to where it no longer existed. Behind them, the trail wound around a sharp bend. Sgt. Costa brought up the rear, stood alert there at the bend.

He made eye contact with her. She gave a curt nod, half turned so as to watch the path they had just taken while still able to keep an eye on the group, some of whom had already begun to settle in for what looked to be a break.

Asher stepped over to stand beside Susan and Church.

"Did we make a wrong turn somewhere?"

Susan gave an uncertain shrug.

Church grumbled. "It is possible, of course. It all looks familiar, but things change out here."

"I'm fairly certain this is the path we took," said Susan. "I could be wrong. A forest trail is... a forest trail."

Church's comment from a moment ago finally registered with Asher.

"Closing one path, opening another? Are we being led somewhere?"

"If so, I see no pattern, no design or direction."

Lt. Quinn turned to face them, focused on Church. "This has the smell of a trap more than a guiding hand, Doctor."

"Perhaps. But again, to what purpose?"

Banister spoke from his seated spot nearby. "This is the Adversary's game, Nate. We have yet to puzzle out the rules."

Church had to agree, if only silently.

Lt. Quinn took the comment to where it led. "We've already lost the captain to whatever is out here, Doctor Banister. Or whatever it is that controls whatever it is that is out here. If we can't figure out these rules, I doubt very much that it will stop with Captain Carver."

"Quite," Banister said crisply.

"What do you suggest we do, Lieutenant?" asked Asher.

Yes, thought Quinn. *What do we do?*

He looked to Church. "You certain this is the right path?"

"Not absolutely certain, no." Church stood under Lt. Quinn's sharp gaze. "I agree with Susan. I believe this is the same path."

Decision time.

"Carmody! Raso!"

They turned to look at their lieutenant.

"Double back and see what you can find," he told them. "Back in twenty."

They dropped their backpacks, left their positions and started back through the group. Sgt. Costa waved a hand to Ramos to move forward and stand watch in place of Raso.

Lt. Quinn turned to the rest of the group. "Take twenty, but stay alert."

Susan found a small hillock to sit on. She dropped her pack to the ground, sat down, elbows on knees, hands clasped.

Asher followed her over, stood above her. "Doctor Bautista... mind if I join you?"

Susan indicated the empty spot beside her.

"Take a load off, Professor," she said. "Call me Susan."

Asher dropped down beside her. "Peter."

"Hello, Peter."

"Hello, Susan," Peter answered. "How are you holding up?"

She gave a halfhearted shrug and a faint smile.

"I've been involved in all this since the day this tower first appeared." A second halfhearted shrug. "But you... you must still be at the overwhelmed stage."

"That is an understatement."

"Hmm," she slowly nodded. "Yes. I know the feeling."

Across from them and a few yards further down the trail, Elizabeth Owen was grumbling under her breath. Ray Do was trying to comfort her as Lisa Powell watched with a hint of indifference.

Asher felt an odd sense of intrusion and turned his gaze away. Susan was looking in their direction as well, but wasn't really looking at them.

"You know," she began after a long pause, "back when Doctor Church was first trying to put a team together, somehow your name kept coming up."

"So I'm told," said Asher. "Not sure why. I'm not as engaging as all that."

"False modesty, Professor?"

"Not at all. My career has been very focused. I'm an anthropologist, and not much else."

"Anthropology has many subsets, and you seem to be involved in all of them."

Asher gave a humble shrug. "And you?" he asked.

"Not much to say. I've been with Dr. Banister a long time. What career I have, I owe to him."

"False modesty?"

"Not at all," she answered precisely. "I'm afraid I don't do very well with people. This personality quirk can have quite an unpleasant effect on one's career. Then I met Doctor Banister. He saw something in me, was willing to overlook my, um... social handicap?"

"You're doing fine right now."

"Give it time," Susan sighed. "It shouldn't take more than..."

Susan's sentence faded as she shifted slowly about to listen to something.

"What is it?" asked Asher.

"D'you hear that?"

Asher listened a moment, then shook his head. He turned fully around, listened more intently.

Slithering , rustling, scratching...

Barely audible at first, the sounds rose slowly up to where everyone could hear.

Suddenly, explosively, branches and vines rushed into the clearing from both sides of the trail, striking at the group, wrapping around them.

As suddenly then... several small shadows came out of the brush, hovered a moment, then quickly clambered on first one then another of the group, jumping from person to person, making it all the more difficult for the humans to free themselves from the vines. Each shadow was about eighteen inches in diameter, and changed shape as it moved.

Lt. Quinn managed to free himself and hurried over to help Banister, who was almost completely hidden beneath the shifting vegetation. He pulled steadily at the vines, had to fend off a thin branch that slapped ceaselessly at him as he worked.

He looked over at Sgt. Costa and Ramos, who both appeared about to free themselves.

"Get the others!" he called out. "Move them out now!"

Costa scrambled over to help Susan free Doctor Church. The two of them helped him to his feet and stumbled toward the head of the clearing, in the direction where the path should have been, had it still existed.

Lt. Quinn helped Banister to his feet, started toward the others.

"Do it!" he called out.

Sgt. Costa lifted up the machete and brought it down.

The vegetation screamed.

Episode One / Chapter Three

The Quonset hut was small enough that its curved, corrugated sheeting seemed to hover over those inside. The interior was cluttered with desks in the middle of the room, wooden tables along the walls.

Corporal Johansen, the young communications operator, sat before the table on which sat the aging olive drab radio. General Wong and his adjutant Captain Adamson stood behind the young soldier. The General had the radio receiver to his ear.

"Of course, Doctor Church," said the General, speaking into the mouthpiece. "Yes. Success is vital. But it will not come if the team isn't around to meet the challenge."

General Wong was an Asian man in sixties with short, salt-and-pepper hair. He was stout in stature, had broad shoulders, and a tough, grizzly gaze.

He stared at his adjutant as he listened to Doctor Church. Adamson was in his early forties, tall, slender yet strong, with a sure manner and crisp dress.

"Yes, yes," General Wong continued. "Absolutely. As I have already said to Lieutenant Quinn." He listened again, glanced at Captain Adamson again before letting his gaze drift to an empty space somewhere above the radio.

"I'm afraid Doctor Lake isn't here at the moment," he said.

As if on cue, Doctor Lake came into the command center, clearly agitated, with SSG Miller right behind him.

He approached General Wong, politely but curtly waving one hand for the phone. The middle-aged scientist was prim-and-proper in both manner and attire.

"Ah," said General Wong. "Doctor Church? Doctor Lake is here now. He just stepped in." He stepped aside and handed Doctor Lake the receiver.

"Church? This is Lake."

General Wong moved away from the radio, waited for Miller to follow him.

"What is it, Sergeant?"

"General... the door is gone."

General Wong gave the sergeant a long, reflective look.

"Say again," he stated flatly.

"The door into the structure is no longer there," said Miller. "Sir."

Over at the radio, Doctor Lake was telling Church that they were on their own.

General Wong looked carefully at the sergeant. After some brief internal evaluation, he looked over at his adjutant, who, as if on orders, moved to the radio and took the receiver from Doctor Lake.

"This is Adamson," he said. "Put Lieutenant Quinn on."

Lt. Quinn was speaking on the radio, Corporal Ramos standing beside him. Across the clearing, Dr. Church was mumbling animatedly to Asher, Banister and Elizabeth Owen. Further down the trail, Ray Do was examining a minor head wound on Lisa Powell, Sgt. Costa standing watch.

"I understand, General," said Quinn. "Yes, sir." He handed the receiver to Ramos and stepped away from the radio. "I need everyone to gather 'round," he urged. Some looked his way, several started moving slowly toward him. "Please. Everyone."

He caught Sgt. Costa's attention. She gave a curt nod in response, remained on watch.

"Well, you've all heard," he said to the group. "We're here to stay, at least until we get to the top floor and accomplish our mission."

There was an undercurrent of mumbling from the group, and Quinn patiently waited for it to die down before continuing.

"Because of the current situation, it is all the more critical that General Wong and his staff be kept up-to-date on our status, and fully informed of any findings."

"And if we lose communication?" Owen asked snidely. "As our host apparently does not want us to leave, he may not want us communicating with the outside world at all."

"A concern of the General as well, Doctor Owen," said Quinn. "However, so long as we do have communications, each team has been directed to make regular reports. I will be reporting to Captain Adamson every eight hours. Doctor Church and his scientific team have been asked to contact Doctor Lake daily."

"Of course," Church acknowledged.

Quinn turned to Elizabeth Owen. "Doctor Owen, your research team is also being directed to provide daily reports to our science advisor." To Asher, then, "As have you, Professor."

Asher gave Quinn a silent acknowledgement, after which Quinn turned to the group as a whole.

"For the moment," he went on, "Make yourselves comfortable. Our missing team members can't be far off."

Owen gave him a dismissive look. "And just what would make you think that?"

Carmody and Raso entered a large clearing and stopped. The only exit was the way they had come in.

Off to their left, above and beyond the vegetation, was the occasional flickering of the wall. The ceiling overhead shimmered, just barely maintaining its illusion of sky.

"Another dead end," said Raso.

They both turned sharply at the sound of rustling brush behind them.

Their only way out had vanished. The vegetation had closed it off.

"Like I said," said Raso. *Dead end.*

As they turned back around, a tall shadow materialized in the center of the clearing directly in front of them, forming out of a slowly thickening, inky mist. After several seconds, it took on the size and shape of a human form, hidden in black, flowing shadow.

Adversary.

It remained little more than a flowing shadow; vaguely human form, about six feet tall.

Carmody and Raso each took a step back, but there was nowhere for them to go.

Small, black shadowy figures began appearing all about the clearing, each just under two feet tall. Their miniaturized human forms altered shaped as they moved, as black amoebas might, returning to a recognizable form only when they weren't in motion.

The figure of the Adversary remained unmoving, yet its form never stopped taking shape. It was as if the black of space was in fact made of flowing, smoky robes shifting in a slight breeze.

"I am... your host," it said. Its voice was smooth, gentle.

Carmody and Raso looked briefly at each other. Neither responded. Carmody looked cautiously at the dozen or so dark shadows that shifted around them.

"I look forward to welcoming you and your companions more formally once you reach the Main Hall." Adversary slowly and smoothly raised a hand, pointing upward with an extremely long, thin finger.

Carmody watched the arm lift up and then slowly lower, finally disappearing back into the flowing, smoky darkness.

"You should be speaking to the lieutenant," she said. "Or to the scientists. I'm just a soldier."

"What would be learned from that?"

Carmody and Raso looked at each other in confusion.

"I don't understand," Carmody said at last.

The shadow of the Adversary shifted and flowed, softened and flowed.

"Quite all right," it said.

Carmody and Raso instinctively moved apart, turning slightly. There was a strange, hollow airy sound, as if the Adversary was taking in a breath. Its black shape seemed to take on a more solid form, held it for several seconds, then returned to its more ethereal existence.

It lifted its arms out and away from its robes, looked studiously at its hands, at its extraordinarily long fingers. It rolled the fingers, and as it did the vegetation that surrounded the clearing rolled in a gentle wave.

"One of you will end existence here," it stated, very matter-of-factly.

"Now *that* I understand," said Raso. He took another step further from Carmody, ensuring two targets instead of one.

Carmody stood unmoving. "And what would be learned from that?" she asked.

"Much," Adversary said silkily.

The shadow entities dashed in and about the surrounding vegetation. The vegetation itself shuddered.

"Oh, crap," Raso said in a hushed whisper.

"The other will return to the others," said the Adversary. "To convey my words of salutation."

Sgt. Costa was standing watch at the far end of the clearing. Lt. Quinn and Church were in quiet conversation, the others dozing or simply resting.

The sudden sound of the cry of pain came from somewhere in the distance, shattering the quiet.

Sgt. Costa started toward the trailhead.

"Stand fast, Sergeant," said Lt. Quinn, his voice calm.

"But—"

"This group stays together." Lt. Quinn spoke slow and deliberate.

"Your pardon, Lieutenant. They need help."

All were on their feet now, most looking to Quinn for direction.

"I will not have people scattered all over the floor."

Costa looked ready to bolt, but held her position.

Asher spoke hesitantly, unsure whether he should step into the exchange between officer and enlisted. "So we go together," he said.

Sgt. Costa waited anxiously for the lieutenant to give her the go-ahead.

Quinn agreed. "Lead the way, Sergeant."

§

The false sky looked about to explode into dawn.

PFC Carmody stood at the ready. At her feet lay the lifeless body of PFC Raso.

The shadowy figures were gone. Adversary was gone.

Carmody was confused and determined and angry all at once.

She heard the rustling of brush behind her. She knew that the path had been cleared for her.

She could hear Sgt. Costa's voice off in the distance, calling out to her, calling out to Raso.

Episode One / Chapter Four

The black sedan pulled up beside the Quonset hut and SSG Miller climbed out and opened the back door. General Wong stepped slowly out, looked over at the mysterious black tower. He gave a sharp nod to SSG Miller before walking stiffly to the wooden door of the command center.

Once inside, he waved Corporal Johansen down when the man started to stand to attention. Captain Adamson, standing at the coffee pot, poured a second cup and had it ready when the general reached him.

"It may have been to test us," he said, handing him the cup. "Or to observe our response."

The general's angry silence was visible. Adamson was uncertain whether to continue, but was desperate to fill the quiet void.

"This character considers this all to be entertainment, General," he went on. "A game, Doctor Banister called it. It watches us, plays with us... tests us."

"A gauntlet," General Wong said absently.

"The Adversary made it very clear. They must successfully traverse these floors in order to reach what it calls the Main Hall, on the top floor; where it will be waiting."

"Yes, well, we knew as much from its earlier blustering." The general gripped tightly to the coffee cup. He had yet to take a drink.

"No one else gets in, and no one gets out," said Adamson. "The people we have in there now is all we get."

"So it would seem."

"And this Adversary has no qualms about killing them, murdering them outright."

The General lifted his coffee to his lips, took a cautious sip, and looked over the rim of the cup.

"A game, Captain?" he asked.

"Sir?"

"A game."

"Yessir," Adamson said uncertainly.

The General took another sip. "A look at the rulebook would certainly be helpful."

For the moment, the vegetation appeared content to let them pass. The team traveled steadily, following what seemed to be the main trail, at least for now, across the floor. It wound like a lazy river through the alien landscape, but always in the same general direction.

Carmody stepped into the clearing, almost stumbling in before stopping abruptly.

A vine-covered wall spanned the opposite wall, no more than five or six steps ahead of her, the rungs of a metal ladder visible in the vegetation.

"This is it." Susan hurried past Carmody.

The rest of the group spilled into the clearing, Lt. Quinn using gestures to silently order his military contingent to stand alert. Asher and Owen approached the ladder mounted on the wall, with Church and Banister coming up calmly behind them.

A thick cloud hovered high above the small clearing, pushing against the wall. The top of the ladder disappeared into the cloud.

Church curled a brow. "Not exactly the way he described it, is it?"

"Perhaps not," said Banister. "But it's the captain's ladder, nonetheless."

Quinn allowed himself to look away from the vegetation that pushed in from the perimeter long enough to look at the ladder; content for the moment. His captain had been vindicated.

Asher jumped up onto the ladder and climbed twenty feet. The cloud was still above him. He looked back across the floor, climbed a few more rungs, looked about again curiously.

"It's there!" he called down, started hurriedly down the ladder. "It's right there!"

"What's there?" Owen asked irritably.

"The landing," Asher jumped down from the ladder. "Where we came in—it isn't more than a few hundred feet away."

Lt. Quinn was lost. "I don't under—"

"It's right beside us," Asher said insistently. "The landing is right there."

Most of the group had turned to look into the alien vegetation, thinking about the route that had brought them here. Church didn't need to.

"That would certainly be in keeping with our host's droll sense of wit," he stated quietly.

Owen looked away from encroaching vegetation and once again let her gaze rise slowly up the ladder.

"I never noticed that cloud," she said thoughtfully. "Not from the landing, not from anywhere."

Church followed where she was looking. "A ladder that appears for only a moment, that may or may not be there. A cloud that—"

Banister cut him off. "I'll bet you a sack of pennies that once you leave this clearing, that cloud can't be seen. It doesn't exist."

Owen was still trying to wrap her head around it. "But how the—"

"It really didn't become clear to me until Private Carmody described her meeting with the Adversary," said Banister. "I had mistakenly assumed this was part of the illusion of the floor."

"I don't understand, Doctor," said Quinn.

"Yes," grumbled Church. "What are you dribbling on about, Banister?"

"I was wrong, you see."

"Hallelujah," Church exaggeratedly fanned his hands in the air.

Banister chose to ignore him.

"We can expect each floor to maintain an illusion of being something other than simply a floor in the building, but I believe this floor's own unique aspect is its constantly changing features."

"And the little things," Susan thought aloud, "like a cloud that is visible from only one location."

"All quite disconcerting," Banister looked to Church. "And quite in keeping with our host's—*drollness*."

"I see," Church nodded. "You might just be onto something, Banister."

"Which is?" Lt. Quinn urged.

Church was looking carefully at his friend Banister. "This Adversary placed the shifting visage concept, and these other oddities, on the first floor, where we must also, simultaneously, come to terms with the concept of the interior of this tower appearing to be larger than the container itself." Church let the thought process itself. "Interesting," he mumbled at last.

"Be careful," Banister frowned. "You'll pop a brain cell."

"But the captain—" Susan started.

"Yes," Owen cut her off. "What about that?"

"The ladder was meant to be seen," said Banister. "At that moment, by Captain Carver."

"To draw us in," Church wondered.

"Possibly, though we really can't know that for certain." Banister breathed out heavily. "We'll need to gather more information."

Lt. Quinn was wondering how he could possibly get this group up through another seventy nine floors, when every floor was... *what?*

"You don't think the other floors will be like this?"

"I doubt it, Lieutenant," Banister said curtly. "More likely, each will be very different; each will have its own distinct properties. Whatever else we may find, the aspects that we are witnessing here may well be unique to this floor."

"Or not," said Church.

"Quite," said Banister. "Or not."

Asher was looking restless.

"Let's do this," he said, and reached out for the ladder.

Lt. Quinn placed a hand on his arm, looked over at his sergeant.

"Sergeant Costa? Lead the way, please."

Sgt. Costa shifted her backpack and approached the ladder. Asher stepped aside and she put one foot onto a rung, then the other onto the rung above. Behind her, the others in the group drifted slowly nearer. Each in turn started up.

They settled into an easy pace set by Sgt. Costa. Asher fell into the rhythm of Costa's boots, the sound they made as they slid onto the rungs just above his head. The cloud that enveloped them hid the rest of the group from his view, though he could hear their breathing, the soles of their boots sliding onto rungs, their shifting gear.

Elizabeth Owen's voice came from somewhere below.

"Anyone counting?"

"I started to," said Church. "Somewhat late I'm afraid. I gave it up."

"Jack and the bloody damn beanstalk," Owen grumbled.

Asher grinned, called up to Costa above him. "Call out if you see a castle, Sergeant."

"Yes sir." She apparently didn't get the joke.

It was another full minute before Sgt. Costa stopped her methodic step, boot to rung, boot to rung.

Asher waited.

Sgt. Costa's words drifted down to him. "We're here, Professor."

"We're at the top," Asher called down. He looked up again toward Sgt. Costa, saw only her boots and her legs. "What do you see, Sergeant?"

"It looks like a submarine hatch," she said. "You know... a wheel in the center."

"Go for it."

"You got it."

Again Asher waited. He thought he heard the sound of metal against metal, but he couldn't be sure.

Owen called out again from somewhere below. "What the hell is happening up there?"

"Ever the restless, eh, Elizabeth?" Church's voice. A few seconds later, he called up calmly. "So, Professor Asher... just what is going on?"

"She's opening the hatch now."

A moment's silence, then Church passed the word down.

"We are advancing, Doctor Owen. Our moment of glory awaits us."

Above Asher, the cloud thinned slightly. He could just make out Sgt. Costa's torso, arms reaching upward, the shadow of the round hatch.

She gave the wheel a final turn. She looked below her at the upturned face of Professor Asher.

"Okay," she sighed. "That's it, Professor... open it?"

"Nothing for us here, Sara."

"Yes, sir." Sgt. Costa turned her attention again to the hatch. "Onward and upward then."

She pushed up. The hatch lifted easily.

Sgt. Costa climbed up through a rusted hatchway and out onto the deck of an aging freighter.

The ship looked long abandoned; rust everywhere, dents in the wall of a small cabin behind her, the railing in front of her twisted out of shape.

Asher climbed up after her. The two of them moved apprehensively toward the railing.

The color of the sea was a strange dark green. A lime green sky hovered above it like a glowing shell. An overly large moon hung low on the horizon.

One by one, the others in the group climbed up through the hatch and onto the deck. Each moved numbly toward the rail. The hint of a warm breeze brushed their faces.

A long, serpentine creature rose above the surface of the sea a few hundred yards from the ship, slid slowly back beneath the gently rolling waves...

~ end of episode one

Episode Two
The Freighter

Prolog

Sgt. Costa climbed up through the metal hatchway and out onto the deck of the aging freighter. The ship looked long abandoned; rusted metal, dents in the wall of a small cabin behind her, the railing in front of her twisted out of shape.

Professor Asher climbed up after her. The two of them moved apprehensively toward the railing.

The color of the sea was a strange dark green. A lime green sky hovered above them like a glowing shell. An overly large moon hung low on the horizon.

One by one, the others in the group climbed up through the hatch and onto the deck. Each moved numbly toward the rail. The hint of a warm breeze brushed their faces.

A long, serpentine creature rose above the surface of the sea a few hundred yards from the ship, slid slowly back beneath the gently rolling swells.

Asher let out a long, heavy sigh. "Okay," he said, to no one in particular. "I'll admit it. I had no idea what I was expecting, but I'm pretty sure this wasn't it."

"Me too, sir," said Sgt. Costa.

"Absolutely amazing," said Dr. Banister. He and Church were standing at the rail beside the sergeant. The others slowly began to move off. Lt. Quinn called to Carmody to take up watch position. Hearing that, Sgt. Costa excused herself. Work to be done.

Elizabeth Owen gave a less than subtle harrumph. "I don't mean to dampen the mood, boys and girls, but we're out in the middle of an ocean. Very few doors; however alien that ocean may be."

"Oh, give us a minute to enjoy the scenery, Liz," said Banister.

"For once I have to agree with Wes," said Church. "I don't want to, but I must. A moment to take it in, and then we'll go in search of your door."

Sgt. Costa stepped in to take charge of posting the watch, leaving Lt. Quinn to return to the rest of the group. He stood with his back to the rail, planted his hands on his hips and studied the rusting hulk. It was like something out of an old black and white movie.

"Doesn't take a scientist to tell me that we're probably going to find the access to the next floor right here on board this ship," he said.

"How do you figure?" asked Owen, a bit of a sneer. "Maybe our host put the opening out there. On an island, or in a floating in a mass of seaweed... inside a whale."

Maybe, thought Asher. *But where would you even begin to look?*

"I'll leave it to you scientists," said Lt. Quinn. "In the meantime, I believe I have a location for our base camp."

Asher turned again to the view beyond the rail as the others began to follow after Lt. Quinn. The surface of the green ocean rose and fell in easy, steady swells. A ripple in the distance suggested where the alien serpent might be gliding just under the surface.

Episode Two / Chapter One

Lt. Quinn's choice for home base on this floor was the ship's lounge. Freighters like this sometimes took on a few passengers to supplement the income received from traditional cargo, and a lounge like this was where these passengers spent their time.

That, at least, was how Lt. Quinn explained it. He more than likely acquired this information from one of the old movies this freighter brought to mind. There was a couch, several small tables with chairs, a six foot bar with a couple of tall stools. The outer wall was lined with a row of round portholes and single metal door.

By the time Asher came into the room, most of the others had already begun settling in. Church and Banister sat at one of the tables and were in a heated discussion. Corporal Ramos had taken over one end of the bar to use as the communications station and was trying to contact General Wong. Lt. Quinn hovered beside him, leaving Sgt. Costa and Carmody outside on watch.

Elizabeth Owen's assistants were on the couch sorting through their knapsack.

Asher took a seat at the other table with Susan Bautista just as Owen came in through the inner door beside the bar.

"Well, the restroom is about what you'd expect." She sat in the chair opposite Asher. "All the comforts of sixty years ago."

"And yet it is <u>our</u> sixty years ago," said Banister, from the other table. "An Earth vessel to be sure, on an alien sea."

"Perhaps our host is confused," smirked Owen.

"Possible, of course, but I sense there is purpose behind each choice that he makes."

"Yeah... that wouldn't make him any less a confused whacko."

"True." Banister shifted position then, looked over that Lt. Quinn and Ramos. "Word from home?" he asked.

Lt. Quinn gave Ramos a pat on the shoulder and stepped away, towards the rest of the group.

"Unable to get through, for the moment. We'll keep trying."

"No filing of reports, then?" said Owen, a big snarky grin. They had been told, through Lt. Quinn, that they would be required to make regular reports; she specifically to Dr. Lake, the science advisor on the outside.

"I would suggest that you have them ready," said Lt. Quinn.

"I'll do that."

"Yes. Thank you." Lt. Quinn looked at the other table. "Dr. Church? Can I speak with you?"

"Of course." Church stood and followed Lt. Quinn to the door and outside. They walked a few yards along the open promenade before stopping. Sgt. Costa stood watch another dozen steps further on, Carmody in line of sight the other direction.

"What can I do for you, Lieutenant?" asked Church. Nathaniel Church was the civilian leader on the mission, though one might not think so the way he and his partner continually squabbled.

"I believe the ultimate goal of our mission, that being to reach the top floor, has taken on a new level of urgency." said Lt. Quinn. With the death of Captain Carver, Lt. Quinn was now military head of the team. "Wouldn't you agree, Doctor?"

"Yes, Lieutenant. But, as you have already pointed out, such has been your take on the mission from the start. Not so?"

Lt. Quinn had made it clear that so far as he was concerned, the science teams were there to aid in getting the military contingent to the eightieth floor. Whatever scientific discoveries were made along the way was fine, but second to the mission.

"Yes, I suppose so," he said. "Nonetheless, circumstances force me to, well—"

"Ask that science take a back seat?"

"Not a back seat, so much as—"

"Science will likely be what gets us through this alive, Lt. Quinn."

"I understand that, Doctor."

"Then what is it you are asking?"

Lt. Quinn leaned forward and placed his hands on the rails. He stared out at the green sea. "Our focus must be on finding the access to the next floor. At each floor, the immediate goal must always be to get to the floor above."

"Of course."

"Your observations, and those of the other science teams, must focus solely on meeting that goal."

"Ah. And thus to your earlier commentary regarding our science serving the military mission."

"I'm sorry, Doctor. I—"

"And so... you will be most grateful of our scientific perspective on the matters at hand, but let us not dawdle unnecessarily."

"Under the circumstances, there can be only one mission."

We're not in the back seat, thought Church. *We're in the trunk.*

"I see," he stated. "You want me to support you on this."

"You are the civilian leader of the mission. Therefore, once you and I reach consensus..."

There were three different science teams. Church led one, Elizabeth Owen another, and Peter Asher was on his own. Dr. Church served as the overall leader of all three.

"You have met Elizabeth Owen, have you not?" Church grinned broadly. "I doubt my siding with you on this will help, Lieutenant. For all matters Elizabeth Owen, I defer to Banister."

"I will handle Dr. Owen," said Quinn. "But thank you for your concern."

Returning to the lounge, Lt. Quinn looked first to Ramos. Nothing yet.

He then turned to the rest of the group. Everyone waited expectantly. He even had Dr. Owen's full attention.

"Our first task is to get a complete picture of this ship," he said. "We need to know what's here, and just as importantly what isn't."

"The crew, for instance," said Banister.

"That would be a definite *good to know*," said Lt. Quinn. "And supplies. We need an inventory, anything we might be able to use."

"If you happen to see a doorway to another world, that'd be great," said Owen.

"Just don't leave without saying good-bye," said Church. There was an uncomfortable chuckle from several in the room.

"Yes," Lt. Quinn managed a smile, despite himself. "Maybe give a quick callout before you go, just to let the rest of us know?"

"Oh, but of course," Owen said slyly.

Lt. Quinn let it go with a slight shake of the head, then set about dividing the group into three search teams. He assigned a military person to each search team, with Cpl. Ramos staying behind in the lounge to man the radio, continue to attempt to communicate with the command center outside.

He also asked Ray Do to stay with Ramos.

"My staff go where I go," Owen stated coolly.

"I'm sorry, Doctor Owen. I'll not have anyone left alone on this ship," said Lt. Quinn.

"So pick someone else."

"Really, Elizabeth," said Banister. "You can do without Ray for an hour."

"That's not the point."

"Just what is the point?"

Elizabeth Owen set her jaw tight, gave Lt. Quinn a cold stare. "I'll not have the military dictating to me and my staff."

"Oh, dear lady," Banister moaned. "You've been answering to the military throughout your entire career."

"Everyone, please," Church stepped up beside Lt. Quinn. "It's circumstance that is doing the dictating here. And the circumstances tell me that we need one person directing traffic, a single goal on which to focus. Now, so long as the lieutenant here remembers that he's dealing with a bunch of hoity-toity scientists and not a crack military unit, then he will be the person running things."

"You speak for yourself, Church," growled Owen.

"As the civilian leader of this mission, I speak for all of us, Elizabeth. That includes you."

"Church, don't you—"

"Liz, please," Banister said softly. "Let it go. For now, let it go."

With that, Elizabeth Owen grew absolutely silent. She had lost this one, and she knew it. She would be the first to admit that she could be a pretentious ass, but she also knew when to call it a day. There would be other days. There were always other days.

Dr. Church pulled Lt. Quinn aside, spoke in barely above a whisper.

"Considering Doctor Owen's current state, it might best serve the interest of us all to send young Ray out in her stead and have her remain here in the lounge with the corporal."

Crew's Row was a narrow hallway with half a dozen doors along one side. The quarters were small, two-person rooms, each with a two-high bunk, a desk and chair, and a built-in dresser set into the wall. An eight-inch porthole provided a bit of outside light.

Asher and Susan searched the first room while Carmody stood out in the hall and kept watch.

The bunks were made, the room neat and sparse. A black and white photograph was pinned to the wall over the desk.

"At least they're human," said Susan, indicating the picture; a woman in her twenties. It was impossible to tell where the picture was taken.

"Look at her clothes," said Asher, studying the picture.

"Yes, I noticed. About sixty years out of fashion."

As with the ship. Asher continued to look curiously at the picture. He touched it.

"The photograph... old style. But I don't think the picture itself has been hanging on the wall that long."

"I see what you mean." Susan looked about the small room. "The crew has been gone a while, but not sixty years."

Asher looked in the drawers of the built-in dresser. He found a couple of shirts, several pair of dungarees. They left the room then, took the few steps down the hall to the next room. Carmody followed silently after, again stood out in the hall.

They found much the same thing in the next quarters. Right down to a photograph on the wall above the desk, this one of a young woman holding a baby. They quickly moved on to the next quarters.

The remaining quarters were the just about the same. A set of bunks, beds made, a desk and chair, built-in dresser drawers, a single porthole, a black and white photograph on the wall above the desk.

They reached the captain's quarters at the end of the hall. It was three times the size of the crew's quarters, with a bunk, large desk and chair, a table, several cabinets and a full-sized chest of drawers. Two open portholes let in light.

Asher sat behind the desk and began opening drawers.

"Not much here," he said. There were a few old pencils, block eraser, an old fountain pen; hanging files in the large drawer, nothing in them.

He pulled out a nearly empty liquor bottle with no label. He unscrewed the cap and brought the bottle under his nose.

"Wow," he said huskily. He held the bottle out to Susan. "About one swig left."

"Thanks. I'll pass." Susan stood in front of a map hanging on the wall beside a narrow door leading to the captain's private head. "An ocean, some islands. I don't recognize any of the names. English, though."

Asher screwed the cap back onto the bottle and returned it to the drawer. He looked up, frustrated. "That's it," he said.

Carmody spoke up from her position at the door. "What about a logbook?"

"Yes," said Asher. He stood, looked about the room. "Yes, don't they always keep a log? There should be a log. I don't see a log. Do you see a log?"

Lt. Quinn stepped out onto the metal gangway, some twenty feet above the floor of the hold. He walked far enough out to allow Lisa Powell and Ray Do to come through the hatch and out onto the gangway beside him.

"Looks a lot like the rear hold," said Ray.

"It's exactly like the rear hold," said Lt. Quinn. Both of the holds were empty but for a considerable amount of standing water. The lieutenant frowned, absently held onto the railing and leaned forward. There was the sound of screeching metal.

He grumbled to himself. Nothing usable in either hold, and nothing much in the handful of supply rooms they had passed while traveling the ship's central passageway connecting forward hold to rear hold.

The inventory won't take long...

"One bit of good news," said Lisa. She gave a nod to the great pool below. "We don't appear to be taking on water at the moment."

It took Quinn a few moments, but he did manage to lose the dark frown.

"Yes," he said, finally. "Quite right, Miss Powell. The situation could certainly be worse."

"Okay," sighed Ray. "Not sinking. I like it."

They had taken a measurement of the water depth in the forward hold. Four feet and stable. Unless there was something unusual about the floor of this hold, it was probably the same here.

Okay, not good, an awful lot of water, but... it wasn't getting any worse.

Lt. Quinn sought out something on the far wall that he could use as a marker to read against the water level. There was a horizontal support I-beam on the hull two feet above the water line.

"All right," he said to the others. "Let's head back to the lounge."

Sgt. Costa stood several steps from the door, watched Church and Banister as they shuffled about the pilothouse, each lost in thought, studying the banks of knobs and darkened thumbsized bulbs. They each gave off the occasional quiet *hmmph*, the soft *ahhh*. Wes Banister would nod knowingly, scratch at his thinning scalp and pull at graying hair.

What an odd pair, thought Sgt. Costa. *Always bickering, always snapping at one another, and obviously inseparable.*

Church stepped over to the forward wall, a bank of windows running the width of the pilothouse. He stared silently out at the alien sea, an unnamable green reaching all the way to the horizon. Light from an invisible sun shone through the dull glass, giving Church's dark skin a strange shimmer.

"It's warm," he said without turning.

"What's that?" asked Banister, standing before the wooden wheel. He placed his hands on it and studied their position, as if this would somehow answer unasked questions.

"The sunlight," Church grumbled. "It feels warm... through the glass."

"Interesting," Banister said absently.

"I know."

"Hmmph," said Banister. He glanced over at the old fashioned engine order telegraph. "All stop," he said, reading the speed indicator.

"So I saw," said Church, his attention still focused on the sea before them.

"No one's been here for years."

"I doubt anyone has ever been here."

Banister mumbled. He let out a quiet sigh. "Quite right."

"Doctor?" Sgt. Costa asked. She couldn't let that comment go. "Either doctor. Doesn't matter."

Doctor Church turned from window, stepped up beside his friend Banister and laid a hand absently on the wheel.

"As our host has created this environment for our benefit, there is no reason to assume that anything we may find has ever existed outside this floor."

"Excuse me?"

"What Church is trying to say is that this ship may never have existed in the real world."

"The Adversary may well have created it from the memory of any one of us."

"Yes," said Sgt. Costa. "Yes, Lieutenant Quinn did say it reminded him of an old movie."

"That could well be its origin," said Banister.

"But then what about that?" Sgt. Costa pointed to the alien sea beyond the window.

Church turned back to the view. "Perhaps it comes from the world of the Adversary."

"Or from the mind of another such as we," said Banister. "A being taken from yet another world."

Ramos tried to ignore the unnerving woman stalking the lounge. He hovered over the radio and adjusted dials, holding the headgear in place with a cupped his hand over the ear piece.

But he couldn't help himself. Each time he glanced up and away from the radio, the woman was looking in his direction. She was never in the same place, but her eyes were always on him, always watching him, always boring into his skull.

What is up with this lady?

Elizabeth Owen, for her part, said nothing. Nothing aloud, anyway. She looked to the radio man, walked to the door, looked out, looked to the radio man; walked to the tables, walked to the couch, looked to the radio man, walked to one of the portholes and looked out.

This is infuriating.

A quick trip to the bathroom. The head? Then back to the lounge. The radio man just about jumped out of his skin when she came back in. Good.

Where are they?

She started toward the door, probably for the fifth or sixth time. She was halfway across the room when the door opened and Carmody came in, Asher and Susan Bautista following behind her.

Carmody set a canvas sack on a table, ignored Owen and looked to Ramos.

"Any luck?" she asked.

"Had 'em for about five seconds," he answered. "Lost 'em before I had a chance to say anything."

"That's somethin', anyway. There's hope."

"Whatcha got?" Ramos nodded to the sack on the table.

"Hope you like spinach."

Susan Bautista had settled into a chair at the empty table. Asher sat on the arm of the couch. He looked at Owen, who by now was rummaging through the sack.

"We didn't find much in the crews' quarters; found a few things in the galley."

Carmody sat on a stool at the bar. "Whatever might have once been in the vegetable bins has long since evolved into something other than food, but we did come across some canned goods."

Owen was looking at a can of spinach. "English."

"Yep," said Asher. There wasn't much on the label other than the word 'spinach' and a small picture of a spinach plant. No dates, no list of ingredients.

Each member of the group had brought their small backpack with them from the first floor, containing basic supplies, a handful of personal items; rations and water to last four or five days at most. If they were going to survive this thing, it was important they supplement en route whenever possible.

"Yuck." Owen put the can back in the sack and continued rummaging. "That's it?"

"Some clothes in crews' quarters," said Asher. "A finger or two of whiskey in the captain's cabin."

"Now you're talking." A quick glance around the room. "You didn't bring it?"

"Sorry." He probably should have... for medicinal purposes.

Church and Banister came through the door, Sgt. Costa at their heels. She went quickly over to Ramos as the two doctors joined the group at the tables and couch. They were exchanging information when Lt. Quinn returned with his small team.

The lieutenant went straight to the military contingent at the bar, leaving Ray and Lisa to tell the others what they had found.

Ray stated categorically that this boat wasn't going anywhere under power. The diesel tanks were empty and the engine room half under water; the holds as well.

None of the three teams had come across anything that might suggest an access to the next floor. For supplies, they could only add eight cans of spinach, which may or may not be any good.

And finally, they were fairly certain they were alone. The crew, if there had ever actually been a crew, was no longer aboard.

Lt. Quinn joined them, leaving Ramos at the radio.

"We remain to our own devices," he said. "Though I believe the corporal will yet make contact with the outside world."

"All right, so what do we do now?" asked Lisa.

Quinn thought that was obvious. A methodical search. Start at the bow, work their way to the stern, deck by deck. This last had been a simple investigatory explore, discover their surroundings. Okay, they had that. They could now focus all their attention on locating the portal to the next floor.

First things, first. He placed a hand on the canvas. "How 'bout we try the spinach?"

"Count me out," said Owen.

"A critical experiment, to be sure," Church said thoughtfully. He raised a brow to the group-wide questioning gaze. "Ladies and gentlemen, we do need to know whether the food we might find along the way is edible."

"Quite right," agreed Banister.

"I'm almost afraid to find out," said Susan.

She nonetheless stood beside the lieutenant and watched as he pulled a can from the canvas sack.

"Sergeant," he said, and gave it to Sgt. Costa. She reached into her shirt and pulled out a simple can opener she kept on a chain with her dog tags. She set the can on the table and set to open it.

She froze, her hand hovering over the can, the opener at the ready.

She glanced up, first to Asher, then Lt. Quinn.

"What's that?" she asked.

A rumbling noise, very faint at first, then it grew slowly louder.

"I don't know," said Quinn.

"Crap," grumbled Owen. "What now?"

It came from somewhere below decks. As it faded, a deep vibration reverberated throughout the ship, a thrumming along the hull and inner walls.

"Did we hit something?" wondered Asher.

"I don't know," Quinn repeated.

"Perhaps we have company," Banister thought aloud.

"Crap," Owen repeated.

Episode Two / Chapter Two

General Wong entered the command center, nodded sharply to Captain Adamson as he walked across the room to the communications station.

"What's the situation, Captain?"

Adamson came up beside the general, the two of them hovering over Corporal Johansen at the radio. The corporal had had a brief communication with the team inside a few minutes earlier, but had since lost contact.

"They're on some sort of freighter," said Captain Adamson. "Nonfunctioning, and they're alone."

"It's abandoned?"

"It would appear so. And while the freighter looks to be one of ours, the ocean is certainly alien."

"Dangers? Threats?"

"Nothing specific," said Adamson. "They did report a single occurrence of some strange vibrations; lasted a few seconds and then nothing. They were unable to identify the source."

There was a crackling noise from the radio, the sound bleeding through Johansen's headset. He pushed himself forward, adjusted a knob on the face of the radio as he listened to a voice from inside the tower.

"This is Command Center," he responded. "Hello, away team... hey, where'd you go off to, Ramos? Terribly rude of you. Over."

Johansen listened to the reply, grinned and gave a chuckle. "I forgive you. Say, I have the General here; pretty sure he'd like a few moments of the lieutenant's time. Over... Okay, great. All yours. Over."

He stood and handed the headset to the general.

"Thank you, Corporal."

"Strong signal, sir. But I can't promise it'll last."

Asher stepped out onto the deck, leaving Lt. Quinn to his radio in the lounge. He found Sgt. Costa standing at the rail, hands clasped behind her back, eyes searching the horizon beyond the green sea.

He stuffed his hands into his pants pockets and stared out at the same horizon. The sea, the sky, the world... all was dead calm.

"Quite pleasant, in its own way," he said after a long silence.

"If you say so, Professor. I find the alienness of it all to be very unsettling."

"Yes. There is that." He so liked the quiet, but there was definitely an unearthly quality to the silence. Giving it a few more moments, he couldn't help but sense that if he let it, it would envelope him, swallow him up and consume him. "I see what you mean."

"A lot different than the last floor. And even more weird."

"If that's possible."

"Oh, it's more weird, all right," she said.

"I suppose you're right," said Asher, thinking it over. He wasn't sure just what made it more alien than the first floor, but it was.

"You know, I crewed on a ship," said Sgt. Costa. She shrugged then and gave Asher an embarrassed half grin. "Well, it was one summer. I was eighteen."

"Really?"

Another shrug. "Well, it wasn't much like this, but..."

"Still... I had the impression you were always army. You know, born in fatigues."

"No, not at all. That came later."

"So how'd you end up on a freighter?"

"My uncle had a friend who had a friend, a favor for a favor; got my brother and me signed on. Nothing skilled, but we managed to earn our keep."

"Of that I have no doubt, Sergeant."

Sgt. Costa gave another half-hearted shrug. "What about you, Professor? I'll bet you were born wearing a corduroy jacket with leather elbow patches."

"Hey, I haven't worn that in years." He grinned sheepishly. "Okay, I keep it on hand, just in case."

The surface of the sea was smooth as silk, not even the slow swells disturbing the glassy surface. So when there was a rippling a few hundred yards distant, it stood out. Sgt. Costa had seen it several times before, and it seemed to be following a schedule.

"I believe our friend is circling," she said calmly. "It always nears the surface at just that spot."

"Feeding, you suppose?"

"You're the professor, Professor."

"I'm afraid this is a bit out of my field."

"You're what we got. You'll do."

The rippling had settled, the pristine surface of green sea restored. Dusk was approaching, and the world slowly fell into a steadily darkening shadow.

Elizabeth Owen appeared to be settling into the Captain's Cabin quite nicely. She had already found the aforementioned liquor bottle and finished off the last swallow. She was now getting the bunk ready.

Ray Do had just left for the crew's quarters that he would be sharing with Ramos. Lisa Powell continued to hover about. Once Owen released her, she would be heading to the quarters she would be sharing with Susan Bautista.

Lt. Quinn wasn't all that keen on having the team scattered along crew's quarters, hidden away in the individual rooms. He would just as soon they all spend the night together in the lounge where he could keep an eye on everyone. But he had been soundly overruled by just about all of 'em; most vociferously by Dr. Elizabeth Owen.

Very well... he would post a guard at the end of the hall. The radio would be unmanned for a few hours, as he wouldn't leave Corporal Ramos up in the lounge on his own. He could have him bring it down with him, set it up on the small desk, but it would be awkward, and truth be told, there was really little reason.

Quinn stood at the end of the hall now, listened to the low rumbling of conversations going on in several of the quarters. Dr. Owen was giving her assistant Lisa a hard time, that disconcerting voice carrying all the way from the opposite end of the hall. Much nearer, Banister and Church were squabbling. They had come to a consensus on top bunk, bottom bunk, and yet both seemed to be voicing objections... not sure what that was about. One of them called out to Susan, asking her to intervene from her quarters next door. She gave them both a kind but firm retort and they grumbled themselves to silence.

Professor Asher came down the narrow stairwell and into the hallway behind Lt. Quinn.

"Lieutenant," he said as he stepped around him. "Getting all the kiddies settled in?"

"Will you be needing a bedtime story, Professor?"

"Oh... would you?" Asher started down the hall, spoke over his shoulder. "I'll see you later, roomie."

The lieutenant mumbled goodnight under his breath. He watched as the professor stopped to say goodnight to Susan before continuing on to the door beyond, the quarters that he and the lieutenant shared.

Corporal Ramos was standing watch at the end of the hall. Sitting actually, in the chair that he had brought out from his quarters when he relieved the lieutenant.

It was late-night peace and quiet. There was a low, dull throbbing sound of the sea against the hull, a sound that he felt more than heard.

That and the growling snore coming from the quarters where the two elderly scientists slept.

He heard a muffled, shuffling sound, and a moment later a door opened midway down the companionway. Carmody stepped out. She quietly closed the door behind her and started toward Ramos.

"Hey," she said sleepily. "You are relieved."

"Thank you much," said Ramos, standing. "All's quiet."

"Yeah..." Carmody sighed and plopped herself down in the offered chair. She rubbed her face with both hands. "Good to hear."

"Okay, maybe too quiet. Don't you go dozing off, Carmody."

"Man, when have I ever..."

"All right." Ramos took a step back, starting to his quarters, then stopped. "Ya' want me to hang around a few?"

"Nah, I'm good," said Carmody. "Really. Go get some bunk time. Expect it's gonna get busy around here in a couple of hours."

"'kay." Ramos turned then and took a step toward his quarters. There was a sudden heave port to starboard and the companionway seemed to rise, glide and fall. He had to place a hand on the wall to steady himself before the world again settled about them.

"Whoa..."

"What was that?" asked Carmody. "We been getting' much of that?"

"Not a smidge." Ramos turned to look back at Carmody, still sitting in the chair. "Dead calm all night."

"Really? Really? You had to go with *dead calm*?"

There was another heave, this one more violent, more uneven. Ramos was thrown against the wall and Carmody out of the chair and onto the floor. There were shouts and cries from the quarters.

The ship shuddered, rose and as suddenly dropped, knocking Ramos off his feet. He struck his head against the wall. Carmody scrambled over to him as he rolled over and sat.

"I'm all right," he said as she reached him. He placed two fingers cautiously against an already growing tender spot on his skull. "Ouch."

"Oh, man. Purple heart, dude," Carmody grimaced, studying the bump.

"I think I'll tough it out," Ramos shifted about to stand.

He was about to say they should check on the others when the ship rocked and jostled about again. He and Carmody both braced themselves against the floor and the walls. More angry and pained cries came from the rooms. Doors opened one after the other and people struggled to maintain balance as they came stumbling out into the hall.

Lt. Quinn and then Sgt. Costa hurried to help others as Ramos and Carmody got to their feet.

Once he was sure no one was seriously injured, Lt. Quinn called for Ramos to lead the way out of Crews Row and up the stairs. Heading for the lounge, they had to first make their way up on deck. The sky was black and starless, the sea choppy and frothy with foam, with rising swells and deep hollows. A strong, warm wind carried a heavy mist that soaked everyone moments after they stepped out into the open. Ramos stayed close to the wall as he led the others from the below-deck hatch to the lounge door.

Entering the lounge, he noticed immediately that the radio was no longer on the counter. He hurried across the room and found it on the floor behind the counter.

"Oh, no," he groaned.

Lt. Quinn was one of the last to come into the room, stepping around others that were heading for the couch or tables.

"How does it look, Corporal?" he asked. He reached the bar as Ramos brought the radio up from the floor and set it on the counter.

"Don't know yet, sir," said Ramos. "Nothing obvious. Give me five. I'll let you know."

"Very well." Quinn turned to the rest of the group. "Is everyone all right?"

There were grumbles, but it appeared injuries were limited to a few bumps and bruises. Ray disappeared into the inner hall, came back a few moments later with a handful of small cloth towels.

"Thank you, young man," said Banister, taking one. His longish salt and pepper hair hung damp from his skull. He started patting himself dry. "How much sleep did we get?" he asked of no one in particular.

"About four hours," said Quinn.

"Ah. Not so bad," Banister said cheerily. "We can make do with that."

"Not much choice in the matter," said Church.

"And so, we make do."

"Yes. I doubt we'll be getting much more this night." Church braced himself, as did everyone, as the ship lifted and dropped, angled precariously as it was pushed to starboard.

The world slowly settled.

"I just had an unsettling thought," said Owen.

"That so?" said Asher, a broadening grin.

"Don't get snotty," growled Owen. Then back to the group, "What if it's like this every night?"

"The thought occurred to me as well, Elizabeth," said Banister. "We have no idea what is normal here. If weather patterns and oceanic conditions are cyclic, it is possible we could face this nightly."

"Then I must insist on a most fervent search for the gateway on the morrow."

And of course they didn't really know when that morrow might be. The first floor had followed a twenty four hour day, with a bit more than eight hours between nightfall and sunrise. They as yet had no evidence that the same pattern would apply here, but if it did they had a few hours to dawn.

Lisa Powell watched the alien dawn from the railing. She noted the time and recorded it in her notebook. Eight hours, twenty minutes from sunset to sunrise. Come evening she would note the sunset and thereby document the length of the full day. It would take several day periods at least to determine whether the cycle was regular.

They would hopefully be gone long before they could draw any conclusions.

She put away her notebook and stepped away from the rail. She briefly considered going back inside, the door to the lounge was behind her, decided instead to take a walk around the ship. The weather had quieted, and the sea was calm. It was turning into a pleasant morning.

She came upon Lt. Quinn up near the bow. He was sitting on a large metal equipment compartment, lost in thought as he gazed outward. He quickly stood at hearing her approach, for some reason embarrassed at being caught in an off-duty moment.

"Miss Powell," he said, stammering slightly. "Doctor."

"Lisa is fine, Lieutenant."

"Ah, yes," apparently unable to reciprocate. "How are you this morning? Get the time of the sunrise recorded?"

"I did," said Lisa. She looked admiringly around them. "It's turning into a beautiful day."

"Yes. It is. Especially after the wild night we experienced."

"I hope it doesn't turn out to be a common phenomenon." Lisa sat on the edge of the equipment box. Lt. Quinn settled in beside her. Their knees barely brushed the lower cross bar of the rail in front of them.

"I expect we'll all do our best today to ensure we don't find out," he said.

"Ah," Lisa grinned. "Doctor Owen's strong desire for a 'fervent search' for the gateway."

"On the morrow."

"And this being the morrow."

"Exactly," Quinn said with a sharp nod. He smiled uncomfortably. "So... have you been with Doctor Owen long?"

"About a year and a half."

"And you... enjoy... your work?"

"The work is very interesting," she said, smiling broadly. She took a deep breath, slowly let it out. "Now Ray, he's been with her a lot longer than I have; quite a few years."

"I see," said Quinn. "I believe I heard that. That he... had been with her a long time."

"I admit, it isn't always easy," she sighed. "As you have seen for yourself. But I shouldn't talk out of school."

"Of course," he nodded quickly. "I don't mean to pry."

"Not at all. I quite understand."

Asher came out of the lounge holding a white ceramic mug in both hands. He stepped up to the rail as he took a cautious sip.

It tasted like coffee, sort of. It was hot, anyway.

He noticed a rippling on the water. It was that sea serpent again. Much closer than yesterday, though; barely twenty yards out. As he watched, the rippling took form, the seawater slid aside and Asher could see the smooth green skin of the creature. The curling hump undulated forward as the animal glided along the surface. It was glistening damp against the orange-red rays of the great ball of sun that was just rising above the horizon.

It slipped back under the surface, leaving only the familiar ripple behind. Asher turned and absently walked in the direction of the bow, following the movement of the sea creature.

The disturbance in the water drew nearer the ship. Asher saw Lisa Powell and Lt. Quinn up near the bow, watched them stand and look beyond the rail.

They saw it, too.

And then the monster rose up from the sea, a massive head on a long thick neck reaching up and up, its jaws parting, its dark eyes rolling back to black and Lisa Powell was suddenly half lost in the great mouth. She beat at it with her one free hand. Lt. Quinn pushed himself up against the broad face of the beast and grasped the upper and lower jaws and tried desperately to pull the mouth open.

Asher grabbed a rescue pike mounted on the wall as he rushed forward, thrust it at the creature's neck like a spear. It dug in deep. He pulled it out and stabbed again. All the while Lt. Quinn pulled with all his strength as he pushed his feet down firmly on the deck and leaned back. If he couldn't get the beast to release the young woman, perhaps he could keep it from returning to the sea just long enough for the professor to dissuade it and let her go.

A shadow spread across the scene.

Sgt. Costa, hammer in hand, ran up and jumped up onto the metal equipment box, used her momentum to leap up onto the monster's head. She pounded at the skull again and again.

The creature pulled back, trying to take Lisa Powell with it. Lt. Quinn used his legs to lock himself to the rail and held on tight. Sgt. Costa slid down and continued beating at the creature's forehead as Asher pushed the pike ever deeper into its neck.

Asher thought Sara Costa was probably doing more to dissuade the monster with the hammer than she would with a bullet, but he nonetheless would have liked to put the theory to the test. He wasn't all that keen on weaponry in general, but he wasn't totally averse to them. Okay, he had never had one in his hands, there was a scary thought, but right now he would have been totally comfortable with Sgt. Costa carrying one.

Since firearms wouldn't fire in here, such was not to be...

Another swing of Costa's hammer and Lisa pulled herself free. She fell backward and Lt. Quinn grabbed for her as he simultaneously let go of the creature. It slid from sight, slid into the sea, and was gone.

Episode Two / Chapter Three

Elizabeth Owen was writing in her notebook when Asher came into the lounge. He went to the coffee pot and poured a cup.

"Coffee?" he asked.

"Oh, is that what that is?" she asked snidely. She continued her scribbling. "I've been intending to ask. I didn't recognize it."

"I'll take that as a no, then." He walked back to the table and sat opposite. He took a sip... yes, it could be coffee. He set the cup down on the table. "How is Lisa?"

"Well enough." Elizabeth closed her notebook, slipped it into her knapsack on the floor beside her. "She's resting."

"She was pretty shook up."

"That she was." Elizabeth reached over and picked up Asher's coffee cup. She took a swig, raised a brow, set the cup back onto the table. "How about you, Peter?"

"I wasn't nearly eaten by a sea monster."

"Perhaps not, but you did do battle with one; came to the rescue of a damsel in distress, no less." She wiped a dab of coffee from the corner of her mouth.

"Say, I did, didn't I?" Asher grinned. "Not bad."

"A regular hero, you are." She leaned back and folded her arms across her chest. She silently watched Asher take another sip from his coffee. He held the cup out to her. She unfolded her arms and took the cup.

"Nothing on the hatch hunt, eh?" She drank down the last of the coffee, handed him back an empty mug.

Asher shook his head no. Most of the team had paired off to do another search for the way to the next floor. He had just returned from exploring the small compartments between the forward hold and the bow with Sgt. Costa. "I have this strange feeling that I've looked right at it and didn't see it for what it was."

"You mean that big orange arrow pointing to a swirling black hole and the sign reading 'This way to next floor'?"

"Do you think that was it?"

"Possibly. Maybe we should throw Quinn in and see what happens." She pointed to the empty cup that Asher was still holding. "Don't you want some more of that curious liquid?"

Asher grinned and stood. He walked casually over to the side table. Church and Banister came in as he was filling the cup.

"Well, there's no going back," said Banister. "Not that it was ever really an option."

"The hatch is gone?" asked Owen.

"Oh, it's there," said Church.

"It just won't open," said Banister. "It may look like a hatch, but I don't think it's a hatch."

Asher thought it was probably good to know there was no going back, not even in an emergency. But as Banister said, there was never really a question about returning to the first floor. They needed to find the way to the next floor.

The problem was, no matter how methodical or organized their search might be, they were still basically just poking a stick into the shadows and hoping something jumped out. They didn't know what they were looking for.

He returned to the table, absently handing Elizabeth the cup as he sat down. "I do have a thought," he said.

"Does it hurt?" Owen asked, deadpan. She brought the cup to her lips to hide a thin grin. She so enjoyed her own sense of humor.

"On occasion," Asher sighed. He looked curiously at the two senior scientists. "You'll remember something similar happening on the first floor. The door leading out vanished; leaving us only to continue forward."

"Ah, yes," said Church. "The way back closes as the way ahead opens."

"A *feature* of the tower floors?" wondered Banister. "It could be."

"Okay, so what does that give us?" asked Owen. "Nothing has really changed so far as options."

"I wouldn't be so sure," said Church. "The access to the next floor may not have been immediately available to us."

"Not until the way back was closed," Banister thought aloud. "And we don't really know when that happened."

"So we'll have to search the ship yet again," growled Owen. "Which we would have done in any case. As I said... our options remain just as they were."

"Yes, yes, right enough, Liz," sighed Banister. He spoke then to the entire group. "Given this, what are our next steps?"

"Well," Church frowned, wandered toward the couch and sat on the arm. "We must of course operate under the assumption that there is in fact a way to the next floor."

"Of course," said Banister. "Otherwise there's no point."

"Exactly so. Given that, there are really only three choices. The way lies somewhere on the ship, in the water just beyond the ship, or is just above us."

"What about on some island a thousand miles away?" asked Owen.

"As the ship will never travel under its own power, that is highly unlikely," said Church. "Again, there would be no point. Therefore, any such option is not really an option. If it cannot be reached, it is not a choice."

"All right," Owen nodded thoughtfully. "I can give you that. Then let us focus initially on the most likely."

"On the ship, then."

"Yes," Owen stated flatly. "The Adversary put us on this ship; the ship is the game board. I am as yet too unfamiliar with the Adversary to ascribe much to his reasoning, so let us for the moment go with the most obvious. At least until we learn more of his thought processes."

"Very reasonable," said Banister. He could see it coming.

"And so, we search the ship. Again."

"Yes..." hesitantly.

"Where have I heard that before?"

Lt. Quinn and Ray were at the bottom of the rear hold, down near the water line. They had found nothing and were starting across the floor toward the steep metal stairs when Sgt. Costa called down from the gangway above them.

"Something curious about the water in the forward hold, Lieutenant," she said. She was leaning against the rail, looking down at them, Carmody beside her.

"What's that, Sergeant?"

"It's warm," she said. "And it's fresh water. The forward hold."

"Fresh?"

He looked questioning to Ray Do. Ray stepped back to the water's edge and knelt down. He held a hand to the water. It was cold. He cupped a hand and brought it up to his face. He smelled it, tasted it.

"Salty," he said, looking up at the lieutenant. He grimaced. "Very salty, as a matter of fact."

Lt. Quinn looked up at Sgt. Costa. "Fresh?" He asked again.

"And warm. We tested several locations."

Quinn turned back to Ray. "Finally something for you white-coats to mull over, eh?"

Ray stood, his back to the water. He smiled as he wiped his wet hand on his pants. "I know a couple of old codgers who are going to—"

He stopped when he saw the disconcerted look on Lt. Quinn's face. "What?" he asked.

Quinn took hold of Ray by the arm. He stepped back as he looked beyond Ray, toward the water.

Sgt. Costa called out calm and cool from above. "Back it up, boys."

"Get outta there!" cried Carmody.

A disturbance in the water; a rippling, and the head of the sea creature rose up from the surface, higher and higher, the long neck undulating.

Lt. Quinn continued to pull Ray back as he stepped further from the water.

Ray turned slowly about. As he looked up, the creature lowered its head, turned slightly and studied Ray.

"Pick up the pace, Lieutenant," said Costa.

Lt. Quinn again took hold of Ray's arm. "Let's go, Ray," he said, forced calm.

The face of the serpent began to morph. Its features slowly contorted. It became the face of the Adversary, as Carmody and Raso had seen on the first floor... when Raso had been killed.

"Oh, my god," cried Carmody, now barely above a whisper. "Oh, my god."

The great serpent pushed its face ever closer to Ray, its grin broadening, growing more menacing.

Church and Banister sat at one of the tables in the lounge, hovering over a collection of pencil drawings outlining various sections of the ship. They talked quietly, and whenever they came to agreement Banister would update one of the drawings.

Asher stood at the counter watching Ramos tweak knobs on the radio. They hadn't been able to communicate with command since before the radio took that spill and ended up on the floor. There was some concern that the inability to make contact might be more than just the Adversary playing games. If the radio was in fact broken, and irreparable, they might be out of communication with the outside world for the rest of the mission.

Owen came into the lounge from the back hall. She wore a worried look. "Did you hear that?"

"Sorry, Liz." Banister looked up from the drawings. "What was it you heard?"

"I'm not sure. Raised voices, maybe?"

"I'm afraid I didn't hear anything."

Asher took a step from the counter. He listened, at first hearing only the background noises of the sea brushing up against the creaking ship.

Then, something...

Owen looked to Asher. "Peter?"

"Uh, huh," he said. "Yes..."

It was very faint. Someone crying out... a man crying out.
Then a woman's scream, also very faint.

"That's Carmody," said Ramos.

"Something is very, very wrong," said Owen.

Asher started toward the door. "Come on."

Sgt. Costa stood on the gangway some twenty feet above the floor of the hold, both hands on the rail. Carmody was sitting beside her, back against the wall, elbows on her knees, her face buried in her hands.

Asher came through the hatchway, took one step and stopped. Costa continued to look down onto the floor of the hold, slowly dropped her hands to her sides. She took a long, shuddering breath.

Asher moved nearer the rail, peered over the side. He looked curiously back to Costa, again down onto the floor.

He was missing something, but he didn't know what. Nothing looked out of the ordinary.

There was Lt. Quinn. He was standing alone near the water's edge, the rippling surface slowly settling.

Episode Two / Chapter Four

Asher stepped through the hatch and out onto the deck. He walked in the direction of the lounge, passing Elizabeth Owen consoling a very shaken Lisa Powell along the way. Owen didn't look that much better than Lisa.

In the lounge, Banister and Church stood near one table, Susan sitting in one of the chairs. Ramos and Carmody were at the counter. Carmody glanced once at Asher as he came in, then looked to Banister and Church.

"Why isn't the ship sinking?" she asked. "If there's a hole in the hull big enough for the creature to get through, why isn't the ship sinking?"

"Buoyancy?" suggested Ramos. He was getting nowhere with the radio.

"The salt content is high, but not nearly high enough," said Church.

Asher sat on one arm of the couch. "How can the water in the forward hold be fresh and warm, while the rear hold is cold and salty? A chemical reaction to something on the ship?"

Banister and Church had already come to a consensus. Banister straightened and folded his arms across his chest. "Hazarding a guess, the water in the forward hold comes from a different source."

"And is therefore the passage to the next floor," stated Church.

"I see," said Asher. "That could also explain... this junction between floors could be working as an air pocket."

"And keeping the ship afloat."

Realization swept slowly across Carmody's face like a gray shadow. "You're not suggesting that we—"

"Yes, my dear," said Banister. "Exactly so."

The team was scattered about on the floor of the forward hold. Several wore their backpacks, others had stacked theirs together in a pile a few yards from the water's edge.

"Even the air is warmer here," noted Susan.

"No doubt radiating from the water's surface," said Church.

Lt. Quinn approached the pool cautiously, squatted down and reached into the water with a cupped hand. He brought up a palm of water, tasted it.

"It's fresh, all right," he said, looking to Sgt. Costa. He stood and looked to the entire group. "And quite warm."

"The environment on the other side bleeding through to this side," Banister stated.

"Great choice of words there, Wes," grumbled Owen.

"What does that tell us about the next floor?" asked Quinn.

"I don't believe it tells us much of anything, Lieutenant," said Susan.

"Doctor Bautista is right," said Owen. "We could walk into a volcano, or a steamy bathroom with a heat lamp."

PFC Carmody had been keeping her distance from the water's edge. She wasn't ready for this. "We're not really going in there? Into the water? With the sea monster?"

"Not to worry, Private," Banister soothed. "This is not the same body of water. The source is the next floor. No creature."

"Not the same creature," Church corrected. "There could be a completely different monster."

"True." Banister bowed his head. "But I suggest that if this is in fact the portal to the next floor, our Adversary would see that it was traversable."

"We have no choice, in any case," finished Church.

"But... but this would take us down," Carmody said, a hint of desperation. "We're supposed to be going up."

"We're not really going up or down, my dear," sighed Owen. She had resigned herself to what they were about to do. "We're going *somewhere else*."

"Exactly so," said Banister. "The entrance can appear to us to be up, down, forward, back, left, right. And we might come out on the other side upside down and diagonal."

Lt. Quinn walked over to the collection of backpacks, found his and began slipping into it. "I'll go first." He started back to the water. "Give me what time you think is sufficient to attempt to get word back if I run into problems."

"Good luck, Lieutenant," said Church.

Quinn gave him a nod in thanks, turned looked to Costa. "Send them through one or two at a time, Sergeant. You bring up the rear."

"Yes, sir."

Lt. Quinn stepped into the water. Each step took him down just a little deeper. He mumbled something about the water being fine and disappeared beneath the surface without looking back.

Ramos set the radio onto the floor and slid out of his backpack. He took out a small pouch and unfolded a poncho. Sgt. Costa looked on doubtfully as he began wrapping the radio. He would never get a watertight seal, but perhaps it would help.

"Who would like to go next?" she asked the group.

Elizabeth Owen rested an uncharacteristically motherly hand on her assistant's shoulder. "Let us be off, Miss Powell."

"Yes Ma'am."

They stepped into the water side by side. A few yards in, Elizabeth Owen turned back to those still on shore. "Oh my, this does feel pleasant. Peter, we should have done a bit of skinny dipping when we had the chance."

"Perhaps on the other side," said Asher, grinning.

Owen had already turned forward, spoke over her shoulder. "It's a date, then."

Ramos had settled again into his backpack. He picked up the poncho-wrapped radio and headed to the water. "See you on the other side."

Costa looked sharply at Carmody. "You. Into the water."

"Sergeant, I—"

"Now."

Carmody stepped forward. She hesitated, held her arms stiffly at her sides, fluttered her fingers. Without looking back, without saying another word, she went into the water and quickly forward.

"Okay." Asher in turn looked to Susan, Banister and Church. "After you."

Susan let out a noisy breath and entered the water. Asher then urged the two scientists with a wave of the hand.

"No, go right ahead, young man," said Church.

"We'll be right behind you," added Banister. "See to Susan."

Both were grinning. They had donned their backpacks. They were ready.

"All right." Asher stepped quickly to the last remaining backpack, swung it up and around. "Don't be long about it."

They watched him disappear beneath the surface. Both then looked back to Sgt. Costa. She in turn looked to them with a raised brow.

"Shall we?"

"Of course," said Banister.

The ship shuddered suddenly. A moment later the water level began to rise.

Church and Banister looked curiously at one another.

"Change in ballast." Church stated calmly.

"Our Lieutenant has reached the other side," said Banister. "The passage is open."

"Water on both sides seeking common level."

There was more alarming movement from the ship. It began to list to one side.

"Doctors," urged Sgt. Costa. "I think we should go now."

"Yes," agreed Banister. "Let us be off."

The small lake, perhaps a thousand feet across, was surrounded by tall, yellow grass and a few scrubby bushes, one gnarly oak tree. The sun was high overhead, the horizon in the distance beyond a flat, open plain.

Lt. Quinn had slipped out of his backpack, waded back into the water and assisted Owen and her assistant to the bank. As he did, others of the team began to appear, the smooth, glassy surface of the still lake rippling and churning.

Quinn hurried back in to help Susan the last few yards. As he went back to see to the others, Susan took another few steps, slowly caught her breath as she casually took in their surroundings.

Ahead of them, just over a short rise, was a tiny, old-west town; little more than a dusty road and a couple of dozen buildings. There was no movement, no sign of life.

Turning about in a slow circle, Susan realized that this was it. They were out on a wide-open windswept plain, with the only features this one small lake and a cluster of old buildings lining a single dirt street.

Sgt. Costa was the last to make an appearance. She trudged out of the water, sputtering, nodded a sharp affirmative to Quinn. She shrugged out of her backpack, looked around them, glanced up at the warm, bright sun.

"Looks like ours, doesn't it?" asked Asher, shading his eyes, also looking up at the sun.

"If you say so, sir."

~ end of episode two

Episode Three
Ghost Town

Prolog

The team was gathered along the shore of the lake. It was small, a thousand feet across at most, surrounded by yellow grass and a few scrubby bushes. Lt. Quinn stepped away from the others and approached a short rise. The cloudless pale blue sky seemed close enough to touch. He fought the urge to reach a hand up and...

A few hundred yards beyond the rise lay a small town right out of the old west. Main Street was a dusty road lined on either side by a handful of assorted wooden buildings.

Sgt. Costa and Asher came up beside the lieutenant, the others following not far behind.

"Waddya say, Marshall?" Asher asked in an exaggerated western twang. "Stand me for a shot a' rotgut?"

Lt. Quinn responded with an awful "*Why shore, pardner.*"

Asher cringed good-naturedly.

Sgt. Costa's expression was slightly more pained. "You might want to work on that, Lieutenant."

"No... no, that's it for that," sighed Quinn. He would not be trying that again. He looked to the group. "Onward, then."

At a sharp nod from the lieutenant, Sgt. Costa led the way toward town, with Quinn and Professor Asher half a dozen paces behind. The bulk of the group, all still soaking wet from their foray through the watery passage from the second floor, followed behind them, Private Carmody and Corporal Ramos bringing up the rear.

The third floor looked to be as different from the second floor, it with its antiquated freighter on an alien sea, as that floor had diverged from the first.

Above the straggling line of travelers, the pale blue sky flickered once, twice... then all was well...

Episode Three / Chapter One

Asher stepped down from the planked walkway that fronted the general store and crossed the entrance of the narrow alley that ran between the two buildings. He took the single step then up onto a similar wood deck that spanned the front of the saloon.

The sloped canopy hanging above the porch shaded him from a warm sun that heated the dirt street. Across the way was the hotel, a big square box of a building with a row of windows spanning the width of the second floor. Standing at the edge of the porch, Asher saw a figure move past one of those windows. It was Elizabeth Owen, settling into one of the rooms.

Asher turned about and pushed through the saloon doors. The air inside was much cooler, and after the glare of Main Street, the room was a bit dark. It took a few moments for his eyes to adjust.

Corporal Ramos had the radio set up on a table in one corner. It had survived the trip through the watery portal well enough, but he wasn't having any success making contact with the outside world.

Lt. Quinn and Sgt. Costa hovered over a table in the middle of the room, were looking down at a roughly drawn map of the town; two rows of buildings facing each other across a thirty foot wide dirt road.

Asher came up to the table, gave the map a quick glance.

"Professor," said Quinn, looking up from the table. "Is Miss Powell settling in all right?"

"Don't know about that," said Asher. "But she's getting Liz settled in well enough."

"Ah, yes... of course."

"She'll be all right, Lieutenant," said Asher. Ray Do's death had been particularly gruesome, and Ray and Lisa had been close friends as well as colleagues for years.

"Yes. I'm sure she will," Quinn stated quietly. He turned back to the map. "To the business at hand, then."

Asher absently nodded in the general direction of map. "It's a doctor's office, all right."

Elizabeth Owen had insisted on finding a room in the hotel, stating that she would *look things over* as she was getting settled in. Most everyone else had been sent out to get an initial impression of the town, to look for any obvious signs of a portal to the next floor. Asher had walked the outer perimeter of the town beyond the buildings on his way to what appeared to be a doctor's office near the far end of town and on the other side of the street from the saloon.

"Did you find anything we might be able to use?" asked Quinn. Obviously, if Asher had seen anything that might indicate a portal, he would already have said as much.

"Not really," said Asher. He had seen nothing out of the ordinary, neither during his walk nor in the small building. "Though, it looks like one corner of the front room has been set aside for a dentist; an archaic dentist. Scary stuff."

Sgt. Costa grinned politely, but Quinn only nodded curtly and made a note on the map at the location of the doctor's office.

"What was your impression of the town," he asked as he finished and tossed the pencil onto the table.

"About what you'd expect," Asher shrugged. "Looks like any small town you'd figure to find in the old west, if you only had old westerns to go by."

Lt. Quinn nodded knowingly. "My thought exactly."

"Another landscape pulled from our own thoughts," suggested Sgt. Costa.

"Makes sense," said Asher. "And I suppose we should keep that in mind as we investigate this new environment."

"Again, my thought exactly." Lt. Quinn folded his arms across his chest and frowned down at the map. "Yes. Well. I think I'll do a bit more of that exploring right now."

"Do you want me to go with you, Sir?" asked Sgt. Costa.

"No need, Sergeant. I shouldn't be getting into any trouble; just a quiet stroll up and down the street, see if I run across any of our fellow travelers.

"Yes, Sir." Sgt Costa watched her lieutenant stroll over to the saloon's swinging doors and mosey on outside. She gave Asher another grin and nodded in the direction of the bar. "I'll spot you a drink, Professor."

"That's Peter, please," said Asher. "Or Asher. You make me sound old." They started toward the bar. "A stocked bar?"

"Haven't looked." Sgt. Costa stepped around behind the bar and began rummaging around. "Not that I myself would do any drinking on duty, Asher."

"Not much of a drinker, myself, Sergeant."

Costa came out from under the counter empty handed and placed her hands flat on the bar. "That's not going to be a problem."

"Probably for the best."

"Actually, I was hoping for something that we could all partake in, like bottled water."

"I think bottled water might be out of place in this setting."

"Yes," She nodded quickly. "You're right. The façade must be maintained."

"At least until we find out differently."

Sgt. Costa looked past Asher and called across the room to Corporal Ramos, who was about to give up on the radio. "Hey, Ramos, d'you find anything resembling water when you searched this place?"

"There's a well out back." Ramos looked dejectedly at the radio as he leaned back in his chair. "Didn't try drawin' any water out of it. Was lookin' for the portal."

While searching for that portal, he had dropped a stone into the well, watched for a reaction that might indicate the passage to the next floor. He had seen nothing; but then, he hadn't heard the splash that would mean water, either.

"You taking a break from that radio? Why don't you check it out?" asked Costa.

Ramos pushed his chair back and stood up. "I don't mind if I do."

Costa spoke then to Asher. "The lake water is drinkable, but just barely."

"We have what we brought with us," said Asher. They had filled their canteens before leaving the last floor. That was a standing directive from the lieutenant. Whenever possible, canteens were to be filled before moving to the next floor. They never knew where they would find themselves.

"Then let us hope we find another source soon," said Asher.

"Yes, Sir." She rested her arms on the counter and clasped her hands. "And food. We didn't come away from the freighter with much."

"Spinach."

Costa frowned. That and what they brought with them wasn't going to last long.

"I'm sure we'll find something." They both knew they had five days rations at best. They would have to supplement food and water en route if they expected to make it all the way to the top floor.

"I hope you're right," said Costa.

"I'm certain of it. If not here, then soon enough. If the Adversary has any expectation that we survive this gauntlet that he's set before us, there will have to be supplies along the way."

"I don't want to live off MREs and spinach for the entire mission."

"I'm sure that won't be necessary."

"It sure won't," said Carmody, pushing her way through the swinging doors. She was dressed in clean, dry civilian clothes and carried an armful of neatly folded shirts and pants. She set the stack down on the nearest table. "Doctor Bautista and I hit the jackpot."

Susan Bautista followed Carmody into the saloon, also dressed in clean pants and shirt, carrying an armful of new clothes, all carefully folded.

"Not bad," said Asher, wandering over to the table. "Not what I would consider edible, but not bad."

"Cute," said Susan. "We thought everyone might like a change of clothes."

"But there's a wall of shelves filled with canned goods and staples," said Carmody. "More than we can take with us."

Sgt. Costa came around the bar and walked to the table. She admired a shirt, then a pair of pants.

"You're out of uniform, Private Carmody," she said, holding up another shirt.

"Yes, Sergeant," said Carmody.

"Don't be hard on her, Sara," said Susan. "I have to say, it feels good gettin' out of those wet, smelly things."

"Understood," Costa smiled thinly. She tucked the shirt under her arm, selected a pair of pants. She focused her attention back to Carmody. "Once our fatigues are cleaned and dried, we will dress appropriately; uniform of the day."

"Yes. Of course."

"You know the Lieutenant's thinking on this mission. Military discipline exists for a reason, and we have a very long way to go."

Ramos stood at the well, his back to the back wall of the saloon. He was tying a thin, discolored rope to the handle of an old, wooden bucket. Beyond the well, the illusion of wide-open prairie spread out to a false horizon. The big ball of the sun hung in the sky overhead, warming his skin, heating his shirt and pants till it was almost unpleasant.

The rope had been in place, a few yards coiled around the crank axle, the remainder suspended down into the dark of the well. He had found the bucket near the back steps of the saloon.

He absently brushed at his face, as if something was there, without really thinking about it, and continued tying the rope.

A few quiet moments later, the hint of a willowy breeze whispered past him; but there had been no wind.

He looked up from his work, glanced curiously about, as if only just realizing that something had been going on and that he had missed it.

Is somebody here?

Some... thing?

Ramos grew increasingly uncomfortable. He didn't see anything, or anyone, but that only made it worse.

What had happened to Raso way back on the first floor was now very fresh in his mind. Raso and Carmody had come face to face with the Adversary, and it hadn't ended well.

It hadn't ended well at all.

Ramos went cold, this despite the hot sun. He couldn't say why.

Something caressed the back of his hand; he jerked it away from the bucket. He took a step back.

I felt that... I did... I felt that.

Uh... what did I feel?

He took another step back, two steps nearer now to the back door of the saloon and the company of another human being.

Elizabeth Owen stood at the window of her upstairs hotel room. She watched a thin, wispy dust cloud drift placidly down the center of the street below. The saloon was directly across from the hotel, with a general store on one side of it, a café on the other.

The world was unnervingly quiet.

Owen spoke to Lisa without turning from the window, her tone deceptively casual.

"I suppose we should be going down soon, join the others in the search."

"Yes, Ma'am." Lisa had just come from her room, having cleaned herself up as best she could. She had earlier done her best to dry their clothes and brush them out. "I'm ready."

"Good." Owen showed no sign of turning from the window. "I think we may soon have fresh clothes. I saw Susan and the Girl Private carrying armfuls of new shirts and pants over to the saloon a few minutes ago."

"Private Carmody," Lisa stated flatly.

"Sure. Whatever." Owen had formed a grudging respect for Sgt. Costa, but the others had yet to prove themselves in her eyes; particularly the Girl Private.

She saw a shadow move across the rooftop of the saloon.

Rather, she thought she saw a shadow. A silhouette, a figure perhaps, something...

Actually, she wasn't absolutely certain that she had seen anything.

She said nothing, focused all her attention on the space just beyond the rooftop façade of the saloon.

"Doctor Owen?" asked Lisa. She stood waiting near the door.

"Yes?" Owen mumbled absently.

"Shouldn't we be going?"

"Yes." Owen kept her attention across the way. There it was again... something... a flurry of dark shadow, as a cape fluttering in the breeze... then it was gone.

"Ma'am?"

"Yes, Lisa... on our way..."

Banister stepped away from the dais and down from the raised platform that served as altar for the small, rustic church. Nathaniel Church sat in the last pew, one arm resting on the back, quietly observing his friend.

"What did you expect, Banister?"

"I expected nothing." Banister walked down the central aisle, passing several pews. He stopped midway, slowly turned about and faced the podium, hands on hips. "And yet, finding the portal in a house of worship would have said something as to our host's mind."

"The Adversary is not so obvious," grumbled Church. He brusquely brushed at his closely trimmed hair with the flat of his palm. "Perhaps the fact that the portal isn't here speaks to us as well."

"Not to me." Banister took a step and leaned against the nearest pew. He studied the very crude wood carving of Jesus on the cross that hung on the wall behind the altar. What paint remained had chipped and faded. "These worlds have such detail."

"I will grant him that." Church leaned forward, rested his arms on the back of the pew in front of him and clasped his hands. "Now if the details would only provide us with answers."

"I'm sure they will come," Banister sighed. He glanced about the room, pulling his own long salt and pepper hair behind his ears. "Perhaps we must first decipher how to ask the questions."

"Come up with the correct questions."

"Correct or not, there are two questions that sit at the top of my list, and they shall remain there until answered."

Church looked up at the exposed rafters and called out, "Who are you? Why this gauntlet?"

"Question one and question two," said Banister.

The front door opened and Lt. Quinn came into the church.

"Important questions, I'm sure," he said. He took off his cap and tucked it under his arm. "However, my own would probably be more immediate; food, water, potential threats... and the magic key to finding the portals on each floor."

"Why yes, of course, Lieutenant," Church said, standing. "And so you see the value in having both military and scientific perspectives on this mission."

"Yes..." he said warily. "Though I'm a bit surprised to hear you admit that, Doctor Church."

"Grudgingly, Lieutenant. Most grudgingly."

"I'll take it, Doctor, however reluctant it comes," Quinn said, almost cheerily, before going slowly silent.

There was something unsettling about the apprehensive expression that Quinn saw suddenly appear on Church's face.

"Doctor? Is something wrong?" he asked at last.

Church watched as an inky black, wormlike shadow slithered across Lt. Quinn's face. It slid across one cheek, up over the bridge of the man's nose and onto the other cheek. It twisted slowly about and moved up to his forehead, across his brow, finally disappearing into Quinn's hair.

"Doctor?" Quinn asked again. He was obviously oblivious to what had just happened.

Church forced himself to turn away. He looked across the pews and out through one of the narrow side windows. He looked then up at the podium standing tall at the front of the room.

Everything seemed to be just fine.

Banister stepped up beside him. "Are you all right?"

"Yes. Of course I'm—" He stopped abruptly.

Banister started to ask what was wrong, instead slowly turned to look where Church's disconcerting gaze took him.

The face of Jesus was no longer that of Jesus; the carved, wooden head no longer slumped down, chin onto his chest.

The head was now lifted up, the face human and yet not quite human. The mouth was upturned, the hint of a demented smile, teeth showing.

And the eyes... bright eyes, shining eyes... as the face looked down on Church, Banister and Lt. Quinn.

Episode Three / Chapter Two

General Wong stood outside the Quonset hut gazing up at the gleaming black tower. It was near dusk, and it seemed that all the sun's rays were being pulled into the great monolith. There was an ethereal purple glow surrounding the tower.

Captain Adamson stepped outside the command center and stood beside the general. The door clattered closed behind them.

"Still nothing, General," he said, looking up at the tower. The purple haze was beginning to fade as dusk grew to dark. "Johansen believes they attempted communication earlier, but the connection was lost before it started."

"That's something, anyway."

"Sir?"

"If they're trying to contact us, it means they made it to the third floor."

"So. A bit of news after all."

At the base of the tower, near where the only door into the tower had once been, two powerful lights mounted on tripods were being turned on, their focus the exact location of the now vanished opening.

An around-the-clock watch detail was posted there. Should the door reappear, General Wong wanted to know about it; immediately.

They had tried cutting their way into the tower using the most advanced equipment available. They hadn't made even so much as a scratch.

They had brought in archeological equipment to measure the density of the material of the tower's outer wall at various locations, looking for weak spots and hidden passages.

There were no weak spots, no hidden passages.

They tried digging down beside the tower. They found only more wall.

There was no way in without an invitation.

The sound of the door behind them opening; Johansen poked his head out. He spoke with a quiet calm.

"Sirs?"

Captain Adamson turned about just enough to acknowledge the interruption. General Wong only clasped his hands behind him and waited.

"Sirs?" Johansen asked again, more of a request for permission to disturb them. "Sirs... I have Lt. Quinn on the line for you."

"Excellent," stated Adamson.

General Wong simply grinned oh so slightly and gave a quick, curt nod.

The saloon appeared crowded, with everyone in the team there. Ramos and Quinn were hovering over the radio, the lieutenant filling General Wong in on their current situation. It was important that he detail as many of the facts and suppositions as quickly as possible, as they had no idea when they might lose communication.

Banister, Church and Liz Owen sat at one of the tables, while everyone else was gathered around either side of the bar. A few had glasses of water close to hand. For the moment, the water came from their canteens. They all still hoped to find water from somewhere other than the lake, but Ramos had yet to return to the well.

"Ghosts?" Carmody asked doubtfully. She was half snickering, but this was more from discomfort than from disbelief. In the tower, it seemed that just about anything could be true. She turned to the brains sitting around the table. "Crazy, right?"

None answered at first. Banister finally let out a low sigh. "I do believe this is meant to be a ghost town."

This brought a low growl from Owen. "Okay, damn it. Whose mind did he pull this one out of?"

"Ghosts?" Carmody asked again.

"What we saw in the church had a supernatural flavor to it," said Church. "Not your traditional ghosts as such."

Costa indicated Ramos, who was still over at the radio with Lt. Quinn. "What Ramos saw was definitely of a ghostly nature."

"What I saw, as well," said Owen.

"All right," said Asher. "What we're talking about here aren't ghosts. What we're experiencing is the Adversary's interpretation of ghosts... or whatever supernatural flavor you want to put on all this."

"The Adversary's minions playing at ghosts," agreed Susan.

"Right."

"But what does that mean for us?" asked Carmody. "How do we deal with the interpretation differently than we would the real thing?"

"You often deal with the real thing, do you?" sneered Owen.

"She asks the right question, Liz," said Asher.

"That she does," agreed Church. "Do these representations follow the same rules that we have given your everyday ghosts and other supernatural phenomena?"

"The rules that whomever the Adversary pulled this little dreamscape from," said Owen.

"Ghosts can't really hurt you, can they?" asked Lisa.

"Ghosts?" asked Carmody, yet again, for the third time. "Really?"

"True or not in the real world," said Susan, "In here, ghosts, or something like ghosts, have been created for our benefit."

"And whether or not they can harm you would depend on the culture or beliefs from which you draw their origin," said Church. "For the most part, the created environments we find ourselves in appear to follow the guidelines of the memory from which they were born."

Banister slowly shook his head. "Ah, but the Adversary has no problem deviating from those guidelines whenever it suits him."

"You don't know that," argued Church. "He may very well be following very strict rules. We just don't know what those rules are."

"If you're right, Doctor, then how do we figure out these rules?" asked Costa.

"By watching for consistent patterns in our interactions with what the Adversary presents to us, through extrapolation from actions and events."

"Holy crap," groaned Owen. She rubbed at her brow as if to work away a deep-seated pain.

"It will certainly take time," Church continued. "We'll not likely resolve it on this floor, or even the next."

"Holy crap," Owen repeated, the groan all the deeper.

When evening came, for most of the team it actually did feel like it should be evening. For the moment the cycle on this floor seemed to match their own. That could change if they spent much time here.

After a leisurely meal from their rations, they headed over to the hotel across the street. They all quartered on the second floor, pairing off to the same room partners as they had back on the freighter. Also, somewhat similar to their quarters on the freighter, a watch was established at the end of the hall near the top of the stairs. Carmody stood first.

There was a primitive water closet at the other end of the hall, though without the requisite water to make it fully functional. Costa and Ramos made a trip to the lake with several buckets each. A bit of water poured into the commode after each use made the water closet workable enough and saved everyone late-night walks to the outhouse behind the hotel.

Once he had finished settling into his room, Asher went downstairs and then outside. He wanted to take one more walk around town before it was fully dark.

He had only just stepped out the front door of the hotel when he met Quinn coming around from the alley. The lieutenant was making the rounds himself. They started together along the planked walkways fronting each of the buildings in town.

As they walked they speculated on where they might find the access to the next floor. It was little more than small talk, since they didn't have much on which to base their conjectures. They didn't see anything in common between the two portals they had discovered so far, the ladder on the first floor leading to a hatch, and the pool of water in the hold of the freighter on the second that led here. And as for trying to guess what the Adversary might be thinking... they didn't have very much to go on there, either; at least not yet.

They were outside the telegraph office when Asher stopped and looked curiously across the street. He thought he saw a light through the front window of the general store. It moved, as if someone was carrying a lantern.

"Is that Sara?" he asked Quinn. Costa had left the hotel a minute or two ahead of him.

"Sergeant Costa and Ramos are making another trip out to the lake," said Quinn.

"Then—"

"Everyone else is accounted for."

"Okay, so then who might that be?"

As they looked on, windows all over town began glowing with the flickering light of unseen oil lamps. Shadows passed before the windows.

"I'm not liking this," mumbled Quinn.

"It would seem our little community has a night life."

Costa and Ramos appeared at the end of town, returning from the lake with buckets in hand. Seeing the lit windows and the shadows, they hesitated, soon stopped.

Asher and Quinn stepped into the street.

"This can't be good," said Quinn.

"Probably not."

A sound then... a low rumbling as of a number of people all talking at once.

"Where's that coming from?" Quinn mumbled. After a few moments, he eyed the saloon. "There."

And then came the sound of the piano playing. Bright and cheery. Lively. Harsh and out of tune.

"Everyone accounted for, eh, Lieutenant?"

"I'm afraid so, Professor."

"Yeah."

"Well, I suppose I should get this over with." Quinn let out a long, dark sigh and started across the street.

Asher followed. Sgt. Costa and Ramos set down their buckets and approached from the edge of town.

The music got louder and more lively as they all drew nearer. The dull roar of voices, though unintelligible, also seemed to grow louder. The light from inside spilled out through the windows and onto the street.

Quinn climbed the steps up onto the porch. "Wait here," he said.

"I don't think so," said Asher. He followed Quinn up the steps. Costa silently followed Asher, leaving Ramos standing on the bottom step.

Quinn raised his hands to push open the swinging doors.

The piano stopped.

The voices stopped.

Quinn pushed his way through the doors and entered the saloon. As he did, the room grew dark. There was only the faint light of dusk coming in through the windows, creating shadows in all the corners, beneath the tables and behind the bar.

Asher and Costa stepped up beside Quinn.

"Must be shy," said Asher.

"I'm pretty sure I asked you to wait outside."

"Yeah, really sorry 'bout that."

Quinn looked side-glance at Costa.

"Keeping an eye on the civilian, Lieutenant," said Costa.

"Uh, huh."

At that moment the oil lamp on the wall above the piano began to glow; dim and first, then increasingly brighter.

A piano key struck a sour note. Then a second key struck.

Then... nothing.

The light from the oil lamp flickered unsteadily but stayed lit.

Outside, Ramos stepped slowly down from the porch step and into the street. The town had grown dark; the graying sky overhead more gray.

A single window began to glow a brownish yellow, the light within shimmered and fluttered.

A second window in another building turned yellow. And then another.

Ramos glanced back to the swinging doors of the saloon. He looked back up the street.

The silhouette of a tall figure stood in the middle of the street near the livery; calm and still as the darkening shadows.

Across from the livery, the windows of the laundry began to glow, spilling yellow light out into the street and onto the figure.

"Lieutenant?" Ramos called softly, a touch anxious.

Episode Three / Chapter Three

Owen watched from her second story window. Ramos was in the street below, standing outside the saloon. Down near the livery, someone stood in the center of the street, the figure mostly in shadow.

Light spilled out then from the laundry opposite the livery and Owen was able to see the shape more clearly. It had the appearance of a man.

Lisa stepped up beside Owen. "A gunfighter?" she asked.

Owen studied the figure. He wore a maroon-colored vest beneath a long, black coat; black pants and boots, a flat-brimmed hat, the brim low and even above the eyes. From this distance, it was impossible to get a good look at the face.

Owen frowned uncertainly. "More like playing at being a gunfighter." She thought he looked like some nineteenth century European nobleman come to experience the American West that he'd read about in dime novels.

Corporal Ramos was joined by Quinn and Costa, coming out of the saloon. A moment later, the three started up the street toward the dark figure.

Quinn stopped when they were three or four paces from the stranger; close enough to comfortably have a conversation. He held a hand up for others to stand fast, *this time I mean it*, and took one more step.

"Are you the Adversary?" he asked.

While the light from nearby windows managed to splash across the figure, the face beneath the flat brim of the hat was still mostly in shadow.

The eyes, however, sparkled in pools of black.

"I am but his humble servant." He spoke with a heavy accent, faintly European and yet not quite.

"Hmm. I see. Well, maybe you can help. We have a few issues that need addressing."

"That is irrelevant. I am not here to *address issues*."

Quinn felt a cold chill. In a previous meeting quite similar to this, the visit had ended with Raso being killed.

He did his best to maintain his composure. "Is this to be a one-sided conversation?" he asked.

"I really wouldn't call it a conversation at all, Lieutenant Quinn. That would imply a back and forth exchange, and as you have surmised, information will for the most part be flowing in one direction."

"I'm always willing to listen to what those on the other side of a disagreement have to say."

"Most wise, Lieutenant."

"I wonder what's going on," said Lisa, watching Quinn and the stranger outside the livery. They appeared to be in polite conversation. Professor Asher, Sgt. Costa and Cpl. Ramos stood a pace behind the lieutenant.

"I expect we'll find out soon enough," said Owen. She was as curious as Lisa, but there was no sense speculating. Her hope at the moment was that the meeting would end without anyone dying. Their number was growing smaller with each floor.

There was a knock at the door, and before Owen could tell Lisa to go see who it was, Church and Banister came into the room.

"Sorry to barge in, Liz," said Church. "We were wondering if your view of the little get-together was any better than ours."

"You're right next door," said Owen.

"The angle, Elizabeth." He stepped up to the window, crowding Owen and Lisa. "It's not much better, Wes."

"Then we wait and hope," said Banister.

"It appears peaceful enough," said Church.

"Right up until it isn't."

"Please, Elizabeth."

"Sorry."

"Looks like it's breaking up," said Lisa. Quinn and the others were backing away from the stranger. The stranger took a short step back, turned and started away.

"That it does, Miss Powell," said Church. He headed across the room toward the door. Banister was right beside him.

Lisa called to them, her focus still on the street outside. "I think they're going to the saloon."

"I suggest we join them," said Church, and he opened the door.

"Right behind you, Nate." Banister looked back to Owen and Lisa Powell. "Ladies?"

"By all means," said Owen.

Ramos was chuckling lightly, and even Sgt. Costa was struggling to hold back a grin. Both were standing near the bar. Quinn stood frowning, arms folded across his chest.

Asher sat down at one of the tables just as the others began coming in.

"What's the joke?" asked Carmody.

Asher smiled now too, but only managed to shake his head.

"Well?" asked Owen. Everyone was settling in around the tables.

"Yes. Come now," urged Banister. "What news did this character bring?"

"We have one day to find a way off this floor," Quinn stated, with no humor whatsoever.

"I don't get it," said Owen.

"Lieutenant..." said Asher. "You have to admit—"

"I do not," Quinn cut him off. It was almost as though he was afraid he might look foolish. "We've been given one day."

Asher sighed, turned from Quinn to look at the others. "This tall dark stranger... he gave us till tomorrow sundown to get out of town."

Owen appeared startled. "He told us to get outta Dodge?"

"That's the gist of it, Ma'am," said Ramos.

"There's nothing funny about this, people." Quinn stepped around behind the bar, set his canteen onto the counter.

"No sir," grumbled Ramos.

"Out of town by sundown," said Church, mulling over the words. He drummed his fingers on the table in front of him. "That does put our situation in a whole new light."

"Yes it does." The lieutenant poured water from his canteen into a glass. It looked like he was pouring himself a stiff drink. "Come dawn, our search goes from haphazard to precise."

"What did he threaten to do to us, Lieutenant?" asked Owen. "Should we yet be here once the sun goes down?"

"The gentleman didn't get into specifics."

"An odd turn of circumstance," said Banister. "From ghost town to Tombstone, one moment to the next."

"Choose your peril, folks," said Owen. "Ghosts or guns?"

A heavy silence in the room, drawn out for several seconds.

The harsh tinkling of the piano keys broke the silence... *dink dink dink dink...*

Ramos, standing at the piano, found himself uncomfortably the focus of everyone's attention. He smiled apologetically and lifted his hand from the keyboard.

The early morning horizon had a colorful autumn glow. The air was cool but already hinted at the warm day to come. The town was still and quiet.

Carmody stumbled from between the laundry and the doctor's office and out into the street. She was in a panicked frenzy, desperately swatting at a cloud of inky black shadows that were swirling about her head; wispy puffs of dust billowed up around her feet at each awkward step, the silence suddenly overwhelmed by a frenetic rush of harsh whispers seemingly from a thousand minds all speaking at once, all demanding attention, demanding to be heard.

Quinn leaned over the table and put another mark on the now much-marked hand-drawn map of the town. Banister stood near the bar. He was filling his canteen from the wooden bucket sitting on the counter. Church waited for him over near the saloon doors. The soft morning sunshine reached in and washed across his dark complexion.

Quinn had given them the general store to search. Yes, it had been gone through once before, but that had been cursory, as had the entire previous day's survey of the town. This was to be much more thorough, right down to physically examining every shelf, every photograph; open up boxes, look in closets. Additionally, they were to go over the exterior of the building, board by board; go into the crawl space below and the attic above, if they existed.

They had from dawn till dusk. After that…

"Oh, my," said Church, looking outside. He pushed aside one of the swinging doors and took a hesitant half-step out.

"What is it, Doctor?" Quinn looked up from his map, carefully set down the pencil.

"Private Carmody appears to be—" Church stepped the rest of the way through and out onto the boardwalk. "Just a moment," he called back, and then disappeared from view.

Quinn and Banister both started toward the front of the saloon. They met Church coming back inside, one arm around Carmody. She was frantically waving both arms, swatting at something that wasn't there. She was mumbling to herself, even as Church tried to soothe her.

He guided her over to a chair and sat her down. She leapt back up once, but he finally calmed her down enough that he was finally able to sit down beside her.

"What happened to her, Nate?" asked Banister.

Church rested a hand on Carmody's arm. He kept his attention on her as he spoke to the others.

"More of those black shadows that we saw back on the first floor," he said. "A cloud of them. I don't think they did her any real harm, though."

"Damned things are everywhere," she managed to get out.

"You're all right now, my dear."

"Yes, you should be fine now, Private," said Quinn. He stood to one side of the table, hands clasped behind his back. "They appear to have left... for the moment."

"You can't walk from one building to the next. And they whisper at you. Sounds like thousands of 'em, all whispering."

"What are they saying?" asked Quinn.

"I couldn't understand 'em. They were all talking at once." She shrugged then. "Maybe they're not saying anything."

Quinn looked to the windows, to the swinging doors and the street beyond.

"Not like any ghost town I've ever heard of."

"Yes, well..." Church gave Carmody another pat on the arm, then stood up. "We may have to endure these minions of the Adversary on any number of floors, whatever the environment."

"So the early evidence would suggest, though it is by no means definitive," said Banister. These minions had shown themselves now on two of three floors. Had the team spent more time on the freighter, might they have appeared on the second floor as well?

"They seem to be more of a nuisance than a danger," said Quinn. "At least, so far."

"Where they are, the threat is not far away?" suggested Banister, raising a brow as he looked to his partner. "Such was certainly the case in our previous encounter."

"I saw nothing in this instance," said Church. "But that doesn't mean it wasn't there."

"And may yet be," said Banister.

Church grew thoughtful. He turned back to Carmody. "They assaulted you only while you were outdoors?"

"They were waiting for me; the moment I stepped outside."

"Yes, and then ceased their attack each time you stepped indoors."

"We saw that here," stated Quinn. He looked in the direction of the pair of swinging doors, the daylight outside. He started toward it.

"So," Church sighed noisily, spoke the group. "Harbinger or not, their presence could make our excursions from building to building most uncomfortable."

"How fortunate the general store is right next door," said Banister. Actually, all the buildings in town were pretty much right next door. There were just five buildings on each side of the street.

"Should be fun," said Church. "Shall we?"

"Oh, by all means."

"It's clear at the moment," said Quinn. He had moved to the doorway. Outside, the street was clear.

"I expect that to change momentarily," said Church. He gave Carmody a final comforting pat on the arm, nodded to Banister. The two of them started across the room.

Quinn stepped through the doors and held one side open. "No site-seeing," he said as first Banister and then Church came out onto the boardwalk.

The two of them hurried along the boardwalk and were quickly starting across the alleyway between the saloon and the general store. They hadn't yet reached the other side when both were swarmed by the inky black shadows, spinning wildly around their heads.

Quinn resisted the urge to rush after them, to assist them he knew not how, and a few moments later the two men were up on the porch and hurrying up to the door. They went into the general store as Quinn went back into the saloon.

Ramos stood at the well behind the saloon, this his second trip out since finding water there. He was using the crank to unwind the rope that eased the bucket down into the well. A handful of canteens were on the ground beside him.

A group of small dark shadows circled a dozen feet above him; ethereal black ghosts caught in a little whirlwind. Occasionally, gray shadows of those shadows could be seen skittering across the ground around him.

He had been startled when they first appeared up there, and he had almost rushed back into the saloon. But they had yet to overtly threaten him, had yet to so much as approach him.

They were just... there.

He heard footsteps pounding along a boardwalk over on Main Street. He hesitated a moment, looked in the general direction of the alley beside the saloon, and listened out for any cry for help. None came.

He continued lowering the bucket.

He stopped. A bitterly cold chill steadily worked its way through him. He actually shivered.

He felt it first, and then he saw it.

A ghostly hand rested on his forearm; a woman's hand, long delicate fingers.

Ramos lifted his gaze without moving his head. The apparition stood beside him, stood beside the well; a gentle face, framed in dark hair that cascaded past her shoulders in slowly moving waves. She wore flowing robes of a silvery gray mist.

She smiled a warm smile. Ramos couldn't help but smile back; a reflexive response, certainly not from any warm and fuzzy. He was afraid, very afraid, something close to terror.

He let go of the crank handle and took a very cautious step back, the rope unwinding another three quarter turn before stopping. He felt the hand of the apparition brush across his arm as he pulled away. And then something about her expression changed. There was a hint of growing darkness. Ramos took another step back, his focus never leaving her face.

Her smile withered away and was gone. Her expression turned cool, then cold. A seething anger slowly rose up within her, shown on that once gentle face.

Her silvery misty form drifted toward Ramos, grew steadily darker as she drew nearer. He stumbled backward and fell to the ground. Scrambling back, the apparition turned ever darker. It hovered before him. It smiled then once more, but it was now a maniacal grin. Her head rolled back and she let out a deep, bloodcurdling cackle.

Above her, the black shadows continued to circle.

Sgt. Costa was poking around in one of the stalls that were set along one wall in the stable. She kicked at the fresh straw on the floor, ran a hand experimentally along the back wall. Asher entered the next stall, pitchfork in hand. He tapped at the back wall using the end of the handle.

The floor throughout most of the barn was covered in straw. The feeding boxes all held fresh hay, and there was a sack of feed grain leaning against the opposite wall. One glance up at the loft and he could see a good supply of hay. Despite this, Asher was certain this stable had never seen a horse.

Sgt. Costa rested her forearms on the top rail between the two stalls. She was back in uniform and appeared comfortable that way.

"I'm not getting anything, Professor," she said.

"Nor I." Asher finished his own search, used his feet to brush away the straw as he stepped up to the fence opposite Costa. "Perhaps someone else is having better luck."

"I hope so. The Count sounded like he was ready to make good on his threat."

"He sounded downright giddy about the possibility." Asher turned and looked curiously at Costa. "The Count?"

"It's what I named him." Costa broke into a half-embarrassed half-grin. "He just, you know... it was like I heard Dr. Owen saying... he's like a low-level nobleman come out to the American West to play at being a gunfighter. He even has an accent."

"The Count?"

"He didn't come across like that to you?"

"Oh, I think you nailed it." Asher clasped his hands together, studied his interlaced fingers. "I suppose he needs a name."

"We gotta call him something. *'Humble Servant of the Adversary'* seems a bit longwinded."

"The Count it is," said Asher. He smiled, but the smile quickly faded. "And I believe you are right, Sara. Whatever form this threat may take, the danger should we remain is most certainly real."

"Too bad, really. I wouldn't mind spending a few days here. We could all use a breather after the last two floors."

"Even with the, uh..." Asher waved a hand in the air, implying the shadowy creatures that were constantly harassing them.

"The Adversary's little minions? Annoying to be sure, but they seem harmless enough, don't you think?"

"I would never assume anything we find in here to be harmless."

"You're right, of course." Costa frowned, let out a quiet sigh. "I still think this could've been a great place to—"

She stopped in midsentence. They both turned and looked to the center of the barn.

"D'you hear that?" asked Asher.

"The scraping noise? Maybe a shuffling, sliding sound?"

"Something like that, yes."

"No sir. Not me." Costa stepped cautiously out of the stall. She saw nothing out of the ordinary at first, but then noticed the horse tack stowed on the opposite wall moving slightly. It shifted to one side, then the other.

"Professor?" she called behind her.

Asher was already coming up beside her.

It wasn't just the tack. The tools at the far end of the barn were moving, shifting, sliding. There was no obvious cause. Everything was just... moving... in tandem. Everything was shifting first in one direction, then another.

Asher placed a hand on Costa's arm and guided them both back several steps toward the front of the stable, stopping a long step from the closed double-doors.

"Do you feel that?" asked Costa. She held out a hand. There was a light breeze, and it was slowly growing stronger.

"No, ma'am. Not me."

The dry straw on the floor of the barn began to stir; several seconds later it was in the air before them, more being drawn from the stalls and into the spinning vortex that had begun to form in the center of the stable. Tools and tack mounted on the walls shook noisily, were threatening to come free and get pulled into the increasingly intense whirlwind.

"We have company." Costa was looking up at the loft; several shadowy minions had appeared.

"And there," said Asher. He nodded toward the dark in the back of the stalls. There were shadows within the shadows.

One came rushing out and darted about the vortex, playing in the draft surrounding it. Another joined it, and then a third. They circled round and round, two in one direction, the third in the other, somehow managing to avoid running into one another. The vortex continued to increase in intensity, drawing in more straw and dirt and dust. Tools and tack clattered. The minions in the loft danced joyously about as the three circling the vortex flew faster and faster.

Without warning all three suddenly hurled themselves directly toward Asher and Costa. They both stumbled backward, arms flailing and feet stomping as they tried to regain balance.

Costa managed to recover, planting one foot behind her and then pushing forward as she leaned in to meet the three onrushing inky masses.

Asher continued stumbling backwards, crashing through the doors and out into the barnyard. He found himself laying face up in the dirt, staring up at the sky.

The pale blue above the town had gone dark, and it was streaked with jagged, blood-red lines. As he watched, the lines slowly spread out like expanding cracks in a glass dome.

Asher scrambled to his feet and marched back into the barn.

Episode Three / Chapter Four

Lt. Quinn knelt beside Ramos, helped him to sit up. He had found him lying on the ground halfway between the back of the saloon and the well.

"Corporal? Are you all right?"

"Yes sir." Ramos rubbed at his temple, turned abruptly to the lieutenant. "Did you see her?"

Quinn looked about them. A group of the minions were hovering above the well, but there was no *her* anywhere.

Ramos started to his feet and the two men rose up together. Ramos turned around in a half circle. The ghostly creature was gone. "Never mind," he said.

"Let's get inside," said Quinn, looking anxiously up at the sky. It had turned a deep, dark blue, and there were jagged cracks the color of blood.

Strange things were happening.

"Come on," he said.

They came into the saloon just as Sgt. Costa entered from the front.

"Sir, we have to get to the stables," she said. There was a definite urgency in her tone.

"What is it, Sergeant? Where's Professor Asher?"

"The stables. He's at the stables."

"Have you found something?"

"Yes, sir. You could say that."

General Wong, Captain Adamson and Dr. Lake were seated around one of the two tables in the Quonset hut. On the table were papers and folders, ceramic mugs, half-eaten sandwiches on little paper plates; everything in disarray. Dr. Lake was leaning forward, elbows on the table, trying his best to make a point. Adamson was shaking his head slowly, mumbling in a low, hushed tone, and General Wong sat with his back straight, arms folded across his chest, frowning darkly.

Corporal Johansen stood at the back of the room. He was leaning against the coffee counter and watching the three at the table as he absently sipped from his cup.

Staff Sergeant Miller came into the command center, glanced in the direction of the group at the table as he walked across the room.

"Good evening, Sergeant," said Johansen. He kept his attention on those at the table, watching them over the rim of his cup as he took another sip.

"Hey, Johansen." Miller served himself some coffee, leaned against the counter beside the corporal. He pointed to the group with his cup. "What's going on?"

"Ramos came face to face with a really scary ghost."

"Wicked. He's all right?"

"Yeah. Shook him up pretty good."

"Gonna happen to anyone, it's gonna happen to Ramos." Miller nodded to the group at the table. "That's got them all stirred up?"

"Nah. After scaring the bejeezus out of Ramos, this ghost insinuated that it was really looking forward to this evening. And this was after somebody called 'The Count' gave them a deadline of tonight to find the portal and get on to the next floor."

"The Count?"

"So Costa tagged him."

"Yeah, sounds like Sara," said Miller. "So there's a lot going down. Like... going down right about now."

"Yeah, with everything else, those minions are all stirred up about something: and to top it all off, Quinn says the sky is breaking."

"Breaking? Actually breaking?"

Johansen shrugged. "That's what he said. Gone all dark, and a bunch of bloody cracks in it. Called it the eggshell from Hell."

"Jesus."

"Weird, huh? And just before we lost contact, Quinn was saying something about somethin' goin' on at the stables and how his team was scattered all over town."

Lt. Quinn approached the stables with Ramos, Church and Banister. He had sent Costa to find the others, to make sure they were all right. He and the corporal had crossed paths with Church and Banister coming out of the general store.

The sky overhead was midnight blue; the jagged bloody cracks continued to spider out and were growing wider.

And now there was something more: a low, rumbling hissing sound. It wasn't coming from any one direction, had no single source. It came from all around them, from everywhere.

And it was growing louder minute by minute.

Susan and Carmody came out of the laundry across the street. The small, squat structure was the last building on that side of the street, and the last building at this end of town. They started across toward the livery, both with an anxious eye to the ominous sky overhead.

Church clasped his hands together in a silent thank you. He grasped Susan's hand.

"Susan, are you all right?" he asked.

"Yes, of course." Susan furrowed her brow. "What is it, Doctor?"

"We're not quite sure, my dear. It would appear that Professor Asher has found something."

"The access?"

"We do not know." Church glanced up at the sky, then to the double doors of the stable. "One can hope."

"It wouldn't be a moment too soon," said Banister.

The town itself was growing dark, the darkness reaching out from the alleyways between the buildings and into the street. The menacing shell of sky seemed to be drawing lower and lower, the cracks ever wider and more jagged.

Looking back up the street, Quinn could just make out Costa coming out of the sheriff's office at the opposite end of town with Dr. Owen and Miss Powell in tow.

"All right, then." Quinn turned back to face the barn. "Everyone stay behind me." He started forward and the others fell in behind him.

Stepping into the barn, Quinn quickly held out his arms for the others to stop. They moved in beside him.

The vortex was five feet across, rose up nearly to the rafters. It continued to draw straw in from the surrounding stalls, creating dusty, brownish whirlwind. Barn implements and horse tack hanging on the walls clattered noisily.

"I'm not going in that," said Carmody. She looked awkwardly at Lt. Quinn. "Sir."

Asher called down from the loft. "Not there. Up here. And you may want to get our gear together."

Quinn looked to Ramos. "Go. Take Carmody."

Sgt. Costa did her best to urge Dr. Owen and Miss Powell along. She had seen Quinn lead the others into the barn at the far end of town, now saw Ramos and Carmody come back out. They were hurrying up the street toward them, Ramos veering off in the direction of the saloon.

"What's going on, Carmody?" she asked. They had gotten as far as the hotel. Across the street, Ramos was pushing his way through the swinging doors of the saloon.

"We need to get our stuff."

Costa looked to the others before turning toward the hotel. "Let's go."

"I am not carrying everyone's crap," said Owen.

"Yes, ma'am. You certainly are." Costa hadn't even bothered to look back. She was up on the boardwalk and stepping through the door.

Two minutes later they were coming back out, all with armfuls of clothes and backpacks and utility belts, including Dr. Owen. Ramos was crossing the street, the radio pack on his back and several canteen belts slung over one shoulder. He reached out with his free hand and took the backpack that Costa offered.

"I don't think we have much time," he said. They started up the street toward the stables. Behind them, the other end of town was in near darkness. The shadowy minions that had mercifully not been harassing them the last quarter hour had reappeared, were now darting in and out of the alleys between the buildings.

Asher helped Church up from the ladder. Behind him, the loft was filled with loose hay, a path cleared to the hayloft doors set into the back wall.

"I see," said Church. He stepped away from the ladder to make way for Banister.

Asher had opened the doors after clearing the way. The open plain beyond the town was visible in the growing darkness, but there was an odd shimmer, as if the world outside was being seen through a thin sheen of water in place at the opening.

"I almost fell through," said Asher. He reached down and took hold of Banister's outstretched hand and pulled him up.

"To be all on your lonesome till one or another of us eventually discovered it," said Church. They had previously found that the portals were one way. No coming back.

Of course, Costa had been down on the floor and would soon have realized that Asher was no longer in the loft. With the hay pushed to the side and the hayloft doors open, she would have seen what they were now seeing.

Asher would have only been on his lonesome for as long as it was taking now to bring the others together.

"That peculiar sound," said Banister. He took a cautious step further into the loft. "I believe it's coming from the portal."

"Yes," said Church. "I observed that, as well."

To now, that low rumbling, hiss had seemed to come from everywhere. Here in the hayloft however, there was direction.

"It's coming from the other side," said Banister, both a question and a statement.

"It started when I opened the doors," said Asher. He hadn't realized the others had been hearing the sound out in the street.

"Interesting." Banister took another step, and another. He held up a hand, palm toward the portal. He thought he felt... *something.*

"Watch yourself, Doctor Banister," said Asher.

Banister brought his hand back, looked at it curiously as he rubbed his fingertips together.

"If you'll recall, there was similar cross-contamination between this floor and the last," said Church, reminded of the water in the hold of the freighter; its source had not been the alien ocean, but the lake outside town here on this floor.

"Talk to me, people," Quinn called up. "How does it look up there?"

Church stepped to the edge of the loft. "Most encouraging, Lieutenant," he said. "Is there any sign of the others?"

"Soon enough," said Quinn. He turned to Susan. "You go on up, Doctor Bautista. I'll wait down here for the others."

"Yes, Susan," said Church. "Please, come up."

Asher and Church stepped back into the center of the loft. Banister took another short step nearer the portal.

"Is it getting louder?" he asked.

"Doctor Banister—"

"Banister, that's quite close enough," said Church.

Banister again lifted a hand, slowly reached out toward the portal.

"Doctor—" Asher stepped forward.

Banister vanished. He was there... he was gone.

"Oh, crap," groaned Asher.

"Nate!" Church lunged forward. One step, two...

Church was gone.

"Oh, crap." Asher took another step and stopped. The sound, the wind...

He called back over his shoulder. "Lieutenant Quinn. I most strongly suggest we get a move on."

The Count was standing inside the enclosure in front of the stables, just inside the fence. He smiled and gave a nod to Costa as she led the others into the barnyard.

"Good evening, Sergeant Costa," he said warmly.

Costa looked over at Ramos. "Get them inside."

"Sergeant, I—"

"Now." Costa said dismissively, and was done with him. She took several steps toward the Count. "Hiya, Count," she said.

Ramos was quietly and quickly encouraging the others through the double doors.

"Count?" said the Count. He thought about it a moment. "Yes. I think I like that."

The space next to him began to shimmer, grew increasingly opaque. Within a few moments a specter that Costa took to be Ramos' ghostly apparition had taken form; white gown, long flowing hair that appeared to drift in a light breeze. It leaned near the Count, rested both hands on his right shoulder. It had a kind face. It smiled at Costa, said nothing.

The Count gave the apparition's hands a comforting pat. "Hello, my dear. Do say hello to Sergeant Costa."

The apparition still said nothing, but her smile slowly grew more broad; impossibly wider...

"Now, now," said the Count, several more pats of his hand. The apparition pouted.

The Count chuckled lightly. He sighed, breathed deeply and looked about them. "Do forgive my dear friend, Sergeant. She had so been looking forward to this evening."

"Sorry to disappoint." Costa gave a quick glance to the barn doors. They were all inside.

"Yes, well..." The Count again looked about them. Darkness continued to close in. The world was growing smaller and smaller and smaller. There was little now but the stable and the barnyard. The shell of midnight blue sky above hovered low and was a shatter of deep red, jagged cracks. His grin was menacing, his bright eyes sparkled. "There is still time."

"We found the access portal," said Costa matter-of-factly.

"You certainly did," said the Count with a nod of the head. "It is, however, in there. You, my very brave sergeant, are yet out here."

Beside him, the kind face of the apparition slowly began to morph.

Ramos and the lieutenant helped Owen up onto the ladder. She was the last.

Quinn started away, toward the barn door. "See they get through the portal, Ramos."

"Lieutenant—"

"We're right behind you, Corporal."

"Yessir." Ramos placed a hand on the ladder, looked back at the lieutenant as he waited for Dr. Owen to take a few more rungs. "I'll wait for you in the loft, sir."

"You follow them through, Corporal. They may need you on the other side."

Quinn didn't hear whether Ramos replied. The corporal had his orders.

Stepping outside, he was at first surprised at how quickly things had changed. It was near pitch black, but for cracks of red overhead. The fence surrounding the yard was a worn gray half-lost in shadow.

Sgt. Costa had her back to him, stood facing the Count, and beside him a silvery flowing form of robes and gently cascading hair.

Quinn spoke calmly, taking slow, methodic steps. "We are ready to leave now, Sergeant."

No response at first, then Costa gave a short nod to acknowledge that she had heard. She kept her attention on the Count.

Quinn stopped three paces short of Costa. He waited.

The Count leaned slightly to his left, looked at Quinn. "Good day to you, sir." He straightened then, smiled at his dear friend the apparition.

And then they were gone.

Quinn saw Costa's shoulders sag. She turned to look at him.

"The Count likes his new name," she said. "And we disappointed his friend."

Professor Asher was standing in the left aisle of the passenger compartment of a wide body jet. His first impression was that he was inside a Boeing 747.

Actually, that was his second impression.

His first impression was that they were crashing.

The sounds were deafening. Engines were screaming, though this was second to the loud roar of wind rushing up at him, threatening to knock him down. Either there were windows broken or there was a door open somewhere.

Owen and Lisa were standing to one side, between two rows of seats; most of the others were scattered about the cabin in various states of panic.

Church came rushing in from the forward cabin, Banister right behind him.

They quelled any remaining doubt, crying out simultaneously.

"We're going down!"

Ramos came hurtling through the portal behind Asher and they both tumbled to the floor of the aisle. Costa and Quinn followed a moment later.

~ *end of episode three*

Episode Four
Another Day at the Office

Prolog

The elevator doors slid aside and everyone began piling out, Quinn and Costa first, taking up defensive positions to the left and right.

"Told you ten people could fit into an eight by eight space," said Ramos, coming out next.

"Yeah, well I'm not quite ready for that level of bonding," said Carmody, right behind him.

All ten in the team had managed to squeeze into the elevator car, even with backpacks and utility belts, but it had been a tight fit.

They found themselves in an elevator lobby; fluorescent light panels in the ceiling, light-gray commercial carpet on the floor. The beige colored wall in front of them was solid but for a single door, a small placard above it stenciled with the word 'Stairs'.

The wall to their left had two doors; large, smoked-glass windows filled the wall on their right.

"I can tell you right now, this beats the hell out of the ant colony," said Owen. She was brushing dirt off her pants.

"I'll withhold my opinion on that until we've had a minute to look around," said Asher. The elevator doors slid closed behind them. The letter '7' was written in bold font above the doors.

"I don't care what we find," growled Owen. "Anything beats giant, six foot long ants."

"Most likely," said Asher. "Nonetheless, I'll have to get back to you on that."

Banister drifted over to the windowed wall. The rest of the group grew quiet and waited.

"Prepare yourselves, everyone," he said after a few moments. "We may well be facing the most horrific world ever conceived."

"What is it, Doctor?" asked Carmody anxiously.

Banister placed a hand on the metal crossbar set about waist high.

"We're in an office building," he said darkly.

Episode Four / Chapter One

Johansen looked away from his radio and turned to the sound of the door opening. Captain Adamson came into the command center.

"Anything?" asked the captain.

Johansen shook his head no in answer. He watched Captain Adamson walk to the counter and pour a cup of coffee, then walk back to the table in the middle of the room. Papers and folders were scattered about on the table; scribblings of facts and suppositions regarding the sixth floor.

"Ants," said Adamson, mostly to himself. He picked up a book, all about ants. He tossed it back onto the table. "Giant ants."

"I'm sure they're fine, sir," said Johansen. "They're bound to be on the seventh by now."

They had last heard from the team five days earlier. At that time, they had already been on the sixth floor for three days, holed up in a dead-end tunnel in the heart of the ant colony. There had been no sign of the portal to the seventh floor.

"I'm sure you're right, Corporal," sighed Adamson. He mumbled then. "Be a helluva way to end things."

General Wong and Doctor Lake came into the command center. They appeared to have been in a heated discussion, now quickly fell silent.

"Good morning, Captain," said the general, a quick look to Adamson and then to Johansen as he continued to his desk. He dropped himself into the wooden chair. "Doctor Lake here is getting bored."

"That's not what I meant, General."

"No new data to process, no way to pass along your well-reasoned recommendations."

"We're all feeling frustrated, General," said Captain Adamson.

The general frowned, let out long, slow breath. "That we are," he said at last. He looked up at Doctor Lake. "I don't mean to take it out on you, Doctor. Well, actually I do mean to take it out on you, but I apologize both before and after the fact. There will most certainly be more snide remarks coming your way."

Doctor Lake stood at the table beside Captain Adamson. He glanced down at the paperwork, selected a file and opened it.

"I will not play the butt of ridicule to your military condescension, General Wong."

"Don't misunderstand, Doctor Lake. I have the utmost respect for you and all the science team members in the tower."

"Our responsibilities on this mission are at the very least equal to that of the military staff, sir."

General Wong had to smile at that. "As regards those within the tower, we are in complete agreement. But to be perfectly frank, my dear doctor, at this point in the mission... your role, and mine, lay somewhere below that of casual observer."

The breakroom was long and fairly narrow, about twenty feet by forty feet. Not small, but not really that large for a breakroom in an office building. At one end stood three vending machines: snack, sandwich, soft drink. At the other end was a pair of shoulder-high refrigerators, beside these a counter and a water cooler. One long wall was floor to ceiling windows.

Six tables were scattered about the room. On one sat the radio, and on another were several backpacks.

Carmody came in through one of the two archways that opened to the hallway. She was carrying another water bottle to the cooler. Owen had pulled one of the chairs up to the cooler and was filling the team's canteens. They were piled up on the floor beside her.

Quinn and Lisa Powell were meanwhile working at prying open the sandwich vending machine. The lieutenant was trying not to look frustrated. Lisa looked willing to stand by and wait for instructions.

Asher walked over to Susan, who was standing at the windows. The world beyond the glass looked like any normal, midsized city, except that it was empty of people and absolutely nothing moved. It could have been a photograph. Even the one lone cloud hovering above the city didn't move. It hung there, small and white and fluffy, set against the backdrop of bright blue sky.

Both Asher and Susan continued looking outside. Neither were quite sure how to get the conversation going.

"It's quite a view," Asher said finally.

"It's eerie," said Susan.

"It is, isn't it? I'm going to think of it as a quiet city in the Midwest somewhere, just at dawn, with everybody still peacefully asleep."

"How's that going to work for you when nobody wakes up? Your city filled with thousands of sleeping people, all lying in their beds for all eternity?"

"Okay, maybe I didn't think that through." Asher grew thoughtful. The silence stretched out until it became uncomfortable. He looked back over his shoulder, into the breakroom. "No word from the doctors?"

Susan gave a slight smile, shook her head and said nothing. Church and Banister hadn't been gone that long.

Asher sighed. "Guess not. They find anything, I expect we'll hear about it soon enough."

"Yes."

Lisa watched Susan and Asher, who were in quiet conversation over near the wall of windows. She could just make out what they were saying, at least enough to know it that was a touch more awkward than either of them would have liked.

"They're not too good at that, are they?" she asked Quinn.

"What's that?" Quinn continued his struggle with the vending machine.

"The Professor and Doctor Bautista," she said, nodding in their direction.

Quinn looked quickly over at them. It took a moment, but then he got it. He as quickly returned to his work. He didn't like that he got it. It made him feel very uncomfortable. It highlighted the difficulty he himself was having.

He didn't want Miss Powell to know that he was uncomfortable, and that only made it worse. His face grew warm. He tried to focus on getting the vending machine open, to get at the sandwiches inside.

Lisa sighed. She looked across the room at Dr. Owen and Private Carmody. She looked at the lieutenant, turned quickly elsewhere. She tried to hide a self-conscious grin.

"I suppose none of us are very good at it," she said at last. She was surprised that she had managed to get that out.

So was Lieutenant Quinn.

He wanted to say something. He <u>really</u> wanted to say something.

Why the heck don't I say something?

He drew a blank.

Anything... anything...

The seconds stretched painfully out.

"S'pose not."

Costa and Ramos stood at ease in the middle of the elevator, looking straight ahead to the closed doors. The eighth floor indicator light on the panel was lit. It dimmed out, and a few moments later the indicator light for the seventh floor lit up.

It too dimmed out... six lit up.

They were heading down.

"Well," Ramos grumbled. "That got us nothin'."

"Pretty much," said Costa.

"Is this gonna get us anything?"

"Doubt it."

Fifth floor...

Fourth floor...

"Suppose we gotta check it out, though," said Ramos. "Cover all the bases."

"Pretty much."

Third floor...

Second floor...

"Here we go," said Ramos.

The main lobby indicator light lit up. There was a soft pinging noise. A moment later the doors slid quietly aside.

Costa and Ramos looked out beyond the elevator car. Neither of them moved.

"Yep," said Ramos. "That's what I figured."

They were back on the seventh floor.

Church and Banister could see from one end of the large room to the other. The open design took up the entire northwest corner of the seventh floor. It was filled with rows of cubicles, the gray cubicle walls just four feet tall, giving the space a wide open atmosphere.

Three aisles ran the length of the room. Church walked one, Banister the center aisle, looking into each of the cubicles they passed. Each eight by eight cube had a gray countertop that served as a desk, with a computer and monitor, the keyboard sitting on an adjustable tray. A wireframe inbox hung on the wall just inside each cube.

A clean whiteboard was also mounted in each cubicle, with dry erase markers of assorted colors sitting in the tray.

Each cube had a single chair, each on a foot base of five small wheels.

"I think I'll take the ant colony," said Banister.

"Not much difference, if you ask me," said Church.

Banister almost smiled, but managed to keep it to himself. They continued down the aisles, pacing each other with easy, casual steps. After passing several more cubicles, Banister came to a stop. He took a step into the cube.

"Curious," he said at last.

Church looked calmly around the room, rubbed a hand across his cheek and the back of his neck. He scratched at his scalp. His black crop hair, which he usually kept short, could use a trim.

"This reminds me of the crew's quarters on that freighter a few floors back," he said.

"Yes, yes, obviously." Banister frowned. "I don't have much experience in this area, but... shouldn't there be phones in these things?"

Church muttered a grumbling *humph* in answer, went into the cubicle directly opposite the one Banister was standing in.

"Let me check something." He sat in the chair, wheeled around and scooted up to the keyboard tray. He pushed the power button on the computer and then turned on the monitor. He waited.

"It lives," he said.

Banister leaned over the cubicle wall. "Yes? Well?" he asked.

"Yes, well, give it a minute, Wes." Church sat patiently eyeing the monitor. "Damn," he grumbled after much less than a minute.

"What is it?"

"It wants my password."

"You can get past that, right?"

"No I can't get past it," Church droned. He nonetheless gave the Enter key a few whacks, then randomly struck at various letters and numbers on the keyboard.

"Makes one wonder," Banister thought aloud as he watched Church methodically striking at the keyboard. "The Adversary gives us computers, but no way to get into them."

Church leaned back in the chair, pushed away from the keyboard. "He knew we'd try to use them to communicate with the outside. Hence... the whole *no phones* thing."

"I know I'm the one who brought them up in the first place, but... would we really expect phones to work in here? I mean, kinda tough getting an outside line."

"If the Adversary wanted them to work, they'd work." He stared intently at the computer monitor. "Maybe one of the others knows how to get past the login. Asher, maybe."

The two of them continued down the aisles, met at the end and started back together along the third aisle running along the wall. They looked into a supply room, noted the shelves of supplies that might come in handy. The next door opened to a smaller room with several printers and a large copy machine that took up a third of the room. Wrapped reams of paper were stacked neatly on shelves set against one wall.

There was no sign of a portal anywhere, but at least they would have pens and paperclips to take with them once they did find their way to the next floor.

In point of fact, since the ghost town the floors had yielded little in the way of supplies, and back on the fifth floor they had abandoned much of what they had when they were forced to leave in a hurry. They were running low on just about everything. The seventh floor looked to be much more promising.

Ramos led the way down the stairwell, Costa following three steps behind him. They reached a landing, continued around past a door with a large black '6' stenciled on it and started down the next flight. Their footsteps echoed hollowly in the narrow well.

They reached the fifth floor landing. Ramos stepped around and started down the next flight of stairs.

Costa stopped on the landing. She gave a determined glare at the door with the number '5' on it.

"Hold it," she said sharply.

Ramos was already a third of the way down the flight. He returned to the top step. "What is it?"

"We both know how this is going to end. There's no sense wasting time and effort." Sgt. Costa reached out and opened the door, stepped through it.

Ramos followed her out, moved up beside her.

In front of them was the elevator, above the doors the number of the floor.

"Okay," said Ramos matter-of-factly. "Seventh floor it is, then."

Lisa carried the packages of sandwiches to the refrigerator as Quinn started on the vending machine with the snacks; mostly cookies, crackers and nuts.

There weren't many sandwiches, only enough for one apiece and one extra for them to fight over. There were no expiration dates stamped anywhere on the packages, but the sandwiches looked okay through the wrappers; not that an expiration would mean anything in here.

Quinn figured they would try out the sandwiches for the next meal. They would pool together the snacks and sodas and ration them out with their remaining supplies.

The door of this vending machine popped open more easily than the last. He began pulling out the contents and piling them onto the nearest table.

As with the sandwiches, there were no dates stamped on the packages. The cookies and brownies felt moist enough. They would have to chance it. What alternative did they have?

He grinned... maybe he'd give Dr. Owen first crack at a sandwich, see if she survived...

Costa and Ramos returned from their search, walked between the tables and approached Quinn. Owen, still sitting by the water cooler, stood and followed them.

Quinn placed a handful of small packages of mixed nuts onto the table.

"What'd you find, Sergeant?" he asked.

"For a start, there's no getting off the seventh floor, sir."

"Excuse me?" said Owen, maneuvering her way between Costa and Ramos.

"I'm afraid she's right," said Ramos.

Owen shook her head sharply. "Come on, of course there's—"

"I believe the sergeant is referring to the, um... *more immediate* seventh floor, Liz," said Asher. He and Susan drifted over from the windows.

"Why didn't she say so?"

"Please, Doctor Owen," said Quinn. He met her gaze, and when she said nothing further, gave a quick nod to Costa.

The sergeant detailed what she and Ramos had found in their search; no sign of the portal, no apparent imminent threat, and no way off the seventh floor.

"And that would be the seventh floor of this office building," Costa clarified to Owen. "And not the uh... larger, all-encompassing seventh floor."

"Our host either has an odd sense of humor, or is a touch OCD," said Susan.

"Perhaps," said Asher. "And there may be some significance to putting us on the seventh floor while on the seventh floor."

"That would be in line with past experience," suggested Costa.

"To get to the eighth floor, we must *get to the eighth floor*," Owen stated. "That much is obvious."

Quinn folded his arms across his chest, pursed his lips and let out a barely audible "hmmm..."

"What is it, sir?" asked Sgt. Costa.

Lieutenant Quinn said nothing at first, finally looked directly at Owen.

"Doctor Owen... would you like a sandwich?"

Episode Four / Chapter Two

Quinn and Lisa sat at a small round table in one of the larger cubicles in the open office space. These slightly oversized cubes were generally assigned to supervisors too low on the food chain to rate a real office but who nonetheless needed a little extra elbow room in which to do their supervising, even if that meant just throwing in a small round table and a pair of chairs.

The cubicle was set against the windowed wall and offered a nice view of the cityscape. Night had come to the city, and while there was still no movement, there were lights turned on in a number of the buildings. Windows had lit up here and there as dusk had fallen. There had been no change since then, no lights turning off, and no darkened windows suddenly lighting up, but there was still something comforting about the scene.

It had been decided that the team would utilize the cubicles as individual quarters so long as they were on this floor. Quinn had settled into this cube, appreciating both the view and the table. He had been going over his notes when night fell and had been drawn away from his notebook, lost in the scene beyond the glass, when Lisa had joined him. She had asked if he minded sharing the view for a few minutes.

That had been more than an hour ago.

They spoke very little at first. They sat facing the window, their chairs on opposite sides of the table, and just took in the view.

At some point they noted the fact that there were no stars. The night sky was dark but not really black; more of a very dark gray.

As Quinn and Lisa grew more at ease with one another, they opened up a bit more. Lisa asked about his family, and she found that Quinn's parents had died when he was very young, that he had been raised by an uncle, his only living relative.

His uncle hadn't been rich, but he was fairly well off and was very well connected. He saw to it that Quinn got into a prestigious school, and later into the military academy. The plan was for Quinn to get a well-regarded education, put in the required years as an officer, and then use this background as access to a high-end business career. His uncle had connections there as well.

However, just prior to the tower mission Quinn had broken the news to his uncle that he planned to make a career of the military.

"He was disappointed, but he covered it well. My uncle is a good man."

"Sounds like it," said Lisa.

"So... how about you?" asked Quinn. "What made you decide to work with Doctor Owen?"

"That is not a decision that one makes. Doctor Owen decides."

"But you accepted."

"Of course. It is a *highly regarded, prestigious* position."

"Of course," said Quinn, the hint of a smile. "Military academy and all that."

"It does look good on a resume," said Lisa. "She isn't really so bad, once you learn how to handle her. Ray was great at that."

Quinn's hint of a smile faded. "I am really sorry about what happened."

"He was a good friend," she said quietly. "I miss him."

Quinn was trying desperately to come up with an appropriate response when he heard Banister and Church come in from the outer lobby. They were bantering back and forth, as always. From what Quinn was able to make out, the argument this time was focused on the pair of restrooms that were accessible from the lobby.

He and Lisa continued looking out the window in silence, taking in the doctors' lighthearted discussion. When the conversation waned, Lisa sat forward and stood up.

"I suppose I should be going," she said quietly. "I need to check in on Doctor Owen before I settle in myself."

"Of course," said Quinn, standing. "Sleep well, Miss Powell."

"Yes. Thank you."

Quinn waited until she left before turning about awkwardly and returning to his chair.

It would be some time before he settled in for the night.

Asher had padded his half-empty backpack with several dozen crumpled up sheets of paper, giving it some semblance of a pillow. Making a space for himself on the floor in one of the cubicles, he tried to get comfortable.

Comfortable or not, he wasn't ready for sleep. He finally sat up, then stood up and settled into the chair. He opened his notebook, read what he had written about this latest day in the tower, thought about how he might improve on his notes.

"Everything all right, Professor?" Costa stood in the opening.

"Yes. Yes, I'm fine," said Asher, looking up from his notebook. He nodded in the direction of his makeshift bed. "Just can't sleep."

"May not be a five star hotel, but it beats the ant colony."

"It certainly does," said Asher. "What has you up, Sara?"

"Watch duty." Costa raised a hand and drew a circle with her finger. "Making my rounds."

"Well, I appreciate you looking after us."

"My pleasure." She took a moment to listen to Banister and Church, parked in side-by-side cubicles some distance down the aisle. They were arguing office supplies. She smiled at their light bantering.

Asher noticed the focus of her attention. "Have you ever known two people as close as those two?" he asked Asher.

"They bicker back and forth like a pair of old hens."

"According to Liz, since the day they met."

"About forty years, I hear."

"I hear the same," said Asher.

Costa looked around them, studied the walls and windows and shadows. She took in a shallow breath, let it out slow.

"This one makes me nervous, Professor," she said, continuing to take in the scene around them.

"Too quiet for you?"

"Maybe. It's just... I don't know where the threat's coming from. We've usually seen something by now. We may not have it figured out, but by now we usually know what *the bad* is."

"Oh, I don't know about that, Sara. We've gotten it wrong as much as right."

"Right or wrong, we usually got somethin'. Here? Here we got nothin'. And that makes me nervous."

Asher gave a soft smile. "Well, thank you for the bedtime story, Sergeant. I should have no trouble getting right to sleep."

"Sorry," she said sheepishly. She stepped out of the cubicle, gave a nod in the direction of Church and Banister. "Think I'll check on the kids."

"Good night, Sara," Asher said to the retreating figure. Once she was gone, he glanced down at his notebook. He was about to append to his latest entry when he heard Banister and Church simultaneously offer their greetings to Sergeant Costa.

He leaned back in his chair, listened to the pleasant back and forth between the doctors and Sara. They liked her, and it was obvious that she liked them, that she enjoyed talking with them.

Asher looked at the notebook lying open on the desk. He reached over and used his pencil to slowly flip the notebook closed.

Ramos was in the breakroom first thing in the morning, sitting before the radio. Carmody sat beside him, watched him as he made one fine adjustment after another.

Nothing worked.

He finally grasped the radio with both hands in frustration, a low grumbling growl rising up from his chest.

Within moments however, the angry expression on his face broke apart and fell away, leaving only surrender. He lowered his head and softly pounded his forehead on the table; slowly, methodically; once, twice... the third time he left his forehead on the table.

Carmody stood up. "I'll let the lieutenant know."

"You do that," said Ramos, his head still resting on the Formica.

Church and Banister sat at a table on the other side of the breakroom. Church nodded in Ramos' direction as he ate from a small bag of mixed nuts.

"It looks like we're still incommunicado," said Church.

"Considering the conspicuous absence of telephones in an office building such as this, I suppose that is to be expected," said Banister. "Our host clearly wishes us cut off from the outside world."

"I wonder why," said Church. He brought another handful of mixed nuts out of the bag. "I mean, he always has a reason, however obscure."

"True." Banister leaned forward, placed his elbows on the table. "It is not by chance that we find ourselves on the seventh floor of this office building."

"The situation is obvious," Church nodded, waving a hand over his head. "The reason for it... obscure."

"As Liz alluded to so eloquently, there is no getting off this floor without getting off this floor. To reach the eighth floor of the tower, we must reach the eighth floor of this office building."

Church snickered. "So this is all about maintaining orderliness in the universe?"

"The Adversary has a compulsive disorder?"

"Banister... we must monitor this." Church turned serious. "If it turns out that he does have some alien form of OCD... we might be able to put that to use."

"Back to the here and now," sighed Banister. "In the matter of getting us to the eighth floor. If the elevator is not an option, and the stairs are not an option, what is your guess as to how we make the ascent?"

"Haven't a clue."

"Open a window and climb up the outside wall? Perhaps pull down a ceiling tile and climb up through the floor?"

"As I said, not a clue. But when we do find a solution, I can assure you that it will not be so pedestrian."

"That would be what you call... a clue."

Lieutenant Quinn came into the breakroom clutching a handful of papers.

"Copy machine works," he said, waving the pages.

"So what do you have for us?" asked Banister.

Quinn handed a sheet to Banister, another to Church; copies of the hand-drawn map that he had made of the seventh floor, as they currently understood it to be.

Quinn really, really had a thing for drawing maps of the floors they were on.

"Ah, I see," said Banister.

"I have to tell you, Doctor Banister, I had a heck of a time figuring out how to work that monster."

"You would think that using a copy machine would be fairly straightforward."

"Not this beast. It's not just a copy machine. It must have five or six different functions. And once you actually get to copy mode, there must be a dozen different options." Quinn looked at one of the copies of his map. "I just wanted copies."

"I suppose that explains why the machine takes up half the room," said Church.

"Copy room," Banister chuckled to himself. "A copy machine that actually does need its own room."

"More like Mission Control," said Quinn, turning away from the table. "That copy machine could land a man on the moon."

Church and Banister looked coolly at one another. Church slowly raised a brow. Banister slowed smiled, absently scratched behind an ear.

Johansen was all alone in the command center. He was often all alone in the command center. He slid back from the communications table and stood up, wandered over to the coffee counter. He pulled the carafe from the coffee maker, frowned, and poured the half-cup that was left into his mug.

He took a sip, grimaced and set the mug onto the counter. He was making another pot when he heard the machine over on the narrow table set against the wall come to life. It woke up, made several obnoxious screeching and beeping sounds.

It was one of those small-footprint tabletop four-in-one machines: printer, copier, scanner and fax.

There was a fax coming in...

Johansen filled the carafe with water from the water cooler, finished getting a fresh pot of coffee going. Once the coffee maker started to gurgle, he went over to the printer-copier-scanner-fax machine and picked up the piece of paper sitting in the tray.

He smiled.

He looked up, looked around the room.

Still all alone...

He looked back down at the piece of paper.

Five handwritten words filled the page:

"Hello out there. Banister here."

Episode Four / Chapter Three

Two of the cubicles along the windowed wall had been opened up, the cube wall between them removed. A table and a number of chairs had been brought into the expanded cube. When not out exploring, many of the team members divided their time between this and the breakroom, and this was where they had gathered the last few evenings before heading off to their individual cubicles for the night.

This was where Owen found Church and Banister. They had been reviewing the latest updates to the map, but were now quietly taking in the cityscape view.

"We stay here much longer, we're gonna run out of toilet paper," said Owen. She dropped herself into one of the chairs with a heavy groan.

"One more reason to be moving on," said Banister pleasantly.

"As a matter of fact, I was in the supply room this morning," said Church. "Liz is quite right."

"Someone's probably stashing a private supply," grumbled Owen.

"Always so cynical, dear Elizabeth," said Banister.

"Warranted, more often than not."

"Cynicism is never warranted, whatever the circumstance. It benefits you nothing, and life is way too short to fill it with valueless nonsense."

Church's mind had been wandering. Hearing this, he snorted, snickered and then spoke up. "Speaking of valueless nonsense, can you imagine coming in here day after day, planting yourself in one of these cubicles, day after day, week after week, year after year?"

"I'm beginning to," said Owen.

"I shudder just to think such a thing," said Church. After a long pause, he turned and looked curiously at Banister. "Say Wes... what if that's what this is all about? What if that is the big, scary monster? There has been nothing else."

"Don't forget Carmody's paper cut," said Owen. At least she wasn't calling her The Girl Private anymore.

"Are you suggesting that this floor's Big Bad is being bored to death?" asked Banister. He would need a little more convincing.

"Just a thought, thinking out loud; but why not? If the Adversary looked into my mind for something bloodcurdling to throw at us, this is what he'd find."

"All right, just for the sake of argument... let's say that your *out loud thought* proves to be true. How do we beat the Mundane Monster?"

"Well, how would I know? I've never faced mundane before."

"And yet here we are," said Banister. "You started this... assume this is where you work."

"Geez, get a different job," Owen sneered.

"Absolutely," Church said quickly; too quickly. Then he thought of something. "No. Wait. Not a different job... a <u>better</u> job."

"Different, better... whatever," Owen said dismissively.

But Banister smiled. "Ah. I see where you're going. What's the saying? Get kicked upstairs?"

"A promotion?" Owen was actually startled. "How the hell are we supposed to get promoted?"

"You know what they say..."

"No. Please don't."

"It's not what you know..." Banister started.

"It's who you know," Church finished.

Ramos leaned close to the radio, as if somehow putting himself nearer to the man on the other side of the signal. "Johansen? Johansen? Come on back to me, man. Johansen, you read? Over?"

Quinn came into the breakroom, Carmody behind him. They hurried toward Ramos, hovered over him as he listened for the faint voice coming through the headset.

"Corporal?" asked Quinn. "You have them or not?"

"Johansen..." Ramos spoke again into the headset. "Johansen, come back, over."

Ramos listened. Quinn and Carmody waited.

Ramos grumbled unintelligibly and tossed the headset onto the table. He leaned back in his chair and rubbed his face with both hands. "Sorry, sir," he said.

Quinn lifted his gaze, looked away from Ramos, out the window.

"But you did get through to them?" he asked, more of a statement. "You spoke with command?"

"Yes sir. Or... they got through to us."

So Carmody had told Quinn. "Either way, we were in communication with the outside."

"For a minute or so, sir. Long enough for Johansen to tell me they've been receiving our faxes."

"That's excellent!"

"Yes sir." Before Ramos could add to that, other members of the team started streaming into the breakroom. Word had gotten out, and everyone had questions.

Quinn managed to quiet them down, then ordered Ramos to fill him in on exactly what he had heard before losing communication.

Ramos had spoken only with Johansen, and only briefly. Yes, they had received the faxes the team had been sending out. He was told that the general and Doctor Lake had both sent faxes in return, but when it looked like these weren't getting through, the general had ordered Johansen to continue to try to reach the team on the radio.

"Good thing, too," said Costa.

"But why didn't we receive the faxes?" asked Lisa.

"The machine is designed to receive as well as send," said Ramos. He pointed up. "He's just not letting it happen."

"Actually," said Asher. "It shouldn't be working at all, receive or send. I mean, it isn't really connected to anything on the outside."

"It works because the Adversary makes it work," said Church.

"Exactly so," said Banister. "Which is how they managed to get through to us on the radio."

"But why?" asked Quinn. "We're missing something."

"We're missing just about everything," said Owen.

For perhaps the first time since the mission began, Lt. Quinn and Dr. Owen were in total agreement. He turned back to Ramos.

"Did you get anything else?"

"Sorry, Lieutenant. Johansen was just about to put Doctor Lake on, and that was it."

General Wong stood outside the Quonset hut, hands clasped behind his back, and gazed up at the black monolith. The top of the tower was lost in the gray blanket of low clouds that hung overhead, threatening rain.

It was very quiet here; an unreal alien quiet. It was unsettling to most, but General Wong found it strangely calming. He would often come out here, stand in this very spot and let the peace wash over him and let all the noise in his head wash away.

The door behind him opened and Dr. Lake came out of the command center. He stepped up beside the general. He stared irritably at the tower.

"This is ridiculous," he stated at last.

"It is what it is," said the general.

"Ridiculous."

"Very well. As you say."

Dr. Lake let out a sigh. "I apologize, General," he said. He frowned at the black tower rising up from the asphalt. "There's no reason to any of it."

"Oh, there is reason, Doctor. And you'll figure it out."

The doctor wasn't so sure. Even if there was reason that he had yet to identify, it was nonetheless a kaleidoscope of moving targets. "He's playing with us," he said darkly.

"That he is." The general turned to look at the doctor. "There are rules to the game, Doctor Lake. That much at least has been evident from the very first floor. The key element of this game is to decipher the rules without benefit of a rulebook."

"We don't even know what the game board looks like."

"Quite right; that would be a second key element."

It took a few seconds, but both men managed to smile. The general mumbled something about needing to go back inside, but for the moment neither made any move to do so.

For just one more minute, they let the peace wash over them.

Johansen had their complete attention. He was sitting at the central table in the command center, papers and folders pushed aside, leaving only the one sheet of paper. Looking over his shoulder, General Wong and Dr. Lake could just make out a long column of numbers very precisely written out. A second column had only the occasional check mark.

"Every thirty seven hours, twenty minutes," he said, for the third time.

"We've gone much longer than that without being able to reach them," said Lake.

"Yes, but the window was there," said Johansen. "Open about three minutes, give or take a few seconds. If we had tried to communicate within that window, I'm certain we would have made contact."

"I see," said General Wong. Looking closely at Johansen's work, he focused on the rows with the checkmarks. Those represented the successful contacts with the team. Each fell to an increment of thirty seven hours, twenty minutes. "I'll be damned."

"Probably," mumbled Lake. He folded his arms across his chest. He continued to study the figures. "We initially had a much longer communications window than three minutes, did we not?"

"Yes sir," said Johansen. "Something happened while they were still on the first floor that changed that."

"We lost the door," stated the general, quite matter-of-factly.

"Just about then, sir," nodded Johansen.

General Wong frowned thoughtfully. "Was that the cause, or were they both symptoms of something else, something of much greater import?"

Johansen wasn't expected to have an answer, and he didn't. He said nothing.

Dr. Lake glanced at his watch.

"A testable hypothesis, corporal," he said. "About seventeen minutes from now."

Asher and Susan sat at one of the tables in the breakroom. They had finished their lunch, half rations, and were now looking over copies of Quinn's latest updates to the map.

The team had explored every square inch of the floor several times. More than several. Ten, twelve times... there was no sign of the access to the next floor. Nothing.

And yet Quinn always had updates to his map. There were daily revisions, and each day everyone was expected to study the updates. Perhaps a correction would reveal something. Maybe a change from one day to the next was a clue. Was there something missing that would lead them to the answer, lead them to the question that would lead them to the answer?

"This is getting us nowhere," droned Susan. "We're going in circles."

"How does he come up with so many changes, one day to the next?" asked Asher.

"Mostly just stuff people overlooked," said Susan. She leaned over the map and pointed. "I mean look at this, Peter. He added trash cans. Lisa noticed trash cans in the cubicles, and they weren't on yesterday's map."

"Hmm," Asher grunted. "They were there yesterday, weren't they?"

"They were there. I use the one in my cube. Don't you?"

Do I?

"I guess so. Not really much call for it." He looked around the breakroom. "We use the cans in here."

Susan slid the map a bit closer, pulled yesterday's map up beside it. Most of the handful of differences between the two were similar to the trash bins. The light switch board in the supply room, a second set of shelves along the north wall. Both should probably be checked out, if they hadn't already. And it looked like a door in the men's restroom had been added to today's drawing. How'd they miss putting a door on the map till now?

"What about this?"

"Utility panel, I think," said Asher. "You know... electrical boxes, water shutoff, like that."

Ramos' radio on the nearby table began ringing for attention. Asher and Susan looked at one another, then to the radio. They finally stood and walked over. They stared uncertainly down at it, neither quite knowing what to do.

Susan looked anxiously at the open archway to the hall.

"I don't think he hears it," she said.

The radio continued its horrendous ringing noise.

"I guess I'll, uh..." Asher fumbled around with the receiver, looked apprehensively at the button on the handle, then at the face of the radio itself.

"Hello?" he stammered, putting the receiver to his ear. He began adjusting and then resetting knobs, clicking and unclicking the button.

"Anything?" asked Susan.

"Hello," Asher said again, continuing to click and adjust and reset. "Hello. Hello. Asher here."

A voice then, coming through the receiver, cutting in and out. "Hello, Professor. Johansen here. You wanna stop doing that?"

Episode Four / Chapter Four

Costa came into Quinn's oversized cubicle and stood before the table. She waited for the lieutenant to acknowledge her.

Quinn looked up from his paperwork. "Inventory completed?"

"Yes sir." Costa handed him the clipboard. One sheet contained the updated list of food and rations, the remaining documents included a final inventory of supplies and equipment they held ready to take with them to the next floor. This second list was divided into two categories: the first was a full inventory, the second that same inventory broken down by members of the team and who was expected to carry what.

"Nice work, Sergeant," said Quinn. He returned to the first sheet with the food inventory. It didn't look good. "Looks like we'll begin to starve right on schedule."

"Yes sir," said Costa. "We've about worn out our welcome, sir. Time we were moving on."

"I'm right there with you." Quinn tossed the clipboard onto the table and leaned back in his chair. "We can't cut rations any further; particularly the civilians."

"The water supply is good," said Costa. "Thank goodness for that."

Quinn leaned forward again, put his elbows on the table. "Put a lock on the bottled water. Everyone is to use the water out of the tap. I want to keep our known quantity on hand, run the unknown until it runs out."

"Yes sir. Doctor Owen won't be happy."

"Doctor Owen is never happy. Being unhappy is what makes her happy."

"Ah, the paradox that is Elizabeth Owen," said Banister. He stood at the opening to the Quinn's cubicle.

Quinn dismissed Costa with a slight nod. Costa nodded in return, turned and left.

"Doctor Banister," Quinn indicated a chair. "Have you and Doctor Church come up with anything?"

"A few theories." Banister came into the cubicle and sat in the offered chair. "Nothing you could hang your hat on."

Asher opened the narrow access door set into the end wall of the men's restroom. Beyond the opening was a narrow passage two feet wide and about four feet deep. Along the left wall were three metal utility panels.

"Like I told you," Ramos said casually. "Utility closet."

"Never doubted you for a moment," said Asher. "Why didn't it get onto Lieutenant Quinn's map?"

"Couldn't tell ya," shrugged Ramos.

Carmody had the map in hand. She stepped up to the access door and looked inside.

"D'you check that far wall?" she asked.

"Of course," said Ramos. "It's a wall."

Carmody frowned at the map. "There's a blank space on the other side."

"Blank space?" asked Asher.

"It's the stairwell," said Ramos.

Carmody continued to study the map. "I don't think so."

"I paced it out myself two days ago," said Ramos. "Other side of that wall... stairwell."

"Not anymore." Carmody squeezed into the access passage.

"What are you doing?"

"Just checking it out."

Carmody shuffled sidestep to the end of the short passage. She rapped on the wall with her knuckles, pushed against it.

"See?" Ramos poked his head into the access. "A wall."

Carmody stared curiously at the wall.

"D'you hear that?" she asked.

"Hear what?"

"That." Carmody put her ear against the wall. "You don't hear it?"

Elizabeth Owen and Lisa Powell started down the aisle at an easy pace, the cubicles on their left, the cream-colored wall on their right. They had finished the rest of the office, this was the last row. Owen stopped and waited as Lisa went into the first cube and poked a yard stick into the trash can. She tapped the end of the ruler against bottom of the bin and watched for any reaction.

Nothing.

She stepped back into the aisle and they moved on. Coming out of the next cube, the doors to the copy room and supply room were on their right. They went into both, flipping switches, examining shelves and looking into boxes and bins.

Back to the cubicles then and the current mission to check all trash bins. Lisa expected nothing from this latest search, and Owen was for the most part disinterested. She looked out across the cubicle jungle spread out over the open floor.

"What a horrifying thought, working in a place like this day after day."

Lisa smiled dutifully and said nothing. She and Dr. Owen had often spent weeks at a stretch working in a small, cluttered three room office.

"Still," Owen sighed, stepped back as Lisa came out of the cubicle and continued on. "I suppose what this replaced wasn't any better. Probably a sight worse."

"Yes, ma'am," said Lisa.

"Acres of floor space, filled with hundreds of small metal desks lined up in perfect rows."

"I'll take this over that."

"Thank goodness you and I had other options, eh?"

"Yes, Ma'am."

"I wouldn't have survived a day."

"Suppose not."

Reaching the end of the aisle, they should have turned left, as this was the only way they should have been able to go. This was the end of the cubicle maze, facing a row of cubes set against the far wall.

Today, however, they turned right around a corner that hadn't been there before. Here in this small side room they found another set of cubicles. They walked cautiously down a narrow aisle that ran along the wall until they reached a door set slightly open.

It was another supply room. Gray metal shelves lined the walls, and on the shelves were supplies from the distant past: typewriter ribbon, small bottles of black ink and white-out, metal paper trays, staplers, inkpads, rubber stamps, calculator paper rolls, index cards...

"Wow," said Owen. "Talk about your blast from the past."

"Do you hear that?" asked Lisa.

"Of course I hear that." It was a dull, distant sound, a faint roar felt as much as heard. Owen stepped further into the room. There was another door set between two of the gray metal shelves that lined the opposite wall. "It's coming from there."

Banister had spent a good twenty minutes relaying to Quinn the various observations and suppositions that he and Church had drawn regarding the peculiar communication cycle that existed between them and the outside.

Their conclusion, such as there was a conclusion, was that their ability to communicate with the outside had as much to do with the mechanics of where they were as with the Adversary allowing it; at least in as much as the Adversary had to work within the laws of those mechanics.

"And just where are we?" asked Quinn. "And what are these mechanics?"

"Where we are is someplace other than our own world, perhaps even some place other than our own plane of existence. Whatever this place, whatever this reality, we are here because here is the limit of the Adversary's reach."

"He has no influence in our world?"

"Which is why he brought this one to us."

"Then how are we able to communicate with the outside at all?"

"The answer must lie in the cycle," said Banister. "Wherever we are, however this place works, there is a mechanism operating that brings us around, lines us up, puts us... *in range*, you might say... every thirty seven hours twenty minutes."

Quinn looked skeptical. "And just how might that work, Doctor, the inside communicating with the outside? What with these being two different planes of existence?"

"Ya got me," shrugged Banister. "We're giving you our best guess based on what we know at the moment."

"What you think you know."

"Suppositions based on conjectures."

Quinn grinned. "I thought as much."

Lisa Powell appeared suddenly in the opening to the cubicle. "We found something."

Asher listened at the door set into the inside wall of the newly discovered supply room. Carmody stood beside him, some of the others just beginning to gather in the small room or just outside. Several backpacks and utility belts were already piled nearby.

"What is it?" asked Carmody. "Is it the same as—"

"Yes. It is."

"Same as what?" asked Owen. She was standing to the side, arms folded across her chest, her brow furrowed.

"We heard this in the restroom; the utility closet."

"All right. What is it?"

"Don't know," said Carmody.

"The sound of the way out," said Asher.

"I figured out that much all on my own, Peter," said Owen. "But I sure wasn't about to step into it alone. Remember the jet plane?"

"Good call." Asher took a step back from the door. He looked to Quinn, who was squeezing past several others as he came into the room.

"Professor Asher," stated the lieutenant.

"Everyone here? We ready to do this?"

"Sergeant Costa will lead the way, Professor."

"I'm fully capable of opening a door, Lieutenant."

"Nonetheless."

"A point of order, Professor Asher," said Banister. He had made his way into the supply room behind Quinn and was standing near the pile of backpacks. He picked Asher's out from the pile and handed it to him. "Can you in fact open that particular door?"

"Right. I'm going to feel awfully foolish if I can't." Asher took the pack and slid into it. He took the utility belt offered and strapped it on as he looked again to Quinn. "If this is the way off the floor, we're all going, whatever we find on the other side. If it's not, or if there's something bad waiting for us, I'd like to go first, knowing Sara is at my back."

Quinn didn't like it, but finally gave Asher a curt nod. He nodded then to Sgt. Costa, who had been standing out in the aisle beyond the open door. She came into the room having already donned her backpack and utility belt.

"Ready when you are, Professor."

"Great," Asher said, just a moment's hesitation. He faced the door, reached down and turned the knob.

They entered a huge room to the overwhelming din of hundreds of old typewriters at work, row after row after row of small desks, where women in conservative fifties dress sat at the old machines.

Lisa Powell turned to Owen. They looked dumbfounded at one another. This was exactly what Owen had described only minutes before.

"Holy crap," whispered Owen.

"This is—"

"Yes, hold that thought. Like... forever."

The floor boss, a middle-aged woman with precisely combed hair and a stern gaze, strode imperiously down the central aisle. She stopped three steps from Asher.

"This way," she stated coolly. Her precise words easily pierced the roar of the typewriters. She turned about and retraced her steps up the aisle, never looking back.

Asher looked at the others and grinned, then followed after the woman. The rest of the team followed Asher.

The woman opened a heavy mahogany door and stepped through, moved to one side and held the door open for Asher.

He entered a large, well appointed office with paneled walls. There was a leather couch and chair to one side, glass-fronted shelves on the other. A large desk dominated the center of the room; a well-dressed, middle-aged man sat behind the desk in a very nice leather chair.

"Ah, Asher," said the man. He waved for Asher to come closer. Asher took several steps toward the desk, and the others moved into room behind him.

"That would be me," said Asher.

"So good of you to come."

Quinn stepped up beside Asher. "And who would you be?"

The man behind the desk took no notice of Quinn, or of anyone other than Asher.

"Nice work on the Higgins account, Asher. A helluva job."

Asher looked quickly at Quinn, glanced briefly back over his shoulder, turned back then to... his boss?

"Um... I did my best, sir."

"Of course you did, son. Of course you did. And don't think you're not getting noticed, my boy."

"I'm... flattered. Just doing my job."

"Oh, don't play coy with me, Asher." The man leaned forward and pointed a thick, well-manicured finger. "You're one of our best and brightest. You are going places."

"Thank you." Asher felt a hand grip his arm. Susan was standing behind him. He could hear her breathing. He kept his focus on the man. "Does this mean—"

"You're moving on up, son." The man put on a wide grin. "You should celebrate. Take the afternoon off. Take the family out for a nice lunch. My treat."

The man gave a nod to the woman who had escorted them into the office. She stepped back to the door, held it open and waited.

Carmody looked up at Quinn. "I don't understand."

Quinn kept his attention on the man behind the desk. "I suppose that's it then."

"Thank you, sir," said Asher. He turned about. Susan stepped aside; they all made way.

Susan leaned near Church. She spoke in a whisper. "Is he saying what I think he's saying?"

"Are you thinking that Asher is being kicked upstairs and we're all going to lunch?"

"And that means..."

"I think so."

Professor Asher stepped through the open door...

The observation room was circular, about thirty feet in diameter, enclosed in a Plexiglas dome. The floor was stone, polished smooth. There were two plastic benches, one telescope mounted on a tripod, and nothing else.

The world beyond the glass was speckled with small impact craters, the landscape barren and gray, stretching out to an impossibly close horizon. The sky was deep black, scattered with extraordinarily bright stars.

"Where are we?" asked Lisa.

Banister stepped up beside Asher, who had walked across the room and was standing next to the telescope.

"Hazarding a guess, Miss Powell," said Banister, looking out beyond the dome. "I would say we're on an asteroid."

Asher pointed to one of the objects in the black sky; a faint, fuzzy blue sphere, appearing no bigger than the larger stars. "I'm betting that's the Earth."

~ end of episode four

Episode Five
Night Train

Prolog

The narrow wooden door opened almost silently. Sgt. Costa came through first and stepped into the passenger car. She felt the easy side-to-side rocking of the train beneath her feet, heard and felt the rhythmic rumbling of wheels on track.

The vintage train car looked like something out of an old mystery novel that she might have read years earlier; the wood floor running the length of the car was scratched and worn from decades of use; a row of thickly padded blue seats with wooden armrests lined either side of the car. Yellowed tulip glass light fixtures hung along the length of the car above the seats; vertical sliding windows were set into dark wood framing.

The others began coming through the door behind her one and two at a time. Susan Bautista was being helped, Banister at one arm, Peter Asher the other. She took in cautious, shaky breaths as she clutched an elbow. They guided her over to the nearest seat and eased her down.

"You all right?" asked Asher.

"Fine," said Susan. She took another cautious breath, the pain showing on her face.

"Nothing broken, my dear," said Banister. "But we should wrap those bruised ribs."

She nodded but said nothing. Banister gave her a pat on the shoulder as he looked up at Church, just coming into the car and looking anxiously about for Susan.

"She'll be fine, Nate," Banister said quickly.

Owen tossed her backpack onto another of the seats. "Well, that was the weirdest thing ever," she said. She looked over at Susan. "You okay, hon?"

Susan managed a nod and slight smile.

"What were those things?" asked Carmody.

"Somebody's idea of a nightmare," said Ramos. "Were those arms or legs?"

"A bit of both, I should think," said Banister.

"Certainly gave them the advantage on the cliff," said Church.

Costa maneuvered herself between several passenger seats and studied the scene beyond the window.

"Doctor Owen, I might just be able to match you on the weird meter."

Owen lowered her head and looked out at the darkness beyond the glass. "I hardly think nighttime constitutes weird, Sergeant," she said at last.

"That's more than just dark, Doctor," Costa stated flatly. "It isn't night out there. It's empty."

Episode Five / Chapter One

Lieutenant Quinn stood at the table with his arms folded across his chest, watched as Ramos began setting up the radio. Costa and Carmody waited at the last table near the far end of the dining car.

"It looks fine, sir," said Ramos. "I think we're good."

"Thank you, Corporal." Quinn looked then to Costa, who slid into the aisle and approached.

"Sir?" she asked.

"You and Carmody search forward, all the way to the engine, if possible. I'll head down train. We'll meet back here."

"Yes sir." Costa led Carmody forward.

Quinn glanced back to Ramos. The next communication window to command was a long ways off. "Do you need anything?"

"I'm good, sir."

Quinn looked at his watch. They had found over the last few floors that no matter what the local time might be on an individual floor, the communication window held consistent: thirty seven hours and twenty minutes, their own time. He kept his watch on that communication schedule.

The next window to command was more than five hours away; plenty of time for preliminary searches and prepare a report for General Wong.

"Very well, Corporal," he said. "I'll be back soon."

Susan sat staring out the window in the train's passenger car as Dr. Owen and Lisa Powell used strips of a cotton tablecloth to bind her ribs. They finished pulling her shirt back into place just as Lieutenant Quinn entered the car and started down the aisle, using the chair backs on either side for balance.

"How are you feeling, Doctor Bautista?" he asked. He had to take a step back to make room for Lisa to move out into the aisle. He smiled awkwardly.

"Quite well, Lieutenant," said Susan. "Thank you."

"Very good. You take whatever time you need. Everything is quiet enough at the moment."

"There hasn't been much of that lately," grumbled Owen. She settled into a seat on the opposite side of the aisle.

"Whenever we can, Doctor Owen." The lieutenant appeared a bit distracted. There was a slight, goofy half-grin whenever Lisa looked in his direction. "We should all take a moment whenever the opportunity presents itself."

"Uh, huh. Right," said Owen.

Lisa finally noticed Quinn's attention. She turned away uncomfortably and reached down to pick up the last of the homemade bandages and bindings that were piled on the seat beside Susan.

"I should put these away," she said, and mumbled an apology as she stepped past Quinn.

Quinn gave his own fumbling apologies to Susan and Owen and continued on down train.

Owen looked first one direction, then the other, watching the door at each end as they slowly closed.

"This is going to be nothing but trouble," she growled under her breath.

"I think it's cute," said Susan quietly. She was still looking out the window, out at that strange black void. There was nothing... absolutely nothing.

Owen plopped her head against the back of her seat. "Cute? I just know that somehow, some way, I'm the one that's gonna get bit in the ass."

The kitchen car was forward of the dining car. Church and Banister had begun searching cabinets for food, were gathering together what little they were finding and stowing it in the tall central cabinet beside the stove. So far... a few bags of flour, rice and ground coffee.

"The thirteenth floor," said Banister, closing and latching one of the overhead cabinets. "You know what they say about the thirteenth floor."

"It is a most peculiar tradition, not naming the thirteenth floor the thirteenth floor. Setting superstitions aside, it is still the thirteenth floor after all, whatever they choose to name it."

"I don't think I've ever been in a building that had that many floors."

"We're in one now," said Church.

Banister chuckled. "True enough. I wonder what's going to come of it, circumstances being what they are."

"I doubt it shall go unnoticed."

Costa and Carmody came into the kitchen on their journey forward.

"Doctor Church, Doctor Banister," said Costa. "Are you finding lots of goodies for us?"

"Ah, Sergeant Costa! How very good of you to drop by." Banister spoke through a broad smile as he closed another cabinet. "The cupboards aren't totally bare."

"We've already found enough to take some of the pressure off our current supplies," said Church. "But we are likely to continue on short rations, I'm afraid."

"Oh, who knows what the next cabinet may give us?"

"Exactly so," said Banister.

"Wow, cool stove," said Carmody. It was a wide cast iron wood stove with an overhead hood and vent.

"Perhaps I'll fix us up something later, eh Private?" said Banister.

"Hey, that'd be great, sir."

"Onward and forward, Private," Costa said to Carmody. She looked a final time to the two doctors. "Steak and eggs for me."

"I'll see what we can do, Sara," said Banister. He and Church watched Costa and Carmody continue forward and through the door.

"What are you staring at?" asked Church, once they were alone.

"A lovely girl. And very kind."

"Of late, I would argue that her most attractive feature is more military in nature."

"Don't give me that, Nate," grumbled Banister. "You have as big a childish crush on her as I do."

"What are you talking about, you old fart? That, sir, is forty years out of the gate."

"Smart, attractive, and can take on all manner of monsters?" Banister let out a very long, very sad sigh.

Quinn walked the length of the baggage car, passing crates and boxes, some sitting loose on the floor, others strapped to either wall. One set of metal shelves was filled with smaller packages that were held in place with stretched netting.

He glanced briefly at several of the labels on the boxes. Most were stamped with individual alphanumeric identification codes and what appeared to be the same three character destination code, though the letters weren't anything he recognized.

The baggage car showed a lot of promise. He would send a team in to do a complete inventory.

The next car down train was the caboose. There were two desks, a padded bench along one wall, and a shelf and locker on another. A cold potbellied stove stood in one corner, a bamboo basket of kindling on the floor beside it.

A cozy little guard shack on wheels.

He would check the desk drawers and locker on his way back. Now though, he was curious as to what things looked like beyond the next door.

He found Peter Asher standing on the rear platform. The professor was standing at the rail, looking out at the tracks disappearing into the void behind them. Quinn stood beside him.

"Professor," he said.

"Hello, Lieutenant." Asher kept his attention outward.

"This is a new one, eh?"

"It certainly is," said Asher. "I'm not sure what to make of it."

Quinn placed his hands on the handrail and leaned forward. He looked down at the tracks, watched them rush from below the train and then away, vanishing into the black only a few yards behind them. He could feel the rumbling of the wheels through his feet, through his bones, the sound pushing in on him from every direction, wrapping itself around him like a fuzzy cocoon.

Costa and Carmody stepped out onto the open platform at the front of the car. Ahead of them was the tender car, gently rocking from side to side. The absolute blackness of this world pushed in on them from either side and down from above. The sound of the engine, just beyond the tender car, had a lost, lonely, haunted quality.

The coupling between cars afforded some footing for crossing over, but the span was wide enough that the slightest misstep could send them to the tracks below and under the train.

Carmody remained on the platform side of the rail as Costa climbed over. Carmody pressed firmly against the rail and held tight to Costa's left hand as Costa eased herself down onto the coupling. She would have to let go of Carmody in order to lean forward enough to take hold of the ladder running up the rear of the tender car ahead of her.

She paused and checked her balance, extended her right arm out as far as she could reach, fingers outstretched. At some unspoken signal, she let go of Carmody's hand, simultaneously leaned forward and grasped the ladder.

She pulled herself forward and up fully onto the ladder. She took a moment to reposition herself. Once she felt secure, she adjusted her footing, placing one foot on one step of the ladder, her other onto the step above. Holding on tight then with her left hand, she leaned back out over the expanse between cars, her right arm outstretched.

Carmody had climbed over the platform railing and was waiting. She stepped out into space as she reached for Costa's offered hand, one foot dropping down onto the coupling below. She started to swing out dangerously to one side before Costa managed to pull her back in.

She spent very little time on the coupling before lunging forward and grasping the metal steps of the ladder.

With Carmody was safely across, Costa climbed the ladder to the top of the tender car. It was filled with cut and dried wood ready for the steam engine's furnace.

Costa climbed onto the wood, Carmody following behind her. They scampered forward on hands and knees, worked their way up to the front of the tender car.

Ahead of them was the engine. Looking down into the open compartment, they could see the engineer, busily going about his business. He wore the coveralls and cap that they would expect an engineer to wear. He turned slowly about and looked up at them...

A distorted, demon-like face, a fiery gleeful grin, both threatening and glowing with demented joy...

Episode Five / Chapter Two

Corporal Johansen handed the radio headset to Dr. Lake as General Wong and Captain Adamson moved off and settled in at the main table in the middle of the command center.

Dr. Lake held the headset to his ear and spoke into the mouthpiece. "Doctor Church? Lake here. Over."

Johansen slid his chair back and stood up, left the doctor to his conversation with Church.

"Yes... yes. I understand," said Lake, glancing first to the receding figure of Johansen, briefly then to the general and the captain. He turned and focused his attention on the radio set as he spoke. "There's not much time remaining to us, Doctor. We'll have to make this fast. Over."

Back at the table, the general and Captain Adamson were discussing the news regarding this latest floor.

It was a black void... nothing but the dark, an old train, and the set of tracks on which it traveled.

And a demon engineer...

"And it's the thirteenth floor, to boot," said Adamson. "Not that I've ever put stock in such things."

"Nor I, but the Adversary has apparently attached significance to it."

"Some sort of supernatural threat this time?"

"A demon engineer driving an old train across a black void? Yes, Captain, I would say supernatural was a safe bet."

Over at the radio, Dr. Lake tossed the headset down in disgust. Time had expired. The communications window had closed.

He turned and looked sharply at the two sitting at the table.

"General Wong! I must insist that I be allowed to speak with the team first at the next window. It is impossible to get a complete report in the time allowed as it is, much less respond with recommendations to their observations. But to be left with only the last remaining seconds at each communication is completely unacceptable."

"Of course, Doctor." General Wong turned to Johansen. "Corporal... at the next communication, excepting immediate military need, please ask Lieutenant Quinn to put Doctor Church on the line."

"Yes, sir," said Johansen.

"Thank you," said Lake.

Wong gave Dr. Lake a slow nod, then slid about in his chair and leaned forward. He placed his elbows on the table and clasped his hands together.

"It is long past time to bring medical in on this, Captain," he said to Adamson. "I would like you to provide them with what we have on Doctor Bautista's condition."

"They'll have to be brought up to speed on the mission, General."

"That's fine. It's about time we expand the circle. I'd feel a whole lot better with some expertise looking over their shoulders. That much, at least, we can do from here."

"Of course, sir." Adamson was confident that the team could handle the majority of whatever medical issues might come up. Each military member had undergone a crash course in field medic training, and from their files he knew that the scientific members of the team all had varying levels of first aid training as well.

As such, it had been decided not to include a dedicated, full time medic on the team. It was felt at the time that should an emergency warrant it, the team could be advised from the command center.

But a lot had changed since those first days on the first floor, and considering the present circumstances, Captain Adamson was inclined to agree that it would be best to have medical expertise much closer to hand.

"I'll set up a briefing with Major Connelly," he said.

Church handed the receiver back to Ramos. "Oh, dear," he said calmly. "I expect Lake is giving the general an earful about now."

Ramos put the receiver back into its cradle. "I expect so, Doctor."

The dining car was empty but for the two of them. Quinn had left as soon as he had provided his report to General Wong.

Church had only begun his own report to Lake when the communication window had closed, had still been detailing their findings of the last floor.

He did find value in providing this information. Doctor Lake was compiling an extensive dataset, and with each new floor came another layer of data elements from which they might be able to extrapolate what may lie ahead.

While it was true that each floor they entered, each world they found themselves in, was unique unto itself, there were universal laws being followed. And there were similarities in the clues that existed on each floor. As had been suggested on several occasions, there were rules to this game, and even the Adversary appeared to be following them.

For the moment, Doctor Lake would have to work with what Lieutenant Quinn had provided in his final report of the last floor and what little they had so far regarding this floor.

Church would have much more data for Lake by the next communication window.

The door at the far end of the dining car opened and Susan came in, stepping delicately, Lisa Powell behind her, ready at her elbow.

"Susan," Church called out. "Up and about, I see."

"I needed a change of scenery, Doctor." Susan walked past a number of tables, settled into the one opposite Ramos and his radio equipment. She looked up at Lisa. "Stop mothering me. Please, go for a walk or something."

"All right," said Lisa. "I suppose I should see what kind of trouble Doctor Owen is getting into."

"Good idea," said Susan. She felt bad then and reached out, gave her a gentle pat on the arm. Lisa accepted the silent apology with a comforting smile, continued forward and through the door as Church settled into the seat opposite Susan.

"You are looking much better, my dear," said Church.

"Thank you." Susan looked out the window. She frowned and sighed. "No getting away from that."

"I'm sorry, I —ah, yes... the view." Church studied the scene beyond the glass. "We have yet to determine just what it is. Our working supposition is that it is... nothing."

"And just how does one leave, depart, exit... nothing?"

"For that matter, how can one travel within... *through*... nothing?" Church shook his head. "We don't even have the terminology to describe our circumstance."

Susan started to laugh at that, but a streak of pain in her tightly bound chest cut it short.

"Susan?" A worried look from Church, it eased when Susan managed a smile. "I'll try not to be so amusing," he said.

"Our circumstance?" Susan's smile broadened. "Our most recent circumstance... we were attacked by bizarre creatures with numerous arms for legs, or legs for arms, not sure which, that live on the face of a cliff two thousand feet high."

"They were arms for legs, I think." Church looked across the aisle to Ramos. "What do you think, corporal? Were those arms or legs?"

"Arms, I figure," said Ramos. "That big fella gave Doctor Bautista one big time bear hug."

"Could have been a leg lock," said Susan.

"Guess so," said Ramos. "My money is still on arms."

"My money as well," said Church.

Asher entered the dining car. Susan scooted over and he settled in beside her.

"How goes the search, Professor Asher?" asked Church.

"It goes." He gave Susan a quick onceover. "You're looking much better, Susan. How are you feeling?"

"I'm perfectly fine, Peter."

Church leaned over the table. "She thinks we're smothering her."

"Tough," Asher said dismissively. "Any word on our engineer?"

"He has made no overt threats, as of yet. Sergeant Costa is keeping an eye on him." Church leaned back in his seat. "And how are things at the other end of the train?"

"There's not much to it, really," said Asher. "I think the lieutenant may turn the caboose into his private office. It's not a bad setup."

"If we're all up here, he's gonna get awful lonely," said Church.

"That may be just the way he wants it."

"I understand there's a baggage car," said Susan.

"We'll start popping open crates soon, see what sort of presents Santa brung us." He looked across at Church. "What about food?"

"Staples, mostly. Flour and such. Few other things. It'll help."

"I heard something about coffee."

"Why, yes, Professor. I believe so."

As if on cue, the forward door opened and Doctor Banister stepped through, coffee pot in hand. Private Carmody was directly behind him, holding before her a tray of white ceramic coffee cups and a second pot.

"Ladies and gentlemen, boys and girls, we bring you the liquid of the gods," said Banister.

"Oh, you sweet, sweet man," said Asher. Ramos was also sliding out of his seat, eager to assist. A moment later, Owen and Lisa came in behind Banister and Carmody.

The dining car was suddenly the place to be.

Lt. Quinn sat at his desk, working on his drawings. The interior of the caboose was warm, a soothing heat coming from the potbellied stove in the corner.

He hadn't really been cold, but he had known that it would add a sense of comfort to his environment. Right about now he could use whatever psychological healing he could get.

Dr. Owen had been right about one thing... they all needed some down time. A few hours of warm and fuzzy and he would think clearer, hopefully make better decisions.

Quinn set his pencil down. He leaned back in his chair and closed his eyes. The heat pushing out from the cast iron of the stove reached him in a gentle wave, brushed across his face. He heard and felt the rumbling of the wheels on the tracks beneath the train, felt the slight swaying from side to side. He found himself sliding into a soothing peace. It felt good. It felt pleasant. Tension began to drain away. The dull headache he hadn't realized was there began to fade.

He took in a long, deep breath, let it out easy as he opened his eyes. Yes, he could get used to this, if he let it.

But of course he knew that he wouldn't.

Too bad, really.

Still leaning back in his chair, he stared at the drawings on the desk; diagrams of the train. One drawing had the cars lined up in order, each one titled. Other drawings detailed the individual cars, with each car's content and items of interest listed, as he understood them at the moment.

They had already discovered some food, water, as well as a few items they would take with them once they moved on to the next floor. They had yet to do a search of the crates in the baggage car, but that would come soon. Quinn had hopes there. This was just the sort of scenario the Adversary would create to provide the team with the gear necessary to continue this crazy gauntlet. After lunch they would conduct a thorough and proper search, complete a proper inventory.

Quinn felt a slight shift in the movement of the train; a barely perceptible change in the weight of his body within the caboose. It felt as though the train was no longer traveling on a straight track that it had these past hours, that it was moving now on a very long, gentle curve.

He left the desk and walked over to the bench, sat and leaned close to the window.

He saw nothing at first. There was, as always, only the void. Doing his best to look directly up the line of cars, it was impossible to tell if they were in fact traveling on a curve. The train was too short; the curve, if there was one, was too slow.

He was about to slide back off the bench when he thought he saw something. He pressed his cheek against the glass.

Nothing...

Then, up ahead. What was that?

A dull glow... far in the distance...

Wait... how could there be *distance* in a void?

Okay, but they were traveling *through* a void, which was another impossibility, so...

If the train was in fact traveling on a track with a long, gentle curve, they could be heading right for that... whatever it was.

Something. There was something there... a very faint glow; fuzzy, indistinct, and they were heading right toward it.

Costa sat atop the tender car, calmly watching the demon engineer at work. For the most part it ignored her, only occasionally glancing up in her direction. When it did, it would smile its eerie mix of warmth and insanity, then return to its work.

Other than the first time the engineer retrieved wood from the tender car, which he did through one of several large open access panels set into the front of the car, Costa hadn't felt seriously threatened. She was ever vigilant, ever expectant, but the sudden attack that she had been certain would come never came.

She shifted position on the cut wood; she realized then that she was feeling a slight push in one direction, as if the train was traveling a curve.

Looking outward, it was impossible to tell. All about them, in every direction, there was only the black.

She focused her attention forward, staring directly ahead of the engine, then slowly lifting up her gaze, if there was such a thing as *up* in this place.

She saw nothing at first. But then, after some time, she thought... just maybe...

Was that a light up ahead? Far ahead, forward and just slightly to the left; a dull, fuzzy glow.

She studied it. It faded in and out, but it was definitely there. It was still very far off, but it was drawing nearer.

They were heading right for it.

She glanced back down at the engineer.

He had ceased his labors. He stood there, looking up at her. And there it was... that knowing, demonic grin.

With the exception of Lt. Quinn and Sgt. Costa, everyone had found their way into the dining car, were sitting at three of the tables in the middle of the car. Their conversations moved quickly from one table to the next, from one subject to the next.

The coffee had run out long ago, but that didn't seem to matter. There had been some mention a while back of making more, but the empty coffee pots sat untended.

Quinn came hurrying into the car. Banister welcomed him, offered him a spot at the table. Corporal Ramos looked to him for possible orders.

Quinn ignored them both. He stood stiffly in the aisle, put a palm down on one of the tables for balance.

"Everyone, can I have your attention?" he started. He waited for some semblance of silence. "Thank you," he continued. "Folks, I really hate to break this up but, well... I think this is our stop."

Episode Five / Chapter Three

The train eased slowly into the train station. It was little more than a small building with a wide wooden platform bordering the tracks and running the length of the station. Pole lamps stood at each end of the platform and gave off a dull, golden glow that did little to push back the surrounding dark. Another lamp hung on the wall next to an opening that served as the one gate access leading from the station's interior.

Quinn hopped down onto the platform just as the train came to a full stop, looking about for immediate threats. But for the sound of the engine settling down after its run, it was very quiet.

Church and Banister followed him out a few moments later. Ramos came out of the train from the forward platform of the dining car carrying the radio equipment, and Carmody and Asher began unloading the team's backpacks and other gear from the passenger car. They had no way of knowing whether the train was going to stay or leave, so thought it best to keep their equipment with them.

Quinn wished they had inventoried the baggage car earlier. If the train left without them, they would lose whatever was in the packages and crates. The same was true for the food supplies in the kitchen car.

Costa dropped down from the tender car and started toward Quinn. He noted that she was doing a careful study of their surroundings as she approached.

"What of our engineer, Sergeant?" he asked her.

"He's doing a visual inspection of the locomotive, sir." Costa stood beside the lieutenant. "You know, a walk-around of the engine, checking it all out, looking for damage and whatnot."

"This whole thing is weird, weird, and still more weird," said Owen.

"That about sums it up, Doctor Owen," said Quinn. He turned back to Costa. "Does it look like he plans on sticking around for awhile?"

"No way to tell. He could hop back in as soon as he finishes his inspection and take off."

"We need those food supplies," said Church.

"Yes we do," said Quinn. "I'll leave that to you and Doctor Banister."

"Of course." Church and Banister turned back to the metal steps and climbed up into the train.

Quinn called after them. "If the train leaves, don't you be on it."

"Yes, yes."

Quinn turned then to Carmody. He told her to wait outside the kitchen car, and if it looked like the train was about to so much as budge, to pull them out. She gave him an affirmative nod and started off.

"And the baggage car?" asked Professor Asher.

"The baggage car," mumbled Quinn. He looked at the group, all gathered now beside him on the platform but for Church and Banister, with Carmody in position outside the kitchen car.

He wanted to get them all inside the station, everyone safely tucked in. He felt uncomfortable about splitting them up without knowing their situation. But those crates...

"Sergeant Costa," he said. "You and the professor. Go."

"Yes, sir."

"And what I told Doctor Church holds just as true for you. If the train starts moving, I want you off. Got it?"

"Absolutely." She looked at Asher, held out a beckoning arm. "Professor?"

Quinn turned again to what remained of the group. He would make certain the station was safe before he let the civilians walk in. "Give me two minutes to make sure there are no surprises." He signaled Ramos and the two of them went inside.

The hardwood floor was faded and scratched, as if from years of foot traffic. Two rows of wooden benches took up most of the center of the room. To the right was a counter with one ticket window. The counter spanned the width of the narrow room. Set high on the wall behind the counter was a plastic message board with one line of plastic letters: "North 8:00AM".

The other side of the room, a wide hallway led to the rest of the small building.

"Quiet enough, Lieutenant," said Ramos. They were alone.

Quinn indicated the hall with the nod of the head. Ramos started toward it as Quinn went across the room to what looked to be the front door of the station.

Costa squatted down beside one of the crates. "What do you think of these, Professor?" she asked, indicating the label.

"They all have the same destination code."

"Whatever those letters are. No language I recognize."

"An inside joke of the Adversary's, no doubt." Asher began looking around for some tool to use to open up a crate. Meanwhile, Costa went to the shelf and grabbed a cardboard box.

She was about to tear it open when she thought she heard a sound.

"Do you hear that?"

Asher listened. It came from outside the car... wheels rolling across the platform...

Metal latches lifting and dropping, and the large side door slid open.

Asher and Costa both stepped cautiously back, moved to the end of the baggage car. A figure jumped up into the car.

He was a small man, barely five feet tall, dressed in coveralls and wearing a well-worn cap. He stood there a moment, in the center of the car, looked calmly at Asher and Costa.

It was a demon face... like that of the engineer. It didn't appear threatening, and didn't appear at all concerned at seeing the two humans standing at the end of car.

It turned about, set about to unload the crates and boxes and packages, handing them down one by one to a second demon that was standing on the platform outside the baggage car. This second demon stacked them carefully and neatly onto a flatbed four-wheeled cart.

Costa held up the cardboard box she was still holding onto. She looked at the destination label. "I guess we are... wherever this is," she whispered.

Lisa Powell opened the front door and stepped out onto the porch. Quinn was standing at the rail, looking out into the black.

"Everyone settling in?" asked Quinn.

"I don't know that I would call it settling, exactly," said Lisa. "Corporal Ramos said it was safe to come in, so we came in."

"I see." Quinn glanced back at the door, turned back to the scene beyond the porch. There was nothing to see, quite literally, but it was better than staring awkwardly at Miss Powell.

Lisa took a step closer to the rail and rested her hands on the banister.

"It would be peaceful, if it wasn't so ominous," she said.

Quinn found it peaceful in any event, but definitely got it; completely surrounded by an emptiness that threatened to swallow them up.

Raised voices came from inside the station; some disagreement between Elizabeth Owen and Corporal Ramos. Quinn took it as an opportunity to shift the subject back to those inside.

"Dr. Owen sounds to be settling in just fine," he said.

"Dr. Owen puts on a strong front," said Lisa.

"You know her better than I," Quinn said doubtfully. After months together in the tower, he had yet to find anything weak about the woman.

"Well, she would never let anyone know it, but she took what happened to Ray pretty hard," said Lisa.

"Really? I mean, I could see how much she relied on him—"

"I know it didn't show, but she felt very deeply for him, almost as a son."

"You're right. It didn't show." He stiffened. He felt his skin grow warm. "I apologize. I'm very sorry. That was very rude."

"No," Lisa grinned. "I understand."

"Yes... well..."

"Neither would ever have admitted it, but Ray was much more than Doctor Owen's assistant. He provided a strength that she depended on. His death left a hole that impacts everything she does, every decision she makes."

"She has you, Miss Powell. And she is lucky to have you."

"Thank you, Lieutenant," she said. "However, whatever my qualifications as Doctor Owen's assistant, I would never attempt to fill the void created when Ray died. And she wouldn't want me to."

"Yes. Well, as I said..."

"Thank you."

"Yes..." he began fumbling with his clasped hands. He struggled to come up with something real to say, was relieved when the silence was finally broken by the sound of Dr. Owen giving Ramos another what-for.

"Oh, dear," said Lisa.

"I believe duty calls," said Quinn. He reached out for the door behind them. "Shall we?"

They entered the station just as Church, Banister and Carmody came in from the platform carrying bundles and bags of food supplies. Over near the counter, Owen was pointing an angry finger at Ramos.

"This isn't over, Corporal," she hissed, then stalked across the room. "Home, safe and sound," she said, speaking in the general direction of Church and the others.

Ramos started toward the hallway on the other side of the room. "This way, please, doctors. We can store that in the supply room."

"I'll show them," said Susan. She was just coming out of the hallway, turned and started back. They followed her, which left Ramos looking uncomfortably in Owen's direction. He then noticed Quinn's return, walked quickly over and began briefing the lieutenant on what he'd found in the rest of the station.

There was a large supply closet, a pair of restrooms, a small break room and baggage storeroom.

And that was it; all of it together not much larger than the size of this one main room.

On the positive side, that meant a smaller area to search for the portal. On the negative, with such a small search area, shouldn't they have already stumbled across it by now?

Nonetheless, Quinn was certain the portal was here. As with the previous twelve floors, they would conduct a methodical search, find the portal and move on.

Quinn looked across the room at Owen. "What was the problem between you and Dr. Owen?"

"Nothing serious, sir," said Ramos. "Some disagreement as to my duties."

Asher and Costa came into the station.

"You are not going to believe this," said Asher.

Carmody burst in from the hallway. "Holy crap!" Something down the hall had definitely taken her by surprise.

"Ah," said Asher, a bit disappointed. "So you've met our friends."

General Wong found Dr. Lake standing in the open lot midway between the command center and the tower. The man was staring off into space, not really looking at the tower; not really looking at anything.

The sun had gone down, and the gray of dusk was growing steadily darker. The cool day was turning into a chilly evening and the doctor wasn't wearing his jacket. He had to be getting cold.

"Doctor Lake? Is everything all right?"

Lake didn't answer, didn't even acknowledge the general's arrival.

"Doctor?"

Dr. Lake stirred, mumbled then without turning. "Yes?"

"Is everything all right?"

"No. No, I don't think so," he answered softly.

General Wong looked at the black tower, looked about at the surrounding lot, at the buildings far in the distance.

"What is it?" he asked. The world was quiet. Nothing looked out of the ordinary, excepting the fact that there was an eighty storey windowless black building where there shouldn't be an eighty storey windowless black building.

Lake watched as a Jeep rounded the far corner of the tower. It followed the base of the tower, approached the nearer corner and finally disappeared around the side. He knew from past experience that the patrol would park at a bivouac consisting of a handful of command tents that were set up just out of sight around the side of the alien tower.

"How many do you have on the watch, General? Thirty soldiers?"

"About that," answered General Wong. "A platoon."

"And you don't find that odd?"

"I'm not sure I know what you mean." The general was beginning to feel uncomfortable.

"Less than three dozen of us, all total. Considering the situation, shouldn't there be like... a battalion? A division? Hell, the whole freakin' army should be here."

General Wong was now truly perplexed. "What are you saying, Doctor Lake?"

"General... I'm pretty sure we're on the inside."

"Excuse me?"

"We're not outside the tower. We're inside."

"No. No, that doesn't make sense," said Dr. Owen. "Lake's wrong."

"It does provide answers to a number of questions," said Church. He and Owen were sitting at one of the two tables in the small breakroom. Most of the others of the team were standing against the four beige colored walls.

"Such as our ability to communicate with command," said Asher.

"No," Owen stated flatly. "It just pushes the questions around, but they're still there."

"And it does create a batch of new ones," admitted Church.

"It certainly does," said Owen.

"How can they be inside and not know it?" asked Quinn. "Don't they periodically go somewhere?"

Owen threw up a hand. "Questions."

They had only just finished their scheduled communication with command. Lake had dominated the session, laying out his theory that command and the area immediately surrounding the tower was actually inside, that it was as another floor.

"It can't be a floor," said Carmody. "When we got here... it was outside. We drove up to the tower. We were outside."

"Were we?" asked Lisa. It was a whisper. "There was something not quite right. It was eerie. It felt... eerie."

"Come on, Lisa," droned Owen. "We had just pulled up outside an alien tower, for Christ's sake."

Lisa gave a weak smile. "I suppose," she said at last.

"To the lieutenant's point," Owen said to the group at large. "Wong and Lake and the others must leave command now and then. They would certainly notice traversing from inside to outside. Or is it being suggested that wherever they go is still inside?"

"Perhaps they only believe they are leaving," said Asher.

"Oh, Peter. That's crazy, even for this place; even for you."

"Just a thought," Asher sighed with a thin smile.

"Keep thinking."

"I'll do that."

Sgt. Costa and Ramos had been standing quietly near the door. Costa shook her head in frustration. "You guys sort this out. I don't see as it makes much difference to us." She looked across at Quinn. "How 'bout Ramos and I head over to baggage storage, sir?"

"Good idea, Sergeant," said Quinn. He turned to Carmody. "Let's you and I check the perimeter outside."

"Mind if I join you?" asked Asher.

"I'd like to tag along," said Susan.

The room began to clear until Church and Banister found themselves alone. Church sat back with a loud sigh.

"That's better," he said. He looked thoughtfully at Banister. "You've been uncharacteristically quiet, Wes."

"Have I?" Banister moved to the table and sat down opposite Church.

"You have." Church wiggled a finger in Banister's general direction. "You workin' on a notion in that web-entangled skull of yours?"

A shrug. "Theory of a sort."

"You're thinking Lake is right?"

"He's onto something, but..."

"Yeah, I know," groaned Church. "No answer fits all the questions."

"And there are a few. You were right about that."

"Alright. Let us assume then that there are several different answers to our multitude of questions."

"I can do that."

Church scooted forward in his chair. "A floor, but not a floor."

"Ah, my dear Doctor Church," said Banister. "You are thinking what I am thinking."

"Perhaps."

"Perhaps command isn't actually within a floor as Doctor Lake has postulated. Perhaps it is rather an event horizon, of a sort, that lay between the tower and the true outside world."

"I am toying with such an idea, though certainly not an event horizon per se."

"Event horizon?" Carmody was standing in the doorway. "You mean like a black hole? We're in a black hole?"

"I doubt that very much," Church stated patiently.

"But isn't an event horizon part of a black hole?"

"An event horizon is simply a boundary that lay between two incompatible environments," said Banister. "It serves as the bridge between them."

"You're oversimplifying, Banister," growled Church. "You can't throw the term 'event horizon' around and ignore where that leads." He looked then to Carmody. "An event horizon is a surface of spacetime. It is by definition the point of no return. Once crossed, there is no coming back."

Carmody wondered aloud. "If the command center is in an event horizon, if it is the boundary between the outside world and tower floors, then we can't go back."

"If command were in fact located in an event horizon, it would mean that we, these floors on which we travel, lay within a singularity." Church looked sharply at Banister. "Infinite spacetime curvature. Zero volume. Does this look like zero volume to you?"

"I never said the floors were within a gravitational singularity."

"You infer it by suggesting the command center is in an event horizon."

"Did you not hear what I said, old man? Only insofar as it serves as the boundary between two incompatible environments."

"Oh, I heard you, all right," said Church. He tiredly rubbed his forehead. "I have the headache to prove it."

Quinn waited for Carmody out on the front deck of the station. He directed Asher and Susan one direction before he and the private began in the other. Asher watched them start away, then looked to Susan.

"Susan?"

They stepped down from the deck and walked the path that followed along the wood-slatted wall of the building. Once away from the light that pushed through the small window set into the front door, they were walking in near darkness. They could just make out the wall beside them, the gravel path at their feet, the shadows of one another.

"I'm glad you're feeling better," said Asher.

"Much," said Susan. "Thank you."

"Sure." They walked in silence for a few moments. Asher wanted to tell her that he was glad she had come along, was glad for the chance for them to spend a few minutes alone, but no matter how he put the words together in his mind, they came out awkward. "Interesting scenery," he said.

"Very," she stated. "You know, Doctor Church has a theory about the void. He believes that, as this is the thirteenth floor, and since we humans have this peculiar habit of removing the thirteenth floor from all our buildings, that the Adversary has done so here."

They stopped. Asher looked out into the black emptiness. "He removed it? This is the absence of the thirteenth floor?"

"That's the doctor's theory. And believe it or not, Doctor Banister is leaning toward agreeing with him."

"Well, then it's gotta be so."

Susan grinned and they started walking again. "That's kinda what I was thinking."

They reached the corner of the building, turned and started along the side toward the back.

"Are they letting you take it easy?"

"I didn't need to be injured for that."

"What do you mean?"

"There's not much call for an assistant these days. I do what I can, but..." she shrugged a shoulder. "They've always been close, if cantankerous, but they keep each other preoccupied like no other project we've been on."

"You been on a lot of these?" he asked lightheartedly.

"Alternate worlds strung together like carnival beads?"

"Let's say... puzzles to be deciphered, mysteries to be solved."

"Many."

There was a shimmer of light up ahead, and they could make out the back corner of the building. Approaching, they found a pair of steps that took them up onto the loading platform that ran the length of station. The pole lamps at each end and the lamp on the wall shone bright enough to push dark from the platform and no further.

Quinn and Carmody were just stepping up onto the deck at the other end of the station, directly opposite the head of the train. Asher waved at them and Carmody waved back.

Steam continued to roll out from under the locomotive, as if ready to pull away at any moment. There was no sign of the engineer.

Asher and Susan met the lieutenant and Carmody near the opening that served as the gate leading into the station. They stood beneath the softly glowing lamp on the wall.

"Anything?" asked Quinn.

"All's quiet, Lieutenant," said Asher. "But to be honest, anything could be hiding out there; so long as it keeps its mouth shut, we'd never know it."

"There could be a horde of demons out there, for all we know," said Susan.

"That was our impression as well, Doctor," said Quinn. "That does appear to be the theme this time around."

At that moment the demon engineer climbed down from the locomotive and stood on the metal step, a lit lantern in one hand. He looked back along the train and slowly waved the lantern.

"The train's leaving," said Susan.

"Sure looks that way," said Asher.

"Should we—" started Carmody.

"We've made our choice." Quinn took a slow, deep breath. "This is where we look for the portal."

A demon leaned out from the rear platform of the caboose, gaily waving an arm at the engineer. He looked like one of those who had unloaded the baggage car.

The door to the station's baggage storeroom a few yards behind Quinn opened. Yet another demon came hurrying out and scrambled across the platform and up into the train's passenger car.

Two more demons came running from around the side of the station and scurried across the platform, reaching the train just as it started to pull away.

"Okay, I know they weren't all on that train when we pulled in here," said Carmody.

"They are certainly eager to be on it now," said Susan.

They watched then as the train disappeared into the darkness. The last they saw was the rear platform of the caboose, a lone demon waving a cheery goodbye.

"How can that be good?" asked Asher.

The train was gone. The world grew silent.

The train station was alone in the black void.

Episode Five / Chapter Four

Quinn stood in the middle of the small breakroom staring at the stuffed doll he held in his hand. It looked like a grinning demon.

Costa and Dr. Church stood beside him. Church fought to keep from smiling.

Quinn was definitely not in a smiling mood. He tightened his grip on the doll and looked up at Costa. He said nothing.

"Every crate, every box, every package," said Costa. "Hundreds of 'em."

Quinn looked down at the doll, then over at Church. Church shrugged.

"May not mean anything, could mean everything."

"Very illuminating, Doctor."

Another shrug from Church. "Most everything the Adversary does has a purpose. The purpose of this? I'm sorry, Lieutenant. I haven't a clue."

"Could just be playing with us," suggested Costa. "Having a little fun."

"That's possible," said Church. "We've seen his attempts at humor on more than one occasion."

Quinn handed the doll back to Costa as he spoke again to the doctor. "This means the only fresh supplies we'll be taking with us are what you and Doctor Banister found in the kitchen car."

"We'll make do."

"We're already down to near nothing."

"Now we have coffee and biscuits. We'll be fine."

Costa was staring down at the doll. "That damned grin. Always that same, damned grin."

Lisa Powell appeared in the opened door, holding up a hand to catch Quinn's attention. "I think you better come out here, Lieutenant."

They followed Lisa out into the station lobby. Owen was sitting on one of the benches. She was calm, and unusually quiet.

The Adversary's acolyte stood behind the ticket window. He was dressed in cap and jacket this time around. He appeared to be going about the busywork of a ticket agent. Noticing the group enter the lobby, his expression brightened.

"Hello there, folks," he said cheerily. "And where might you be heading?"

Church stepped around the benches and approached the ticket window.

"Ten tickets to the fourteenth floor, if you please."

The ticket agent looked genuinely puzzled. "I'm sorry, sir. I'm afraid I don't understand."

"The fourteenth floor," urged Church.

The ticket agent glanced down at a schedule on the counter behind the window. "I don't recognize that location." He continued to study his schedule.

Church glanced back at the others. Owen sat silent on the bench; Quinn, Lisa and Costa stood behind her.

Church turned back to the ticket window, glanced up at the wall behind the counter.

North 8:00AM...

"Ah!" he beamed. "We are traveling north, my dear man! North!"

"Yes sir!" said the ticket agent. "We have a train leaving first thing in the morning!"

"Then put us on it, man!" Church slapped the counter with the palm of his hand. "Ten tickets, one way."

Owen and Lisa came into the station lobby from the hallway. Owen and Ramos had gone at it again, and Lisa suggested they take a few minutes.

Most of the team was in the little breakroom getting their gear ready for the departure, and it was crowded in there. Carmody was in the baggage storeroom digging through crates and packages on the off-chance that there may yet something useful.

And Banister was in the lobby. He was standing near the end of the counter in quiet conversation with the ticket agent. Owen watched as the agent handed him the bundle of tickets.

Banister didn't look nearly as pleased as he should, considering the circumstances.

"Now what do you suppose that's about?" she asked.

"Our tickets," said Lisa.

"Hmm. Yes." Owen stepped around one of the benches and sat down. She watched the ticket agent give a polite grin and start back around behind the counter. Banister started across the lobby toward the hallway.

"Everything all right, Wes?" asked Owen.

"Yes, of course," answered Banister. He held up the tickets. "All set."

Something's not right... thought Owen.

Banister continued down the hall. Poking his head into the breakroom, he saw that everyone looked about ready. He caught Asher's attention.

The two of them continued down the hallway and went into the restroom.

"Something wrong?" asked Asher. He noted the tickets in Banister's hand.

"I'm afraid so." Banister held the tickets up between them. "It would appear we are two tickets short."

"What? Well let's—" Asher was ready to head out to the lobby.

Banister put a hand on Asher's arm. "Our friend out there tells me there are only eight seats available."

"What?"

"Full up, I'm afraid."

"What does he expect us to do? We're not going to leave two people behind."

"That's exactly what we're going to do." Banister handed the tickets to Asher.

Looking at them more closely, Asher could see the tickets had names on them. "Assigned?" he asked. He saw his own name on the first ticket.

"That's right."

"Who does he plan on—"

"Myself and Private Carmody."

Asher stared numbly down at the tickets. He swallowed hard, took a deep breath and then pushed the tickets back to Banister. "We're not doing this. Not a chance."

Banister refused to take the tickets. "Yes. We are. The situation was made very clear. Private Carmody and I are to remain behind. There is no alternative."

"Of course there is. We're all staying."

Banister smiled tiredly, shook his head. He tried to give Asher a consoling look, but it only looked sad. "I'll speak with the young lady. In the meantime, you must keep this to yourself until the train pulls away."

"We can figure something out."

"I'm sorry, Peter. I'm only telling you because you'll have to explain to the others what's happened. But you must wait until you're well away from the station." Banister grinned. "We can't have Church jumping off the train."

The 8:00AM northbound train arrived at the station at 7:57 and, planned or not, there was a mad rush to get aboard before it departed. Everyone was gathering gear, hauling and dragging it out onto the platform and handing it to others on the train, hurriedly following after.

Dr. Banister and Carmody boarded the train with the others. They as quickly stepped off on the other side, quietly and quickly walked out into the black, leaving their gear just inside the door. Once beyond the reach of the light that spilled out from the passenger car windows, they stopped and waited in the darkness.

Banister could hear Carmody's short, shaking breathing. He reached an arm around her and tried to comfort her. They watched as the train cars jerked and pulled and the train slowly began to pull away.

Asher stood on the rear platform of the caboose. He watched the train station drift into the dark until there was only the soft fuzzy glow of the lamps that stood at either end of the platform. Then that too was gone and there was only the dark.

The door behind him slid open and Church stepped outside.

"Ah, Peter," said Church. There was a hint of concern in his voice. He stood beside Asher, looked back into the train. "Say... I seem to have misplaced Wes. I don't suppose you've seen him?"

Banister sat on the bench beside Carmody. The station was quiet. More quiet than it had been since they first arrived.

Banister looked around them, then at Carmody, then forward. *Alone...*

"Well," he sighed. "I suppose that's it, then."

"Yes sir."

They sat silent. Their gaze was in the general direction of the ticket counter, but they were looking at nothing in particular.

"It could be worse," he said after a long, uncomfortable minute.

Another few moments of stark silence.

"I don't think so, sir."

Carmody was calmer than she had been. The situation still sucked, but she had resigned herself to it. Whatever happened now, the team had made it to the next floor.

She had made thirteen floors. She had barely made it off the first, and since then had nearly bit the dust a dozen times.

She looked side-glance at Dr. Banister. So had this old guy. Probably came close to buying the farm even more often than she had.

It's been one hell of a ride.

But damn it, they had only just started. Eighty floors, and she falls on the thirteenth...

Damn it.

"We didn't get very far," she mumbled.

Banister grinned, chuckled lightly. "I was just thinking the same thing, my dear. All these so many weeks, all these floors, and there is so very far to go."

"I guess they'll have to do it without us, eh?"

"I'm sure they'll do fine," said Banister. "A more difficult task without us, to be sure. But they'll make it."

The ticket agent came around from behind the counter and walked towards them. They hadn't noticed him back there, but then the Adversary's acolyte had a way of doing that.

He came up to them and took a slight bow. He held a pair of tickets out to them.

"Your tickets," he stated.

Banister reached up hesitantly and took them. He handed one to Carmody without bothering to look at it. "Tickets?"

"You can't board without a ticket."

"We going somewhere?" Carmody looked at her ticket, saw that it had Dr. Banister's name on it. She reached over and traded with him.

"You certainly don't expect to stay here," said the ticket agent.

"But I thought—"

"We have an unscheduled train arriving within the hour. You must be on it when it departs."

The ticket agent turned sharply about and returned to his position behind the ticket counter.

Banister turned to Carmody. "Well, my dear. A most curious turn of events."

"I'm good with that, sir."

"Me, too."

They sat quietly then, and waited for the arrival of the unscheduled train.

Banister and Carmody were standing in the lot outside the tower. The sky overhead was slate gray and the air smelled of rain. A pair of powerful industrial lights mounted on tall poles lit up the wall of the tower where the door had once been located.

There was no one around. Looking back over his shoulder, Banister saw the Quonset hut that served as the command center. It stood alone a couple of hundred feet away.

If they listened very closely, they could just hear the sound of the train in the distance. It faded, drifted, and was gone.

"Doctor?" Carmody turned slowly about. "Is this real?"

"That is a very good question, my dear."

~ end of episode five

Episode Six
Fog and Shadows

Prolog

A thick fog drifted across the world. It glowed, as if there was a sun up there somewhere shining down on it. Beneath their feet, the ground was as smooth and as cool to the touch as linoleum, the same color as the fog.

There was no horizon; there were no objects visible. There was only the fog, slowly drifting, shifting in this strange, alien light and shadow. There was an odd feeling that there was something out there, something almost within reach, almost within sight; take a few steps in any direction, reach out your hand and…

"Nobody wander off," said Quinn.

"That would involve moving, and I'm not going anywhere," said Owen. She dropped her pack to the ground and sat on it.

"I believe we could all do with a break," said Church. Except for the incident with the pterodactyl, the last floor hadn't been particularly dangerous, but the low oxygen atmosphere and the steep trails had made the journey to the summit an exhausting one.

Quinn directed Sgt. Costa to set the watch and dropped his own gear to the ground. He took two steps out as everyone began settling in. He stood gazing out into the fog.

Asher came up beside him. "Are you thinking on going against your own orders, Lieutenant?"

Quinn looked back at the rest of the team. Costa and Ramos stood to either side of the main group, still settling in amongst the gear. He guessed visibility at no more than twelve feet. Costa was little more than a silhouette in the bright, silvery gray of the fog.

He looked outward again. "It would be nice to know which direction we should go. A few degrees one way or the other could make all the difference."

"I agree," said Asher. "But having no clue what's in any direction really makes the choice an easy one."

"I don't follow you, Professor."

"We just a pick a direction and go."

Quinn curled his brow and frowned. "What say we try to gather a little intel, eh Professor? Who knows? We might catch a break. I would rather not take the team into that completely blind. Not if I can help it."

"It's up to you, Lieutenant."

"Just a quick peek at what's out there."

"Dip our toe in the water, so to speak."

"Something like that. Twenty steps out. Fifty feet, see what's to see." He turned quickly to the rest of the team. "We'll be right back."

Costa took a step forward from her watch position. "Sir?"

"Just a few yards, Sergeant, and right back again."

"I thought you said no wandering off," said Owen. She turned to Church. "Didn't he say no wandering off?"

"That's what the man said, Elizabeth."

Owen watched Quinn and Asher disappear into the fog. "Oh, this is not going to end well."

Episode Six / Chapter One

Carmody was sitting with Johansen at one of the six tables in the mess tent. Several of the other tables were also occupied, but for the moment they had this one to themselves. Their empty food trays were pushed aside and they were talking quietly over their forgotten cups of coffee.

Carmody had picked up a promotion since coming out of the tower with Dr. Banister several weeks earlier, PFC insignia pinned on her collar. After almost a week of extensive debriefing, she had been assigned to the command staff, purportedly as part of Sgt. Miller's team but in truth assisting Dr. Banister as needed. This had meant that she and Johansen were required to work together quite a bit; neither seemed to mind.

It had taken almost that entire week's debriefing for Banister and Carmody to believe they weren't in some duplicate universe created by the Adversary. Though, according Dr. Banister, they weren't really outside at all... the command center and the area around the tower was somehow inside.

Even after all that Carmody had been through while in the tower, she just didn't get this. This was the command center and these people were real, but they weren't really outside?

So, they _were_ back at command, but command wasn't where they thought it was...

As it turned out, General Wong had been just as suspicious of Carmody and Banister. He didn't think they were real at first; magically appearing outside the tower, claiming to have taken a ride on a special train? Yeah, right...

It wasn't until after some intense conversations with Church on the inside, first to convince Church, and only then convince the general, that they were finally accepted to be who they claimed to be.

Carmody knew that it was all tied into this whole idea that they weren't really on the outside, that this was somehow like the floors in the tower... and yet different...

Geez...

Johansen looked down at his watch. Twenty minutes to the next communications window. They turned in their trays and started back to the command hut.

At last communication, the team had still been on the sixteenth floor, but had been fairly confident they would soon reach the portal to seventeen.

Carmody had left the team back on the thirteenth... back at the train station in the void.

Entering the Quonset hut, she moved off to one side as Johansen walked over toward the radio. He had to maneuver between Banister and Lake, who were already hovering near the communication station. General Wong and Captain Adamson came in a minute later, sat at one of the two tables in the middle of the room.

Johansen sat down, calmly watched the clock on the wall and waited. The final seconds passed... He put on the headset, flipped a switch on the radio set.

"Tower team, this is command. Do you read? Over." He looked up at Banister, who was standing to his right, then to Lake standing at his left. He smiled and turned back to his radio. "Command to tower. Command to tower. Over."

Five seconds passed.

"Well?" asked Lake.

Johansen started to turn to Lake, quickly turned back to the radio.

"There you are, Ramos. How's tricks? Over." He slapped a hand on a timer that he had fastened to the top of the radio set. It was preset to 3 minutes, letting everyone know how much time remained in the communication window. He listened a moment, smiled uncomfortably up at Lake, then Banister, turned away from them both. "All right. Thanks much, Ramos. I'll let 'em know. Here's Doctor Banister. Over."

"What?" Lake had expected first crack at the team.

"Doctor Church is asking to speak to Doctor Banister." Johansen handed the headset to Banister as he stood up. He looked across to the general. "They're on the seventeenth floor, General. Ramos said something about London fog."

Captain Adamson caught his attention, nodded to an empty chair at the table. Johansen went over and began filling the general and the captain in on what little he had been told.

Carmody took a few steps closer to Banister, curious to know all about the next floor.

"I agree absolutely, Nate," Banister was saying. "No. No, you best stay put for now. Better they come back to you."

"What is it?" Lake asked impatiently.

Banister only raised a brow and turned away. "They know better where you are than you them. If you're not in any immediate danger, then heck, give 'em a little more time."

"Banister," grumbled Lake. The timer continued to wind down, the seconds inexorably being eaten away.

Banister's hint of a frown began to turn dark. He wasn't happy with whatever it was Church was now saying.

"Banister," said Lake, now more forcefully.

"Oh, come on Nate." Banister was suddenly exasperated. "Really? Are you really going to bring that up again? Now? Get over it, old man. I'm the one put Asher in that spot. And a damned tough spot it was."

Dr. Lake gave Banister the sternest gaze he knew how to give, held out a hand for the headset. Banister finished listening to Church's response to his chide. It was his attempt at being polite.

"Of course, Nate. Of course. Okay. Okay, I need to turn you over to Lake now." He grinned broadly. "No... no, I'm afraid I do." He pulled off the headset and handed it to Lake. "I do apologize," he said, starting toward the table. "He's all yours."

Quinn and Asher had paced out the twenty steps, found nothing, turned around and paced those same twenty steps back. They had returned to what should have been the location of the rest of the team. They found themselves standing alone in the fog.

They took five steps to their left, came back, and took five steps to the right. There was no sign of the rest of the team. They called out. No one was out there.

They continued in their original direction for another twenty paces. Still nothing. They were lost. They shouldn't have been, they had taken every precaution outside of not taking the walk to begin with, but they definitely had no idea where the rest of the team might be.

They began pacing out a grid pattern, keeping each grid small enough so as not to miss any part of the floor.

A few steps, turn, a few steps, turn...

All the while, one fact continued to nag at them.

Even if they had gotten turned around, they should be able to hear the team.

Should be able to hear Owen, if no one else...

And the team should be able to hear them. They continued to call out to the others at each point in the grid. They had yet to get a response, had yet to hear any sound coming from the fog.

"Lieutenant, do you see that?" asked Asher. A shadow in the fog, one of many shadows in the fog, wasn't moving. Straight ahead, appearing and fading in the fog that was drifting across their path.

There's something there, all right, thought Quinn.

They approached a wide chasm. The smooth, hard ground beneath their feet ended abruptly at the jagged edge, the fog spilling over and down into the abyss, and outward across the empty expanse.

Directly in front of them were two vertical posts three feet high set four feet apart, anchored near the edge of the chasm. These formed the anchor of a narrow rope bridge that stretched out across the chasm, disappearing into the fog. There was no way to tell how wide the gulf might be, or where the bridge might take them.

Quinn took one step out, held tightly to the hand ropes and looked down. "It could be twenty feet to the bottom, could be a thousand," he said.

"Same for the bridge," said Asher.

Quinn steadied himself, looked outward and rocked cautiously one side to the other, testing the stability of the bridge. "It looks scary as hell, but it should bear our weight."

Asher looked left and right. They now had a boundary. "We shouldn't cross the bridge until we find the others," he said. He moved out of the way as Quinn stepped off the bridge.

"Exactly my thought," said Quinn. "The chasm forms one boundary of our search area."

With their backs to the bridge, they started away from the edge of the chasm, returning the way they had come.

Costa and Church stood in the center of the makeshift camp, the others in the team standing around the perimeter, facing outward, each well within sight of Costa. They were taking turns calling out for Quinn and Asher. As yet there had been only silence coming back to them.

Church had convinced the others that for the time being they should wait there, but as the minutes passed there was growing concern that more than just getting lost, that something may have happened to Quinn and Asher. The fact that Doctor Banister had agreed with him that it was best they hold their position had bought some time, but now even Church was considering going in search of their companions.

He and Sgt. Costa were discussing ways of conducting a search without everyone getting lost when Owen calmly called out to everyone.

"We have company," she said.

Shadows in the fog materialized into two figures. One figure raised a hand as they approached. "Hey."

"Welcome home."

"Thank you, Liz," answered Asher.

"So what happened? You two got lost, eh?"

"In a manner of speaking," mumbled Asher. "The weirdest thing... everything moves in here."

"Moves?" The others were gathering behind Owen.

"Yes. Moves," said Quinn.

"Yeah," said Asher. "You can't count on something that you know to be behind you to be there when you turn around."

"Exactly," said Quinn. "Walk away a few steps. You turn around, walk back... it's gone."

"Of which you have direct observational experience," said Church.

"Yes," Quinn sighed.

"And more than that," said Asher. "You can walk away from something, never turn around, and find yourself right back at what you just left behind."

"We came up on that rope bridge four times. I still don't know how we finally made it back here."

"Dumb luck," said Owen.

Church shook his head from side to side. "Likely the Adversary's doing."

"You give him too much credit, Nate."

"Luck or not, we're glad to see you back safe," said Susan, looking first to Quinn, then Asher. "You really gave us a scare."

"For which I apologize," said Quinn.

"To the positive... we did learn something from the experience," said Asher. "We may not know how things work in here, but we have an idea what to expect, what to watch out for."

"And in all your wandering, that rope bridge was the only object you came across," Church stated thoughtfully. He was speaking to Quinn. "I suggest we take it as a signpost; our first milestone on our journey across this floor."

"Precisely what Professor Asher and I were thinking," said Quinn.

"Well then," Owen sighed noisily. "What say we see if we can find it again?"

"We can but try, Doctor," said Quinn. He turned to the group. "You heard her. Gather up your gear, ladies and gentlemen."

Once General Wong had accepted the fact that Banister was in fact Banister, the doctor had quickly become an integral part of the staff. His direct experiences inside the tower and his relationship with the members of the team, with Dr. Church in particular, provided a unique and invaluable perspective.

The general also appreciated the fact that Dr. Lake understood Church's value to command. He not only accepted and listened to Church's observations, he actively sought them out. What was his take on an observation made by the team? What did he make of a comment or thought, or of the way the comment was presented? What of the Adversary's interactions with the team? What of the consistencies and inconsistencies from floor to floor?

Taking it beyond this, General Wong was genuinely impressed with the way Dr. Lake had brought Church into the process of refining Lake's dataset of information that he had compiled over the last sixteen floors. Gaining a solid understanding of the how and why of each floor, of those very consistencies and inconsistencies between floors, and then correctly interpreting the data and being able to provide to those within the tower an accurate analysis, could be critical to getting the team from one floor to the next; could very well provide the tools they would need when they finally confronted the Adversary on the top floor.

Of course this also meant that their meetings always ran two to three times longer than they had prior to Dr. Banister joining the command staff.

The general leaned back in his chair, took a drink of his coffee, long since gone cold. He listened to Lake and Banister going back and forth about Quinn and Asher's little walk into the fog. At the time of the last communication, they had been gone about twenty minutes. Unsettling yes, but it could mean anything.

They would just have to wait for the next communication for news, hope for the best.

This had been the nearest the communication window had come to the time of the team's arrival on a floor. On the positive side, it was great to hear of a successful move from one floor to the next so soon after the trip through the portal. And it also allowed command to get an early peak at the conditions on the next floor.

On the downside, it also meant that the inside team didn't yet know that much about the new floor they found themselves on, and command wouldn't hear from them again for more than a day.

Major Connelly entered the command center. She acknowledged those sitting at the table before heading to the coffee station. Lake eyed her warily, while General Wong simply sat patiently drinking the last of his cold coffee.

"And how are you today?" asked Banister. He agreed that Major Connelly was likely not the person she presented herself to be, but for the moment there was no reason to be uncivil.

"I'm doing quite well, Doctor Banister. Thank you for asking." Connelly sat at the table, fresh cup of coffee in hand. "I understand the team has made it to seventeen. Is everyone all right?"

"Quite," stated Lake.

"Though several of the team has since decided to go for a walk, and have yet to return," said Banister. He explained the environment of the new floor and the situation with Quinn and Asher.

General Wong looked on in silence, listening to Major Connelly's questions, observing her body language as she listened to the answers.

Major Connelly was a good looking woman in her forties, the medical officer brought in to consult should the need arise.

The problem was, if the scientists were to be believed, command and the area immediately around the tower had somehow become part of the "inside" at the moment the door into the tower disappeared.

They weren't on a floor exactly, but for all intents and purposes, they were just as isolated.

Lake believed that there had been no real contact with the outside world since that time. No one had left command, which really blew the general's mind. What of his trips to headquarters?

And no one had entered.

Which meant that Major Connelly wasn't Major Connelly.

According to Dr. Banister, that wasn't a problem. As long as this Major Connelly performed all the duties required of her, what did it matter?

General Wong would accept that for now.

He was still trying to wrap his head around the fact that no one ever left and that no one noticed that fact.

The Adversary wasn't just messing with their surroundings. He was screwing with their minds.

Episode Six / Chapter Two

Sgt. Costa led the way through the fog, traveling in what they hoped was the direction of the bridge that spanned the chasm. Asher followed well within sight of her, with the others trailing along behind, all within sight of the person in front of them.

Susan Bautista and Church walked side by side, speaking in hushed tones. The fog seemed to bring that out.

Officially, Susan was Dr. Church's assistant, but had really served as an associate to both Church and Banister for years. Her duties had often focused on keeping the rest of the world from getting in, whether it be through her direct intervention or simply serving as a conduit. She wasn't a social person by nature, but was able to hide herself when she was representing the doctors.

Unfortunately, her responsibilities along those lines had greatly diminished since entering the tower. Her attempts at helping them to organize and process their ideas and theories often only got in the way and she frequently found herself standing to one side and waiting for one or the other to turn to her in search of mediation.

Much of that changed after the thirteenth floor. Dr. Church was depending on her more now that Banister was on the other side of the radio. While there was no replacing Banister, she was accomplished in her own right and fully capable of working through ideas with Church. She could stand in for Dr. Banister between communication windows.

Finding out that Doctor Banister had made it to the command center had made those communication windows difficult. Church had been unable to understand his friend agreeing to stay behind without a putting up a fight, and without telling him. Certainly together they could have come up with something, some way of keeping the team together.

But Susan got it. There had been no options. Banister and Carmody would stay behind no matter what they did. And she knew that if Banister had told his friend, Church would have absolutely stayed behind in some vain attempt to get them all to the next floor. The mission would have been lost.

Banister had only told Peter so that they would know what happened after the fact. He hadn't wanted his friend left wondering.

Professor Asher had understood as well. He had been put into a terrible position, but he had kept Dr. Banister's secret. He had waited until they were well on their way before telling anyone.

Dr. Church had been very, very upset. Even hearing that Banister and Carmody had survived and were back at command, he hadn't forgiven Asher.

Susan wondered if this breach of trust could ever be overcome.

"Susan... do you see that?" asked Church. He was looking to their left.

Susan's mind had been elsewhere. "What?"

"There." He slowed his step. Susan slowed to match.

Asher, walking ahead of them, sensed something and looked back. "What's going on?"

"I see," said Susan.

There was something in the fog. Movement... something...

"People," mumbled Church. "There's someone there."

Shadows, shadows within shadows. People moving.

"Is that—" Susan started.

"It's Wes."

They watched as Dr. Banister stopped in front of the Quonset hut that served as the command center. He looked in their direction. He took a step toward them. He started to lift a hand.

And then the fog rolled in from both directions and the shadows washed away.

"Dr. Church?" asked Asher. "Susan?"

"Gone now," said Church. "Never mind."

Banister stood just outside the Quonset hut. Across the open lot stood the tower, rising up into a thick, off-white cloud deck that lay heavy over everything. The sound of muffled voices came and went from the bivouac that was set up around the other side of the tower. Other than that, the world was quiet.

Had he just seen what he thought he had seen?

The thin strands that had drawn out from the layer of cloud above now began to retreat; the strange fog winnowing its way across the asphalt began to fade, vanishing as a whisper into the mist.

The Quonset hut door opened and Carmody came out of the command center. She held the door open and Lake came out behind her. Banister had to step to one side to make way for them. He kept his attention on the peculiar cloud formations. A last fingerling strand was drawing back up into the cloud deck.

"Doctor Banister?" prompted Carmody. "Doctor Lake has been looking for you."

"Thank you, Private," Lake said patiently. "I can speak for myself."

"What is it, Lake?" asked Banister.

"Yes. Well I..." Lake looked sharply at Carmody, then looked across to the tower, clasped his hands behind his back. "I believe we had a meeting scheduled, Doctor Banister."

"Did we?" he asked absently.

"Yes. We did. We do."

"I don't suppose you saw any of that?" Banister said abruptly, pointing in the direction of the clouds bumping up against the tower.

"Excuse me?"

"No, I suppose not." He turned to look at Lake for the first time. "I'm sorry. We had a meeting, didn't we?"

"We were to review our data regarding our plane here and its relationship to the floors."

"Hmm, yes." Banister turned slowly back to the tower. "I may have some additional information to contribute."

Costa rested her hand on the top of the anchor post and turned about, waited for the others to gather up close. The rope bridge disappeared into the fog behind her some ten feet beyond the post.

"Nice work, Sara," said Asher. He slipped out of his backpack and set it at his feet, pulled his canteen from his belt.

"Yes, very good," said Church. He and Susan stepped around Asher. He studied the bridge, or what little was visible, stepped near the edge of the chasm and looked down.

"I doubt we could have missed it," grumbled Owen. "Not after what Peter said. How many times did you find this thing?"

"Four. Nonetheless," said Asher, nodding politely to Costa.

"Absolutely," said Church. "Thank you for successfully guiding us to our first milestone."

"Sure. Any time, Doctor Banister," said Costa. She looked over at Lieutenant Quinn, who was just finishing a few words with Ramos. "Lieutenant?"

"Lead the way, Sergeant," said Quinn. "When you reach the other side, you stay well within sight of the bridge."

"Yes, sir."

Quinn turned to the group. "The bridge certainly looks strong enough, but we're not taking any chances. I'll be sending you across half a minute apart. Take it slow, and when you get to the other side, stay together. Hold hands if you have to, but no wandering off."

With that, Costa moved out onto the bridge. She held onto the two rope handrails, put one foot in front of the other and started out over the chasm. She stopped two steps out and looked back over her shoulder. Professor Asher and the lieutenant were standing at the head of the bridge watching her. She could just make out the silhouettes of the others standing behind them.

She started forward across the bridge. Another two steps and there was nothing but the fog, the bridge disappearing behind and before her. She heard Dr. Owen's voice drifting toward her. She was griping about something, probably something to do with poor Ramos, but that faded as well... and then she was utterly alone.

Asher paced his steps slow and easy, sliding his hands along the rope hand rails to either side. The bridge faded into the fog several steps ahead. Sergeant Costa was up there somewhere.

Liz Owen was behind him. He knew that because he occasionally heard her.

"Peter!" she called out. "You still on the bridge?"

"Yes, Liz. I'm still on the bridge."

"Peter? Peter?"

Asher stopped and twisted about so that he could call out behind him. "Here, Liz. Still on the bridge."

He started forward then. There was only silence behind him. He had lost her again. She should only be thirty seconds behind him, assuming they were travelling the same pace, but there was something very strange about this floor... strange even for the tower.

It took him at least four minutes to cross the bridge, perhaps longer. He really wasn't very good at judging time. However long it took, he knew it was a really long time. It was a very wide chasm.

"Sara? Sergeant Costa?" Asher stepped off the bridge. He couldn't see anything beyond the two anchor posts. Shadow-filled fog drifted slowly past.

He let out a long, exhausted sigh and let his pack slide from his shoulder.

"Crap."

He was alone.

Johansen entered the command center a couple of minutes ahead of the next communication window. Lake and Banister were huddled together at one of the tables, heavy into some deep discussion, their hushed voices seldom carrying beyond the table.

Carmody was over near the radio, her back against the counter, arms folded as she watched the two doctors.

"What's that all about?" he asked her.

"As best I can tell, before they went all hush-hush on me, our bubble wall is touching the bubble walls of all the floors."

"Huh?"

"Yeah, that was my thought."

"Bubble wall?"

"Ya see," she sighed, "Each floor has a connection to the floor below it and the floor above it; though they're not really above and below."

"Yeah, I get that."

"Now... our own little acre has a simultaneous connection to every floor. A wall of our plane is actually touching every floor, all at the same time."

"Okay..." Johansen glanced up at the clock above the radio. "Okay... hey, about that time, eh?"

He settled himself in before the radio, put on the headset. Behind him, Lake and Banister slid their chairs back and stood up, wandered over to stand behind him.

Johansen flipped a switch, rested two fingers on a dial.

"Tower, this is command. Tower, this is command. Over."

Ramos was sitting on the ground a few yards from the end of the bridge, the radio set up beside him. He had the receiver to his ear.

"Yeah, hey there Johansen." He looked at the world around him. He was all alone. "We have a bit of a problem here. Over."

Episode Six / Chapter Three

Susan Bautista had been walking for hours. She kept a steady pace, stopping just three times to drink from her canteen and once to have a light meal from the dried berries and jerky she had in her pack. She had called out to the others at each of those stops, not expecting a reply and not getting one.

She had known midway across the bridge that she was alone, and so was not surprised to find no one waiting when she stepped off on the other side. She had waited there just long enough for anyone who might be coming across the bridge behind her to finish the crossing, just in case. When no one showed up, she had started off, marching directly away from the chasm.

They had been on this floor for several days. By now Cpl. Ramos had no doubt been in communication with command a second time. They were probably freaked, what with the team scattered across eight flavors of the floor with no obvious way to get back together. Command certainly wouldn't have an answer.

Susan was just as certain they would all be together again, sooner rather than later. Just as the bridge had been an unavoidable milestone, so too would be the threshold connecting these different realities of this floor together. It would be a simple matter of recognizing it when she saw it.

She came upon the apple tree only moments after seeing its large shadow shifting into and out of focus in the fog.

This has to be it...

The tree was big, the lower branches barely within her reach, the higher branches lost in the fog. She set her pack down against the trunk and pulled down an apple. Sitting next to her pack, her back against the tree, she munched on the fruit and waited.

Asher stood under the orange tree. It grew right out of the smooth hard surface of the floor. And it was big, the biggest orange tree he had ever seen. He could barely reach the fruit hanging from the lowest branches.

Sitting with his back against the trunk, he peeled an orange as he thought about what to do next. There was no day and night on this floor, no light and dark. There was only gray, but by the reckoning of the team time they went by, it was late evening. His own internal clock told him the same thing.

He decided he'd have a good night's sleep and then start out again in the morning. He assumed the others would be stopping for the night as well, wherever they might be; he'd hang around until mid-morning before heading out to give anyone who might be out there on this variation of the floor time to show up.

Not that he expected anyone would be making an appearance. He was pretty sure it was just him and this tree, but he would stick around long enough to be certain.

Sleep was a long time coming, despite how tired he was. He couldn't get comfortable and his mind refused to quiet down. The strange fog drifted slowly past, fingering its way through the branches overhead, gray and shadowed.

Morning came and he started awake, somewhat surprised that he had finally drifted off. He ate a little from his rations, peeled and ate another orange, and washed his breakfast down with a few swallows of his water.

He collected as many oranges as he could carry in his pack and stuffed another couple into his shirt to eat as he walked. Finally, gathering branches and leaves and orange peel, he created an arrow on the ground indicating the direction he would be heading. You never knew...

He walked for several hours. He was about to stop for lunch when he noticed a dark swath of shadow running left to right across his path. Another four steps and he came up to a wooden rail fence. It disappeared into the fog a few yards to his left and to his right, posts every eight feet, horizontal split wood rails set at one foot and at three feet above the ground.

Another boundary, thought Asher.

Should he climb over the fence and continue on, or follow the fence and stay inside the boundary?

Lunch... he decided. He sat with his back against the nearest post; another orange, a half ration, and half of his remaining water. A sure sign that he had to get wherever it was he needed getting to.

General Wong handed the radio headset to Captain Adamson and went over to the table. The captain would give any final instructions to the corporal in what few seconds remained in this communication window, the third window since their arrival on this floor.

Banister and Lake were already hashing over the most recent news. There was some disagreement as to the underlying meaning of the walnut tree that Cpl. Ramos had come upon.

The general hadn't gotten any underlying meaning from it, but from what Ramos had reported, several things were immediately evident. First of all, this didn't look to be a threshold or portal. This was no junction point of the multiple realities of this floor. It was a walnut tree.

And second, being that it was a walnut tree, and as it was currently bearing lots and lots of walnuts, it was a much-needed food source.

"Gentlemen, please," said General Wong.

Banister and Lake turned their heads in unison.

"Yes?" asked Banister.

"You're arguing over the meaning of the walnut tree?"

"Absolutely," said Dr. Lake. "Properly interpreting the meaning of the tree on this floor will add to what we already understand of the Adversary and could help us in safely guiding the team across later floors."

"Yes, of course, but—"

"It is the reason I am here."

"Yes, I understand. But for the moment the team would be better served by our focusing on next steps."

"At the moment we have no recommendation beyond what we have already suggested," said Banister.

"Exactly so," stated Lake.

The general looked up at Captain Adamson's approach. "Captain."

"I didn't mean to interrupt."

"Please," hint of pleading. "Interrupt."

"Corporal Ramos will be getting a few hours rest. He'll then harvest as many walnuts as he can carry and continue on."

"Very good, Captain." General Wong leaned forward and set his elbows onto the table. He rubbed his face with his palms. "I wish we knew how the others were doing."

"I am fairly confident they are no worse off than the corporal," said Banister. "With or without walnuts."

Sgt. Miller came around the corner of the tower from the mess hall on his way to the command center. The sky was a dull, flat gray, the air damp enough that he frequently had to wipe the wet from his eyes. The clouds had been dark and threatening for days, and with each passing hour they seemed to push down lower and lower.

Reaching the command center, he turned back to look at the tower once more before going in. The lights that had once been set up near the now-absent door access had long since been removed, but a detail still patrolled the base of the tower. He saw the two-person team come around the far corner, little more than dark silhouettes in the thick mist.

Miller was about to turn back and open the door when he noticed something odd happening to the low cloud layer near the tower. The clouds were beginning to bulge and swirl, and thick streamers of fog began reaching down toward the ground.

This is what Doctor Banister saw...

Sgt. Miller stepped away from the Quonset hut, took several steps toward the tower. He noted that the two soldiers on patrol had stopped and were also watching what was happening.

Good... witnesses.

The fog strands reached the ground, drifted out and coalesced with one another, puffing and expanding and contracting. A large, dark shadow began to form within this cloud bank. The shadow eventually took on the shape of a tree.

The door opened behind Miller. Johansen came out of the Quonset hut.

"Hey, Sarge. I was just— whoa, what the hell is that?"

"What does it look like? It's a tree."

"Hey... is that—"

"I think so."

The shadow drifted into and out of focus, but they could see a figure sitting on the ground beneath the tree. It looked like Ramos. He was trying his damnedest to smash a walnut with the butt of his canteen.

Asher followed the fence all through the morning and well into the afternoon, when it abruptly ended in the side of a dune rising up from the floor, the slope of sand disappearing into the drifting fog overhead.

He decided to climb the dune. It was hard work, as the sand was soft and his feet went deep with each step. His weight pushed the sand downslope and with each step up gravity pulled him down a half step.

Still, he did make progress. The fog grew thicker and less gray. He had the sensation of climbing into a cloud. Continuing on for several more minutes, he finally had to stop to take a break. Catching his breath, he considered giving up and heading back down, maybe try to walk the base of the dune, see where that took him.

He finally decided to give it another couple of minutes, to see if he could get to the top of this thing. He had some faint hope that it might get him above the fog and shadows.

A few more steps then and all of a sudden there was no more *up*. He was at the top. There was no panoramic view. Looking straight out, there was only the fog. It was whiter and brighter than down below, but there were still the dark shadows swirling within the mist, drifting along in a breeze that Asher couldn't feel.

He was about to start down the other side when a voice came from out of the fog.

"Professor Asher, it is so good to see you."

A shadow formed in the fog to his left along the ridgeline. It drew nearer, and as it did it took on the shape of a man.

Asher was certain it was the Adversary's acolyte, though it was difficult to tell by looking at him. His guise was always different; this time he had long, flowing gray hair and beard, wore a loose robe with numerous folds, and he carried a tall staff.

But with each appearance there was always something familiar about the Acolyte's face, particularly the eyes. It was the same, no matter the persona.

"It's been a long time," said Asher. They hadn't come across the Acolyte for several floors. "Love the new look."

"Thank you. I put a lot into it."

"And it shows." The niceties were out of the way. "So... I don't imagine the visit is a social call."

"My dear friend," said the Acolyte, taking a step nearer Asher. "I come bearing... *opportunity*."

"Is that so?"

"Yes, Professor." The Acolyte rested his free hand on his chest. "It pleases me very much to bring this gift to you."

"I am intrigued." And he was. He was also very wary. Interactions with the Acolyte seldom ended well. "What might this gift be? This *opportunity*?"

The Acolyte lifted his hand, two fingers raised. Behind him the fog brushed aside, forming a tunnel seven feet high and three feet wide. Sunlight shone through the tunnel. Asher could see people beyond the tunnel, walking about, going about their activities, unaware of the portal. Some wore military uniforms, some were dressed in civilian clothes.

"The opportunity to go home, my friend," said the Acolyte.

"Home," mumbled Asher. "So I see."

"A few steps, and there you are. What do you say?"

Oh, to be home again... three meals a day, regular showers, clean clothes and a bed.

"If I say no?"

"It is your choice, Professor Asher. Stay or leave. But why would you not avail yourself of the chance to go home?"

"I'm not quite finished here, Acolyte. We have a few floors yet to go."

"Many. Many floors, and then many more." The Acolyte leaned forward onto his staff. "I tell you true, Professor. Not all will make it to the Great Hall."

"And so you give me this chance to get out alive?"

The Acolyte answered only with a smile, a slight shrug.

"Why?" asked Asher.

"Because I like you." Another bright grin.

"Uh, huh." Asher frowned. "Banister and Private Carmody. You didn't give them a choice. You made them leave."

"Different circumstances, different times."

"Uh, huh. Well, thanks all the same. I think I'll hang around a bit longer."

"This is a onetime offer, as they say. That is what they say, is it not?"

"That's what they say." Asher looked away from the Acolyte, turned away and looked downslope. He could see nothing. "Are we done here?"

The tunnel behind the Acolyte vanished.

"Yes, Professor Asher." The Acolyte sounded disappointed. "We are done here."

Working his way down the other side of the dune was a clumsy and awkward affair, and more than once Asher had to lean back and fall on his butt to stop from falling forward and tumbling down the slope.

The fog slowly dissipated as he descended, and by the time he reached the bottom it was clear enough that he was able see across the depression that he had come down into.

Dozens of trees stood in a handful of clusters a hundred yards ahead. He realized as he approached that it was an oasis. The clusters of trees surrounded a pool of water some forty feet across. Another dune rose up beyond the oasis, the ridge disappearing into a cloud.

There were a number of shrubs scattered about, and as he entered the perimeter of the oasis he found the sand beneath his feet had turned to soil. He stepped up to the edge of the pool and knelt down at the bank. Cupping water in his hand, Asher took a sip.

It tasted good, much better than what remained in his canteen.

He stood again, looked across the pool to the opposite side. He saw what looked like a campsite. There was a fire pit, and beside this what looked from this distance to be palm leaf fronds laid out to form a bed. There were piles of neatly stacked kindling... and a backpack.

Just beyond the campsite, near the base of the far dune, were large shrubs clustered near a couple of date trees.

Lieutenant Quinn came around from behind the bushes carrying an armful of twigs and branches.

Episode Six / Chapter Four

Quinn had been at the oasis for four days, this after traveling three days to get there. Asher was certain that he hadn't been walking for seven days; this had him wondering about time flow differences within the different variations of the floor. He hoped these differences weren't too extreme; who knew how that would affect the rest of the team arriving at the oasis?

The lieutenant had been busy. He had decided to operate under the assumption that the portal was there at the oasis, and hoped that it would also be the location of the threshold that would bring his team back together.

While waiting for the others, he had conducted an initial survey of the area, and then followed that with a more extensive one. He also had time to establish a campsite, gather what kindling and firewood there was to be had, collected fruit and nuts from the trees and bushes.

He couldn't lose the nagging feeling that if he went too far from the oasis that when turning back it would be gone. He didn't really think so, as the oasis was clear of fog, but the concern was there nonetheless. So on the second day he defined a perimeter of the oasis. For the most part this followed the border where soil transitioned to sand. There was an outlying tree all by itself at one point, and there was the base of the far dune. He planted fallen palm fronds stem down in the ground along one empty stretch, forming a fence line of sorts, and another single frond midway between a garden of stones and a large berry bush.

He also decided that while walking this perimeter he would never turn his back completely to the oasis. He would always remain in direct line of sight with some object well within the perimeter.

Hearing this, Asher said they were probably safe so long as they stayed out of the fog, which was well beyond the perimeter, but agreed that it was best not to take any chances.

"I'll not be making that mistake again," said Quinn. "We'll not get separated again."

"I don't think you really had a choice in the matter," said Asher. "What happened is exactly what was meant to happen."

"The Adversary's game plan for this floor?"

"That and what happened up on the ridge."

"So you saw him too; the Acolyte." Quinn nodded. "I suspected as much; had to be a test of some kind, to see if we'd abandon one another."

Though the whole affair concerning Banister and Carmody had long been settled between Quinn and Asher, the comment nonetheless brought it all back. Asher had taken a lot of heat from Quinn as well as from Dr. Church, and it had also affected his relationship with most of the others. It said something about Asher that he had known what the fallout would be and had accepted it.

Given the perspective of time and several floors distance, Quinn had eventually been able to understand what Banister had done. To have told everyone that he and Private Carmody were going to have to stay behind would have risked everything. Church and Dr. Bautista at the very least would not have gone on without him. And what would Lieutenant Quinn have done? Certainly he would have tried up to the last possible moment to find an alternative, but then what? Would he have forced the others onto the train and then left Church and Carmody to their fate? How could he do such a thing? And if not, then what? They couldn't all stay behind. Could they?

Quinn would have done whatever it took to keep to the mission. That had priority over everything and everyone.

Dr. Banister had no doubt reasoned all this out. And wanting the others to know what happened, but only after the fact, he had chosen Professor Asher to bear the burden.

It had taken a while, but Quinn finally got that as well. Poor Asher had been the obvious choice.

"He was probably looking to assess our spirit, our resolve," said Asher. "We've been through a lot these seventeen floors, Lieutenant. Looking ahead, we still have a very long way to go."

"That's no exaggeration." Quinn studied the young professor a moment. "Did you consider it? Going home?"

"No. A tantalizing offer to be sure, but no. I did not."

The lieutenant smiled. "I thank you kindly for sticking around."

"My pleasure, sir." Asher munched on a date. At least, he thought it was a date. He had never seen one before, much less eaten one. "What about you? Did you think about leaving?"

Quinn tapped the lieutenant's bar on his collar. "Nope."

"Right."

"How many do you think are going to take him up on it?" Quinn assumed everyone would have to face the Acolyte's test.

Asher was looking past Quinn, at something behind the lieutenant. "I believe one less than you're probably thinking," he said, standing.

Quinn stood and turned, couldn't help but grin and shake his head.

Reaching the two men, Elizabeth Owen stopped and put her hands on her hips. She breathed out a heavy, tired groan. "You won't believe the crap I had to go through to get here. Why the hell didn't I walk around that damned dune? Are those dates any good?"

The three of them were sitting around a small campfire. The clear day had turned to dusk and dusk was slowly turning to night. This was something they hadn't seen since coming onto the floor, and it had them feeling positive about the oasis. The oasis was key to getting them to the next floor.

Quinn was pulling apart dry branches that he'd brought in from a cluster of berry bushes and was stacking them into piles according to size.

"I've found nothing so far," he said. "And yet everything tells me the portal is here."

Owen shook her head. "Not necessarily. To be sure, everything tells us this location is important; it's the threshold that will bring us back together, after all. That doesn't mean the portal is here."

"If not the portal, a sign as to where we go next," said Asher.

"No portal, no path," said Quinn. "Not yet."

"Still, I do love what you've done with the place," said Owen. "And the change in diet is a nice touch."

"Your own contribution is most welcome, Doctor Owen."

"Yes, love the plums," agreed Asher. He had brought a supply of oranges, Quinn had brought apricots, and Owen had brought plums. With this and what had been found at the oasis, they were a lot better off than they had been. Their existing meager supplies would only have lasted a few more days, even at half rations.

"Just doing my part," said Owen. "Considerate of the Adversary to provide us with such variety."

"Most curious," said Asher. "Each variation of the floor with its own variety of tree."

"Be great if one of the others comes in with the fruit of the 'steak and eggs' tree."

"I'll take whatever we get," said Quinn.

And with that the conversation shifted again to their individual journeys in getting to the oasis. At one point along the way Owen was certain she had seen the command center in the fog, someone standing in front of the Quonset hut waving at her. Later, arriving at the tree, she had considered planting herself beneath its branches and waiting for others to show up. In the end, she had continued on.

"I spent the night there," said Asher. "What about the fence? What made you decide to follow it and not climb over?"

"A no-brainer. I didn't want to climb over a fence."

"And from such, worlds are changed," said Asher.

"And yet you climbed the dune," said Quinn.

"Yes, and I don't know why. It is so not like me."

"You were drawn to the top."

She frowned and shrugged one shoulder. "You're probably right, Lieutenant. The bridge, the tree, the fence, the dune, and here to the oasis. Gotta be more than chance."

"You turned down the Acolyte's offer," Quinn stated.

"Hell, not turning back now. I'm just gettin' started." Owen stood up with a groan that was half growl. "I'm tired. Where's my room?"

Lisa stood before the Acolyte, the tunnel leading home several paces behind him, its walls swirling and shadowy, the image of those beyond the portal sharp and clear.

"I'd like to be on my way, please," she said.

"Come now, Miss Powell. Where do you think you can do the most good? Tagging along with the others, struggling from floor to floor with barely enough to eat? Or back home, assisting those working hard each and every day to help the team survive? Be honest."

"If it's all the same to you, I think I'll continue to tag along with the others," said Lisa, trying her best to sound sure and decisive. She wasn't completely successful, but she believed she was making her point. "The choice is mine to make, is it not?"

"As I said. I leave it to you."

"Then I choose to stay."

The Acolyte bowed his head and slowly dissolved into the mist. Fog drifted into the tunnel, shadows formed and faded. After a few moments the shadows took on a new shape. It looked at first to Lisa like someone walking. He stopped, looked in her direction. He started to raise a hand, and the image dissolved. It formed into a new image...

Quinn and Ramos were at the radio, the lieutenant talking with command. Nearby, Costa was working her way up a tree, Owen standing below. Beyond, Susan and Church walked along the oasis perimeter.

Asher, kneeling at the bank of the pond as he filled canteens, stood when he saw Lisa approach.

"Miss Powell, it's great to see you."

"Thank you, Professor," said Lisa. "It's not here."

"Excuse me?"

"It's not here. The portal. It's not here." She half turned and pointed back the way she had come. "It's up there."

Asher immediately took her meaning. "Come on. You need to speak with the Lieutenant.

General Wong absently handed the headset back to Johansen.

"I believe they're on their way," he said. "They're at an oasis of some kind, but they're on their way to the next floor."

"That's great news," said Captain Adamson.

"Wonderful, just wonderful," said Banister.

"Yes," said the general. "Miss Powell found it. Apparently it's a grape vineyard."

"A vineyard?" asked Lake. "But how could they know that?"

"A well-manicured vineyard. I believe she could see it."

The team stood at the edge of an expansive vineyard, row after row of vines, heavy with ripening grapes. The vineyard was set on a sunny, gently sloping hillside.

"This... this I can handle," said Owen.

~ end of episode six

Episode Seven
The Tunnels of Hades

Prolog

Sgt. Costa led the way into the narrow tunnel, moving out ahead far enough to make room for the others of the team to come through the portal behind her.

The rough rock walls were the color of rust; the floor was worn smooth from millennia of dragging footfalls. The low ceiling hung oppressively above them.

There was a bend in the tunnel about twenty feet ahead. From around the bend came an orange-red glow that shimmered along the reddish walls.

Church stepped around Costa. "What do you suppose?"

Costa held out an arm and barred his way. "Let me, Doctor." She glanced back at Lt. Quinn, who gave her a silent go-ahead.

Costa moved cautiously forward, her right hand resting on the hilt of the knife sheathed on her belt. Church gave her a few steps before starting forward again. Quinn had to reach out and gently take hold of his arm.

"Give her a sec, Doctor."

Sgt. Costa stopped just before the bend, took another half step and stopped again. She was silhouetted in the orange-red glow. The light shimmered, creating shadows across her face.

"Oh, boy," she mumbled.

"What is it, Sergeant?" asked Quinn.

"I'm not sure, Lieutenant." She hesitated. "I think it's the Ferryman."

"You mean—"

"Shall we?" Church pulled away from Quinn, followed after Costa as the sergeant disappeared around the bend.

The tunnel opened into a great cavern, the ceiling so high above them there were hints of wispy cloud in the air. The walls stretched out for a thousand feet in both directions before gradually curving around and reaching to the distant far side of the cavern.

The world glowed a dark, shadowy orange-red, the light reflecting from the dark rocky dome of the cavern; the light emanated from a wide river that flowed across the heart of the great chamber. The water was black and red and orange and rust.

It moved slowly, gently, winnowing its way across the cavern, passing directly in front of them.

A small dock jutted from the bank directly ahead. Tied to the dock was a wooden longboat. Glowing lanterns hung from its high stern and bow. Near the stern stood a tall, dark figure dressed in black cloak, his face hidden in shadow beneath the hood. Several small cloth sacks hung from a thin rope tied around his waist.

He said nothing. He waited.

"Crap and double crap," grumbled Owen. "We're in Hell."

Episode Seven / Chapter One

"If that's the Ferryman—" Quinn wondered aloud.

"Of course it's the Ferryman," said Owen.

"Then that would be the River Styx."

"Of course it's the River Styx."

Somehow, Owen's grousing always put their troubles into a bizarrely twisted perspective. It was how she dealt with the world, and Quinn had begun going along for the ride.

"Styx?" asked Ramos.

"From Greek myth," Quinn said quickly, before Owen had a chance to jump on the corporal. "One of a number of rivers of the Underworld. The Ferryman takes the souls of the dead across to the other side."

"To Hell," Owen said sharply.

"More precisely, to the realm of the dead," said Church. "For many, the Underworld is where life originated and where all must return."

"And for many, it's Hell," Owen stated. "Which do you think they're going for here?"

Church sighed. "Yes. There is that."

"What do you suggest we do, Doctor?" asked Quinn.

"The intent is clear. The Adversary would have us cross."

"Yeah... you all let me know how that works out for you," said Owen.

"Oh come, Liz. You would abandon us now?" asked Church. "Is your curiosity not piqued?"

On the boat, the Ferryman lifted a hand, held it out palm up.

"I am curious about one thing, Nate. How do you suggest we pay the man? Anyone here carrying any half-pennies? Drachmas? Anything? How 'bout quarters?"

"Oh my," sighed Church.

"Ya' gotta pay the Ferryman. Them's the rules."

"And if we don't?" asked Ramos.

"If you can't pay, you wander the banks of the River Styx as a wraith for eternity."

Asher took a step calmly forward, looked up and down the river. The bank sloped gently to the water's edge, the soil dark and barren. There were no signs of wraiths, wandering or otherwise.

Asher was tired. The last few floors had beaten him down, mind, spirit and body. He was tempted to drop to the ground, to sit and just wait for the whole wraithing thing to happen.

But of course he couldn't. He would push on. He would always push on.

This was the twenty-first floor. Oh man, they had a long way to go.

He walked to the river's edge and up onto the wooden dock. The floating pier shifted slightly as he approached and stepped down into the boat.

The Ferryman continued to hold out his hand, palm up. The long, bony fingers were pale and leathery.

"Sorry friend," said Asher. "I must have left my wallet in my other pants."

The Ferryman stretched his hand out another few inches. Asher could just see the darkly shadowed face beneath the hood. The cream-colored skin was stretched taut across bone and streaked with thin dark lines. The eyes were hidden in black sockets.

Asher stepped back and sat on a wooden plank bench. He could feel a trembling in his chest, tried mightily not to let it show. He had thought he didn't care anymore, and was surprised to realize that he did. A helluva time to find that out.

"Actually, I believe our host has already made arrangements," he said. He stared down at the bottom of the boat, guardedly lifted his gaze up toward the Ferryman.

As he watched, two silver-colored coins materialized in the palm of the outstretched hand. The Ferryman curled his fingers closed. He brought his hand back and dropped the coins into one of the sacks hanging from his belt.

Asher let out a long shuddered breath. After taking in and letting out another, he looked over at the rest of the team. They were still standing on the bank, but had gathered nearer the dock.

"We're good to go," he managed to say, and with that Lieutenant Quinn started ahead, the others falling in behind him. The Ferryman collected two coins for each passenger as each stepped into the boat and settled onto the benches.

"This is so not a good idea," said Owen, finding her spot.

Sgt. Costa released the lines and was the last to climb into the boat. "What other choice do we have, Doctor Owen? This is the path we've been given, our passage paid for. The portal to the next floor must be on the other side."

"Oh, we have most-assuredly paid for our own passage, Sergeant," Owen stated ominously. "On credit. There will come a reckoning."

The crossing itself was uneventful, for the most part. The Ferryman never spoke, seldom looked at his passengers. He guided the boat as it wound its way through currents and eddies and worked its way toward the far shore. Twice something in the water bumped into the wooden hull, but it never showed itself.

After about twenty minutes, Lt. Quinn stood and studied the approaching cliff wall of the distant shore. A few minutes more and he could make out a small pier jutting out into the river from an inlet set into the base of the cliffs. This looked to be the only location anywhere along the shore that was accessible, with the sloping riverbank at that point some forty feet wide and twenty feet deep. To either side of this little beach the towering cliffs rose directly up from river and reached nearly to the ceiling of the great cavern in tall, thin spires.

There was movement part way up the cliff, a shifting of shadows among the shadows.

"What is that?" asked Quinn.

"Some kind of creature," said Lisa. She was standing beside Quinn now, as were several others.

"Cerberus," said Asher. He had remained seated, and spoke without looking to the shore.

"I believe you're right, Peter," said Church. He could make out the creature more clearly now. Jet black, three large heads and a single thick, writhing mane.

"What do we do now?" asked Ramos.

"Not to worry, Corporal," said Church. "Cerberus is there to keep folks from leaving, not entering."

"That's gotta make you wonder now, doesn't it?" Owen said with a sly snicker.

The longboat glided the rest of the way to the pier, bumped up beside it and came to an easy stop. Sgt. Costa climbed out and fastened the lines.

"What now?" she wondered aloud, not really asking anyone in particular. She glanced up the cliff, but couldn't see Cerberus. His shadow had blended fully into the other shadows.

She looked back then at the others, all of whom were standing now and making ready to disembark. Behind them in the stern, the Ferryman raised a hand and pointed.

There was a tunnel opening directly ahead at the base of the cliff. Appearing at first as a smear of black set into the rock wall, rust-colored light began to bleed out from within and out onto the sandy ground outside.

The group gathered near the mouth of the tunnel, some glancing anxiously about, several nervously adjusting their small backpacks.

Costa looked determinedly into the tunnel. It led straight into the hillside for twenty paces before fading into darkness. The light came from a pair of torches mounted on the wall midway along the tunnel.

Quinn stepped up beside her. "Slow and cautious, Sergeant," he said.

Owen moved up beside them both. "Might I suggest running headlong into the mouth of the beast and we'll see what happens?"

Costa shifted the shoulder strap of her backpack. "I think I'll follow the lieutenant's orders, Ma'am."

"Of course you will, dear," Owen said smoothly.

The tunnels wound and twisted, forked and forked again, descended and then ascended again. The rough-hewn reddish rock walls and ceiling forever pushed in on them from either side and from above, the smooth-worn floor a constant reminder that the route they travelled had been trod a million times before over thousands of years.

Each time it grew almost too dark to see, there would come a flickering of light from beyond the next bend, and beyond the next bend they would find torches mounted on the walls. These they would take and use to guide their way so long as the flames lasted.

After uncounted hours in the claustrophobic tunnels, the cavern they stepped into felt large. It was perhaps a hundred feet across, the dome-like ceiling forty feet above them reflecting back the glow of the lava that bubbled in a dozen pools that pockmarked the floor.

"Someone's been watching way too much Doug McClure," said Owen.

"I'm glad of the opportunity to stretch my arms," said Lieutenant Quinn. He stepped out ahead of the others, studied the chamber more closely. "A dead end?" he asked.

"There's a way out over there." Lisa pointed directly across the way.

"Don't look now, boys and girls, but we are not alone," said Owen. She indicated the walls around them.

"I don't see anything," said Lisa.

"Them ain't shadows, girl." The walls were covered in black splotches, each one to two feet across. They seemed to writhe, shrink and expand.

"We haven't seen our friends in a while," said Church. They had been crossing paths with the Acolyte's minions going all the way back to the first floor.

"The Acolyte," Asher said calmly. He was looking at another tunnel access far to their left. A tall, thin figure stood unmoving, hands clasped before him.

Even at this distance, Owen thought she could see a thin smile cross the Acolyte's face. The expression sent creepy-crawlies up her spine. She looked quickly back to the walls.

"Oh, this can't be good," she grumbled.

As they watched, the inky black masses began to take shape; swelling and writhing, taking on form and dimension. Thin, spindly legs sprouted, each ending in a set of sharp claws. The creatures' heads were rat-like, with long snouts, ears set far back on the skull. As the creatures continued to evolve, their fur turned from pitch black to gray and then to dark brown.

Their tails were monkey's tails; tails that rolled and unrolled, curled and twisted.

The creatures all turned their heads at the same time; big, bulging black eyes, all looking to the group of humans standing just inside the chamber.

"Holy crap," whispered Owen.

"Yes ma'am," said Ramos. "We finally agree on something."

"Shall we take our leave?" asked Church.

"Yes we shall, Doctor," said Quinn. He reached back and brought out the crude knife he kept in a sheath pocket on his pack. "Everyone... back away easy, no sudden moves."

The soft, hushing sound of shoes sliding across the floor. At that very instant, the sound of sharp claws scratching across rock; a shudder of movement as every creature moved just a fraction.

And they waited.

"Oh, boy," Owen sighed. "This is so not going to end well."

"New plan," said Quinn. "On the count of one, we run like hell."

"Yes, sir," said Costa. "I like that plan."

Again, the sound of sharp claws on rock, all in a rush, and another shudder of movement. The creatures had all inched another fraction closer. All those black, empty eyes watched.

"Everybody ready," said Quinn. "And... one."

Quinn made sure the others made it back into the tunnel ahead of him before leaving the cavern himself. Backing out and then turning and running, he heard the creatures' scrabbling and scratching as they rushed toward the tunnel.

As they drew nearer, Quinn could sense them closing in on him as he hurried through the tunnel. He could feel their presence. As he ran, the others ahead of him, he knew the creatures were right behind him. He heard the whispering rush of claws and fur getting nearer and nearer.

And something more...

That faint whispering was reaching into his mind; ethereal tendrils just touching his thoughts, brushing across random images, past and present and some not his at all.

The walls to either side were suddenly alive with the creatures. They leapt at the running humans, grabbed at them, grasping and clawing and biting. Everyone kept running, pulling and swiping at the little monsters. Those with knives in hand, however primitive, stabbed at them.

Quinn pulled one off and swung it hard against the wall. He quickly reached out and grabbed at another that was holding onto Owen's backpack with its hind legs as it repeatedly scratched and clawed at her arm and shoulder. Pulling it away by the head, he stabbed at its throat.

Sgt. Costa had worked her way to the front of the group, slashing at creatures attacking her comrades as she passed, fighting off those that dared to attack her directly.

There was an opening up ahead on the right. Costa recalled that it led to a small cave, large enough to accommodate everyone, at the same time defendable. She stopped before the opening and directed the others in as she fought to keep the creatures out.

She and Lt. Quinn were the last into the cave, fighting the creatures off with knives and fists until the attackers finally gave up and retreated back down the tunnel.

Episode Seven / Chapter Two

Quinn gave Asher a pat on the shoulder and left him to stand watch at the opening to the tunnel. Looking about the small chamber, he had to fight back a grimace.

Everyone had visible injuries. Most were minor, some not so minor. Lisa Powell was tending to Dr. Owen, who had suffered a number of deep claw scratches and bite wounds. Susan was looking after Sgt. Costa, with Church hovering over them both. The sergeant had taken the brunt of the attack during her defense of the rest of the team. She would be all right, but could be counted among the walking wounded.

They had used the majority of their first aid supplies many floors ago and now relied primarily on water from their canteens and strips of cloth torn from the most ragged of their clothes. Alcohol had come in handy when they had it some floors back, but that was long gone. They did make use of needle and sewing thread they had acquired somewhere along the way.

Quinn stepped past a grumbling Dr. Owen and knelt down beside Cpl. Ramos, who was fussing with the radio.

"Corporal?" he asked.

"Nothing serious, sir." One of the creatures had gone after the radio during their run through the tunnel. The radio's canvas jacket hadn't fared too well, and one of the knobs was missing, but other than that it had survived the ordeal better than had some of the team members.

"Good to hear," said Quinn. "How about yourself?"

"I'm fine, sir. He was after the radio more than me."

"Smart little buggers." Quinn rose to his feet. His bandaged right hand throbbed where he had taken several deep claw wounds. He also had scratches to his back, which would need cleaning when he had time. He turned and spoke to the group.

"It looks like we're about as safe here as we can hope for, so we'll stay put for a bit and catch our breath."

"What then, Lieutenant?" asked Asher. He glanced over at Quinn before turning his attention back to the tunnel. "Sooner or later, we're back out there."

"I'm all for staying right here for just as long as we can," said Lisa. She was busily cleaning a bite wound on Owen's arm.

"We don't have the supplies to stay here," said Owen. "Nor the restroom facilities."

"Yes, well, Doctor Owen's facility concerns aside, Professor Asher is right," said Quinn. "The portal to the next floor is somewhere out there. So out there is where we have to go."

"After we catch our breath," Lisa stated firmly.

"Yes, Ma'am," agreed Quinn. He looked back to Ramos. "How long to the comm window, Corporal?"

"About forty minutes, Sir."

"Comm window? Really?" asked Owen. "What the hell can they do? And I do mean that literally."

Susan and Church sat with their backs against the rear wall of the cave, Susan wiping her hands clean with a damp cloth. Church watched Sgt. Costa move across the cave toward the opening leading out to the tunnel, to where Asher stood watch.

"A nice job dressing the sergeant's wounds, Susan."

Susan only shrugged. They had all become quite skilled at dressing one another's wounds.

"She is quite the competent young woman," Church said casually.

Susan glanced over at Costa, who was now relieving Asher. "We wouldn't have survived this long without her."

"I suppose not," he sighed noncommittally. "But then, we each have our part to play."

"Don't give me that," Susan chided. "The way you and Doctor Banister go on and on about her..."

"Hmm... I suppose so."

Asher stepped around those sitting about the cave and worked his way over to the wall on their left. He sat, leaned his back against the wall and closed his eyes, arms resting on his raised knees.

"I grow increasingly concerned about our young Professor Asher," said Church, watching Asher. "He is... darker... of late. These past floors in particular have taken their toll."

"Peter takes this place more personally than the rest of us."

"More so even than the lieutenant?"

"For Lt. Quinn it is a matter of duty. It is much the same with all of us, one way or another. We all have something. Responsibilities. For Peter, there is only the immediacy of the floor we are on, and the mind games."

"I do regret that I was quite harsh with the man regarding his role in Wes and Private Carmody being left behind."

"The Adversary and his Acolyte created those circumstances, Doctor. And just who was the real target of that exercise?"

Church looked in Asher's direction and considered. Susan may well be right. How many the times over these twenty one floors had their situation drawn particular focus to the young professor?

"The Adversary may have plans for our Professor Asher," said Church. "At the very least, the gauntlet set before him may not be the same as that which the rest of us walk."

Carmody and Johansen sat down opposite Sgt. Miller. The mess hall was almost empty, the dinner rush was past and most were now going about their evening duties.

"How'd the comm go?" asked Miller. He pushed his plate aside and took a drink from his water glass.

"Weird," said Johansen.

"Really weird," agreed Carmody. "They're in Hell."

"What's so weird about that? Sounds par for the course."

"No. Really," said Carmody. "They're really in Hell. Hell. River Styx, Ferryman, tunnels and devil's minions and everything."

"Wow. Weird."

"Yeah."

"Are they all right?"

"They got into it with a bunch of vicious little monsters or demons or something, but they came through it," said Johansen.

They watched Banister and Lake enter the mess. Banister sat at a corner table as Lake went to the coffee counter and returned with two coffees. They both looked exhausted.

"Doctor Banister didn't take the news too well," said Carmody.

"He never does," said Miller. "Processing data and dispensing advice from the outside is pretty weak duty after being inside."

"It could save their lives one day," Carmody said defensively.

"I'm sure it will," said Miller. "Did it save anyone today?"

"That's cold, Miller," said Johansen.

Miller frowned and rubbed at his temple. "Yeah... this place is starting to get to me. I could use a vacation."

"Hey, check it out." Carmody nodded in the direction of Major Connelly, just coming into the mess. Seeing Banister and Lake, she went over to their table and sat down.

"I'm seeing 'em hang out a lot together lately," said Miller.

"That lady gives me the willies," said Carmody.

"That's no lady," said Johansen.

"That is Major Connelly," said Miller. "So long as General Wong says that's who she is, then that's who she is."

"Yeah, I get that," said Johansen. "That's about how the Docs see it, too."

192 David R. Beshears

"You need to make clear what you mean when you say we're going to stay a while, Lieutenant." Owen stuffed the last of her meager belongings into her small backpack.

"I do apologize, Doctor Owen," said Lt. Quinn. He stood at the opening leading out to the tunnel, his arms folded across his chest. He was dividing his attention equally between the team preparing to leave and the tunnel beyond the small chamber.

Susan slipped an arm into one of the shoulder straps of her pack and walked over to Asher. He was on one knee, putting the last of his gear into his own pack.

"Are you ready for this?" she asked. She tried her best to make the question sound conversational, but it came across as anxious.

"Ready as I can be, I expect." Asher closed his pack and stood up. Seeing real concern in Susan's eyes, he nodded in Owen's direction. "Liz has a sixth sense for these things. If there was something bad on the way, she wouldn't be grumbling so dourly. The way she's going on, I figure we'll be on the next floor by bedtime."

Susan shook her head and slipped the rest of the way into her pack and started toward Lt. Quinn. "Geez, Peter, you are so full of it."

Peter managed a sad, fading grin and followed her.

The air in the tunnels grew warmer and drier with each passing hour. There seemed to be less oxygen and their breathing became more labored. Sgt. Costa continued to lead the way, Ramos and Lt. Quinn bringing up the rear. At each intersection, the team stopped and Quinn pulled out his notebook, expanded on a hand-drawn map that now spanned several dozen pages.

There was no sign of the minions that had attacked them earlier. Asher silently wondered whether even they dared not travel this deep into the Otherworld, but he kept that to himself. The thought had probably occurred to the others as well, but no sense getting Owen started again. She had been blessedly quiet for some time.

Susan walked beside Asher. They occasionally glanced at one another, occasionally spoke a clumsy word or two. Asher's increasing melancholy made their exchanges all the more awkward, and neither was very adept at such conversation to begin with.

Following one particularly graceless exchange of meaningless one and two word sentences, Owen groaned "jeezus people, get a room."

And thus concluded any further conversation for the foreseeable future.

Up at the front of the group, Sgt. Costa stopped. She wasn't at an intersection this time, but rather a few yards from a bend in the tunnel. She was listening at something.

"What is it, Sara?" asked Church.

"Not sure just yet, Doctor."

"Oh, god..." groaned Owen. "It's not—"

"No, Ma'am," Costa said softly. It wasn't the minions.

"I hear it," said Church.

"Me, too," said Susan. It was a distant, haunting whisper; a hollow moan of wind that brushed across the soul.

Overwhelming despair...

Costa looked back at Dr. Church, at Susan Bautista. At the back of the group stood Lt. Quinn; the expression on his face was grim, hard.

He gave a short, sharp nod. "Continue," he stated brusquely.

Costa steeled herself and started forward.

She led them into a small, round chamber, some twenty feet across. A pit twelve feet in diameter took up most of the floor, leaving only a narrow path running along the wall. They would have to traverse this path around the pit to get to where the tunnel continued on the other side.

Costa tried to keep herself as far from the open pit as she could; not easy, as there was less than four feet between the rough rock wall on her left and the lip of the pit on her right.

She glanced then into the pit for the first time. She had to reach out and grasp at the rock of the wall, or she would have fallen into the abyss.

Glowing a deep rust-orange, the pit grew darker and darker as it descended, yet never really seemed to end. It went on and on, deeper and deeper into the very bowels of the Underworld.

And clinging to the walls of the pit were dozens upon dozens of barely recognizable humans; naked, skeletal, their gnarled bony fingers grasping at the almost smooth stone, their faces twisted in torment and despair, all looking up, looking up toward the top of the pit.

Church stood beside Sgt. Costa. He sighed sadly as he looked down at the lost souls.

"They climb and they climb... but never make progress. The way out is always in sight, yet forever beyond their reach; for eternity."

"Doctor..."

"I know." Church lifted a hand and touched her arm. "Please, Sara. Take us out of here."

It took almost everything she had for Costa to look away from the horror in the pit. Finally though, she was able to turn her attention to the dark opening in the wall up ahead... the tunnel that would take them from this terrible place.

She kept the palm of her left hand on the wall beside her and started forward again. She took slow, steady steps, each taking her a few feet closer to the tunnel and the way out. The others followed, Church right behind her and the others trailing after him. Costa could hear them; their hesitant, shuddering breaths, their feet dragging across the rough stone...

The tunnel they entered was narrower than the one before the pit chamber, and the ceiling was much lower. It grew darker, much darker. There were no side tunnels; it wound and twisted without interruption.

Suddenly then the tunnel opened into yet another chamber. This one was lit only by a single torch hanging on the wall just to their left. It had come to life as Costa entered the chamber.

Visible in the faint light were twelve dark openings set in the walls about the cave.

Twelve tunnels to choose from.

"Oh dear," sighed Church. He took off his pack and tossed it against the wall behind them.

"Crap," grumbled Owen. "And you just know there's only one right way out of here."

"We can't do this," said Lisa. "We're almost out of water. We're almost out of food."

"Oh, we will do this, Miss Powell," said Lt. Quinn. "We will absolutely do this." He stepped further into the cavern, stopped, turned slowly about. The others watched, waited.

Twelve tunnels.

It could be any one of them. There was no way to tell.

They would just have to check them out one by one.

Quinn looked at Sgt. Costa. He pointed at the nearest tunnel.

"That one."

Episode Seven / Chapter Three

Sgt. Miller had taken to walking the base of the tower each morning after breakfast, following the same route as the watch. He didn't expect to find anything, but you never knew. Maintaining a consistent routine, he would notice if there were any changes from one day to the next.

The two guards of the watch were well ahead of him, walking at about the same pace. They rounded the corner to what was generally thought of as the front of the tower, the side that had once held the only opening into the building, and the side where the command center had been set up.

Miller rounded the corner several minutes later. The two guards were midway along the base of the building. Further ahead and off to the left, far across the empty lot, sat the small Quonset hut that served as the command center. The door had been propped open and several people were sitting at one of the two picnic tables that were set out in front. Though it was still early, the day was already warm.

It was going to get a lot warmer. It had been this way for days now, cool at night but growing warm soon after the sun came up, and then hot by midday. By late afternoon the air would be stifling and it would be difficult to breathe.

Miller crossed the asphalt lot and approached the tables. Dr. Banister invited him to sit down with a wave of his hand. Dr. Lake barely gave him a nod, but then Miller and Lake had never really hit it off; no reason really, and he supposed they got along well enough, but Miller doubted they would ever go out together for a beer.

From their expressions, it looked to Miller that another communications window had come and gone with no contact with the team in the tower. That was the fourth straight with no contact, more than six days with no word. Considering the nature of this floor, this had everyone more than a bit anxious.

General Wong came out of the command center, paused a moment, and then walked up beside the pair of tables. He stood gazing up at the black tower, clasped his hands behind his back.

"There will be another opportunity in thirty seven hours, gentlemen," he stated casually.

When neither of the doctors responded, Miller thought to jump in.

"Absolutely, General," he said. "I'm not too worried. They're a seriously tough bunch."

"Quite so, Sergeant," said Wong. "The silence is undoubtedly due to our Adversary once again playing games with us."

"No doubt," Banister said quietly. "No doubt."

"As with this weather," said the General. He lifted his gaze to the sky, breathed cautiously through his teeth. "It is already quite warm. Another very hot one on the way."

No coincidence, no way, thought Miller. And he knew that Banister and Lake didn't think so, either. Not for the first time, the conditions in the tower appeared to have had an effect on conditions out here. The last word before losing contact with the team had them descending ever further into the Underworld, and it had been getting warmer.

And that was when things started getting a lot warmer outside the tower.

Captain Adamson came out of the Quonset hut.

"All set, sir," he said, stepping up beside the general. He looked over at Miller. "If Major Connelly shows, please ask her to meet us in the mess."

A lot of meetings happened in the mess these days.

"Yes sir." He watched the captain and the general start in the direction of the mess tent. Behind him, Banister and Lake had returned to the analytical back and forth on what the lack of communication might portend.

He left them to their thing and went into the Quonset hut.

Just another day at command.

The cavern was several thousand yards across, the ceiling overhead almost lost in great swathes of dark shadows streaked with golden rays of light. The floor was covered in a forest of towering rock spires that stood like majestic redwood trees a hundred feet tall, trunks ten feet and more in diameter.

And yet the great chamber felt eerily empty. There was a peculiar hollowness about it.

Quinn called for a halt a hundred yards in. Several dropped to the ground right there; others dragged themselves to one or another of the massive stone columns and sat with their backs against the rock.

No one spoke. There was nothing to say.

They had been wandering the tunnels for days. They were out of both food and water. They had been attacked twice more by the shadowy rat-like creatures, and it was during one of these attacks that the radio had been damaged. Ramos had so far been unable to repair it.

After ten minutes rest, Quinn paired off the team members and sent them in four directions across the cavern floor. Each was to go all the way to the wall and then return.

Asher and Owen left their nearly empty backpacks behind and headed out together, walking silently through this bizarre rock forest. They reached the cavern wall finding no sign of water or food. Owen insisted on taking a break before starting back. Asher didn't argue. He was as spent as she was. It was taking all he had to keep going, and this little side trip had taken just a little bit more.

They sat in silence, staring out across the chamber. At times they could hear the others, their voices drifting across the great cavern, making the quiet all the more ominous.

"Crap," Owen growled after a minute, and struggled to her feet. "Come on, damn it."

She started back without another word, without waiting for Asher. After a few seconds, he rolled onto one knee, stood and followed after her.

None of the other search teams had found anything useful. Ramos was already hunched over his radio, trying yet again to repair it.

"Give it up, Corporal," said Owen. She repositioned her backpack and sat on it. "Even if you could fix that thing, what do you expect them do? Record our demise into the daily log?"

Ramos did his best to ignore her.

"We're not dead yet, Liz," said Church.

"This radio is," said Ramos. He sat back and held his head in his hands, ran his fingers through his non-regulation length hair. "It's done."

"Then we are alone," said Lisa. "Really alone."

I could deal with that, Asher thought. *But they'll never know what happened to us. They'll never know whether we managed to get off this floor, or of our progress to the next floor and the next.*

In the end, he said none of this aloud. In the end, it came down to just what Lisa had said. They were truly alone. However much or little command had actually been able to do to support the team in the tower, having that connection had meant something. And now that connection was broken.

Everyone watched in silence as Lt. Quinn lifted his backpack and slipped into it. At first, only Sgt. Costa followed his lead, standing and picking up her gear.

"Let's go," she stated. Once she noted everyone making at least some show of getting up, she started out.

Seeing Ramos kneel beside the radio, Quinn moved toward him and placed a hand on his shoulder.

"Leave it, Corporal," he said quietly.

"Sir?"

"It's not worth the weight."

"Who knows," said Owen, following after Costa. "Maybe we'll come across a Radio Shack on the next floor."

The tunnel was long and straight, and it was the first level stretch they'd seen since leaving the stone forest chamber hours earlier. Until now they had been slowly descending ever further into the bowels of the Underworld.

The Acolyte walked beside Owen. He was dressed in a black robe, the hood thrown back to reveal long, flowing salt-and-pepper hair. He appeared content to walk in silence, and was quite comfortable in the silence of the others.

Owen glanced at him from time to time, seemingly unconcerned at his presence. She also did not seem to be surprised that clearly no else could see the Acolyte in their midst.

She had a pretty good idea what his being here meant, and the reason she could see him when the others could not.

After some time had passed, she stirred up the courage to push the issue along.

"So," she said quietly. "You here to take me away from all this?"

"Oh, madam, I took you away three minutes ago."

"I see." She thought about that, tried to sort out what it might mean. No matter where her thoughts took her, it didn't come out so good for her.

Still, there wasn't a whole lot she could do about it.

"It couldn't have happened at a better time." She mulled that over for a moment. "Well, maybe yesterday would have been better. Today's been a bit of a drag."

The team continued along this long stretch of straight, level tunnel. Sgt. Costa led the way, as always. Lt. Quinn and Cpl. Ramos brought up the rear, as was the norm.

There was no sign of the Acolyte. There was no sign of Elizabeth Owen.

No one noticed.

Sgt. Miller was halfway along his routine morning walk around the tower. It was already very warm out, and was shaping up to be the warmest day yet. As he rounded the corner he considered picking up the pace, thinking to get himself under a canopy and out of the sun before it climbed much higher. There was a box fan sitting on one of the tables over in the mess tent with his name on it.

He saw two figures walking up ahead that he took at first to be the pair of guards walking the watch. But he knew they were much further ahead and were already beyond the next corner.

He recognized the person on the right then as Major Connelly. She was dressed in a clean, crisp uniform. As always, she was unaffected by the weather.

The one on the left took a bit longer to identify. He could tell that it was a woman, of average height. From the back it was impossible to judge her age. Her clothes were ragged and dirty. There was a beat up old backpack strapped to her back.

The two were in quiet conversation and seemed to be oblivious to the world around them.

Miller walked more quickly, and began to close the gap between himself and the two women.

The woman with Major Connelly turned her head slightly, and her profile came into view.

It was Dr. Owen.

The women reached the corner and continued around it. Miller hurried, broke into a jog and then finally began to run. He rounded the corner.

There was no sign of the women. Another dozen steps and Miller came to a noisy, stomping halt.

Ahead a third of way along the base of the tower walked the two guards. One looked briefly back over his shoulder at Miller, turned forward then and continued.

Miller wasn't sure what to do. What was there to do? Nothing, really. What did it mean? Had Major Connelly been in the tower, or had Dr. Owen been here?

Or had they both been somewhere else?

More likely. They hadn't disappeared, rather one of those weird windows Banister and Lake talked about had opened and closed.

Yeah... take this to Dr. Banister...

Episode Seven / Chapter Four

Elizabeth Owen and Major Connelly were sitting opposite Banister and Lake at a corner table in the mess tent. While Banister knew that Connelly wasn't who she appeared to be, he had no problem seeking her opinions on medical issues. After all, that was supposed to be the medical officer's reason for being there. Connelly, for her part, played her role well, despite the fact that no one believed her to be the person she purported herself to be.

At the moment they were discussing how long Major Connelly believed the team in the tower could survive without food and water under their current conditions, or rather the conditions they were believed to be in at the moment. They hadn't heard from the team in many days, and at that time supplies were reported to be extremely low.

"Okay, I get that they can't see or hear me," Owen said to Connelly. She leaned forward across the table and looked up into the face of Banister. He obviously couldn't see her. She turned her head then and looked side-glance at Connelly "But I'm having a bit of a time grasping that you are having two conversations at once."

One instance of Connelly was speculating to Banister on the team's probable current health. Another Connelly smiled and placed a hand on Owen's arm.

"I wouldn't want to leave you all alone, Elizabeth," she said.

"All alone where? And... just why am I here, wherever this is?"

"Ah, yes... well... you might say there has been a change in, how do you folks say, a change in your job description."

Sgt. Miller came into the mess tent. Seeing Banister and Lake at one of the tables, he hurried over and sat down opposite them.

"Sorry to bother you, doctors," he said quickly. "But I just saw something weird."

"Quite all right, Sergeant," said Banister. "What is it?"

"I just saw Doctor Owen taking a leisurely walk with Major Connelly."

Banister and Lake both looked quickly at Connelly, who was sitting placidly beside Miller, then back to Miller.

"Excuse me?" asked Banister.

Miller glanced curiously at the empty space next to him, looked again across the table.

"They were taking a walk around the tower. Doctor Owen looked like hell, but the major looked the same as always."

"I see," said Banister.

"I don't," said Lake.

Owen was completely bewildered.

"What the hell?"

"Yeah, I know," said Connelly proudly. "Enough to make your head spin clean off. Right now, I've got a bunch of different *'me'* going on all at once, or in the sergeant's case *not* going on, or both, or... and that's just here at this table."

Owen shook her head in frustration. "But... there's like... at least three different scenes going on here. All at the same time. And I can see all of them; how can I see all of them?"

"Most interesting." Connelly looked directly at Owen. "Don't you think?"

Most of the team waited midway along a long, wide section of tunnel, with Quinn standing apart from the others a few yards further on. He had his back to the group, kept his attention focused forward, focused on the bend in the tunnel another dozen yards ahead.

There was no sign of Elizabeth Owen. When they had first realized that Owen was no longer with them, no one had been able to pinpoint exactly when they had last seen her. All had just assumed she was there, until faced with the fact that she wasn't.

Had she dropped back to quietly take care of business? Had she turned left when everyone else had turned right? Had she just slowed and then finally stopped?

However it had happened, how had they not seen it?

Backtracking had revealed nothing. They had searched every side-tunnel, every cave and crevasse. Elizabeth Owen was gone.

Please... let her be back at command.

Please, let her be with Banister and Carmody.

At this point, it was all they had to hang onto. And they needed it. They needed something. Physically, they were almost done. They were now just hours from being too spent to walk, and their mental faculties were almost as affected by the hunger and dehydration. And then with Owen's disappearance... it weighed heavily on them. The thought that she might be thoroughly annoying Banister at this very moment was all they had left.

It brought a smile to one's face.

"Hey," Susan said tiredly. She nodded in the direction of Lt. Quinn; beyond Quinn. "The sergeant's back."

Asher leaned forward enough to see around the others. He saw Sgt. Costa coming around the corner. She approached Quinn. Reaching him, she stopped and nodded wearily.

Whatever it was, she wasn't all that pleased about it.

"All right. Thank you," said Quinn. He turned to face the group. "Everyone wait here."

"Lieutenant?" asked Ramos anxiously.

Quinn ignored him, turned back to Costa. "Give me five."

"Understood," Costa stated coolly.

Quinn stepped around his sergeant and started forward.

Lieutenant Quinn moved out of the narrow tunnel and into a cavern quite different than any they had seen previously. Directly ahead of him, stone steps were set into the side of a wide stone tower that rose up some forty feet and dominated the center of the chamber.

Quinn hesitated as he reached the top step. The top of the tower was flat, some thirty feet across. The creature was standing near the center of the dais, looking patiently in his direction.

"Approach," said the creature. The voice was deep and hollow.

Quinn left the top step, moved a few yards from the edge and stopped, still some eight feet from the creature. It towered above him and he had to look up to look it in the eye. It wore no clothes. Its skin was leather the color of dark burgundy. Its feet were cloven hooves. Two massive horns curled forward and up from its forehead and its chin protruded out impossibly far.

It lifted one of its hooves and took a single step forward.

Quinn almost took an involuntary step back before catching himself. He held his ground.

As the creature brought its other foot forward, it began to change shape. Its physical presence slowly morphed, growing increasingly less tangible, a dark, murky cloud. The cloud continued to push forward, and as it did so it continued to morph, slowly solidified into a form almost human.

The being was about the same height as Quinn. His face was thin and pale, seemingly more so with the jet black hair and nearly black eyes; eyes that sparkled with life.

He wore dark slacks, a black shirt, beneath a black jacket. They fit him well.

He took another step forward; a smooth, easy glide.

"Oh, that's much better," said the Devil. "Now perhaps we can have an intelligent conversation."

"Where is Doctor Owen," demanded Quinn.

The Devil smiled sympathetically, took another step forward and just a bit to one side. He studied Quinn; his facial expression, the way he stood, the defiant glare in his eyes.

"You have come so very far, my friend."

Quinn started to respond, in the end stood silent.

"Your journey through my realm, to be sure," the Devil continued. "But the path that has brought you to this moment is so much more, is it not?"

"We've managed."

"Yes. You have... managed."

"And now?"

The Devil grew thoughtful. He looked about them, stepped further to one side. "These tunnels and chambers that you have traversed these many days, you did not recognize them?"

"Should I have?"

"It would have changed nothing."

"All right... then what's the point?"

"No point." The Devil gave a casual shrug. "It would have been nice. There was much effort put into it."

Damn. Quinn couldn't help himself. "Into what?"

The Devil turned slowly about and grinned. "Ah... it was quite the accomplishment, my dear friend. For you see, the path that you and your comrades have trod through these tunnels and chambers, through the small caves and the grand caverns... it is the same journey as the twenty floors that came before."

"Yeah..." Quinn slowly drawled out. "I don't get it."

The Devil held up a long, bony finger. "My friend... by your journey through the Underworld, you have retraced the very path that brought you here."

What a load of gibberish, thought Quinn. And yet, it had to mean something to the Acolyte, or the Adversary... whoever this was.

"Let's assume that makes sense," said Quinn. "How does it get us out of here?"

"Much the reverse, I'm afraid. Think, sir, on what I just said. You have retraced the path that brought you here."

"Yeah, I heard. And?"

"You, my friend... are back at the beginning." He raised an arm and lifted his hand in one smooth, easy movement. He pointed at a glowing portal that had appeared a dozen yards away. "There lay the way to the Underworld. Yes. The Ferryman awaits."

"That's not possible."

"Of course it's possible." The Devil looked genuinely surprised. "I have made it so."

"We'll never survive. You know the condition we're in. Another day of this and we'll die. You know that."

"So sorry. The rules of the floor, my friend. The floor is the floor."

"And every floor has a way out. There has to be a way out."

The Devil cocked his head to one side, then to the other. He looked curiously at Quinn. Washing across the Devil's face was an ethereal shimmer of burgundy-colored leather and monstrous horns, and then he smiled.

"You would make a deal with the Devil?"

Elizabeth Owen stood passively six steps from the open portal in the middle of a field of wildflowers. Sgt. Costa stepped through, passed to Owen's left without seeming to notice her standing there. Owen was not surprised.

Lisa Powell came through next and passed to Owen's right. As with Costa, Lisa said nothing, saw nothing, her half-dead eyes staring dully ahead. The others came through then, one at a time, walked silently past Owen and continued on.

Lt. Quinn was the last to step through the portal. Owen sensed immediately that there was something different about him. Different from the others, but more than that... there was something not right. Owen couldn't put her finger on it, but there was definitely something different, something wrong.

There was an air of resoluteness about him. His gait was different. His step was slow and paced, but also steady, certain. It shouldn't be. Owen just knew that it shouldn't be.

It was wrong. It was all wrong.

And the eyes... the eyes didn't have the look that Owen just knew she should see. That gaze... saw too much.

And then, just as he reached her, passing on her left... Owen felt a bitter cold chill.

Quinn's eyes turned to her, looked directly at her; saw her. Those cool, clear eyes...

And then he was past.

Elizabeth Owen and Major Connelly stood outside the command center, Owen gazing up at the tower.

If the floors were actually floors, then the team would be just about... *there*.

"They're on the next floor," she said, her focus never leaving the tower.

"That is good," Connelly stated. "I'll let the General know."

"Yeah," Owen said softly, almost a whisper. "Yeah, you do that."

~ end of episode seven

Episode Eight
The Neighborhood

Prolog

Peter Asher stepped out onto the front porch of the comfortable two bedroom house, closed the door behind him and started down the front walk to the sidewalk. He was clean-shaven, his hair recently trimmed. He was dressed in clean clothes, nothing too heavy as this was clearly going to be another very pleasant day.

Walking up the street, he only occasionally glanced at the homes that he passed. It was by now all warmly familiar to him. This was a nice, middle-class neighborhood; nice homes, green lawns and shrubs, and healthy trees that provided shade wherever shade was needed. There were a few light, wispy clouds drifting slowly overhead, set against a sky that was a very nice shade of blue. The morning sun was still low on the horizon, would be hidden from view for another hour or so.

Reaching the corner, Asher had to step around the little boy on the tricycle.

The tricycle wasn't moving. The little boy wasn't moving. His eyes never wavered, never blinked.

Asher moved around and passed by the little boy, giving him a casual, disinterested glance before continuing up the side street.

He had places to go; there were things to do on this fine day...

Episode Eight / Chapter One

Ramos stood in the middle of the small parking lot, frowning at the little strip mall before them.

"Not much to offer," he said. The building held a Laundromat, a nail salon, a pet groomer and a dollar store. They would have to check them all, of course, on the off-chance that one of them held the portal to the next floor. But Cpl. Ramos continued to hope he would find the materials that he needed in order to put together a new radio, and so regain communication with command.

They would not be finding those materials here.

"Not much," agreed Lisa, though to be honest she thought they might find a few useful odds and ends in a couple of those shops.

"So, start with the Laundromat?" Ramos started across the lot without waiting for an answer. Lisa followed beside him.

They had been teamed together for the last several days. It had been awkward at first, for though they had been living and working side-by-side for months, they had until now never been paired together.

Just the way it sorted itself out, she supposed.

The parking lot was empty. But then, every parking lot was empty; as was every road, every driveway and every garage.

There were no cars. The Adversary wanted the team on foot.

The lieutenant had the teams searching the floor in a circular grid, working out from the street they had settled into and were using as their home base. They had named the block "the neighborhood".

They had been on the twenty-seventh floor for eleven days. They had yet to find any real threats, and the environment was pleasant enough. They had quickly found food and water, clean clothes and comfortable beds. It had been their first real opportunity at genuine rest and recovery since their escape from Hades, some half a dozen floors back. While the intervening floors had provided some food and water, between the unrelenting meteor storms on twenty three and the insect-infested jungle on twenty six, there had been little time to recuperate from the horrors of the twenty-first floor.

Lisa Powell was more than happy to take advantage of what peace this floor offered for just as long as it was offered. She was certain the dangers of this floor would make themselves known soon enough.

The Laundromat smelled of oft-used washing machines and dryers; of wet, soapy clothes and of hot, drying clothes. They found a young woman sitting on a wooden bench before a front-loading dryer. She appeared quite bored.

Lisa stood in front of the woman, looked dispassionately down at her. The woman didn't move, didn't raise her gaze to look up at her. She didn't acknowledge the fact that Lisa now stood between her and the dryer she was absently watching.

Ramos searched the Laundromat while Lisa studied the unmoving woman. Once he was certain that the portal wasn't hiding in one of the washing machines, he came up beside Lisa. He gave the young woman only a passing glance.

"Come on, Lisa," he urged calmly. "Let's have a look in the nail salon."

"Yeah... okay." Lisa sighed and looked up from the motionless figure. "Nail salon it is..."

Quinn sat at the picnic table in the small park, fastidiously updating his maps. With each passing day his picture of the floor grew more accurate, more complete, expanded further.

At least that was the intent.

He had kept the team together during the first few days, until he felt confident they wouldn't get separated and suddenly find themselves scattered to alternate worlds. He then sent them out in two-person teams to different directions on the compass, each day shifting the direction slightly; each day pushing several blocks further out, and then further out still.

He frowned now as he studied his maps, gripping the pencil and absently tapping it on the table.

Something was very odd.

It wasn't coming out right. He couldn't get his maps right.

It was as though the teams were going out further each day, but the distance they were travelling each day was actually less...

And no one was noticing.

Either he was doing something wrong, or every team was consistently providing inaccurate data, which seemed unlikely.

But whichever it was, it didn't bode well.

"Sir?" Costa had just come into the park. She stood beside the lieutenant. "Is everything all right?"

Quinn continued staring down at the maps that were scattered across the table.

"Yes. Everything's fine," he said at last. "What do you need, Sergeant?"

"We're back, sir. The others should be back shortly." Costa had been out on recon with Dr. Asher. They had met Church and Susan Bautista coming back in.

"Very good," Quinn said distractedly. "I'm on my way."

Costa waited a few moments for something more; there was no more. The lieutenant stared at his maps, tapped his pencil, and said nothing further.

She turned away and started back across the neighborhood park.

Quinn glanced up once, just as his sergeant stepped off the grass and started along the side street.

Solid, efficient Sergeant Costa. He could count on her. He could rely on her.

She would do well in his place once he was gone.

Quinn turned his attention back to his maps.

What am I doing wrong? What am I not seeing?

The small café had a row of booths set along the windowed wall, a handful of tables in the center of the room. Several of these tables had been pushed together for the daily team meetings and the occasional get-togethers.

Peter Asher, Susan Bautista and Dr. Church sat at the tables, absently drinking freshly brewed coffee, snacking on cookies.

Elizabeth Owen watched in silence from a nearby booth, forever unseen, unheard. She showed no emotion. She was there. She observed.

Church set his white ceramic cup onto the table in front of him and leaned back in his chair.

"Very much in spite of myself, I could get used to this."

"Take advantage of it while it lasts, Nate," said Asher. "I wouldn't go getting used to it."

"Oh, dear Peter..." Church sighed contentedly. He grinned. "That won't be easy. That won't be easy at all."

Asher thought a moment about the very nice day he had had so far. An enjoyable morning walk from his house, breakfast with the team, an uneventful recon. He and Sgt. Costa had even grown their supplies.

He had needed this timeout. He was almost back to himself.

"I totally get that, Doctor," he said. "It's the first real break we've had in six months."

"After twenty seven floors, we certainly deserve it," said Susan. She didn't look or sound at all content with their situation. When she let her comment hang there in empty space, both Asher and Church subconsciously leaned a little bit closer to Dr. Bautista.

"What is it, Susan?" asked Church.

"Don't misunderstand, Doctor; I do enjoy the break. But there is something so... *haunting*— about this place."

"Yes. The citizenry can be rather unsettling," Church said softly. He had done his best to set aside his feelings regarding these motionless people while at the same time trying to understand what they represented, what they meant to the larger picture.

"And the silence," said Susan. "And beyond that... what is to follow the silence."

They all appreciated the quiet, Asher as much as anyone. He also understood where Susan was coming from.

The other shoe would most assuredly fall.

That was why he was not going to get used to this. He would take it while it lasted, and all the while would stand ready for whatever was to come.

His own bit of discomfort lay in the fact that he was having trouble anticipating what that might be. They all were.

The front door opened and Sgt. Costa came into the café.

"The Lieutenant is on his way," she said.

"Very good, Sara," said Church. He indicated an empty chair. "Have a seat."

"Don't mind if I do, Doctor."

Once settled in, she asked Church and Dr. Bautista about their morning. She had gotten a quick brief when they had met coming back in, and would hear the details once the meeting got going. At the moment, she was just looking for general impressions.

She too was waiting for the inevitable. She was looking for a sign that might tell them that *it* was coming. She didn't expect the forewarning to be written across the sky, but there might subtle indicators. If they were there, she wanted to find them.

Costa and Asher had seen nothing out of the ordinary. Other than those weird, motionless people, the world was totally pleasant.

Too pleasant. Too quiet. Costa was getting jumpy.

Church was telling her about his own totally wonderful morning when Lisa and Ramos came into the café. They were just finding their way to their chairs when Quinn followed them in.

"Good afternoon everyone," he said. His maps were stuffed into the large portfolio that he had tucked under one arm. "Let's get this meeting going."

Dr. Owen settled back in the booth, what she thought of as her own personal booth. The others seldom used it. She tapped her fingers on the tabletop. God, she hated these meetings. Actually, she hated any meetings, but poor ol' Quinn had a way of taking the most interesting fact and making it dull.

But what made it just about unbearable for Owen was that she couldn't participate. She could do nothing but sit quietly and observe.

Oh, please... just once... just one of my classic retorts...

Dr. Banister had spent the morning reviewing data with Dr. Lake, and the meeting had lasted well into lunch. After a sandwich in the mess, he had gone for a long walk, giving him a chance to clear his head and take in the nice afternoon.

He found himself walking along the tower wall near where the door into the structure had once been, the only access in gone now for nearly half a year. A month or so ago someone had put a bench and long planter box there. The flowers were in bloom.

Major Connelly was sitting on the bench. She appeared to be lost in thought... but then, who knew where she was when that happened? Banister sat down beside her and waited, letting the warm afternoon seep in. He was content to let the day pass as it would.

"Hello, Doctor Banister," said Connelly, easing out of her reverie.

"Good afternoon, Major," said Banister. "How are you this afternoon?"

Connelly smiled gently as she came fully back to the moment. "I am well," she said. "Thank you for asking."

There were a few more pleasantries exchanged, which was the normal protocol whenever they met, whatever the circumstance. Banister held no illusions about Major Connelly's loyalties, but he also appreciated her value to the mission.

He would weigh carefully every item of information she offered. The validity, accuracy, even the very color in which the information was provided was always to be questioned. Some still doubted that Major Connelly was actually in communication with Elizabeth Owen. But after having key questions answered, Banister accepted that Dr. Owen had somehow found herself in a median plane between the tower floors and the command center.

Unfortunately, Owen was unable to communicate directly with those in either. The one positive they had going for them was that Elizabeth could witness the events occurring on the floors and could communicate with Major Connelly.

This was of course not an accident of circumstance. This was undoubtedly a creature of the Adversary or of his acolyte.

Very well. Bannister would take it.

"Thank you for your input this morning, Major," he said.

"Of course, Doctor Banister. I wish I could do more."

"Yes, well, we work with what we are given. Do we not?"

"That we do," said Major Connelly, accepting the statement at face value.

Banister leaned forward, rested his elbows on his knees and clasped his hands together.

"Very little news regarding Nate of late," he said quietly.

"I believe that may be due to the rather tranquil situation in which they currently find themselves. Be assured, Doctor Church is well."

"I suppose so," Banister sighed.

Major Connelly sat forward now, edged closer to Dr. Banister. She placed a comforting hand on his arm.

"I understand that this must be frustrating for you."

"To be observers only." Banister shook his head despondently. "Second-hand observers at that."

More frustrating still, he thought, was that the team inside the tower had no way of knowing they were being observed. If they had known, there could at least be one-way communication. As it was...

"Second-hand observers," he said again.

Church sat down on the park bench with a soft, tranquil sigh. He leaned back, placed an arm on the back of the bench and glanced over at the figure sitting on the bench beside him.

Carl, that's what Church called him, showed no sign that he recognized he had company. He was an elderly gentleman, probably retired. He had a small paper bag in his lap. From his earlier visits with Carl, Church knew the bag contained a handful of bits of bread.

No doubt for pigeons, although Church had yet to see a single bird.

"Good evening, Carl," he said. He looked out across the park. It was a wide expanse of lawn, bordered by trees on three sides, opening to a quiet street on the fourth. The picnic table over to the left was where Lt. Quinn spent many an hour sweating over his maps.

"Oh, Carl, Carl, Carl," droned Church. "What does it all mean? What are you not telling me, my friend?"

That this was a test, he had no doubt.

And the impending doom and gloom? After the first few dozen floors, one came to expect that.

But what was the test? And what form would the threat take?

"Don't take this the wrong way Carl, and please don't say anything to Banister, but I do miss the old man."

Church looked over at Carl. "You're good company, dear sir, but to be perfectly honest, you're not much for scientific discourse." He looked back out across the park. "Wes is an annoying old fart, but the back and forth had its merits."

Church leaned back until he felt the wooden slats of the bench against his back. His pleasant evening was losing its pleasantness, and he wasn't happy about that. He was annoyed with himself. This morose tone was gaining him nothing.

"The old man doesn't even know whether we're alive or dead," he said. "And that's the worst of it, Carl; the absolute worst. I can't even let him know we're okay."

Episode Eight / Chapter Two

Dusk... that quiet time just before the fall of night when it isn't yet dark, when the world gradually fades to a calming, restful gray. Here in the neighborhood it seemed to hang on a lot longer than Owen thought normal. Not that she minded, really. It was kind of nice.

She strolled along the sidewalk that ran between the wide strip of parkway and the lawns of the middle-class homes. She passed by the first house, the windows warmly glowing from the light of life within. Church lived there with his young associate Susan Bautista.

A bright enough girl, Owen supposed, though she was certainly no Ray Do.

Owen missed Ray much more than she would ever admit.

The next house held the military team: Quinn, Ramos and Costa.

Owen held a grudging respect for Sgt. Costa. She had found her to be most efficient in her duties.

Cpl. Ramos, on the other hand, annoyed her no end. Always did, always would. It didn't matter that she was now, well... as she was.

She still wasn't sure about Quinn; even after all this time. The lieutenant seemed sincere, and to his credit he was not your typical gung-ho, by-the-book, just-following-orders-sir type. And he had done all right by the team. She'd give him that, if she was forced on the matter.

Lisa Powell lived on her own in the small house directly across the street. Dear, sweet Miss Lisa Powell. A bit of a dove in the beginning, working in Ray's shadow and happy to do so from what Owen could tell.

The girl had come such a very long way in twenty-seven floors; still a dove, perhaps, but starting to stand on her own.

Good. The team would need that.

Owen heard someone coming up the street behind her. Turning about, she watched Asher approach. He passed by her, oblivious to her presence, and continued on to the house that he called home here on this floor.

Peter was doing much better these days. This floor had been a great healer of whatever psychological wounds he had suffered on those earlier floors.

Owen was glad to see it. She had always liked Peter. Though they had never worked together out in the real world, their paths had crossed a number of times and she had always enjoyed their interactions, however brief and trivial. She had been delighted to see him on the team, and his presence had helped make her time in the tower just a little more bearable. Excepting Ray, Peter had understood her like no other.

She knew she needed handling. She had been okay with that.

Now of course, things were very different. How many floors had it been since her sudden departure? Six? And she still didn't know how to deal with it.

When she was on a floor in the tower, she was totally on the floor. She could hear things, smell things, could feel the wind against her face. She could touch things; most things.

She couldn't touch the other members of the team. And of course they couldn't see, hear, or touch her.

Such was the same when she was at the command center. She could sit at the table with the staff there, could smell the coffee they drank, could hear their inane banter, but they couldn't see or hear her.

That drove her batty. They needed some serious talking to and she would have been quite willing to provide that talk.

But only the creature that was Major Connelly could see and hear her. This was both a curse and a blessing. Whoever or whatever Connelly was, at least she was someone Owen to talk to. Owen wasn't totally alone. Connelly was less than the ideal target for Owen's sharp repartee, but at least she could hear her and could talk back.

Connelly no doubt had many secrets, but there was at least the illusion of openness within their relationship. Owen appreciated that. And she understood that it was a very narrow path Major Connelly must walk.

Still, the one question Elizabeth Owen wished Connelly would answer but would not, or could not...

What was to come of her?

Major Connelly stood near the coffee station in the command center. She leaned against the counter, arms folded, and watched as Cpl. Johansen finished up another unsuccessful session at the radio. On schedule every thirty seven hours twenty minutes, the corporal attempted to contact the team in the tower. This, despite the fact that Connelly continued to advise that Cpl. Ramos had not yet been able to put together another radio on their end.

Johansen slid back from the radio, glanced over at Major Connelly as he slowly turned about in his chair. She gave him a supportive smile. He gave her an acknowledging nod in response.

The door opened and General Wong came into the Quonset hut. Johansen spun about another quarter turn and stood up. The general waved him back down as he crossed the room.

"No contact, sir," said Johansen.

"Thank you, son." The general reached the command center's main table and turned his attention to Major Connelly. He indicated a chair as he pulled one out for himself and sat down. "And what do you have for me, Major?"

It was time for the daily update. Connelly relayed Elizabeth Owen's latest observations of the team's activities as had been recounted to her during their periodic exchanges over the previous day.

Of late there had been very little new information to pass along. The team in the tower continued to go out on their daily recons in search of the portal to the next floor. There was nothing new on that front, no sign of the gateway, though in truth the general was more concerned with the lack of news regarding what threat lay in store for them on this floor than he was the portal. The portal would come. It always did.

It may not have been a matter of choice, but the team was walking a fine line. Yes, since arriving on this floor there had been very real healing happening, both physical and mental. The team had needed this period of recuperation. This should not be minimized.

But while this healing progressed, the unknown threat continued to close in. Of this, the general was certain. The threat was certain.

Everyone knew it was coming.

How seriously are they taking this imminent danger, he wondered.

"I do not know," Major Connelly had told him.

They must feel some sense of relief each day they return from their recons without finding the portal, he thought. *Another day away from the nightmare of the floors.*

"I do not know," Major Connelly had repeated.

Each day the threat didn't reveal itself was another day they dodged the bullet. Was it not?

Major Connelly held her silence. General Wong wasn't looking to her for answers to any of these questions.

Wong felt the same frustration as Dr. Banister at having to play the role of observer. He had never been comfortable with command being so apart from the team on this mission. He, and command in general, had been relegated to the role of spectator. Since the loss of the radio, the title of observer had taken on a whole new meaning.

But for Elizabeth Owen, they wouldn't even have had that.

It had been Dr. Banister who had convinced General Wong that the Owen scenario was real. It had been Banister who had first appreciated the value of Major Connelly, whoever or whatever she truly was, no matter her true loyalties.

"Does Doctor Banister have anything new?" he asked the Major.

"As regards the threat?" asked Connelly. "He and Doctor Lake continue to document what information Doctor Owen relays through me, but analysis of the data to date has yet to reveal any answers. I believe they are focusing on the residents of the floor. They suspect that they may play at least some part in whatever danger looms over the team."

"And what do you think, Major?" asked the general. "I would be most interested in your opinion; your thoughts, from your perspective."

"I am afraid I have very little to contribute, sir. As you know, my expertise lay in the medical field."

"You have no opinions from your own observations."

"As I have stated, sir," said the major. "My observations do not reach any further than yours. I have no more information than you. I leave the analysis of that information to Doctor Banister and Doctor Lake."

"Very well, Major." General Wong frowned, pursed his lips and let out a noisy sigh. "Should anything... *come to you...* any thoughts that might be helpful, I do hope that you will bring them to me."

"Of course, General." Major Connelly looked genuinely surprised. "Without hesitation."

"Yes," said the general with another low sigh. He leaned back in his chair. "Of course."

Quinn and Ramos stood at the curb of one of the main thoroughfares. Across the street was a young woman, long dark hair, dressed in slacks and a light shirt. She was silent, unmoving, as all the residents. Her unwavering gaze could have been directed right at them.

"Are you sure?" asked Quinn.

"Yes sir. Absolutely, sir," said Ramos. "It's her, all right."

"Well then," sighed Quinn. He stepped off the curb, took one step into the street. He stopped, studied the woman for some sign.

There was nothing.

But if Ramos was certain, then it was so. And if it was so, then it meant... what?

Asher walked out of his house, closing the door behind him as he stepped down from his porch.

He stopped suddenly, startled.

There was a woman and her little girl standing on the front walk, a pace from the sidewalk.

They hadn't been there before...

They weren't moving, and yet they were most certainly coming up the walk to the house.

"Oh, boy," mumbled Asher.

Church and Susan were making their way up the street to the café.

Two people were at the bus stop, one sitting on the bench, the other standing beside it. The figure standing appeared to be looking expectantly up the street.

Church and Susan continued. They passed a store window. Beyond the glass, a middle-aged man was in the act of dressing a mannequin.

There was a small group standing at the intersection, waiting to start across the crosswalk.

It was as a three dimensional photograph; a snapshot of a single moment in time, capturing the residents of this community going about their daily lives.

Entering the café, they found Asher and Lisa sitting at the tables. Sgt. Costa was standing near the counter.

A waitress stood behind the counter.

The café cook was visible through the order window, standing before the stove in the kitchen.

Episode Eight / Chapter Three

The café was eerily quiet. Half the team was gathered around the cluster of tables, with only an occasional soft-spoken comment breaking the silence. Over at the counter, Ramos sat on the stool directly opposite the waitress. He was leaning slightly forward, hands clasped before him, studying the woman's face. Her unblinking eyes stared back at him.

Quinn and Dr. Church were in the last booth at the far end of the café, Quinn's hand-drawn maps spread out on the table between them. It was Elizabeth Owen's booth. She sat beside Church, leaning near to better see the drawings.

"I see," mumbled Church. He moved one of the hand-drawn maps aside, compared it to the one beneath it. "Yes. Most odd."

The spectral Elizabeth Owen agreed. She frowned. "It certainly is."

"Though not unprecedented, I should think," Church said, mostly to himself.

"Oh, of course not," said Owen, dripping sarcasm.

Quinn shuffled through the drawings, found the one he was looking for. He pointed to a building he had labeled "strip mall".

"Six days ago," he stated. He pulled a second map over. He found the strip mall on this drawing. "Three days ago."

Church nodded, his hand resting on a third drawing. "And yesterday," he said, pondering.

"Our little world isn't just getting smaller, Doctor. It's shrinking,"

"A bit of both, I believe." Church noted that while the distances between some locations were growing shorter, other locations had indeed... *dropped off the map.*

"Either way, Doctor Church; it doesn't bode well for us."

"No, it doesn't," grumbled Owen. She furrowed her brow as she continued looking at the maps.

"No, it doesn't," said Church. They had come across somewhat similar phenomenon in the past, going all the way back to the first floor, where distances were dependent upon perspective. But while the first floor had been disconcerting, it had been the third floor that had been the most threatening. They had only just escaped through the portal before that old west town had been devoured by the black that had been closing in on them.

Dr. Church saw their current circumstance as a somewhat twisted amalgamation of the two, all made possible by the very nature of the floors.

"You're running out of time, Nate," said Owen.

"Our time here is limited," said Church, looking up from the maps to Lieutenant Quinn.

"A few days at most," agreed Quinn.

Asher looked over at the row of booths lining the wall of the café. Quinn and Church sat in the last booth, hovering over the lieutenant's drawings.

Meanwhile, over at the counter, Cpl. Ramos was poking the waitress in the forehead with a finger.

"Ramos, leave the lady alone," ordered Costa.

Ramos lowered his hand, leaned forward and moved his face in close, almost nose to nose with the waitress. "She's new," he said.

"No kidding," said Costa.

"No. I mean new. A lot of 'em are moving around, disappearing one place, showing up in another, but not her. She's brand new."

"Maybe we just didn't come across her before," suggested Costa. "We haven't been absolutely everywhere."

"Nah, I don't think so. I think she's new. And the cook, too."

Asher thought Ramos was right. A lot of the residents were on the move, but just as many were making their first time appearances. The mother and child on the walk outside his house, for instance.

The world was starting to get crowded.

Down at the far end of the café, Quinn and Church slid out of their booth. The lieutenant gathered up his maps as Dr. Church approached the rest of the team.

Asher didn't much like the dour look on the doctor's face.

Quinn stood waiting outside the café. He had sent three of the team to the left, and Professor Asher and Dr. Bautista to the right.

There would be no dilly-dallying from this moment forward. The portal must be found. It must be found quickly. Everyone understood the urgency.

Sgt. Costa stepped out of the café.

"Ready, sir," she said.

"Very good, Sergeant." The two started across the street. Reaching the other side, they had to step around a group of residents who were lined up at the curb before they could enter the alley.

Asher and Susan turned right onto the narrow side street, continued for three blocks and then turned left. They were headed for the six block square in the northwest quadrant of Lt. Quinn's search grid. Mixed in amongst the familiar and expected shops, the area had a handful of pawn shops, a couple of secondhand stores and a swap meet. Ramos and Lisa Powell had been the first to map it, and Asher had been involved in a later sweep. Both searches had been rewarded with useful supplies.

This third search was not about supplies. They were looking for the portal first and foremost. Second was to survey geographic changes.

Rounding the corner and starting up the main street of the neighborhood, the first of the pawn shops was ahead on the left.

"I don't remember it being this close the last time," said Susan.

Everyone found it unsettling that no one had noticed the diminishing distances during their explorations. How could you not notice a store or a street or a mall was closer this time than the last?

"I think you're reading things into it, now that we know what's happening," said Asher.

"We know what's happening?"

"We know he's playing with our minds," said Asher, meaning the Adversary.

As they got nearer the pawn shop, they noticed a figure standing with his back to the door. Any other place or time, he could well have just stepped out of the store.

"Well, he's new," Susan said casually. The figure was blocking the way in. Since the store had been searched previously, he couldn't have been there before.

They passed by the pawn shop and continued up the street.

Susan stopped outside the used book store three doors down from the pawn shop. Asher stood beside her, looking inside. There were several rows of tall bookshelves.

The detail on this floor was beyond anything they had previously seen. There were thousands of books in there. Asher had examined at least a hundred of them his last time here. This could have been any used book store he had ever visited back in the real world.

Susan lifted a hand and carefully placed a palm on the glass of the window.

"Are you all right?" he asked her.

"Yes."

"Spoken with true conviction."

Susan smiled. "Sorry. I don't mean to be melancholy."

She turned away from the window and they started walking again.

"No. I get it," said Asher.

He knew how she felt. The thought of going back *out there* wasn't at all appealing. But this little bubble of cozy that was floor twenty seven was being eaten away before their very eyes. This home and hearth that had done so much to heal them was inexplicably dissolving beneath them. They were being thrown back into the pit.

Walking side by side, their hands touched. Without thinking twice, their fingers intertwined.

Quinn and Costa returned to the café half an hour before sunset. Quinn hesitated at the door, his hand on the knob.

"Are we good?" he asked.

"Yes sir." Costa was a strong spirit, but she was still shaken by what Quinn had told her on their way back. It must have shown on her face or in her manner. "I'm fine, Lieutenant. Really."

"Very good." His own expression softened. "No need to worry, Sergeant. A few floors to go, yet."

"Yes sir."

"No surprises. I wanted you to be ready."

"Thank you, sir."

Quinn opened the door. "You coming?"

"Not just yet."

Quinn gave a nod and went into the café.

Costa was still standing outside when Ramos, Lisa and Dr. Church returned. Church appeared lost in thought, Lisa a little bewildered, and Ramos just plain excited.

"Helluva thing, Sarge," said Ramos, watching the others go inside. "Weirdest damn thing I ever saw."

This just managed to bring Costa out of her own wandering reverie. "That's a very high bar, Ramos."

"Hence, my enthusiasm. So... two buildings that I swear on my mother's pinky ring were at least a good three blocks apart just two days ago... are now side by side. I mean they're sharing the same damned parking lot."

"What?"

"And lookin' like they belong together." Ramos nodded his head up and down a couple of times. "Eh? See? Weirdest thing, or what?"

"Yeah. Weird." Costa decided she could let this go for the moment. She stole a quick glance through the window into the café, then turned to start up the street. "Walk with me if you please, Corporal."

Oh, this can't be good, thought Ramos.

They walked in silence till they were far enough from the café that Costa was certain they wouldn't be overheard. She stopped then, faced Ramos.

She wasn't sure where to start.

"What is it, Sarge?" asked Ramos.

"It's about the lieutenant." She hesitated. "About our escape from the Hades floor."

"Yeah... the lieutenant found the portal. What of it?"

"It was a bit more complicated than that," said Costa. "Ya' see, Quinn made a deal. With the devil."

"I don't get the joke, Costa. What are you talking about?"

"We get out of Hades, Quinn gets to stick with us till we get to the 37th floor. When we leave the 37th floor, the lieutenant stays behind."

"But that's crazy."

"No doubt. That was the deal."

Ramos turned away from Costa. He growled low and shook his head, stepped stiffly off the sidewalk.

"Damn," he grumbled quietly, then more forcefully. "Damn."

"That's about how I feel about it."

"You went along with this?" Ramos turned around and again faced Costa. "Sergeant?"

"Didn't know about it. Quinn just told me. Now I'm telling you."

"Damn," Ramos said again. "Okay, so what do we do?"

"I have no idea."

"We can't let this happen, Sarge. We gotta do *somethin'*."

"I don't know that there's anything we can do. The Lieutenant only told me now 'cause he wanted me to be ready. I'm telling you for the same reason."

"Oh, I'll be ready, all right."

Costa glowered at him. "We'll do what we can, come to that, but whatever happens on thirty seven, I need you ready for thirty eight. Understood?"

Ramos frowned darkly, set his jaw tight and made ready to say something. In the end he fought it back. He half-turned, eventually nodded in the direction of the café. "And what about them?" he asked.

"Let's keep this just between us for now," said Costa. "They need the lieutenant just as he is. Invincible."

Banister sat with an elbow on the table, his chin in his hand, only half listening to Lake. The man wasn't saying anything that he hadn't already said a dozen times before. Banister was looking past Lake to the radioman Corporal Johansen.

Not that he was expecting anything new from that, either.

Johansen thumbed the switch on the radio to the off position. He looked up at Carmody, who was standing beside him.

"Why do I keep trying?" he asked dejectedly. "They don't even have a radio."

"You don't know that for sure," Carmody stated flatly.

"Major Connelly says they don't."

"And that makes it so?"

"Doesn't make it not so."

"What does that mean?"

Banister spoke up then, deciding to jump into the conversation. "It means, my dear, that we should not dismiss the Major's words out of hand."

Dr. Lake grimaced. "You give her words way too much credence, Banister. If you cannot trust the source, you cannot trust the data."

"One should never trust any data unreservedly, whatever the source," said Banister. "But do we disregard completely the information offered simply because her motivation may not serve the same end as our own?"

"That's the point. We don't know her motivation. It may yet prove counter to ours, perhaps even dangerous. Lest you forget, she is a servant of the Adversary."

"Not a servant, Doctor Lake." Major Connelly stood in the open doorway. The sunshine behind her put her form into dark silhouette. "A creation."

The door closed slowly as she stepped fully into the Quonset hut. Lake stood and gave a brisk nod as Connelly approached the table.

"Pardon, Major," he said. "But if I might speak frankly, such a distinction does nothing to allay my concerns."

"Then you do not fully understand that distinction, if I might also speak frankly." Major Connelly pulled out a chair and sat opposite Lake and Banister. "As a servant, my role would be, by the very nature of the position, to serve the needs of the Adversary. But I am a creation. This creation is Major Connelly. My role is Major Connelly. My purpose is to be Major Connelly. The goals and the desires that would be Major Connelly... these are my goals and my desires."

Dr. Lake gave a sly grin. "But then, we come back to it, do we not? You ask that we trust this is so."

"We will always, as you say, come back to it," said Connelly. "That would be true in any event. And I myself, if I am who and what I claim to be, do I not face the same dilemma? At some point, must I not choose to accept or deny that the persona of Elizabeth Owen that is presented to me is in fact Doctor Owen and not a construct of the Adversary? And take that then one step further. Whether she be Doctor Owen or not, is she in fact witnessing the true events of our team in the tower? Might she instead be witness to a fabrication of the Adversary?"

"You make my argument for me, madam," said Lake. "Given this, what would you have us do? Take it all on faith?"

"You have a choice, Doctor Lake." Connelly slid her chair back and stood up. "You work with what you are given, doubts and all, or you do nothing."

At that there was a slight snicker from Dr. Banister.

Episode Eight / Chapter Four

There were several boxes stacked in one of the booths in the café; supplies that had been collected from the most recent explorations.

Quinn, Costa and Dr. Church stood around a table in middle the room, the chairs pushed aside. All three were staring down at the map.

"The rate at which our universe is collapsing in on itself appears to be accelerating," said Church.

Costa sucked in a shallow breath. "As Doctor Owen would say... holy crap."

"Yes. Well." Church rested a fingertip on the map. "The axis of the collapse is right here."

"The park," said Quinn.

"None other."

Scraping and thumping sounds came from the door and Ramos pushed his way through, cardboard box in hand. Lisa was right behind him with a second box.

"A few things, Lieutenant," said Ramos. "Nothing to write home about, but I couldn't just leave the stuff."

"Yes, that's fine." Quinn absently waved a hand in the general direction of the booths without looking up from the map.

"I recommend we move home base to the park as soon as possible," said Church.

"How much time do you estimate?"

"A day, half a day; maybe less. Moving to the park buys us something."

"Very well." Quinn spoke then to everyone in the café. "Gather your gear, back here in fifteen. We move out in twenty with what supplies we can carry."

Church looked up from map, surveyed the café. "Where's Susan? And Peter?"

"Not back yet." Costa looked questioningly to Quinn. "Northwest Quadrant?"

"You take charge here," said Quinn. "I'll go find them. If I'm not back, we'll meet at the park."

"Yes sir." Costa made ready to head to the house and collect her gear. She looked again at the map. "Doctor Church, we set up shop at the park, okay... we buy ourselves a little time; then what?"

"The portal must be there," Church stated calmly.

"I've spent more time there than here, Doctor," said Quinn. He was also making ready to head out. "There's no portal there."

"Either you are wrong, Lieutenant, or our situation will quickly become increasingly uncomfortable."

Asher and Susan hurried down the middle of the street. Several blocks behind them rose up a silvery-white wall of empty space.

They stepped up onto the sidewalk just outside the bookstore. Susan came to a sudden halt.

"Peter? Peter, look." She was looking through the window.

Asher stood beside her, saw what she saw.

There was a man inside, standing at the register in the act of making a purchase. Behind the counter was the cashier.

"It's the guy from the pawn shop, right?" Susan turned as if to walk the three doors down to the pawn shop.

But the pawn shop was no longer three doors down. It was now right next door.

"Oh my," sighed Susan. "It's getting very peculiar out here."

"You're right about the guy."

The resident who had been standing at the pawn shop door was now buying a book in the bookstore that was now right next door.

Up the street behind them, the edge of the world crept ever closer, buildings on either side of the road slowly dissolving, becoming part of the nothing.

Asher took Susan's hand, pulled her along as he started again down the street.

"We better get back while there's still a back to get to."

Ramos and Costa were moving back and forth between the boxes stacked in the booths and the backpacks sitting on the tables in the middle of the café. They were scrounging through the supplies and stuffing what they could into the packs.

Church and Lisa came in, Church looking quickly about.

"The lieutenant hasn't returned?" He sounded anxious. "Susan? Peter?"

"Not yet, Doctor," said Costa. She took one of the two packs that Church was carrying. "This is Dr. Bautista's?"

"Yes, yes," Church mumbled distantly.

"I'll pack it up." Costa indicated the boxes scattered about. "Gather what you can. We're out in five."

"But Susan—"

"They'll meet us at the park. Quickly now, Doctor."

"I'll not leave without Susan." Church was near to pleading.

"Doctor," Costa stated forcefully. "I'll be carrying three backpacks as it is. I'll carry you as well, if I have to, but it'll really slow me down."

Church took a moment to consider the sincerity of the sergeant's words. He reached out then and took back Susan's backpack.

"You'll have your hands full with the lieutenant's pack. I'll take care of Susan's."

Quinn turned a corner, followed the narrow side-street for a block and then turned again. He knew from his maps that this should take him right into the heart of the northwest quadrant.

The world sounded strangely hollow. There had always been an emptiness about the place, but this was different. It was more... the absence of sound. It was as if sound itself was being drawn into some void. Even his footsteps were muffled.

There was movement up ahead. After another dozen steps, he saw the movement as two figures coming toward them. They were moving quickly, at a quick walk at least. He soon recognized Asher and Dr. Bautista. No more than a few hundred yards behind them was a great wall of white.

"Professor, Doctor Bautista," Quinn said. "I am very glad to see you. We must hurry. Time is quite short."

"No argument, Lieutenant," said Asher. "We are real fast running out of world back there."

"So I see," said Quinn. He turned and started away at a quickening pace. "We won't make the café. We'll meet the others at the park."

Their fast walk turned into a steady jog as Quinn led them down first one side street and then a second, bringing them quickly to a larger avenue that he knew should take them to the vicinity of their neighborhood park.

The occasional glance back showed him that the white wall was following.

He recognized the intersection up ahead. The cross-street should take them the rest of the way to the park. He was about to say so when he saw a figure run into the intersection and continue across. This was followed by another and then another.

It was the rest of the team. The first figure returned and waited.

"Good to see you, sir," said Costa. She handed him his backpack.

Church was right behind her. "Susan, my dear!" He gave her a hug.

"Time for that later," urged Quinn, then a mumbled "I hope" as he slipped into his pack.

"Yes, yes. Of course," Church said hurriedly, grinning broadly. Still holding Susan's backpack in place across one shoulder, he took Susan's hand in his own. "Let us be off."

Owen stood in the middle of the park. She turned slowly about, but saw nothing out of the ordinary.

She hadn't come here of her own accord. Something had brought her here. She assumed there had to be a reason. She turned about again, looking for some indication as to what that reason might be.

There were several benches scattered around the park. There was a picnic table. Over in one corner was a small playground with a swing set, climbing bars, teeter-totter, and a small, metal merry-go-round. The park was bordered on three sides by fir trees; a narrow street ran along the fourth side.

She looked over at the little playground. Was that here before? Owen had only been to the park once. She knew that Quinn liked to work on his maps here.

She looked closely at the playground. There was a little boy sitting in one of the swings. He hadn't been there a moment ago. He was looking right at her. She was sure of it. He wasn't moving, but he was looking right at her.

The little merry-go-round was turning. Slow, steady. She thought she could hear the screech of metal on metal as the six-foot diameter base plate spun slowly about on its central axis.

She started across the park, approached the playground. She stepped up onto the heavy timber that bordered the yard and then out onto the sand. She looked to her left, to the little boy in the swing. He was holding onto the chains with both hands. And he was looking at her. She hadn't seen him move, but his head was turned now and he was looking at her.

She forced herself to look away, looked to the merry-go-round. A simple metal platform with four waist-high handrails. It was still turning. Slow, steady. There was a faint *screech*, pause, *screech*, pause...

The team turned up the side-street, coming out of the main thoroughfare that held the café and across from the street they had taken to calling "The Neighborhood". To their left was the park. Asher, second in line behind Costa, could tell immediately that something was different.

There was something in the far corner of the park. From this distance, it looked like a children's playground.

"That's new," said Ramos as they stepped off the street and started across the lawn.

"I believe it is," said Asher.

As they got closer, Asher was able to make out the figure of a small boy sitting in one of the swings. From here it looked like he was staring right at them.

"Do you hear that?" asked Ramos.

Nothing at first, but then Asher thought he could hear a metallic screeching sound. It seemed to be coming from the playground. They continued to draw closer. There was a small merry-go-round just to the right of the swing-set. It was turning.

And then... just a shimmer at first, but then something began to take form, to take shape near the merry-go-round.

"Elizabeth," Asher whispered. He spoke louder then to the group. "It's Doctor Owen."

Owen was waving at them. She was near frantic. *Quickly, quickly. Hurry, hurry...*

Asher picked up the pace, stepped up beside Costa.

"Come on," he said. His walk became a jog. Costa started then, and then the others picked up the pace just to keep up.

Asher took a glance behind them. The world was disappearing. The houses across the street were gone. Beyond was a silvery-gray void.

Owen was indicating the slowly turning merry-go-round.

screech, pause, *screech*, pause...

Asher and Costa stopped beside it.

"Professor?" asked Costa.

"It sure looks that way." He held out a hand. "I suggest you lead the way, Sara."

Elizabeth Owen was pointing directly into the center of the merry-go-round. She looked at Asher, at Costa, and then pointed again, sharply.

The others were right behind them. Quinn was studying the children's ride, while the others were focused more on the specter of Elizabeth Owen.

"Doctor Owen?" Lisa asked. Owen gave her a sympathetic smile, then indicated the ride.

Quinn spoke matter-of-factly, with a hint of urgency. "After you, Sergeant Costa."

"Yes sir." Costa stepped up onto the small ride, maneuvered between the raised handrails and stepped assuredly into the very center.

A thousand tiny sparkles enveloped her, swirled about her in a cloud, and then she was gone.

The others followed one by one, stepping up onto the turning ride, maneuvering between the rails and moving into the center. One by one, they were enveloped by the cloud and disappeared.

On the other side of the park, the silvery-gray wall of nothing began to creep across the lawn.

"Quickly, Dr. Church," Quinn urged. "No time to waste."

Church nodded silent agreement, turned to Owen and bowed his head in a silent thank you. Owen smiled, then frowned and shrugged one shoulder.

Church stepped up onto the ride, moved into the center and was quickly enveloped by the shimmering ice-colored cloud.

Quinn offered Owen a quick, curt nod and followed the others to the next floor.

Major Connelly found Banister and Lake over near the tower, at the bench where the door into the structure had once been located. They had taken a liking to the spot.

They looked up from their papers at her approach.

"Good afternoon, Major," said Banister, hesitantly. There was something about her manner. Something was up. "Is everything all right?"

"I wanted to let you know that they've left twenty seven." She didn't sound as pleased by her own news as she might.

Lake remained seated, clutching his papers.

Banister stood up slowly. "Are they okay?"

"They all made it through just fine. Doctor Owen was there, she watched them go."

Major Connelly hadn't answered the question.

"Major?" There was concern in Banister's voice.

"I'm sure they're fine, Doctor Banister. I wouldn't worry just yet." This, despite her own worried expression.

Lake stood now. "What happened?"

"Yes, Major," urged Banister. "What happened?"

"I'm sure that it's nothing; just that... well, Doctor Owen hasn't been able to find them."

"What?"

"I am as perplexed as you."

Lake looked confused. "I doubt that. How could she lose them? Doesn't she just *will herself* to wherever they are and there she is?"

"It's not that simple, Doctor. She has no real power of her own. However," she conceded, "I do agree that is generally the end result."

"But not this time," stated Banister. It was not a question.

"She followed them to the next floor, but they had already moved on."

"So quickly? It couldn't have taken Liz that long to get there."

"A few hours at most. I asked her that very question."

"Is she certain they actually left the next floor?" asked Lake. "Is it possible they are still there?"

"She was quite sure they had moved on. They arrived and then left."

"Why doesn't she just follow them on to the next?"

And in that question lay Major Connelly's apprehension; the cause for the disquiet that Banister had seen in her manner.

Owen had attempted to continue after the team. There had been no sign. Unfortunately, she could not be certain that she was in fact travelling the same path they had taken. Was she even going to the same floors? Was she even in the tower?

The Adversary could be sending her anywhere.

And now... there had been no word from Dr. Owen for some time.

"That may well be good news," suggested Banister. "Perhaps she finally found them, is with them now, observing."

Connelly looked doubtful. "I do hope you are right, Doctor."

"Here I am attempting to calm <u>your</u> fears, when you were so concerned with mine."

"I certainly didn't mean to burden you."

"Not at all, Major," said Banister. He raised a hand and tapped his chin with a knuckle. "There is something else to consider in all of this. You understand, if they are indeed travelling the floors as quickly as you suggest, then they are finally making some real headway."

The hint of a whispering wind. A dark, blackened landscape, hot whorls of wispy gray smoke spiraling from burnt pits in the barren ground. The sky above, black as pitch but for the hundreds of small meteors trailing long, thin tails of fire.

Puffs of brownish black dust billowed up with each muffled footfall as they ran...

~ end of episode eight

Episode Nine
Storms

Prolog

Sgt. Costa kept up the steady pace as she led the team through the woods at a measured run. The world was gray, the air thick with a warm, drifting fog. From above, dull rays of light pushed through the mist and trees.

She leapt over a fallen, moss-covered tree, dashed left and skirted between two massive ferns. Up ahead then... a gleaming sphere in the center of a large clearing. She came to a sudden stop directly before it, waved the team forward.

Lisa Powell ran unhesitantly into the shimmering, ethereal globe and disappeared. Church and Susan followed, but Asher and Ramos stopped and took a moment to catch their breath, using the opportunity to look back behind them.

There was no sign of Lieutenant Quinn.

"Go, go, go," hissed Costa.

Asher took a last look back the way they had come, turned forward then and stepped into the portal.

Ramos faltered, reluctant to leave. "Sergeant," he pleaded.

"Go," Costa insisted.

The corporal glanced back into the woods one last time, desperately willing the lieutenant to make an appearance. The spears of misty rays of light stabbed through the canopy, the fog rolled slowly through the trees.

And there was a sound; a distant whispering murmur that crept progressively closer; ominous, menacing.

Swallowing the world...

"Ramos," Costa urged quietly, evenly. "We're done here."

Costa led the team along a sandy beach, the calm waves pushing gently up onto the shore. Above the distant horizon, three moons shone against a violet-colored evening sky.

A few moments peace...

A sound subtly crept up, little by little overwhelmed the soothing resonance of the soft waves.

A distant whispering murmur... ominous, menacing...

Corporal Ramos, bringing up the end of the line, stopped and looked back behind them. He spoke calm and matter-of fact.

"Here we go again."

They picked up the pace, taking it to an easy jog. Behind them, the distant, muffled sound steadily increased, swelling as a rolling, growing physical thing.

"Uh, Costa…" said Ramos, a bit more concern now.

She said nothing, but the team's pace quickened.

The world was a giant black and white chessboard.

Costa, Ramos, Asher, Church, Susan Bautista and Lisa each stood on their own square. Large, plastic chess pieces towered above them.

Costa pointed to an empty square. Asher moved forward, stopped on the indicated position.

Church looked guardedly toward an unseen horizon somewhere beyond the board. A moment later, Susan followed his gaze.

"Yes," she said. "I hear it."

"We're running out of time," said Lisa.

"What say we hurry up and win this thing," said Ramos.

Episode Nine / Chapter One

Asher stood just inside the mouth of the cave, one shoulder set comfortably against the rock wall, his arms folded across his chest. Inside the cave behind him, the others sat around a small campfire, their shadows reflecting as shifting silhouettes on the cavern walls.

In the world beyond, the night was near black, wet with a gentle but persistent rain. Moisture dripping from leaves and branches throughout the world, out there in the dark, created a continuous thrumming sound.

Susan Bautista stepped up beside him. She looked into the night.

"I don't think the rain is going to stop," she said.

"I think you're right," said Asher. He pushed off from the wall. He was protected from the rain by the overhang above him, but there was a light breeze blowing in and he could feel the moisture on his face. "But I'll take it."

Susan agreed. And yet, "It's still out there, Peter. This is but a short reprieve."

"And I'll take it," Asher repeated.

"Yes..." she said, glancing behind them at the others in the cave. "We were lucky to find shelter."

Asher smirked. "I put nothing that happens in here to luck."

"You think we were led here?"

"I think we were intended to find it."

Susan thought about that. She wasn't sure Peter was right, but she gave him a thin smile. "I'll take it," she said.

Owen sat in the wooden chair. It had a straight back and gently curved arms. The floor beneath her feet was black, smooth, stretched into empty black in all directions. There was nothing above her.

She held out a hand, reached out. She could just see it. There was a world out there, gray and wet; a flickering light in the distance. A campfire? She believed so.

And there... Peter. He was standing at the mouth of a cave. The campfire was in the cave behind him. And there was the rest of the team.

A sound then... again that horrible sound... and then the vision was ripped from her; yet again.

She was alone in the black. She gripped the arms of the chair; waited for it. The visions rushed at her, swept past her, floor before floor before floor, reaching back the way she had come, the way they had come, waves that washed away space and time swept across the floors, leaving in their wake... nothing.

There... the team was just ahead of that nothing... running, running, rushing from floor to floor. They stumbled into a field that was enclosed on all sides by a thick, dark forest. They hurried across to the wall of trees on the opposite side. Quinn had been with them then.

Quinn saw Owen. She was standing just in the tree line, off to the left. He looked back behind them, then up ahead to Sgt. Costa. She was leading the way, slowing as she reached the trees. She stepped aside and waved the others through. She looked at Quinn.

Quinn looked from Costa to Dr. Owen. Owen was holding out a hand, beckoning.

It was time.

Quinn understood. He took only a moment, slowed and drifted left... toward Owen.

"Lieutenant," called Costa.

Lieutenant Quinn ignored her.

Behind him... the sound... that horrific sound... eating the world.

"Sir, please!" Costa took a single step forward.

Quinn reached Dr. Owen.

Sgt. Costa watched as the running figure of her lieutenant transformed into an opaque cloud and then quickly dissipated.

Elizabeth Owen sat alone in the dark. The wooden chair had a straight back and curved arms. The floor beneath her feet was black, smooth, stretched away into the void...

Susan came out of the cave with a cup of thick broth and handed it to Asher, who was still standing watch at the entrance. He smiled a silent thank you and took a tentative sip.

Not bad. He took a deeper swig.

"Nice to not eat on the run," he said, took another swallow.

"Thirteen floors in five days," said Susan. She shrugged a shoulder. "I've been keeping track."

"Uh, huh. And *whatever that is* following right behind us all the way." They had been chased by this phenomenon going all the way back to the neighborhood floor. It was always a bit different, but it was always the same thing; a wave of nothing sweeping across the landscape.

"Dr. Church was describing it as the absence of space and time."

"I heard," said Asher. "That's what it leaves behind. But what is it?"

"It reminds me of a weather front."

"Portending one helluva weird storm." He finished his broth, stared absently down into the empty cup. "Not bad."

"It's the last of it."

"About the last of everything," said Asher. "Not much time for shopping these days."

"Speak of the devil." Susan said darkly. She was looking at the distant horizon beyond the trees.

"Damn. Waddya think? Coupla' hours?"

Susan half turned and spoke back into the cave. "Uh, Sergeant Costa? Would you come out here, please?"

Sgt. Miller followed Captain Adamson into the Quonset hut and quickly pulled the door closed behind him, shutting out the violent storm that was continuing to rage outside. They were both soaked through. The heavy rain beat down hard on the corrugated metal shell of the command center, creating a loud, deep thrumming sound.

Miller pulled at his wet clothes as he took in the room.

Adamson had already reached General Wong and Major Connelly over at the coffee counter. Johansen and Carmody were sitting at the radio station, and Dr. Banister and Dr. Lake were at the round table in the middle of the room.

"I'm afraid we're all out of dry towels, Sergeant," said Banister.

"That's all right, Doctor. I'll make do."

Carmody could see that there was nothing new and so turned back to Johansen. He flipped a switch and set the receiver in the cradle.

Another comm window come and gone.

He spun slowly about in his chair, saw that Adamson and Miller were back. Miller had moved over to the corner, had taken off his shirt and was wringing it out.

"Looks like no change," Johansen said to Carmody.

Carmody nodded in the direction of Adamson. "I expect that's what the captain's telling the general."

Johansen looked about the room. The Quonset hut was small, would have been crowded all by itself with just a table, a couple of desks and counters. Bring eight people inside and a pounding storm outside, and Johansen was one more claustrophobic sardine in the can.

Not that there was a choice. The storm had been extremely destructive. Dark, intense rain and violent winds had been beating at them non-stop for a week. All the tents were gone. Moving about outdoors was dangerous. The command team was confined to this last small structure.

Johansen looked up at Carmody, then again at the others in the room.

Miller had put his wet shirt back on, walked over to the coffee counter. Adamson and the general moved aside to allow him access, continued their discussion as Major Connelly listened in. The doctors meanwhile were in their own conversation at the table.

Everything seemed okay.

Yet something was off; something beyond the unrelenting storm outside and the command team waiting it out here in the Quonset hut.

Johansen had yet to make contact with the team inside the tower, but that wasn't new.

There had been no word from Doctor Owen for almost a week. Again, that wasn't new.

So what was bugging him?

He tried to shake it off.

But he couldn't.

Over at the coffee counter, Captain Adamson slowly lowered his cup. He hadn't yet taken a drink. He looked studiously about the room, a look of unease on his face.

Wong and Adamson had quit talking. They were both looking in Johansen's direction. Wong looked then to Carmody, to Banister and Lake, then uneasily, uncertainly about the room.

Okay... obviously not just me, thought Johansen. *The world is wrong.*

"Hey, Johansen..." Carmody said, more than a hint of quiet worry.

"Yeah. Yeah, I know..."

Episode Nine / Chapter Two

Elizabeth Owen walked the long, wide hall at a comfortable, casual stride. The way was bordered on both sides by towering Roman style columns spaced two paces apart. Darkness lay beyond the columns and hovered overhead as a dark shell over the world. The floor shimmered bright black and her footfalls echoed out away from her before fading into a dull, soundless nothing.

She had been walking a long time; thinking about that, it struck her that she couldn't remember what she had been doing before she had been walking this hall.

She had been walking the hall for as long as she could remember.

How odd...

The corridor stretched ahead of her as far as she could see. She slowed and glanced back over her shoulder. She saw only the column-lined way stretching away behind her... as far as she could see.

She faced forward again and returned to her easy pace. She continued on for what seemed to her like a very long time.

And then up ahead, far up ahead... there was something there, something at the corridor's vanishing point on the horizon.

As she drew nearer, she could see that the hall ended at a massive set of double doors standing twice her height.

Nearer still, she saw that a figure stood before the great doors.

It was the Acolyte. He was dressed as a monk, or rather as Owen's interpretation of how a monk would dress; heavy, hooded robe tied at the waist with a thin rope.

"Welcome, Doctor Owen," said the Acolyte. He pushed back the hood. "I am so glad you could make it."

"How could I not? I mean, really. How could I not?"

"I don't understand." It was obvious that he truly did not understand.

"Nevermind." Looking about, there was only the column-lined corridor and the massive set of doors. "Where am I? Why have I been brought here?"

"The Great Hall."

Owen looked back the way she had come. Seeing this, the Acolyte smiled amiably and shook his head.

"That is but the corridor, Doctor Owen. The Great Hall lay beyond the doors."

"Ah. I see. And... why am I here?"

"I'm sorry. I thought that was clear, considering where you are."

"Not really, no."

"The Creator of All Things," stated the Acolyte matter-of-factly.

"Yes?"

The Acolyte reached behind him and gently pushed the left door open a few inches. Dull, gray light shone through the opening.

"I'll be waiting here for you when you have finished," he said. He stood patiently waiting, hands clasped, fingers intertwined.

"Oh. Yes." Owen stared blankly at the slight opening, looked side-glance at the Acolyte. "You're not going in?"

"My presence was not requested." He took another step to one side. "Doctor Owen?" he urged.

Owen approached the door. She stopped. "He's in there?"

"He is seldom anywhere else."

"I see," she grumbled uncertainly.

When Owen still hesitated, the Acolyte attempted as best he could to encourage her forward.

"I do not believe he would have brought you before him if the intent was to do you harm, Doctor Owen."

"Yeah? Just what would lead you to that conclusion?" she asked sardonically.

"Observation only," said the Acolyte. He had yet to get the whole sarcasm thing. "I consider the path that has been set before you to now."

"Uh, huh..." Owen pushed the door fully open. "I feel so much better now..."

All eight members of command were squeezed around the table in the middle of the room, having pulled up the assortment of desk, counter and table chairs from around the Quonset hut. They had just finished their breakfast, meager half rations from four now-empty packets of MREs that were scattered about the table amongst cups, mugs and water glasses.

"Well, that wasn't as satisfying as it might have been," said Banister. "But it could be worse."

"It soon will be," said Dr. Lake. Even at half rations, they would be out of food in another day at best. They all knew what the cupboards looked like.

Teams had begun going out into the storm twice each day looking for the strewn contents of the long-gone mess and supply tents. At the time the storm had first swept in, there had been stores of food and cases of packaged MREs in both tents. So far, they had found a few cans and one rain-soaked cardboard box of rations.

And that was about to run out.

"Man, I could really use some coffee," mumbled Johansen. He picked up his water glass, lifted it in a mocking toast to the group, and took a drink.

"A crisis if ever there was one," said the general, holding up his own water-filled coffee cup. "Which will be resolved."

"And best we be about it," said Captain Adamson. He stood up, and with that so did the others. They set about putting on what foul-weather gear they had; what they had initially brought in or what had been found on their recent searches.

Two teams of three would be heading out. Johansen and Dr. Lake would stay behind to monitor the radio. The two who remained in the command center changed with each search.

Captain Adamson pulled on an olive-drab rain jacket as he walked over to Banister, who was struggling to get into a pair of plastic rain pants. The jacket and pants had both been found on previous excursions.

"You're with me this trip out, Doctor, if that's all right." Adamson held Banister by his elbow to prevent him from falling.

"Thank you, Captain," said Banister. "Yes, that will be fine."

Adamson called over to Carmody. "You're with us, Private."

"Yes sir." Carmody was putting on a clear plastic poncho. It looked homemade. There was even duct tape.

General Wong waited at the door for the others of his own team, Connelly and Miller. He glanced over at Adamson.

"You have your mission, Captain," he stated.

"Yes sir." Adamson's team would go to the tower, turn right and follow the base to the first corner, then the second corner, then move away from the tower a hundred yards and return along the same route.

Wong's team would head for the tower and turn left.

Wong and Adamson both knew how important it was to find supplies soon. They were doing what they could to minimize the dangers in these searches, but they were quickly running out of time.

The rest of Wong's team joined him at the door. They left without another word.

Carmody joined Banister and Adamson, absently tying twine around her waist to keep the poncho in place.

"You ready?" Adamson asked her.

"Honestly?" she asked with an anxious grin.

Adamson took that as a yes, looked over at Johansen and Lake, standing now near the radio station counter.

"Keep a light on, Corporal."

"Yes sir."

Carmody started toward the door, spoke over her shoulder in Johansen's general direction. "Back in a flash."

"I'll be here." Johansen watched the second team leave.

Lake returned to the table and pulled out a chair. Johansen pushed off the counter.

"Say... Doctor Lake..."

Lake waited a moment, and when Johansen didn't finish, "Yes?"

"I was just wondering... about the others."

"What about them? I wouldn't worry."

"No, no... not these others. The others."

"The others," Lake said thoughtfully. "By others, you also do not refer to those in the tower."

"No sir."

"I see."

"There was a platoon here with us. I remember 'em. A platoon."

"And now there's just the eight of us," the doctor stated, quite matter-of-factly.

"They were here, with us, and now they're... not. Am I missing something?"

"No, Corporal. You are not."

"They were here? Right?"

"I do not believe so."

"But Doctor Lake, I—"

"Those no longer with us were never really here."

Johansen sighed, shaking his head tiredly. "Oh, I just knew you were going to say that. I so wish you hadn't, but I knew it. I just knew it."

"I do apologize."

"Yeah, well..." Johansen frowned. "I figure you're right. It does make you wonder..."

"Ah... you are concerned as to what this might suggest about the rest of us."

"Yes sir."

Ramos leaned into the iron gates and pushed them open, the sound of screeching hinges reaching out into the silent, eternal night. He stood to one side, his back to the wrought iron bars, and the rest of the team walked into the cemetery. Once inside, he pushed the gates closed and followed after them, now bringing up the rear.

Costa led the way up a tall, grassy slope to the top of a round hilltop. She stopped then and waited for everyone to gather together.

"We'll take five here." She slipped out of her backpack and set it down against a nearby tombstone.

The others did the same, and several sat down alongside their gear. Ramos took up watch nearby, Costa walked a few yards off and took in the scene, planning their route across the floor.

The cemetery stretched away to the distant horizon, a succession of low rolling hills illuminated only by a thick, cloudy band of stars sweeping across the night sky. Church stepped up beside her. He was about to ask a question when the sight laid out before them took him aback.

"My. That is quite the view."

"Yes it is," she said softly, self-conscious at disturbing the quiet. She looked back the way they had come, beyond the gate that stood at the foot of the slope. It was black beyond the gate and the stone fence that ran to either side of it. For the moment, all was peaceful.

It wouldn't last, of course. The storm was out there, somewhere, eating the worlds.

Costa glanced once to Church before looking again to the rolling hills of the cemetery. As with every floor, there was no indication as to where the portal might be. The clues would come when they came.

But what was most important with these most recent floors was first to put distance between themselves and the oncoming storm front. Costa would have the team strike out straight ahead, directly away from the cemetery gate. She set her sights on a structure that sat on a hilltop several hills distant, little more than a silhouette against the dark purple horizon.

"We could all do with a few hours rest, Sara," said Church, speaking up at last. "When you feel it safe to do so, of course."

"Of course, Doctor." Costa nodded in the direction of the distant structure. "There. That mausoleum or whatever it is."

"That will do." It was now Church's turn to look back behind them. The world remained quiet. "An adequate distance, I should think."

"That was my thinking." Costa looked to the rest of the team as she started back toward her pack. "Sorry, people; movin' out. Up and at 'em."

She went over to Ramos, her gear in hand. It looked to Church like she was advising the corporal of her plans, of their route and destination. Ramos was nodding silently as he listened.

Asher slipped into his backpack as he approached Dr. Church.

"A mausoleum," he said. "I hope this isn't more of the Adversary's warped sense of humor."

"Sir, I believe we are in the very heart of his sense of humor."

Ramos stepped past them and started downslope into the heart of the cemetery.

"Ya' comin'?" he asked without looking back, without slowing.

"After you, Doctor," said Asher.

"No, no Peter... you first." Church grinned playfully. "I insist."

Asher gave an exaggerated nod in thank you and followed Ramos. Church and the rest of the team trailed along behind and they started down the hill.

The lush green lawn beneath their feet was well-manicured, and the sweet-scented aroma of freshly mown grass hung in the air. There were hundreds of tombstones scattered across the landscape, all shapes and sizes, some quite old, some appearing fairly new; all were cast in an eerie pale glow, the world illuminated by the hazy band of stars that spread across the otherwise empty, inky black sky.

Many of the tombstones were blank. Some had names carved into their faces, nothing extraordinary. There were a few with phrases: 'beloved wife', 'our sweet daughter', 'I told you I was sick'. When there were dates, they were often only years, though occasionally more. None were dated more recent than the nineteen fifties; not even the newer tombstones.

Ramos led the way; quiet, calm and a steady pace. No one was very talkative. There was something about walking a cemetery at night... they didn't like the quiet, but there was something unsettling about breaking that silence. There were a few hushed comments, an occasional awkward attempt at humor, but for the most part they kept their heads down and walked, one behind the other.

They crested one hilltop, then another. They stopped at each, confirmed their direction, and took in their surroundings. The cemetery continued all the way to the horizon; to all horizons. Behind them, as yet no sign of the impending storm.

Ramos held a protective arm out to one side for those behind him to stop. He continued forward another step.

"Wait here." He continued forward then.

Costa moved quickly past the others. "Wait here," she said, echoing Ramos, and she followed after him.

Together they approached a heavy, sarcophagus-like stone. The words 'Your guess is as good as mine' were carved on the marble face. Sitting comfortably atop the stone was a very thin, extraordinarily pale man, dressed all in black. He had jet-black hair, a small tuft of beard on a pointed chin, and the short bony nubs of a pair of horns protruding through the pasty skin of his forehead.

Asher and Church stepped up beside Costa. Lisa and Susan weren't far behind. Church took a moment to study the smiling face of the strange being looking down at them.

"Our friend the Acolyte," he stated calmly, to no one in particular.

Costa frowned at Church, glanced quickly at the others and then again to Church. "I thought I asked you to wait."

"Oh, I believe we are well beyond that sort of thing, Sara. Don't you?"

"I do now," she grumbled. She focused her attention fully to the being sitting on the stone.

"What do you want?" she asked him.

The Acolyte lifted his hands before him, rolled his long, bony fingers, and then slowly, delicately pointed a yellowed, claw-like fingernail randomly at one person and another, "eenie, meenie, miney, and... mo," stopping decisively at Susan. Those who were nearest her quickly closed ranks to stand between her and the Acolyte.

The demon chuckled happily. "Oh, dear, dear, my dear comrades. My fellow travelers. I joke with you. Yes I do. Most certainly."

"We are not amused," Church said frostily.

"Not even a little bit," said Costa. She repeated then, "What do you want?"

The Acolyte responded lightly, "Sergeant, my sergeant, I drop in only to say hello. I wish to see how you are doing."

"Hello," she responded dryly. "We're doing fine. Kinda' busy. Maybe we'll talk later."

"No." The Acolyte hopped down from the stone. There was a dramatic change in his tone and manner. "We talk now."

"All right," said Costa. The Acolyte's sudden personality shift had taken her by surprise.

"But really, do make it fast," said Asher. "We are in rather a hurry." He gave a gesture to the scene behind them. The storm front had arrived. A great wall of gray nothing was just now pushing onto the floor.

"Yes," said the Acolyte. "Yes, the *storms,* as you call them. The very matter to which I will speak."

"I thought you just dropped in to say hello," said Ramos.

The Acolyte kept his attention on Sgt. Costa. "My master, the Creator of All Things, would acknowledge his distress as regards the phenomenon."

"I'm sorry," said Costa. "Perhaps I'm just thick-headed, but I don't get it."

"Apologies," the Acolyte said with a slight bow of the head. He continued. "The *existence* of the... *storms*... was not intended. The Creator of All Things is attending to the issue."

"You mean make them stop? That would be appreciated."

"Yes. He will make them stop."

"Great," said Ramos. "He should get about doing that."

The Acolyte continued to speak to Costa. "The Creator of All Things would also recognize your stalwartness, Sergeant Costa; your strength during these unfortunate times."

"Simple desperation," stated Costa.

The Acolyte bowed his head again and offered another thin smile.

"The Creator of All Things would know otherwise," he said gently. He slowly then, very slowly, faded to a thick mist, the last wisps drifting on the hint of a breeze.

"Well. That was interesting," Asher said thoughtfully.

"Quite," said Church.

"How so, Doctor?" asked Ramos. "They screwed it all up and now we're the ones paying the price."

"It means, Corporal Ramos, that our host is not infallible."

Episode Nine / Chapter Three

Carmody was leaning back in one of the chairs near the radio station, her clasped hands resting on her belly, her thumbs tapping together in rhythmic boredom. She looked over at Dr. Banister, over at the table looking through the same paperwork for the thousandth time.

What could possibly be so fascinating?

She spun slowly about in her chair.

They were pulling radio monitoring duty while the others were out on the afternoon search runs. The day was warm, the wind and rain continued to beat down on the metal shell of the Quonset hut with a loud, deep drumming.

Carmody continued to absently spin... around... around...

"Hey, Doc... how about we play some cards?"

Banister set a sheet of paper aside, studied the next. He spoke distractedly, without looking up. "I don't believe we have playing cards, my dear."

Carmody held her feet to the floor, stopping the spin. "I could make some."

"A most worthy endeavor," said Banister, just as distracted.

She sat up straight, leaned forward. "Yes sir. It most certainly is."

Carmody started to stand, to go in search of materials to make her deck of cards, when something caught her attention. She wasn't quite sure at first just what it was, but then...

The thrumming noise... the deep drumming of the wind and rain pounding against the Quonset hut... it was fading.

It had been with them for days, beating down on the corrugated metal, creating a hollow bass that was almost physical, pressing in on chest and skull.

Its sudden absence was strangely unsettling.

Carmody and Banister stood in unison, slowly, warily. They walked to the door without saying a word. Hesitating a moment, Banister reached out and turned the knob.

The world outside was wet and ugly gray, but the rain had stopped and the wind was dying down. Blowing debris was slowly settling wherever the last wafts of breeze would take it.

"Oh, my God. Doctor... what is that?" asked Carmody.

There was something on the wall of the tower. At this distance, it was impossible to tell what it was; from here they were discolorations, blemishes...

"I don't know, my dear," said Banister. "Let us find out."

Major Connelly, Sgt. Miller and Dr. Lake stood several dozen yards back from the tower, took another step back, and then another, their heads tilted back, as they tried to take in the entire view.

Seven vortices... appearing like open wounds on the wall of the tower; each a spinning, shifting whorl of gleaming, shimmering mist.

Banister and Carmody joined the others.

"What have we here?" asked Banister, conversation more than query.

"I just got here myself, Banister," said Lake. "Could be tears in the membranes between worlds."

"Portals," Banister stated.

"Yes, portals," said Carmody. "They look like portals."

She and Banister had seen a few of them up close and personal. To her, these looked a lot like portals.

One of them was set low to the ground, very near the base of the tower. Two others were thirty feet up and a few yards apart. The remaining three were set in the wall well above these.

"You figure that one opens to the first floor?" asked Carmody, indicating the one at ground level.

"It could lead anywhere, my dear," said Banister.

"Perhaps we should find out," said Miller. He started forward, took a several steps toward to the portal.

"And if there be no way back?" asked Banister.

Miller moved to within three paces of the vortex and stopped. He looked back at the general, and then to his captain.

Connelly stepped up then and held the sergeant by the arm.

"No," she said firmly.

"Major?"

"There's something wrong." She wore a haunted look. "It's wrong. It's... empty. There's nothing there. Gray. Empty gray..."

"Perhaps they are not portals at all," suggested Lake. He was still quite partial to the torn membrane theory.

"I believe Doctor Banister is right," said Connelly. "I believe they are indeed portals. But they were not meant to be. They are... wrong."

The monk-robed Acolyte was waiting for Dr. Owen when she stepped back through the set of double doors following her audience with the Adversary. He said nothing to her at first, simply held out a hand indicating they should walk.

They started down the walkway, the vast emptiness visible beyond the tall columns lining either side.

"I apologize for being unable to stand with you," he said at last.

"No problem," answered Owen quietly, nearly absent of emotion.

"It was not an option."

"I get it," she mumbled.

They walked in silence for some time. The walkway was as long on the return as it had been on her journey in. Behind them, the great doors were eventually lost beyond the vanishing point on the horizon, ahead the corridor stretched as far as she could see.

"I trust it went well," the Acolyte said at last.

"It could have gone better."

"That's too bad." He knew just what she was feeling. "Such is the way of it."

"He can be quite abrupt," she grumbled.

"Yes, I suppose that is so," the Acolyte spoke easily now. "But then, there is much demanding his attention just now."

"I don't think that was it."

"You don't." The flat comment was an observation more than a question.

"No. I don't," she stated.

They continued on for another along while. She thought she heard something then, very briefly; as if a whisper, heard from a distance. She slowed her step. She listened.

It was nothing. She went on.

"He's a real pompous sort, if you ask me," she said. "Rather full of himself."

"Well," the Acolyte just managed to get out. This was getting uncomfortable. "He is Creator of All Things." A clear justification, he thought.

"Uh, huh... yeah. About that. I think I'll stick with 'Adversary', all the same to you."

Quinn stood atop the thirty-foot wide pillar, a stone cylindrical tower standing in the dark, rising up from the depths of the void that surrounded him. Several hundred yards distant, he saw a row of columns spanning the black, hanging in empty space like a bridge across the void.

There was some illumination within the columns. It was as though this ethereal bridge was some strange, alien corridor spanning an alien abyss.

Voices then, reaching across the night. Quinn couldn't make out the words. He took a few cautious steps nearer the edge of the top of the pillar. He listened.

Someone was talking. He took one last step, now just a foot from the edge. He looked up and down the column-lined corridor in the distance.

Movement; two figures walking the corridor. At this distance, it was difficult to know for sure, but Quinn was fairly certain that one of them was Dr. Owen.

He called out to her. His voice sounded muffled, dulled and lifeless. It rolled out a few yards and faded away. He called out once more. There was no sign that she had heard him. She continued along the walkway, moving further and further away.

Quinn watched until he could no longer see them; waited until he could no longer hear Dr. Owen. He stepped back then, backed his way to near the center of the pillar.

He was alone.

Church worked his way up the slope to the top of the hill. The mausoleum was a small building, a single room with a wall of individual tombs set opposite the front door that now stood open. The doctor stopped at the foot of the steps and turned about, looked out across the cemetery world. From behind him came the voices of several others of the team inside.

Asher came around from behind the building. Neither had found any signs of the portal during their brief searches.

"We'll have to move on soon, Peter," said Church. He was still looking out across the cemetery. The gray wall of the storm took up the entire horizon.

They had been at the mausoleum a little over two hours. By his calculations, Church believed they had less than that amount of time remaining.

"It hasn't stopped," noted Asher. "It hasn't even slowed."

"It would appear the best efforts of our distraught host are as yet ineffective."

"I'm still not a hundred percent sure that this isn't just one more tiresome game the Adversary is playing on us."

"It may well be, Peter," said Church. "I certainly do not trust the Acolyte, but in this case I do believe he spoke the truth."

Asher let out a barely audible *hmpth* and said nothing.

"You do not believe he spoke the truth?" asked Church.

"It isn't that," said Asher. "I was just thinking... either this is a game that sooner or later we're going to lose, or we're in the hands of a being not in control of the universe that he's created, and this universe is trying to kill us."

"Ah, Peter," Church sighed. "You don't get invited to many parties, do you?"

"I can't say as I do."

Susan appeared in the open doorway behind them. She managed to maintain a quiet calm.

"Doctor Church, Peter. We found it."

"You found it?" asked Church. Curious only, he was not yet ready to voice true enthusiasm.

"The portal. We found it. It's here."

"Really?" Asher asked cautiously. He wondered about Susan's subdued enthusiasm. "That's great."

"Um... yeah... you're probably not going to like it."

They were all crowded into the small room that made up the interior of the mausoleum. Several of the individual tombs set into the far wall had been unsealed and stood open.

Susan casually indicated one of them.

"It's in there," she mumbled.

Episode Nine / Chapter Four

Banister was sitting on a bench outside the command center Quonset hut, legs crossed, hands clasped at a knee. The day held a hazy, filtered sunshine and a thin evaporating mist hung just above the pavement.

Banister was looking at the tower across the way. The earlier seven vortices set into the side of the tower had increased in number to twelve. And this was just on what they had taken to calling the front wall of the tower. There were as many on each of the other sides.

He couldn't help but wonder how many more before the integrity of the tower was compromised; or more accurately whatever it was the tower represented was compromised.

Banister was certain that whatever was happening could not be intentional. This didn't look or feel like the Adversary's doing. Quite the opposite; it was very likely a serious threat to what the Adversary had created.

And by inference it was a danger to those within the tower.

Sergeant Miller, Carmody and Johansen approached the Quonset hut, each carrying overstuffed olive-drab colored canvas bags. They set the bags on the nearby picnic table.

"Doctor Banister, we're eating well tonight," said Carmody. She opened her bag and reached in, pulled out a couple of plastic MRE packages with one hand, a can of peaches with the other.

"Wonderful, my dear." Banister stood from the bench and walked over to the table. "I must say, I'm a bit surprised that you were able to find such treasure after all this time."

"We stood with our backs to the tower and just walked away. We walked until there was nothing but gray, and then we walked some more."

"We weren't all that sure we'd find our way back, to tell you the truth," said Johansen. "We lost sight of the tower; lost sight of everything."

"Are the others back yet?" asked Miller.

"Not yet, Sergeant." The second team had gone the other direction along the base of the tower, and Lake was inside monitoring the radio.

"Right." Miller turned and looked at the tower, noted the vortices. "Looks like another one on this side as well. We counted two more on the east wall."

"There they are," said Johansen. He nodded at a group of three figures in the distance. They had come around from the far corner of the tower and were walking in the shadows along the base, were already a third of the way before they had been noticed.

They stopped midway along the wall. From this distance, it looked to those outside the Quonset hut that a new vortex was forming directly beside the other team. This one though appeared a flat gray, without the shimmering, gleaming whorl of the others.

"Oh my God," said Carmody. "What are they doing?"

As they watched, General Wong, Captain Adamson and Connelly stepped into the opening.

The general stood just inside the jagged opening in the wall, the outside world clearly visible on the other side. Adamson and Connelly stood to his left, Adamson mumbling something to himself, Connelly apparently at a total loss for words, mumbled or otherwise.

Set before them was an expansive, empty floor; concrete walls, concrete pillars set in perfect rows forty feet apart.

The dimensions of the floor matched those of the outside.

It was a space waiting to be used.

"What the hell?" came from behind them. General Wong turned half about and saw Carmody standing in the opening. Sergeant Miller and Doctor Banister were just coming into view behind her.

"What the hell, indeed," said General Wong, turning forward again.

Ramos wriggled his way through the crevice and crawled into the open. He stepped away as the others clambered out of the narrow fissure, studied the scene around him looking for signs of potential danger to the team.

Behind them was a steep cliff rising up from a sandy beach. Directly ahead, a narrow promontory of rough, rocky terrain reached several hundred yards into the sea from the shore.

Near the end of the rugged cape stood a tall lighthouse; the ocean beyond was a greenish blue, calm and quiet but for the steady roll of low, gentle waves upon the shore and foaming against the rocks.

The clear sky overhead was a light blue and the single midday sun was warm but not hot. A slight breeze carried a thin, cooling mist.

"It appears peaceful enough," offered Susan.

"Downright pleasant," said Church. "Which I find to be most unsettling."

"I hear ya', Doc," said Ramos. "It always comes with a catch, and that's for sure."

Costa looked up and down the beach, then to the end of the cape toward the lighthouse.

"I don't know about water and food, but at least there's shelter."

"But what about the storms?" asked Lisa.

"We have nowhere to go, Lisa."

"Very well, then. Let's hope that was it," said Church. "That they don't follow us."

"Yes sir," Costa sighed.

A shadow then, danced across the rocks around them. Something overhead... they all looked up, searching. Not a cloud in the clear, blue sky.

Ramos saw it first...

"Oh, crap..."

Quinn stood near the center of the flat top of the thirty-foot diameter pillar. His arms were folded across his chest, and he was frowning.

The Acolyte sat along the edge, his legs dangling over the side. He was wearing his demon persona, dressed in black, the nubs of a pair of horns on his pasty forehead.

He had been there for some time, jabbering away about one thing or another, about nothing in particular. At first, Quinn had been glad for the company, whomever or whatever this creature might be. But as time wore on, he had been getting on the lieutenant's nerves.

Holy Jesus, this has to be another test...

"Oh, Lieutenant... did I tell you? I was conversing with Doctor Owen the other day. A lovely lady, really. A dear, dear lady. I do believe she brings out the best in me. The same for you?"

"Not exactly," grumbled Quinn.

"No?"

"No." Quinn folded arms contracted slightly. He was looking across the empty, black void to the column-lined corridor in the distance. It just hung there in space.

"That's too bad. It really is." The Acolyte was leaning out over the abyss, hands planted on the pillar, legs swinging absently. "A lovely lady."

"How nice."

"She was concerned about you. No idea what happened to you after she directed you from the floor some ways back."

"And what did you tell her?" Quinn was wondering that himself.

"That you were well." The Acolyte leaned just a bit further out, looked curiously down into the black emptiness below as he tapped his heels together. "Oh, hey, I think I see your friends," he said chirpily.

That caught Quinn's attention. He unbound his arms and looked now directly at the Acolyte.

"The team?"

"Yes, yes... the team." The Acolyte was carefully eyeing the void. "I'm certain it is them. Yes, yes."

Quinn took a single step closer. "Are they all right?"

"They are arriving on another floor."

"That's good," Quinn said hopefully.

The Acolyte said nothing for a few long, drawn-out moments. He pursed his lips then and shook his head slowly, sadly.

"Geez," he sighed. "Can't they ever get a break?"

~ end of episode nine

Episode Ten
Lighthouse

Prolog

The lighthouse stood at the end of a long, rocky outcropping that jutted out from the thin strip of beach into a blue-green sea. Ramos stood watch on the catwalk outside the lantern room near the top of the lighthouse. The lantern inside was dark.

The ocean was calm, the low waves foaming amongst the rocks of the cape, pushing gently onto the sandy shore on either side of the promontory. The shoreline ran along the base of a steep cliff, the cliff wall high enough that even from the catwalk Ramos wasn't able to see what lay beyond.

For them, the world was the lighthouse, the rocky cape, and the narrow bands of sand to the north and the south.

Asher stepped out onto the catwalk and up next to Ramos. He was there to relieve the corporal on watch.

"A little early, aren't you, Professor?"

"Maybe a minute or two," said Asher. He looked out at the horizon, then glanced down at the rocks a hundred and fifty feet below. "Anything interesting?"

"Nothing to speak of. Our feathered friend was here a bit ago. Checked us out, then headed back north."

Asher looked up the north beach. But for the gently rolling waves, there was no movement, land or sky.

"Did he look hungry?" he asked.

"Seagulls always look hungry."

"True enough. I expect a gull with the wingspan of a condor must look downright ravenous."

"He looked that way to me." Ramos had stood by the open door, ready to head inside should it come at him. He hadn't dared to leave the doorway until the giant seagull was well out of sight.

Clicking sounds, the scrambling clacking of hard shell on rock, rose up from the rocks below. Asher leaned over the rail and tried to identify the source.

"What the heck is that?"

"Crabs," Ramos stated calmly.

"What?" Asher didn't see anything.

"Crabs," Ramos repeated. "Bunch of 'em. Shells gotta be three feet across. Showed up about twenty minutes ago."

Asher straightened. "When I asked about anything interesting, crabs with shells three feet across didn't come to mind?"

"Okay," shrugged Ramos. "Nothing 'cept for that."

Episode Ten / Chapter One

Sgt. Miller stood at the table unpacking the few supplies they had recovered during their latest search, handing the items one by one to Carmody, who was taking them and storing them away in the nearby cabinet.

There wasn't much left to find, and the only items they came across these days were out in the gray, well beyond the shadow and sight of the tower.

The only other person in the Quonset hut was Johansen. He was leaning against the coffee station counter, cup in hand.

"Where are the others?" Miller asked him.

"I think some of 'em went back over to the tower," said Johansen.

"That place is creepy," said Carmody.

When an opening into the first floor had appeared in the side of the tower, everyone had expected to see the alien jungle that had covered the floor so many months earlier, and for it to extend far beyond the outer dimensions of the tower, just as it had before. What they had found instead was an empty space, concrete floor and walls and ceiling, support pillars set in rows, the individual posts spaced forty feet apart.

It looked more than anything else like an empty parking garage.

"C'mon, Carmody, it's not so bad," said Miller, half-smirking. "A few well-placed lamps, toss down some throw rugs..."

"I don't think so."

Johansen cleared his throat. "Seriously, though. I was thinking maybe we should move in there. It's probably safer."

"Are you kidding me?" Carmody thought it had to be more sarcasm, but it didn't sound that way. "We have no idea what that floor will look like five minutes from now. It could change into anything, take us anywhere; or just disappear."

"And? You think it's any different out here?"

Banister and Lake were far into the cavernous expanse that had been the first floor, near the farthest wall. They each had a flashlight, the fuzzy beams stabbing into the gloom, occasionally dancing across the ladder that was mounted on the wall and led up to nowhere.

"Just what are you expecting to find today that we didn't find yesterday, Banister?" asked Lake.

"Things change, Lake," mumbled Banister. Unfortunately, the ladder and its lack of destination were just as they had been the day before. His retort fell flat.

He swung the focus of his flashlight around and back out onto the floor.

Empty. Empty and yet more empty.

He ran the beam of light up the nearest support pillar, taking it from the floor base up to the ceiling.

"Most peculiar," he said.

"Peculiar. Yes. But just at the moment, I don't see how that helps us. No answers. I don't even know what question to ask."

"I have a question for you, my friend," said Banister. "Query... what does this say about the Adversary? I mean, this can't be the natural state of the floor."

"Why not?"

"Because, my dear Doctor Lake, there is no actual floor, as there is no tower. All is generated illusion, created to give us a landscape upon which to traverse. Therefore, what we see before us is as much a creation as what it replaced. Yes? Yes? So... why this?"

"It looks incomplete. Unfinished."

Banister shook his head. "What I see is a *placeholder*. I do not believe this was planned. The Adversary was confronted with something he hadn't expected. This was his response."

"And the opening?" asked Lake. The portals that were appearing all over the walls of the tower were gateways, similar to those taking the team from floor to floor, but the opening here into the first floor was an actual hole in the wall; whether that wall and that opening be real or illusion.

"Most odd," said Banister. "The implication is that the Adversary intended for us to enter. If that be true, then why?"

"That should have been your first question, Banister." Lake focused his flashlight back to the ladder, lifted the beam up the sixteen feet to the ceiling. "There's nothing here. Nothing."

Church came out of the stairwell and down into the ground level room of the lighthouse. Susan was sitting at the heavy wooden table. Light shone through the few narrow windows and through the open doorway leading outside.

"Our room is much roomier than I expected," said Church. The lighthouse had two bedrooms. "Yours?"

"Comfortable enough." Susan was sharing a room with Lisa and Costa.

Church went over to one of the counters set along the curved walls and began opening cabinets. He rummaged through the team supplies and took down a cup. He filled it from one of the canteens that were sitting on the counter.

"I hope we have the opportunity to take advantage of those rooms." Church sat opposite Susan. "Oh, to have real beds again. It takes me back to that quiet neighborhood, houses and bedrooms, that little café; so many floors ago, now."

"That was the floor where we first saw the storm."

"Ah... yes." Church lost the smile he had been wearing and a frown formed. "There was that, wasn't there?"

Costa appeared in the open doorway, stepped through and into the lighthouse.

"You two interested in doing a little exploring?"

"Absolutely, Sara," said Church. "Where are we headed?"

"North. Follow the beach."

"That shouldn't take long," said Susan. "We can see where it ends."

That was true. The beach ended well within sight of the lighthouse, where the cliff wall met the water.

"I want to take a look at the cliffs en route." She also wanted to see if there was a way to get beyond the beach.

Susan started toward the stairwell. "Just let me get my jacket."

"No rush." Costa sat on the corner of the table. She looked down at Church. "Were you two taking a trip down memory lane?"

"More a casual stroll," said Church. "How about you, Sara? Has this quiet locale generated any pleasant reminiscing? Brought back any mind-repairing memories?"

"Not as yet, I'm afraid. I haven't sat still long enough for anything to take hold."

"Oh, you must, my dear. Doctor's orders."

"I'll see what I can do," said Costa. She smiled warmly at the elderly doctor. Doctor Church gave her a comforting pat on the leg.

Sgt. Costa had done well as the leader of the team, taking over after they lost Lieutenant Quinn more than twenty floors back, the storm right on their heels every foot of the way.

Church could see that the marathon over these score of floors had begun to take their toll on the sergeant. She was an incredibly strong person, but the responsibility must weigh heavy. She looked very tired.

"Thank you, Sergeant Costa," he said, breaking a long silence. "Sir?"

"I appreciate all that you've done for us."

Costa looked uncomfortable. "My pleasure, Doctor."

She stood then as Susan returned from upstairs.

"Okay, we're off."

Ramos and Lisa had finished their search of the south beach and were working their way back. Ramos walked with a five-foot staff, an item that he thought might come in handy should that giant seagull make another appearance.

Ramos had an uncomfortable suspicion the big bird had it in for him.

Here the strip of beach was forty feet from the water's edge to the base of the cliff. The fine sand was dry and didn't look to have spent any time under water. Either they were at high tide or there was none.

They approached the rocky promontory that divided the shore into north and south beaches, climbed twenty feet up the rocks before starting toward the lighthouse. As they got nearer, they could hear the native crabs scrambling about just out of sight.

"Home, sweet home," said Ramos.

They worked their way around the lighthouse and met Sgt. Costa, Church and Susan Bautista coming out.

"Excellent timing, Ramos," said Costa.

"Hey. I am just that good." He handed her the staff. "Nothing to see to the south, 'cept some nice scenery."

Costa weighed the staff in her hand. It was heavy but had a comfortable balance.

"Not bad workmanship, Ramos."

"I'm not finished." In truth he had done little more than cut the heavy stick to length and peel off the bark. He indicated the north. "The gull went that way."

In answer, Costa held the staff at the ready, then gave a quick nod and started away. Church and Susan followed. Ramos and Lisa watched them work their way down the rocks to the sand and then start north up the beach. They could hear Dr. Church saying something to the others, but couldn't quite make it out over the muffled background noise of the waves rolling up onto the beach and foaming against the rocks. There was the whisper of breeze coming in from the sea.

That and the click-clack sound of the giant crabs scrambling about amongst the rocks and small tide pools.

Lisa put a hand on her belly. "I'm feeling mighty hungry, Jerry. Dinner will come none too soon." Lisa was the only member of the team to refer to Ramos by his first name.

"I doubt tonight's dinner is going to help much with that empty belly, Lisa."

"I will gratefully accept whatever is on the menu." She knew that would come to very little. There wasn't much left.

Ramos thought on that and began shaking his head. "No, no, no. I think it's high time we got us a brand new menu. After all, we got us a brand new restaurant."

The north beach was a few yards wider and a few hundred yards longer than the south beach. Other than that, there wasn't much difference between the two. The sand was fine and mostly dry; the low waves were gentle and constant and didn't travel far up onto the shore.

The cliff wall rose nearly two hundred feet from the beach. It was steep, rocky, with occasional tufts of hardy vegetation.

There didn't look to be much to discover along the way, but one never knew. Surprises, both good and bad, could show up anywhere; as could the portal that would take them to the next floor.

Costa walked distant enough from the cliff to be able to see most of it without having to tilt her head back too far, yet near enough to be able to study the details hidden in the shadowy crevices. Church and Susan walked beside her, a step or two nearer the water. Church managed to study the cliff while also conversing with Susan about one thing or another, with an occasional comment or question to Costa.

He was for the most part able to keep the conversation pleasant, but the subject of the storm inevitably came up. He suspected it was over, though there was no way of knowing that for sure. It seemed to him that if it was to make another appearance, it was long overdue, at least as evidenced by past experience.

Also from past experience, the storm had always come onto each floor from the same direction as they had entered, as if following their path through the portal. And each time it had arrived, they had seen it coming, there had been at least the opportunity for a timely escape; such was the way of the Adversary.

Church pointed out that their arrival through the portal onto this floor had come from the cliff wall and onto the lighthouse cape. As such, should the storm follow them, it would come from the cliff.

This would leave very little warning. None at all, in fact.

Very unlike the Adversary.

It would make no sense.

All this led Church to the optimistic view that the storm was at an end.

His dear friend Wes Banister would no doubt have been quick to highlight the flaws in this thinking.

He sure missed the old fart.

A shadow danced across the sand. They all glanced up at once.

It was the seagull circling about overhead. Wings outstretched, it had to be ten feet across.

"Quickly, this way," said Costa. She led Church and Susan to the base of the cliff, hoping this would provide at least some protection.

Their backs against the rock wall, they watched as the gull landed clumsily not far away. It folded its wings and began to strut up and down the beach near the water's edge. It appeared to be searching the wet sand for food, though it always kept an eye on the humans.

After a time, its investigative wandering had it drifting just a little inland, further from the surf and nearer the cliff, eyes always side-glance to the humans.

All too intentional so far as Costa was concerned. She stepped forward and stood protectively in front of Church and Susan, holding the staff at the ready.

The seagull continued to drift nearer, now a dozen feet from the humans. When holding its head up straight, it stood almost five feet tall, near to Costa's shoulders.

Costa took a quick step forward and jabbed the staff in the bird's direction. It flapped its wings and hopped backward, was quickly out of range of the staff. Costa took another two steps forward and jabbed again. Again the gull leapt back and away, squawking loudly; an angry, screeching cry.

Costa kept at it. She took another step and made ready. The giant gull stomped backward, quickly took a short step forward and gave Costa an indignant look.

Costa pointed the staff threatening in the gull's direction. The bird suddenly spread its great wings wide and made to assault the human. Thinking better of it, it turned aside, beat its wings and took flight.

Church and Susan moved away from the cliff.

"Well done, Sara," said Church.

"That is one big, scary bird," said Susan.

"Eh, not so bad," said Costa with a playful smirk. "You've seen one monstrously ginormous seagull, you've seen 'em all."

"Uh, huh. No doubt."

"Yes, well, now that we have that taken care of, shall we continue? Doctor Church? Doctor Bautista?" Before starting out again, she looked back toward the lighthouse...

Asher watched Costa fend off the seagull from his position on the lighthouse catwalk. Once she had chased the bird off, the sergeant looked back toward the lighthouse. She must have seen Asher, because she lifted her staff over her head to show that all was well. He acknowledged her with a wave of his arm. Costa and the others started again up the beach.

Asher walked around the catwalk to stand facing seaward. He leaned forward with his elbows on the rail, clasped his hands and took in the scene. With the background white noise of surf and wind, it was easy to imagine this little bubble of universe was all there was.

Elizabeth Owen walked the circle of catwalk around from the back side and joined him. An invisible specter, she stood beside him, leaned against the rail beside him.

"Hello, Peter," she said, looking out at the same sea he was looking at. "Nice view."

Asher took in a long, easy breath, let it out slowly as he glanced down at his hands, unclasped them and rubbed them together. It had the feel of a response, though of course he couldn't hear her, couldn't see her.

She went on. "I'm so glad to see that you're safe. I had my doubts for a while there."

Asher leaned forward and looked down. There was movement over near a collection of tide pools near the base of the promontory, down where rock met sand.

Several crabs were scrambling about.

Asher turned away, straightened, put his hands on the rail. Looking to his right, he could just make out the three figures of Costa, Church and Susan far up the north beach.

Way back when, back before the storm and everything had gone crazy, Asher and Susan had been cautiously growing closer. Since then however, there hadn't been much opportunity to pursue the relationship further.

Not that he had a clue what that meant.

But it would have been nice to find out.

Maybe now; maybe now that the storm had stopped, if it had stopped, maybe they could stop running and start taking the floors at a more normal pace.

Normal.

Now that was funny. How the hell had he come up with the concept of normal in this place?

He sensed movement below, leaned out and looked down.

Cpl. Ramos had come out of the lighthouse and was walking in the direction of the end of the cape. He had something in his hand. From way up on the catwalk it looked like a length of pipe.

Owen also leaned forward and glanced down. She shook her head and frowned.

"What the hell is *he* up to?" she sneered. "Certainly can't be anything good."

"Corporal Ramos," Asher called down. "Is everything all right?"

Ramos stopped and looked back, looked up to the top of the lighthouse. Asher was leaning out over the rail.

"Everything's fine, Professor."

"What's up? Do you need any help?"

"The cupboards are bare." Ramos held up the pipe. "I thought I'd fetch us some dinner."

"Mmm... crab meat," Owen said conversationally, as if she might actually be part of the conversation. "Wish I could join you."

"Crab meat?" Asher called down.

"Yes sir, that's the plan." Ramos turned back around and continued away.

Asher considered, finally called out again. "Ahead another couple of paces, then to your left and down to the tide pools."

"Thank you, Professor."

"Okay," Owen sighed. "So every now and then the little corporal isn't completely intolerable."

Quinn was sitting on the edge of the top of the pillar, looking down into the empty black below. He wasn't really looking for anything in particular... just looking. There wasn't much else to do.

The Acolyte claimed he could see the team down there, but that could have been a lie.

Right on cue, the Acolyte settled in beside Quinn.

"Hello, Lieutenant," he said. He leaned forward and looked down into the void. "Kinda quiet, eh?"

"As a graveyard," Quinn said darkly.

"How very macabre," said the Acolyte.

"That's kind of the point."

The Acolyte went quiet as he thought about that. "Ah... I believe I understand," he stated calmly. "A comment on circumstances, yours and theirs."

"Yeah, sure."

They sat quietly side-by-side for a few moments.

"Feeling down, are we?" said the Acolyte finally. He continued to stare into the black. So did Quinn.

"What was your first clue?"

The Acolyte gave a sage smile, nodded. "We each have our role to play, Lieutenant Quinn. We may not know fully what that role is, but I can assure you, each is important. Take comfort in that."

"Yeah, sure," Quinn said again.

Something down in the black caught the Acolyte's attention.

"Oooh... crab legs."

Episode Ten / Chapter Two

The team sat around the table in the main room of the lighthouse, eating a meal of crab and a little of what remained of their supply of dried fruit. Only Susan wasn't present, as it was her turn on watch.

As they pulled apart strips of crab meat, they went over what they had found during their surveys of both the south and north beaches. Neither search had revealed a way beyond what beach they could see. The cliff wall turned into the water at the end of each beach and effectively closed off their exit. Ramos had attempted to work his way around, clambering out onto the rocks of the cliff, but he didn't get far and that route appeared hopeless. Costa had fared no better.

As for ways up the cliff wall, there were several possibilities, though none appeared particularly promising, and they all looked far from safe. Closer examination might reveal a potential route.

And as for the portal off this floor, there was as yet no clue as to what form it might take.

It all seemed very reminiscent of the floors they had travelled before the storm.

After thirty minutes of bantering back and forth, Church stood and began preparing a plate for Susan. As soon as Asher realized what the doctor was doing, he offered to take it to her. He took the plate and left by way of the staircase.

Susan was circling the catwalk and Asher stepped through the door just as she reached it.

"I come bearing gifts," he said, and held the plate out to her.

"How thoughtful, Peter." She took the plate and they both moved to the rail.

"A team effort," said Asher. "I just brought it up."

"Then thank the team for me," said Susan. "And thank you."

The sun was setting and the sea was just taking on the orange and red hues of sunset. They admired it as Susan ate her dinner.

"Wow," said Asher. "I should volunteer for the evening shift."

"It is beautiful, isn't it?"

The conversation drifted to some of the sights they had seen on other floors, for despite all the terrible things they had faced over these fifty-eight floors, some of the scenery had been spectacular, going all the way back to the alien jungle of the very first floor.

Susan stopped in midsentence, leaned against the rail. She was looking out to the horizon.

"Peter... do you see that?"

A thin, dark band had formed on the horizon, just formed, just visible. It cast a strange outline against the sunset.

"A storm front?" asked Peter.

"Maybe. I really can't tell."

"It can't be our old friend. Church is right. That would come from the other direction. From the cliff."

"So then, a good old fashioned tempest?"

"With our luck? It's probably a hurricane."

Major Connelly stood alone in the middle of the empty first floor. What little light there was came in through the opening in the distant wall, splashing onto the concrete floor and not quite reaching her.

She was trying to make sense of what was happening to the tower, and she wasn't getting very far. From what she knew of the Adversary, and from what little she had discerned of the Adversary's plans, none of this should be happening. It didn't fit. It didn't fit at all.

Which left her with the uncomfortable thought that this wasn't the Adversary's doing.

But how could that be? The Adversary was the creator of all things.

And now, of late, Connelly had started seeing things, hearing things; pictures of places she had never been, words and thoughts that were not her own.

Something was happening, and it frightened her.

Owen came quietly up beside her. Connelly hadn't seen Dr. Owen in a very long time, yet for a few moments they stood silent, saying nothing.

"I love what you've done with the place," Owen said at last.

"Thanks. I was going for simple."

"Success."

There was an uncomfortable pause.

"So... should I ask?" asked Connelly. "How is the team?"

"I had a helluva time running them down. Then I lost 'em. Then I found 'em again."

"And?"

"They're well enough, considering. Oh... Quinn's no longer with them."

"What? Is he all right?"

Owen shrugged. "I suppose so. They lost him back on, geez... thirty seven?"

"Thirty seven? Where are they now?"

"Fifty eight, I think."

This took Connelly by surprise. "That's good news, at least. Very good news. Isn't it?"

"Sure." Another shrug. Owen hesitated then, shifted uneasily. "I don't know if you know this from your connections and what-not, but I was hauled up before the Adversary a while back."

"No. I didn't know. To be honest, I've been pretty much out of the loop; out of all the loops. You've been my only connection to anything outside the command center here, and I thought I'd lost you."

"Hey, I thought I'd lost me too."

"Well, it's good to have you back, Doctor Owen. So, what about your audience with the Adversary?"

"It was weird. Really weird. You know, I think I was on the top floor."

"I expect you were in the Great Hall. From what little I know, the Adversary seldom leaves the Great Hall."

"So I heard."

"I've never been in the Great Hall."

"But what about, you know... you and the Adversary?"

"He speaks to me sometimes. At least... he used to."

"What, like a voice in your head?"

"Yes. A voice in my head."

"But you've never seen him?"

"No." Melancholy shadowed Connelly's face. "That makes you kind of special."

"I'm not too sure about that," said Owen. "I met him and I'm not sure I saw him."

"I don't understand."

"I don't think I do either." Owen thought a moment, tried to come up with the right words to describe her experience in the Great Hall. "Nothing was quite real. It was like... a strangely colored cloud; lots of clouds, drifting into and through one another. It wasn't really a hall. It wasn't a room or even a place. It was lots of places all at once. Reality within reality within reality."

"And the Adversary?"

"He was there. I knew that, without coming face to face with him. He was one of the realities. I sensed his presence. Amongst chaos, he was order." Owen hadn't been looking at Connelly. She turned to her now. "I had no choice but to move toward that calm. I was drawn to it."

"And he spoke to you then?"

"Yes. I have to do something. I'm pretty sure I have to do something." Owen became very confused. "Quinn. I have to... I have to..."

"Doctor Owen? Are you all right?"

"Yes. Yes, I'm fine," Owen said dreamily. "I have to go."

Quinn had taken to doing exercises; push-ups, jumping jacks, running in place, squats. At the moment he was doing sit-ups, lying on his back near the center of the top of the pillar. He was midway through his set when he noticed a figure watching him from a few yards away.

It was Dr. Owen.

Quinn finished out another half-dozen sit-ups before stopping. He lay back, looking up into the black, his hands clasped behind his head.

The black hadn't changed. It was still black everywhere beyond the top of the pillar that was his home, his prison. The only break in the void was the column-lined corridor in the distance, hanging suspended in nothing.

It had been a while since he last had company It had been days at least, probably weeks, since the Acolyte had last dropped in for a visit.

Quinn spoke without turning his head. "Doctor Owen," he said casually. "To what do I owe the pleasure?"

He could hear her soft footsteps as Owen approached.

"The Adversary sent me," she said.

Quinn sat up with a quiet groan, brought an arm out and leaned on one hand. "Are you working for the man, now?"

"I was drafted."

"Drafted..." Quinn leaned slowly to one side and came to his feet. He stretched and worked his shoulders and arms. With a nod of the head he indicated the corridor. "That was you I saw a while back, wasn't it?"

Owen appeared to notice the corridor in the distance for the first time. She stepped away from Quinn, walked toward the edge of the pillar top.

"Probably," she said at last. She was captivated by the sight. She spoke over her shoulder. "Have you been here long?"

"Ever since you took me off the floor."

"Right." Owen turned and looked back to Quinn. "Would you like to get away for a bit?"

"Am I being drafted now?"

"Most definitely."

"Then how can I say no?"

"You won't want to." Owen took the several steps back toward Quinn. "They don't know it yet, but the team is in a fix. You can do something about that."

"Me?"

"I'm as surprised as you, Lieutenant."

"Oh, nothing surprises me anymore, Doctor Owen."

Good point, thought Owen. She looked around them as she continued.

"The floor the team is now on wasn't planned, wasn't part of the original, how would you say... *itinerary.* From what I'm able to gather, they were rerouted there by the Adversary in order to take them out of the path of the storm."

"He rescued them?"

"I guess so," Owen shrugged. "The storm wasn't his idea. He can't have it finishing off our people before he has the chance to do it himself."

Quinn wrinkled his brow, studied on what that meant. "That makes some twisted sense. Setting aside the thousand questions it brings to mind, the one I gotta ask first is... if they're out of the path of the storm, what does the Adversary want me for?"

"Yeah... that one took me a bit to sort out, myself," said Owen. "You see, that floor they're on? It's kind of a dead end. There is no exit. You? You are going to go get one."

Asher was in the lower bunk in the men's sleeping quarters midway up the lighthouse. He had managed a few hours sleep, was awake now, and was staring up at the springs of the bunk above him.

The room had two sets of stacked bunks, a small desk and chair, and a narrow window. The door to the stairwell stood open. A cool breeze worked its way up the stairwell whenever both the door downstairs and the door leading out onto the catwalk upstairs were open. Some of that breeze would occasionally find its way into the sleeping quarters.

Asher heard thumping on the stairs, looked over just in time to see Lisa rush past on her way down. She was breathlessly calling out "You gotta see this, you gotta see this."

By the time Asher got to his feet and made it to the door, Lisa was hurrying back up the stairwell. Costa and Church were right behind her.

Following them up the stairs, Asher reached the lantern room and then stepped out onto the catwalk. Costa and Church were standing beside Lisa. Asher moved up next to them and looked outward.

The storm front was much nearer, which created the illusion of drawing the horizon nearer. But Lisa was pointing to something else.

There was a dark shadow set against that gray storm wall.

It was the silhouette of a ship.

Episode Ten / Chapter Three

Ramos slowly worked his way up the cliff face. Every handhold, every foothold, was a carefully thought-out action. Even with that, there had been more than a few close calls, and he was less than halfway to the top.

Lisa watched from the beach below, far enough out from the wall of the cliff that she could observe, on occasion recommend a move to the left or the right. They had planned Ramos' route before he started up, but he hadn't been able to follow that path exactly as charted.

At the moment he was in a difficult spot. There had been no way for him to continue up. He had hoped to move to the left, thought he saw a foothold; but it had broken loose from the wall when he put weight on it, and his handhold had been precarious at best. It had been a desperate scramble to stop his slide and now he simply held on tight, the side of his face planted firmly against the rock.

Lisa called up to him. "I don't think this is such a good idea."

"Yeah, well... let's discuss the merits of the plan once we get my butt down from here."

"Maybe I should go get someone."

"No..." Ramos sighed tiredly. "I'd rather you didn't."

"Why not?" She thought a moment. "You didn't tell Sergeant Costa what we were going to do, did you?"

"Not in so many words."

"Jerry..."

"Not a problem," he droned. "Not a problem."

He very slowly took his weight off one foot and tried to find a foothold further down. The left side of his face was still pressed against the cliff, his cheek slid against the rock as he eased down a few inches.

He saw a shadow drift across the face of the cliff.

"Oh, crap," he grumbled.

Costa leapt out of the stairwell and ran across the main floor room of the lighthouse. She rushed past Church and Asher at the table on her way out the door.

Both Church and Asher were on their feet and hurrying after her. Something was obviously terribly wrong.

Scrambling down onto the beach, they could see Lisa in the distance. She was throwing rocks and sticks and Ramos' wooden staff up into the air, all in the general direction of the oversized seagull.

The giant gull wasn't having much trouble avoiding the flying objects as it focused its attention on something that was on the face of the cliff.

As they got closer, they could see that the something was *someone*, and that someone was clinging to the cliff wall as the seagull attempted to get at him, pecking at him with its beak and pushing at him with its feet. The gull wasn't having an easy time of it, as it couldn't hold its position very well. The protruding rocks of cliff were getting in the way of its flapping wings. Still, it was managing to reach in enough that at any moment Ramos would be torn loose and would plummet to the beach below.

Costa reached Lisa, picked up the staff and threw it like a spear at the seagull. The dull tip of the staff struck the bird on the body just under the wing and the bird squawked in pain and in anger. It moved off, but quickly hurled itself back toward Ramos.

Asher had a fist-sized stone, threw it toward the bird, leading enough ahead of it that the stone hit home just as the bird reached Ramos.

By then Costa had retrieved the staff. Using staff and stones, those on the ground eventually managed to drive off the bird.

Once the world had calmed down, they looked up toward Ramos. His shirt was torn, his hair was mussed, and he wasn't moving.

"You alive up there?" asked Costa.

It was quiet for what seemed a very long time. They finally heard Ramos mumbling loudly, the side of his face still against the cliff wall.

"I'm going go to have to get back to you on that, Sarge."

"Uh, huh. While you're figuring that out, get your ass down here."

Asher came down the stairwell and into the main room. He tossed a shirt to Ramos, who grabbed it out of the air and began putting it on.

"Will he live?" he asked Susan. Susan was closing up the small first aid kit.

"The cuts aren't as bad as they look. I expect he'll have some painful bruises, though."

"Well deserved," said Lisa. She and Church were sitting at the table opposite Ramos.

"Thanks for the shirt, Professor," said Ramos, buttoning it. "The next floor needs to be a shopping mall." He turned to Lisa. "And I apologize. I am sorry."

"Hey, I'm easy. Sergeant Costa, on the other hand..."

Costa had not been happy. Ramos and Lisa had been directed to inspect the cliff face more closely, to search for anomalies. There had been nothing in the instructions about trying to climb it. Any such attempt, should it come, was to be a full team affair.

Costa came into the room from the stairwell. "And the court martial will have to wait."

No one knew whether or not she was joking; all chose to ignore it.

"The storm front?" asked Church.

"Much closer. An hour or two out at best."

"And the ship?"

"Oh, it is definitely a ship. And it's still there, pushing in ahead of the front."

"There has to be a twisted sense of humor underlying all this," said Susan. "We finally land on a world where the storm doesn't follow us, and what are we faced with? A storm."

The sky turned a dark, menacing gray. At first a deep quiet lay over the world, but then the winds came, and then the heavy rain. The sea grew angrier, violent waves began crashing against the rocks.

Asher and Costa stood on the catwalk, straining to get a better look at the ship. The others were just inside, looking out from behind the glass wall of the lantern room.

"Sara... I think that's our freighter," said Asher.

"You mean from the second floor? It can't be."

"I'm pretty sure."

"But... *the second floor*. And a different ocean."

"I know. But look at it."

The ship was a thousand yards out, looked to be at the mercy of the tide and the wind. It continued to approach the shore.

"I don't see how, Professor," said Costa. "Similar, maybe, but I don't think it's the same ship."

The door behind them opened and Church came out onto the catwalk. He struggled against the rain and wind as he pushed his way to the rail.

"Peter! Sara! It's the freighter! Our freighter!"

The ship rose high on the crest of a wave, pitched broadside and slid back.

"And it doesn't look like there's anyone at the wheel," said Asher.

Lieutenant Quinn stood before the wheel in the wheelhouse of the decrepit old freighter. Elizabeth Owen stood beside him. Beyond the forward windows, they could just make out the lighthouse through the heavy rain. It was coming up fast.

Quinn's handling of the wheel seemed to have little effect on the ship's direction or its momentum. One moment the shore lay directly ahead of the bow, the next it was gone and they were looking at open sea. Quinn continued to turn the wheel to port, to starboard, and back. The beach, the rocks, the lighthouse... continued to draw nearer.

Episode Ten / Chapter Four

The ship ran aground on the north beach less than a hundred yards from the rocky promontory on which stood the lighthouse. Despite the wind and rain, everyone left the safety of the lighthouse and worked their way down onto the sand. As they trudged up the beach, there was more speculation about this being their freighter.

"Of course it is," said Ramos. "Just look at it."

"We'll have to wait until we're aboard to know that for sure," said Church. They had never actually seen their freighter from a distance, as they had never left the ship.

"How do we get on board?" asked Lisa.

Church stopped, frowned, and studied the hull of the ship. It was a long way up to the twisted railing and the deck. The forward third of the ship was up on dry sand, leaving most of it still sitting in the water.

"There," said Costa. She pointed to the hull about two thirds of the way toward the stern.

"What is that?" asked Asher.

"Ladder." Costa took a few steps nearer the water. The waves had settled some, but the wind continued to create whitecaps.

The ladder was recessed into the hull itself, the rungs within a narrow cavity. It began up near the deck and ended a few feet down below what would normally be the waterline. Now though, the ship beached as it was, the bottom rung of the ladder was at least four feet above the waves.

Ramos looked to Costa, who gave a sharp nod. He walked into the water, worked his way along the hull until he reached the ladder. The water there was about two feet deep, though the rolling swells sometimes added another foot or two to that and made it difficult to stand in place.

Ramos reached up and just managed to take hold of the first rung in the ladder. He pulled himself up to the take the next, and then the next. Only then was he able to bring one foot up and gain a foothold.

Okay, so several of the team might benefit from a boost up…

Seeing that the water depth was at least manageable, the others started into the surf. Reaching the ladder, Costa and Asher stood to either side and, steadying themselves against the swells, helped the others up onto the ladder.

Stepping off the ladder and onto the deck, Asher looked fore and aft and quickly turned to Costa, coming off the ladder right behind him.

"Looks awfully familiar to me, Sara."

"Yes, I see what you mean."

They followed after the others, Susan directly ahead of them. They were all going into the lounge, which had been the common meeting area for them so many months ago.

Ramos came from somewhere forward just as Asher and Costa reached the door to the lounge.

"There's no one in the wheelhouse."

"Naturally," sighed Costa.

In the lounge, Church was standing near the table, tapping at the surface with his fingertips. He and Banister had spent quite a bit of time sitting at this table.

Susan and Lisa were over at the bar, where Ramos had once had their radio set up, back when they had a radio. Susan saw something in the small trash bin next to counter. She bent down and brought out an empty can of spinach.

"Remember these?" she asked.

"Ah geez, the spinach," groaned Ramos.

"Well, well… there's little doubt now," said Church.

"It followed us here?" asked Lisa.

"I doubt it took the same path," said Ramos.

"That's not what I'm suggesting, Jerry."

"So…" Susan wondered aloud. "If this is the same ship, might the portal in the hold be here as well?"

"That portal took us to the ghost town," said Lisa. "Wouldn't we end up all the way back on the third floor?"

"Oh, dear… there's an unsettling thought," said Church. "I suppose the answer very much depends on just how this freighter got here. And why."

"Before we start making vacation plans, let's take a look in the hold," said Costa. "The issue may be moot."

They were fairly confident that they were in fact alone on the ship. Nonetheless, while Costa took Church and Susan down to the forward hold, she sent the others to investigate the rest of the ship.

The crew's quarters looked just as they had left it, including their unmade bunks; small rooms set along a narrow hall, the larger captain's quarters at the far end. There was even the chair that had been left in the hall that those standing night watch had used during their time on board.

Finding nothing else, Ramos led the way then to the mess, supply, and finally to the engine room. There was no sign that there had been any visitors since they had last been aboard the freighter.

"It sure is peaceful," noted Ramos. "I'd forgotten just how quiet it was on this old heap."

"You mean other than the sea monster?" Lisa asked pointedly.

"Right. Sorry." Ramos straightened, uncomfortable. The rear hold of the freighter had been where they had lost Ray Do, Lisa's friend.

"It's not all that quiet," said Asher. He was looking up, as if he could see through the metal to the world outside the ship. Even down here in the bowels of the freighter, he could hear the strong winds and heavy rain. It was getting worse. The heart of the storm had followed the ship ashore.

"It sounds like a hurricane out there," said Lisa.

"Time we joined the others," stated Ramos. He turned about and retreated back through the door, leaving the others to follow.

Costa, Susan and Church stood on the metal walkway twenty feet above the hold.

"It's dry," said Susan.

"The bow of the ship is aground above the water," said Costa.

Church lifted a hand and raised a finger. "But if you will recall, my dear, the water in this hold did not come from the sea outside. It was fed from the lake beyond the portal."

"The lake outside the ghost town."

"Exactly."

"But if there's no water here in the hold, that means there's no portal," said Costa.

"Or the portal is here still, but it is no longer opening to the lake." Church started toward the steep, rickety metal stairs that led down to the floor.

Susan was leaning against the rail, carefully studying the hold below. "I don't see anything, Doctor Church," she said.

"Come, come, my dear. Let us take a closer look." Church moved quickly to the stairs and led the way down onto the floor.

As they started across the hold, Costa placed a gentle hand on Church's arm.

"Take it slow, Doctor," she said. The words echoed hollowly throughout the hold.

"Yes, Sara. Of course." He slowed his pace just a tad, and the others followed suit.

There really was nothing to see. The great cavernous chamber was empty, bulkhead to bulkhead. They stopped. Church turned about, his eyes taking in everything. He was looking for something, anything... a flicker, a shimmer, some indication that something was there.

"Well, this is very disappointing," he sighed at last.

Susan placed her hands on her hips and frowned. "What do we do now?"

"I don't know, Susan." Church shook his head and started forward again. He took a step, and then another. "I suppose we must—"

Church vanished. He was there, and then he was gone.

Costa held her arms out wide. "Everybody freeze."

"Oh my God," said Susan, a hushed cry.

"What the hell?" came from behind them, from up on the walk.

Costa turned and looked back. Ramos, Asher and Lisa had come into the hold.

"Go get our stuff, Ramos," Costa called up.

Up on the walk, Ramos turned to Asher. "A hand, Professor?"

"Of course."

"Lisa, you wait here."

Lisa was looking numbly down at those on the floor of the hold. Ramos placed a hand on her shoulder.

"Lisa? How 'bout you go down to Costa? Wait for us there."

Lisa nodded, said nothing.

Ramos and Asher worked their way up from the bowels of the ship and eventually out onto the open deck. The storm had definitely gotten worse and they were quickly soaked. They made their way over the side and down into the surf, now white and foamy and churning violently.

It took another several minutes to make it the hundred yards up the beach and up the rocks to the lighthouse. Once inside, Asher went upstairs to gather gear from the two sleeping quarters while Ramos collected the supplies from the cupboards.

"Make it fast, Professor," Ramos called up to him. He was piling everything onto the table. "Only what the two of us can carry."

Only moments later he heard the thumping of footfalls on the stairs and then Asher was coming out of the stairwell. He had three backpacks in each arm.

Together they stuffed what supplies they could into the already half-filled backpacks. Once these were closed and secured, they each took three, wearing one and carrying two. They grabbed up the utility belts and were back out the door and into the storm.

The giant seagull was waiting for them.

It stood six feet from the door, head hunched low against the wind and rain, and warily eyed the humans.

It looked miserable.

Asher and Ramos stepped out onto the metal walkway above the hold, soaking wet and struggling with the assortment of backpacks and utility belts. They set the gear down beside them and looked down to the floor. The others had moved away from the center of the hold and were gathered directly below them.

"There you are," said Costa, looking up at them. "I was about to go looking for you."

"Sorry, Sara," said Asher. "It is really, really bad out there."

"And we had to say good-bye to our friend," said Ramos.

"Problem?" asked Costa. She waved for Ramos to drop the packs down to her.

"Nope." Ramos began lowering the packs over the rail and dropping them down to her one at a time. "Not once we stepped away from the door."

"It was the oddest thing," said Asher. "Damn bird just wanted out of the weather. He almost got stuck squeezing through the door."

The team began sorting through their gear as Asher and Ramos came down the steep stairs. Costa had her utility belt on and was putting her arms through the shoulder straps of her very wet backpack. "Who ever heard of a seagull afraid of bad weather?"

"Like the professor said, Sarge," said Ramos. "It is really bad out there. I mean, like end of the world bad."

"We've been feeling a little of that down here," said Lisa.

A deep, hollow rumbling sound of creaking metal reverberated throughout the freighter and down into the hold.

"And hearing it," said Costa. "Perhaps we should be going."

"And if we end up back on the third floor?" asked Ramos.

"Let us hope our assumptions are correct and that doesn't happen," said Asher. "We can't stay here."

"And we have to find Doctor Church," Susan stated firmly.

"Absolutely," said Costa. She took several steps back toward the center of the hold, stopping well short of where Church had disappeared. She looked to Ramos. "Corporal, if you please."

Ramos hesitated a moment, took a deep breath and then started forward. He passed Costa. Another three steps and he vanished. Costa waved a hand for the others to follow.

The weather around the tower had taken a turn for the worse, pounding the Quonset hut with gale force winds and heavy rain. The general, Dr. Lake, Carmody and Johansen waited it out there in the command center while the others hunkered down in the tower's empty first floor.

The thrumming sound of wind and rain against the metal shell of the building had a soothing, almost hypnotic effect. General Wong was leaning back in his chair, half dozing. Dr. Lake sat opposite the general, lost in thought, one hand resting on the tabletop, fingers drumming.

Johansen and Carmody sat together off to one side. They were leaning close to one another, whispering below the level of the white noise. Whatever the conversation, it seemed to be quite genial.

The sound of the storm began to change. The wind eased first, and then the rain. General Wong opened his half-closed eyes, leaned slowly forward. Dr. Lake, staring down absently at his drumming fingers, stopped drumming. His gaze drifted up to the general, then to the corrugated shell of the Quonset hut.

Johansen and Carmody drifted slowly apart, Carmody sitting back in her chair, Johansen finally standing. He went to the door, opened it a few inches and peeked out. Sunlight streamed past him and into the room. He looked back at the others and smiled, then opened the door wide and stepped outside.

Everything was wet and shining bright. The sun was high in the sky and the world glistened. Thin mist began to form as the damp evaporated.

"It's beautiful," said Carmody. She came up beside Johansen. General Wong and Dr. Lake stepped around and walked several paces ahead.

"How many of these storms must we endure," grumbled Lake.

General Wong considered reminding the doctor of what this sort of thing meant. It was believed that many of the phenomena the team in the tower faced was often reflected to a lesser degree here at command. What then might the team inside have just... endured?

In the end, the general said none of that.

"Oh, we've all faced a lot worse out in the real world, Doctor Lake. We can take it."

"Hmmph," managed Lake.

Johansen stepped forward, moved up beside the general.

"What do you think that's all about, General?" he asked. Miller was standing just outside the opening into the tower. It looked like he was waving for them come over.

"Let's go find out," said the General. He started across the lot. The steaming mist hovering above the shining black asphalt grew thicker as the bright, warm sun evaporated the glistening moisture from the surface. Dr. Lake kept pace beside him; Johansen and Carmody followed behind, bantering back and forth about what this all meant and speculated about what Miller wanted.

Johansen and Carmody had continued to grow close. The general figured that if they had been out in the real world, they'd have been a couple by now. Here in this microscopic world where nothing could be assumed and anything could happen, forming deeper relationships must be difficult and tenuous.

Once they were within a comfortable distance for conversation, General Wong gave Miller an acknowledging nod.

"What do you have for us, Sergeant?"

"Best you see for yourself, Sir."

"Mystery. I like it. Lead on, then."

They followed Sgt. Miller into the cavernous first floor. The sudden change from bright sunshine to gray gloom was startling. It took a while for eyes to adjust, and so the general just followed the silhouette of Miller's frame and the sound of his footsteps, the others close behind.

"Ah, there you are." Banister's voice came from somewhere ahead of Miller. "So glad you could join us."

"But of course, Doctor Banister. What have you found?"

Sgt. Miller stepped to one side, allowing the general to step forward. Directly ahead stood Dr. Banister and Major Connelly. Directly behind them stood an elevator door.

"Oh, I see," General Wong said softly.

"Quite," stated Banister.

There was a single pinging sound, and the down arrow light set above the elevator doors came on, glowing a soft green in the gray gloom.

"Now this could get interesting," said the general. Everyone took a few steps back and watched.

And waited.

Several in the group began to shuffle anxiously. The general placed his hands behind his back, slapped hand against palm.

There was another soft ping.

The down arrow light went out.

The elevator door slid aside.

Inside the elevator car stood Lieutenant Quinn. He looked most bewildered.

~ *end of episode ten*

Episode Eleven
Sandcastles

Prolog

Asher followed the winding path through a thinly treed forest of birch, the branches bare and trunks white. Veiled sunshine streamed through and down to the thickly mulched forest floor. Ramos walked the trail some distance ahead. The others were following well behind Asher, with Costa bringing up the rear. It was quiet. No one spoke.

Ramos disappeared from Asher's line of sight as he rounded a bend in the trail. Half a minute later, Asher followed and almost immediately came out into the open. Ramos was already halfway across a sprawling meadow and was approaching a mansion that stood on the other side. Asher could just make out a lone figure standing atop the set of front steps, directly before an open doorway. At this distance, Asher could only guess that it was Church.

The others of the team came up beside Asher and they started across the field together. As they walked, they watched the figure at the top of the steps move down a step and greet Ramos.

Yes, it was Church.

"Thank God he's all right," said Susan. Church had gone through the portal quite some time before the rest of the team, and it hadn't been his idea. Susan had been in a quiet panic ever since.

"I never doubted it for a minute," said Asher calmly.

They continued to approach the castle-like structure.

"Them's some digs," said Costa.

"A bit upscale for my taste," said Asher. "It certainly takes the word *mansion* to a whole new level."

"No kidding," said Costa. "It's a freakin' castle."

"Look at that," said Lisa as they reached the foot of the steps. She was looking at the open threshold behind Church. "There's no door."

"Oh, but that's nothing, my dear," said Church. He stood as a doorman before the entry. "Take a peek inside."

Ramos, standing beside him, waited long enough for the others to start up the stairs, then turned and led the way inside. They gathered together in the middle of the great front hall. The walls and high ceiling were rough-surfaced and tan-colored. The floor was smooth, the color of dry sand.

There was no furniture. The walls were bare, there were no fixtures or outlets; there were no lights hanging from the ceiling.

There were no doors in the doorways, there was no window glass in the numerous openings that were set into the exterior walls and that let in natural light.

The group spread out and began poking their heads through the open thresholds to the other downstairs rooms. Asher started up a staircase with no rails. After three or four steps, he held a hand against the wall for support.

He stopped. He looked curiously at his palm, lightly brushed it with his other hand.

"It's all sand," he said as he tried to get the attention of the others. "The whole building is made of sand."

Episode Eleven / Chapter One

It had become standard operating procedure that once a base camp was established on a new floor that the group split into two-person teams and conduct an initial survey of the immediate area. So Costa sent two teams in opposite directions on the ground floor and then she followed Asher up the staircase to the second floor.

The rooms upstairs were as bare and empty as was the front hall. The compact sand of the walls, ceilings and floor felt firm and solid. The structure wasn't going to collapse around them. But there was no furniture, there were no fixtures; there were no doors in the doorways, the window openings had no frames or glass.

It gave Costa the impression of a sandcastle on a beach.

She and Asher worked their way quickly from room to room, looking for anything out of the ordinary; searching for potential threats, items they could use, and of course any sign of the portal to the next floor. Light streamed into each room through the window openings, spilling out beyond the rooms and into the wide hallway that ran the length of the second floor.

They reached the end of the hall and entered the corner room. It was large and empty. There were two window openings in one wall, a single, larger opening in another. Asher went to the larger window and looked outside.

Sparsely treed woods spread out across low, rolling hills in all directions. The sky was pale blue and brushed with bright, thin clouds.

The world was still.

Costa, standing in the middle of the room, turned about and took in the sight of yet another empty room.

"This snipe hunt is getting us nothing."

"They seldom do." Asher continued staring out the window. "I'm certain this place means something, that it has some significance. Every floor does."

"Church keeps saying. So what's this floor about?"

"I don't have the slightest idea."

"He says that a lot, too."

They both turned at looked out into the hall. There were raised voices echoing through the empty sandcastle. Costa thought she heard Ramos calling for her.

"You think they found something?" asked Asher.

"Or something found *them*."

§

When Costa and Asher appeared at the top of the staircase, Ramos called up to them from the front hall below.

"There you are. You're going to want to see this."

They hurried down the stairs and followed the corporal through a passageway and down the first floor hallway toward the back of the mansion. They joined the others of the team in a small room. There was an open threshold leading outside, and beside this a large window opening.

Through the threshold they could see a desolate expanse of hardpan dune, with occasional tufts of short, hardy bushes. In the distance stood another castle, looking very much like the one they were standing in.

"Interesting," said Asher. "That's not the scene you see from upstairs."

Church was at the window, an elbow on the sill. He pointed outside. "It's not the scene from this window, either."

Asher stepped to one side and glanced out the window. The view here was the same as that from upstairs; sparsely treed forests blanketing rolling hills.

He stepped back before the door.

"A portal?" It didn't look much like a portal. It didn't look anything like the portals they had grown so accustomed to these past months.

"That would be my guess," said Church. "Though not to the next floor; to the next castle."

General Wong was standing with Captain Adamson and the venerable Doctor Banister just in front of the opening into the first floor of the tower. The day was bright and clear and the warm breeze felt good on the skin. Of late they spent too much time either in the tower or in the Quonset hut. It was good to get out in the sun.

The general could see Quinn in the distance. The lieutenant had made his way fully around the tower and was walking now toward the picnic table in front of the Quonset hut. The man looked very tired.

He had appeared in the elevator just that morning, lost and confused, and they hadn't given him much of a break before putting him through several hours of debriefing.

The general wasn't sure what to make of Quinn's story. He had no doubt that it was all true, and it was great to hear that the team was alive and still moving up the tower, but the lieutenant had given them a whole lot more to chew on. There was a helluva lot going on.

And what about that elevator?

Was its sudden appearance due to Quinn? Had the Adversary created it for the sole purpose of delivering the lieutenant? Would it vanish just as quickly now that he was here?

Or was it intended to deliver them all somewhere else within the tower? Perhaps all the way to the Great Hall and the Adversary...

So the decision was made.

"Do you two have any immediate plans that you can't put on hold?" he asked. Adamson looked puzzled. Banister just grinned.

Quinn climbed up onto the picnic table and sat with his feet planted on the attached bench. He looked across the lot at the tower. It didn't look so good. It had lost much of its luster since he had last seen it from the outside.

It looked a bit old and worn out.

Coincidentally, that was exactly the way he felt.

He had no idea how he had ended up in the elevator. He hadn't even known there was an elevator. The last thing he remembered was beaching the freighter.

Maybe Owen had said something at the time... he wasn't sure. The next thing he knew, he was in the elevator car, heading down. It descended for what seemed like forever. When it finally came to a stop, the doors opened and there they were: General Wong and the command team.

Just at the moment, Quinn could see the general, Banister and Captain Adamson standing over near the base of the tower, in front of that entry into the first floor.

It was certainly not the same first floor that Quinn remembered.

Man, that was a really, really long time ago.

What do I do now?

He felt as isolated and useless out here as he had during his time alone atop that pillar in the void.

He didn't belong here. He had no function here. He belonged in the tower with the team; with *his* team.

What could he possibly do out here?

Over by the tower, Banister stepped away from the others and started toward Quinn. Quinn watched him approach, waited until he was near before sliding off the table and standing.

"Doctor Banister," he said, barely above a mumble.

Banister waved for Quinn to sit back down. Quinn sat, this time on the bench. Banister sat beside him.

"Don't you worry, Lieutenant. It does get better," said Banister.

"Doctor?"

"I know a little of what you're going through, you'll remember. I too was taken from the rest of the team and delivered here, left seemingly without a purpose."

"You were able to continue your research, working with Doctor Lake."

Banister grumbled dismissively. "Yes, yes. And for a time was able to communicate with Nate, as well. It's not the same thing. You know that."

Quinn stared down at his clasped hands. "I suppose I do."

"I do understand," said Banister. "Nothing we do here can compare to walking side-by-side with our companions across the floors in the tower."

"Brothers in arms," Quinn sighed, managing a thin smile.

"Exactly." Banister hesitated then. He shrugged. "But it does get better. We do find a purpose. We serve how we can."

"I'll do that," groaned Quinn doubtfully.

"You already have, my friend." Banister gave Quinn a pat on the knee. "The information that you brought back with you is invaluable to us. The data posits many questions and many possibilities."

"I *posit* a few questions of my own." Quinn nodded in the direction of the tower, the walls dull and scarred with what looked like withered portals. "You weren't kidding about the changes to the tower. What the hell's going on?"

Banister glanced toward the tower. "Opinions differ; differences which I'm afraid your tale only exacerbates."

They sat then in silence, staring across the lot at the tower, their individual thoughts drifting. Near the recently formed opening into the first floor, General Wong was alone now, appeared reluctant to leave. He stood with his face lifted to the sun.

Ramos stood watch on the sandcastle's front porch. The meadow was spread out before him, and beyond that the woods. A warm sun shone high in the sky above, paling the colors of the wildflowers in the field and lightening the white bark of the trees in the forest.

The front hall was visible through the entryway behind him. Inside, Church and Susan were sitting on the steps near the bottom of the staircase. Lisa stood beside them, leaning a shoulder against the wall. Ramos could hear their muffled voices but couldn't quite make out what they were talking about.

He sensed movement to his right and stiffened, relaxed again when he saw Costa come around the corner and walk toward the front of the building.

"What's the plan, Sarge?" he asked, once she had reached the foot of the steps.

"I wouldn't go enrolling the kiddies in school, if that's what you're asking."

"You don't like the neighborhood?"

Costa climbed the steps, turned around looked outward.

"It's quiet, I'll give it that."

"But?"

Costa turned about again and started inside. "Shopping's a bitch."

Church smiled warmly at Costa's approach. "Sara... the consensus here is that we move on. What do you say?"

"I would agree," she said. "There's nothing for us here. No food, no water."

"And the only portal is the one to the next castle."

Costa gave a sharp nod. "So, what say we see what's at that next castle?"

"Very good," said Church.

"Where's Professor Asher?"

"He went that-a-way," said Lisa. She indicated the downstairs hallway.

Costa started in the direction of the hall, spoke back over her shoulder. "We'll head out after lunch."

She glanced only briefly into each room as she followed the hallway to the corner room. She found Asher standing just beyond the threshold leading outside, actually within the portal, his back to her. His movements suggested that he was talking to someone, though there was no one there. He looked to be alone.

She crossed the room and stopped at the opening. She heard nothing, but he was definitely in conversation with someone. He was talking, and was responding to whomever he was talking to.

"Professor Asher," she called. He didn't react, apparently didn't hear her. "Peter," she said, louder.

He still didn't hear her. She was about to step through the portal when Asher took a step back, turned and came into the room. Costa had to step aside to let him in.

"Sergeant Costa," said Asher, somewhat startled.

"Professor," Costa nodded. "You mind telling me what that was about?"

Asher looked back through the portal. "The Acolyte," he said. "A bit overdressed, I should think."

Costa figured Asher thought she could see the Acolyte. She didn't bother correcting him. "What did he want?" she asked.

"I don't really know," he wondered aloud. "He was as cryptic as ever."

"What did he say?"

"Not much, really." Asher shrugged. "He seemed curious more than anything else."

"Curious? Doesn't he know, like, *everything* that goes on around here?"

"That's the impression I always had. Now though, I think he was a little confused."

Costa thought about what this might mean. "That doesn't sound so good."

"All I really got out of it was that we have to reach the Great Hall at all costs."

"Wasn't that already the plan?"

"Yes, but..." Asher hesitated. "This sounded ominous."

"Damn," grumbled Costa.

"Yes."

"I don't like it."

"No."

Episode Eleven / Chapter Two

Major Connelly was sitting on a park bench, a wide walkway running past her. On the other side of the walk was a freshly mown green lawn and beyond that a pond. There were several ducks gliding about on the surface of the pond.

The day was pleasant. There was a gentle breeze that kept the air from getting too warm. Connelly could see no one else in the park, but she thought she heard children playing somewhere.

But of course, none of this was real.

Connelly was afraid. She didn't know why she should be afraid, but she was. She didn't know how she had gotten here. She wasn't here and then she was. She couldn't remember where she was before she was here.

She couldn't remember *anything* before she was here.

That was what frightened her. She wasn't anywhere before she was here. This was the beginning.

And yet that could not be so. This couldn't be the beginning. There had been something before.

Had there not?

Far to her right then, some distance up the walkway, a figure. Someone was approaching. He had a tranquil, easy walk... serene, unhurried. He was enjoying this pleasant day.

It was *him*. The one. It was the Creator of All Things.

He was tall and slim, light-complexion and jet-black hair pushed behind his ears. He was dressed in casual dark trousers, a button shirt and a light windbreaker. His eyes sparkled, as if there was a constant smile somewhere behind them.

Connelly was no longer afraid. She felt calm. She felt at peace. Everything was going to be all right.

He reached the bench and sat down beside her, turned about slightly to face her more directly.

He placed a hand on her forearm. "You have done well, child," he said. His voice was as gentle as the expression he wore, sparkled as warmly as the smile behind his eyes.

"Thank you," she managed to say.

"The time draws near. There are things that you should know."

And so they talked. And as they talked, Connelly drew in the essence of the one as one might draw breath from the air.

When they were finished and Connelly knew the things that she should know, the Creator of All Things smiled kindly and gave her arm a tender touch before standing. He continued on his walk, enjoying this pleasant day. In moments, he was gone from sight.

And then Connelly was alone once again.

She had always been alone, here, in this park, on this bench.

But now... now it was all right.

By the time Asher got to the portal room, the rest of the team was already there and getting ready, donning their worn, frayed and faded backpacks and strapping on their utility belts with canteens and the occasional knife.

Costa started them through the portal, sending Ramos out first. Unlike the portals they were familiar with, the world beyond this one was visible to them, and watching Ramos step into that world was unsettling. It should have been comforting, being able to see what they were about to walk into, but it wasn't. This just wasn't the same, and in the tower what was unfamiliar was always unsettling.

Lisa Powell followed Ramos through, and Church followed Lisa. Once on the other side, each started along the path toward the next sandcastle, visible in the distance.

Susan hesitated. She looked through the portal, glanced back to Costa and Asher.

"Always hate this. Always."

"It'll be fine, Doctor Bautista," said Costa.

"That doesn't lessen the hate any," Susan said halfheartedly.

Asher shrugged a shoulder. "Hey, this time we see what we're getting ourselves into."

"Do we?"

Susan stepped into the portal, leaving only Costa and Asher. Asher mumbled in the direction of Susan's retreating figure.

"Hope so."

"Okay, Professor," said Costa. "After you."

"Thank you, Sara," Asher said with a nod, and stepped through the threshold.

The sky was a light gray, the air smelled stale. The others of the team were walking ahead of him, set a few paces apart, already beginning to stretch away.

Asher started forward, four or five steps behind Susan. Moments later, he heard Costa come through the portal behind him.

As he walked, a steady pace, a growing sense of discomfort welled up within him. Barely noticeable at first, it crept up and took hold.

This didn't feel right. The path they walked, the peculiar world they found themselves traveling through... it was... *not right*.

And then the discomfort grew heavy. The world began to weigh on him, but more than that, there was something very disconcerting happening. It seemed to Asher that with every step he took, Susan took two. And with each two steps that Susan took, Church took four... and so on up, for all those walking before him. Within half a minute of Asher stepping through the portal, the team was spread out in a long, straggling line. He couldn't see Ramos at all.

It became more and more difficult to walk. The air that Asher was moving through felt thick, felt rough against his face. He had to struggle to lift his hand and hold it out before him.

The air... it felt like sand.

Susan, now more than a hundred feet ahead, looked back at Asher. She said something, but it was impossible to hear her words. She pointed then. She was pointing behind him.

Asher looked back over his shoulder. He stopped and turned around.

Costa was thirty paces back along the path. She too had stopped and was looking back the way they had come.

The sandcastle, now distant, was disintegrating. The sky above it was dark and menacing, hanging heavy with ugly clouds. Great shifting whorls of brown rose up from the decomposing castle, the sand drawn up into the mass of blackish sky.

Back along the path, Costa waved for Asher to continue on as she herself started forward again. Walking looked to be as difficult for her as it was for Asher.

He turned and leaned into the thick, gritty air, took one step and then another. Susan was even further ahead now, the distance between them growing ever greater. The second sandcastle didn't look any closer.

He lowered his head, leaned forward and pressed on. As the seconds passed, his sense of discomfort grew worse. The increasing uneasiness came up from somewhere deep within him. It felt like the sand was on the inside of his skull as much as the outside. It tickled at his mind.

A figure appeared a few yards ahead and a bit to one side. The Acolyte was dressed in tan-colored flowing robe and hood, and had his mouth and nose covered. He was looking at the disintegrating castle in the distance behind Asher and was shaking his head sadly.

"This does not look good, my friend."

Asher ignored him, continued plodding forward.

Owen found Connelly standing some distance from the black tower, looking back at it, lost in thought and probably not really seeing anything.

"Major... are you all right?"

It took Connelly a few moments to respond. "I'll be fine."

"That would suggest that at the moment you are not fine."

"I'm fine," Connelly said gently.

Owen decided to let it go, or at least to look for another approach. She stood beside the major and studied the tower.

The blemishes they assumed to be misshapen portals leading who-knew-where were gone, had disappeared overnight. Yet the surfaces of the walls were not the gleaming black polish as before. The walls appeared now rough and faded.

If Elizabeth Owen had to put it into words, she would say the tower was dying.

And Elizabeth Owen was never one to shy away from putting it into words.

"It's dying," she stated, calm yet firm.

"Yes," said Connelly. "It would appear so."

This led Owen to another possibility. "Is our Adversary dying as well?"

"That is an interesting postulation."

And that was an interesting response, thought Owen. She would set that aside for the moment, as well. "Where would that leave us?" she asked. "What happens when we reach him, and the Adversary is... um... no longer in any condition to confront us?"

"Doctor Owen, you misunderstand. Adversary. The Adversary. He is not... *your*... adversary."

"No?"

"He is mine."

Whoa, that is most telling, thought Owen. "Okay. That begs the question. You are... who?"

"I am..." Connelly had to think about that, to let the truth come to her. The words came slowly. "I am of the one who sleeps. I am the manifestation of the one. I am..." she smiled then, but it was a haunting smile. "I am the dream given breath."

She hesitated again, turned her head slightly to one side. "We... have become adversary to the one who walks."

"So there's two?" asked Owen.

"There is one."

"But you just said—"

"There is one," Connelly stated firmly. "I am of the Adversary. I am of the one who sleeps."

Owen persisted. "And then there is the one who walks."

"Yes," said Connelly. "Adversary. The one who walks."

"The one who walks, and the one who sleeps."

"The One. The Creator of All Things."

And that was it. Major Connelly was finished. She continued to study the tower, seemed almost entranced by it. Owen looked more closely at it then.

There was something happening. She could swear there was something happening. She took several steps forward.

The wall... it looked... alive. There was movement. There was a thin, tan mist hovering just on the surface.

Owen continued to walk nearer. As she did so, she thought she felt something in the air. There was a grittiness to it. She stopped and looked back to Connelly. Connelly's focus continued to be the tower itself. Owen had to call to her to get her attention. She held out a hand, rubbed her fingers together.

"Sand?" she asked. "Major? Sand?"

Major Connelly finally lowered her gaze and looked at Owen. "I don't know."

"Oh, it's sand all right. But... what does it mean?"

"I don't know," Connelly said again.

They both turned at the approach of Banister and Lake. Asking Major Connelly if she was all right, she said only "Sand."

Lake gave her a blank stare, but Banister turned quickly to the tower.

"Oh, dear," he said.

Dr. Lake also then looked to the tower. Setting aside any further questions, such as where had the major been, "Perhaps we should be going," he said.

"Perhaps so," said Banister. "No sense having an elevator if we don't put it to use, eh?"

It took a bit of encouragement, but they finally managed to get Major Connelly to go with them. Owen followed along, unseen by all but Connelly.

The others of command were already milling about near the elevator, making preparations to move out. At the news of the most recent change to the tower, General Wong gave the word. Calm, but definitely an order.

"Grab your gear, everyone. We're heading upstairs."

At least that was the hope. They didn't really know if the elevator would work; and if it did, they had no way of knowing where it would take them.

To Banister's mind, that it would work and that it would take them upstairs were reasonable assumptions. He was first to the elevator. He pushed the button and the door slid aside. Standing to one side, the others started into the elevator.

Banister looked then to Connelly.

Connelly took a step back. "No. No, you go on ahead," she said.

Banister blocked the elevator door from closing. "Don't be silly. Time to be on our way, Major."

"I think I'll stay here awhile."

"Why would you do that?"

Connelly shrugged. "I don't know."

"Hmm. I see," Banister said thoughtfully. "A directive from above, then."

Connelly shrugged again. She wasn't sure. She knew only that she was to stay behind.

General Wong stepped out. "Major?"

"I'm sorry, General."

The general moved away from the elevator and stood directly before Connelly. He studied her a moment. "Quite all right, Major," he said at last. "If you think this best."

"Best, Sir."

A slow nod. "Very well, then."

Owen stood beside Connelly. She placed a hand on her elbow. "Oh, I guess I'll stick around for a bit as well, Major."

Connelly turned side-glance at Owen. "You don't have to do that, Doctor."

Banister looked to where Connelly was looking. "Doctor Owen, I presume? Staying behind as well?"

"So she says," said Connelly.

"Doctor Banister," the general urged, backing again into the elevator.

"Yes," Banister sighed softly. He stepped in as the others made room for him, continued to hold the door open. He looked to Major Connelly, said nothing further.

"We'll see you upstairs, Major," said General Wong.

Major Connelly gave the general a sad smile as Dr. Banister let the door close.

Looking at the panel, Banister saw only one button. He reached out and pressed it. There was a slight shudder and the car began to move.

The command team was moving up into the tower.

Episode Eleven / Chapter Three

Asher made his way up the front steps and through the threshold into the second castle. It wasn't until he was inside that he felt the pressure fade, the air grow lighter and less gritty. He was immediately able to breathe more easily, move without the sensation that he was pushing against a thick, membranous layer.

The main hall looked very much like the main hall of the previous castle. Lisa and Ramos were sitting on the floor with their backs against right wall, their backpacks beside them. Susan and Church were sitting on the bottom steps of the staircase. Susan didn't look well and Church looked concerned.

Asher slid out of his backpack and tossed it aside as he walked across the room. "Susan, you all right?"

Susan nodded without looking up. Church placed an arm around her shoulders.

"The journey across was rather difficult for all of us," he said.

Asher certainly agreed with that. He looked around the room again, then more closely at Susan. She looked drained. And she looked dazed. "Susan?"

Susan managed to lift a hand and wave dismissively.

"The fog is beginning to clear," said Church.

Asher scratched at his scalp. "That was unsettling, wasn't it?"

"And just what was it, this unsettling thing?" asked Ramos.

"I do have a thought," sighed Church. "I could very well be wrong, but... a thought." He pulled his arm back from around Susan's shoulders, leaned forward and placed his elbows on his knees. He gave a welcome smile to Costa as the sergeant came in.

"Is everyone all right?" she asked. She looked as though she had come through a great challenge still strong.

"Doctor Church was just about to tell us what it was we just experienced," said Ramos.

"Then don't let me interrupt. Do continue, Doctor." Costa slipped out of her backpack and set it down beside Asher's.

"Yes," Church went on. "As I said, I may be wrong. However, I do not believe that our journey from the previous castle to this one was a physical journey. I think the landscape that we traversed was in fact a mental landscape."

"Illusion?" asked Costa.

"Interpretation. We conferred a physical representation of our journey between castles as best our minds were capable."

"But the same interpretation?" asked Asher doubtfully.

"A shared landscape."

"This isn't like the floors, is it, Doctor?" asked Ramos.

"Nothing like the floors, Corporal. As ethereal as the floors we have come to know and love may be, they do have a real physical presence. What we traversed just now... did not."

The elevator door slid open. Captain Adamson and General Wong stepped out first, the others coming out behind them and moving to either side.

They were on the top landing above an open-air, Greek-style amphitheatre, with terraced rows of stone bench seating descending down to a small stage at the bottom of the half-bowl. Above them was a clear night sky filled with unfamiliar star constellations.

Banister turned at the sound of the elevator door sliding closed. It was set into a high wall that enclosed the back of the amphitheatre.

Sgt. Miller sent Johansen and Carmody to the right before he started in the other direction. Lt. Quinn asked if he'd like some company and followed after him. They would look for any potential threats and then a watch would be posted at either end.

Adamson and General Wong looked to Quinn's retreating figure before looking at one another, both wondering the same thing.

"He'll be fine, sir," Adamson said at last.

"I'm sure you're right," said the general. And at that they let the matter drop. He looked about them, at the rows of seats below them. "Ancient Greek amphitheatre," he suggested.

"Or someone's impression of one," said Dr. Lake. Lake and Banister were standing several rows below them.

"Why a theater, do you suppose?" asked Adamson.

"Show time," offered Banister.

"Yes," whispered Lake. He nodded thoughtfully. "This could be it, then."

"Perhaps she can shed some light on matters," said Wong. He indicated a figure that had appeared on the stage floor below. It was Elizabeth Owen.

"Let us find out," said Banister. He started down. Lake and the Wong followed a few steps behind.

"Elizabeth," called Banister. "So good to see you."

"Hello, Wes," said Owen. She smiled, waited then for Banister to reach the first row. "It is good to be seen."

Once down on the stage floor, Banister reached out and gave Owen a hug.

"Doctor Owen." General Wong was still several rows up. "You appear well. Might I ask... where is Major Connelly?"

"Hell if I know, General. We were talking, and then she stopped talking. And then she mumbled something, and then she was gone." She looked from the general to Lake and finally back to Banister.

"Ya' know, I was hoping for a little more enthusiasm. You don't seem all that surprised to see me."

Banister turned about and looked up into the rows of seating rising up from the stage floor. He spoke casually.

"I am not. I expected it; considering where we are." He cocked an eyebrow back in Owen's direction. "Just where are we, anyway?"

"Not sure. Somewhere on the eightieth floor."

Asher came into the front hall from the direction of the downstairs hallway. He found Susan sitting at the foot of the staircase. She looked a lot better than she had a few hours earlier. She glanced up at him.

"How're things looking, Peter?"

"I'd have to say this castle looks a whole lot like the last castle," said Asher.

"And I'd have to say it looks <u>exactly</u> like the last castle." Susan turned side-glance to Asher. "Do you think it could actually be—"

"That's kind of where my thinking is taking me." He sat down beside her. As they talked, a gray shadow drifted up the staircase behind them and into the upstairs hall.

A few moments later, Connelly stepped out onto the balcony of an upstairs room at the back of the castle. The Acolyte stood beside her. They remained silent for a time, taking in the scene before them. A sandcastle was forming in the distance. As it did so, a path began to take shape leading from one castle to the next.

"What brings you here, Major Connelly?" asked the Acolyte. "Shouldn't you be with the others?"

"I was drawn here."

"Ah. There are strange happenings, to be sure."

They fell silent again. Connelly finally turned to look directly at the Acolyte.

"I know who and what I am," she stated.

"I am glad. It should always have been so."

"And you. You serve the one who walks," said Connelly.

The Acolyte smirked. "To serve the one is to serve. There is no other. Though, meaning and direction are not always clear."

"Less so as the time of change draws near, I would imagine."

"Let us say that it is good that it comes soon." He indicated the landscape before them. "As is evident before us, the Creator of All Things has experienced complications during his recovery."

"I have sensed there was something wrong for some time, but have been unable to attribute these feelings to anything specific."

"All to be sorted out soon enough."

Major Connelly considered the Acolyte's tone. "You don't sound pleased."

"As I said, it is good that it comes soon."

"And yet?"

The Acolyte looked sharply at Connelly, then focused his attention again to the evolving landscape spread out before them.

"What of us? When the one who sleeps awakens?" he asked.

"I don't understand. What does it matter? There is but the purpose."

"The purpose," the Acolyte sighed darkly.

"As his manifestation in the waking world, I serve the one who sleeps until he wakes. That is my purpose."

From behind them, within the castle of sand, there came the sounds of conversation as the members of the team gathered together in the main hall downstairs. It was warm, and bonding... and alien.

"That is so," conceded the Acolyte. "But what will the awakening mean for you and me?"

She did not answer. In truth, she did not have an answer.

Banister and Owen had been sitting at the bottom row of the amphitheater for more than half an hour. Banister had said little during that time, leaving Owen to detail Connelly's revelations about who she was and of what she knew of the Adversary. Finishing, Owen leaned back and folded her arms.

"Interesting, eh? Worth the mystical reappearance of one such as myself?"

Banister furrowed his brow as he sought out some deeper meaning to it all. "One who sleeps and one who walks," was all he could manage to say.

"And let us not forget... there is in fact *only one*," said Owen. "Major Connelly was quite insistent on that point."

"A curious riddle. When is two but one?"

"Maybe the Adversary is dreaming."

"And while the Adversary sleeps, the dream walks? I don't think so. Too many questions it does not address." He turned and looked questioningly at Owen. "But you were there. You were in the Great Hall. You saw the Adversary."

"Hell, I don't know *where* I was. It could have been the Great Hall. It could have been the Great Bathroom. And I never said I saw the Adversary. I said I felt his presence."

"Hmm. So you did." Banister thought a moment. "So, which flavor of the Adversary did you brush shoulders with?"

"Hazarding a guess... the one who sleeps."

"Hmm," Banister muttered again. "Why so?"

"He seemed less antagonistic."

"I see." Banister scowled. "And we're dealing with the one who walks?"

"I don't think it's that simple, Wes," said Owen. "Remember what Connelly said. There is one."

"Perhaps two personalities fighting it out for control. That would explain the adversarial aspect to our little game."

Owen shook her head. "Eh... you're not thinking nearly alien enough."

Episode Eleven / Chapter Four

Asher waited outside the front threshold of the next castle, looking back the way they had come for some sign of Sgt. Costa. The air was filled with blowing sand and visibility was very limited. This latest crossing had been worse than the last, and as they grew further and further apart everyone had quickly lost sight of one another. Then, midway across, came the sandstorm.

Church came out onto the landing and stood beside Asher.

"Any sign of her?" he asked. Sgt. Costa had brought up the rear, as always, and she was still out there somewhere.

"Here she is now," said Asher. He could just make out Costa's silhouette a few yards beyond the foot of the steps.

Once they were inside, Costa scanned the faces of those in the room as she slipped out of her backpack. "All safe and sound; good."

"Welcome home," Ramos said cynically. "Same... damn... home."

Costa began brushing sand out of her hair. "So I see."

"Do we just keep slogging our way from castle to castle, knowing we'll always come right back to the same one?"

Costa looked to Church. "What say, Doctor?"

"Considering what happens to each that we leave behind, I wouldn't recommend staying."

"The castles do seem to be less than permanent." The last castle had begun to disintegrate while they were still inside.

"I still don't get it," said Ramos. "How is it we can see the next castle while we're in the last one, and the last one is always destroyed after we leave it, and yet when we go to the next one we always end up right back at the same castle that we just saw destroyed?"

"Careful there, Ramos; you'll hurt yourself," said Costa.

"As I have said, Corporal," said Church. "I do not believe we are at present in a physical realm. What we see is our interpretation of a mental landscape. The sandcastles, their disintegration and rebirth, and our journey between them, all are representative of what is happening at this moment in the mind of our host."

"If that be so, Doctor Church, then our host is one seriously messed up dude."

"Quite so," said Church.

"So what do you suggest we do, Doctor?" asked Lisa. "Keep on going? To what end?"

Asher had been leaning a shoulder against a wall, listening to the back and forth. He nodded now in the direction of the front entrance.

"I don't think we have a choice," he said.

Sand from the storm was working its way in, and the jam around the threshold looked to be dissolving.

"Okay folks. Break's over," sighed Costa. And with that everyone grudgingly got to their feet and grabbed their gear, began dragging themselves down the hall to the room at the back of the castle.

The view through the portal looked inviting. The world beyond was bathed in sunshine and clear skies. Ramos gave a thumbs-up and went through first. The others followed in the same order as always; Lisa, then Church, and then Susan. Asher gave a positive wink to Costa and followed Susan.

Once through, Asher started away from the castle portal, took in the warm sunshine and the brush of a breeze against his face.

He noted then something quite odd.

Ahead of him along the path was Dr. Church; and ahead of Church was Lisa and then Ramos.

There was no sign of Susan.

A clear plastic canister rested on a narrow table in the center of the amphitheatre stage. Standing beside the seven foot long canister were Major Connelly and the Adversary.

The Adversary was tall and slim, a light-complexion and jet-black hair pushed behind his ears. He was dressed in casual dark trousers, a button shirt and a light windbreaker. His eyes sparkled.

He was just as he had appeared to Connelly in the park.

He and Major Connelly were looking at the prone figure within the canister. It was also the Adversary; it was the Creator of All Things. He appeared to be sleeping.

The others of the command team had been scattered about the amphitheatre. None had seen just when the canister had appeared, but seeing it now they stood and slowly descended the rows of seats to the stage.

"Major Connelly..." the general said softly. "Who is your friend?"

"This is the Creator of All Things." She may have been referring to the figure standing beside her, or the figure in the canister. Perhaps it didn't matter.

"I see."

Connelly rested a hand on the canister. "The one who sleeps."

"It is a dream then?" Banister asked skeptically. "All of this? I can't believe that."

"No, Doctor Banister," Connelly stated. "Not a dream."

The one standing beside Connelly looked down upon the canister, placed a hand beside Connelly's on the plastic lid. "I sleep, and I walk."

Susan walked cautiously across a chamber of bright white floor and walls and high ceiling. The great room was empty but for a sarcophagus-like canister resting on a table.

Susan stood beside the canister, looked down at the face of the figure sleeping within. The Acolyte stepped up beside her. He was dressed in his monk robe. He pulled back his hood.

"Hello, Doctor Bautista."

Susan glanced briefly up at the Acolyte but said nothing.

The Acolyte looked warmly at the figure in the canister. "A kind soul," he said. "Quite gentle, really."

"Evidence to the contrary," said Susan.

"Yes, well..." the Acolyte smiled sympathetically. "There is much you do not understand."

"What am I doing here? Where are the others?"

"To be honest, Susan, I am a bit surprised to see you." The Acolyte stepped around the canister, placed a hand affectionately on the clear plastic lid. He looked in at the face.

"The Creator of All Things has been traveling the galaxy for thousands of years. An explorer; no... *a seeker*, a seeker of knowledge, of understanding, of wisdom." The Acolyte took in the room around them. "He survives the long journeys between the stars here, in this chamber."

"He's asleep?"

The Acolyte shrugged. "Awake, asleep... the same. His mind is always active."

"And this is a spaceship?"

"The one who sleeps and the ship are one."

"A mental connection?"

"There is but one. The Creator of All Things. The one who sleeps..." the Acolyte looked from the one in the canister to the room around them. "The one who walks."

Reaching the steps, Asher knew that this time it was going to be different. At first glance, the sandcastle looked the same, but it was a little out of focus, as though he was seeing it through a filter that put the image slightly out of kilter.

Taking the steps up to the front landing, he felt as though he was walking through a thousand spider webs. He couldn't help but brush his hands at the air as he went through the threshold...

And through a portal... leaving behind the bizarre landscape of the sandcastles and coming onto the eightieth floor.

Worn, tattered tapestries hung on the walls of the Great Hall. Hovering thirty feet overhead, a shadowy vaulted ceiling was criss-crossed with a pattern of dark, wooden beams.

A dilapidated, high-backed chair sat on a raised platform in the center of the hall. It was the only furniture in the room.

The others who had come in ahead of Asher had moved off to one side. Ramos and Lisa were looking at one of the faded tapestries. Church was studying the chair from a safe distance, his hands clasped behind his back.

There was no sign of Susan.

A tall shadow materialized beside the chair, forming out of a slowly thickening, inky mist. It had a vaguely human form, though it never stopped taking shape. It was as if the black of space was made of flowing, smoky robes shifting in a breeze.

Asher recognized the entity as that described by Carmody. She and Raso had faced the Adversary all the way back on the first floor. They had lost Raso.

Asher approached the entity. "Adversary," he stated calmly.

The Adversary's face took on a more human appearance. He tilted his head. "I am the one who walks."

Church was now standing beside Asher. "You are the ship then," he said.

"The one who walks," stated the Adversary.

"Where is Susan?" demanded Asher.

"Susan?" The one who walks sorted through the question. "Susan. Doctor Bautista."

"Where is she?"

"Doctor Bautista is with the one who sleeps."

Connelly and the traveler stood on one side of the canister, facing Banister and General Wong who stood opposite. The others were crowded about on the amphitheatre stage watching the exchange.

The Traveler looked up from the canister and directly at Banister, responded to a comment from the doctor.

"I travel the great distances between the stars by shifting from normal space to a layer of space consisting of billions of folds in the fabric. Rather than years or even centuries, I need only sleep for weeks or months."

"And thereby avoid the speed limit issue regarding the speed of light," observed Banister.

"The ship envelopes itself within its own bubble of space, crosses into folded space and travels along the folds, returning to normal space light years distant."

"Ingenious." Banister thought a moment. "I take it something went wrong?"

A shadow of weariness wafted across the traveler's face. "There was a malfunction when returning to normal space," he said softly. "I found this planet. The landing was... difficult."

"You crashed," stated the general.

"The bubble of alternate space surrounding the ship remains intact. I sleep yet, recovering."

"I understand," said Banister. "And the one who walks... the ship, is also... intact. And active."

"The one who sleeps," the traveler said, a hand on the canister. Looking outward then, "and the one who walks."

The robed Acolyte stood several paces from the canister, his outline forming a silhouette against the white walls in the white room.

"The one who sleeps reached out to intelligent life on Earth seeking assistance. The one who walks was hurt and frightened and didn't want anyone to come near."

"The one who sleeps reached out to us for help, as the one who walks pushed us away," said Susan.

"And so... the tower."

Dawn was coming, the sky above the amphitheatre turning from black to purple to dark blue. The horizon was burnt orange and deep red. Rays of early sunlight burst forth and streaked across the stage.

Dr. Banister walked around the canister and looked directly into the eyes of the traveler. "The tower."

Owen stepped up beside them. She too looked directly into the eyes of the traveler. "It was created by the ship."

"As the one who sleeps sought to welcome those who came, the one who walks used the ability to generate bubbles of space to create barriers to bar the way to the ship and the sleep chamber."

"A gauntlet," stated General Wong.

"A gauntlet, yes. A gauntlet of realities, born from your minds and from the memories of past worlds visited by the Creator of All

Things, to stand between you and the ship," agreed the traveler. "The one who sleeps has done what he could to help you."

"S'pose that explains the incongruities," said Owen. She turned to Major Connelly. "Why didn't you tell us all of this before? It would have made things a helluva lot easier."

"I did not know before," said Connelly. "I am a manifestation of the one who sleeps. I serve the one. I know what I am meant to know."

Susan stood now beside the Acolyte in the heart of the white room. "Why couldn't you tell us all of this before?"

"I did not know it before."

"How could you not know?"

The Acolyte looked somber. "I am a creation, Doctor Bautista. I know what I am meant to know, and no more."

"Now... now you know."

"Now it is necessary," said the Acolyte. He looked tired. "The one who sleeps and the one who walks grow weaker. As they grow weaker, faults and flaws form. Realities deteriorate."

Susan frowned thoughtfully. "Time is running out."

The inky shape of the Adversary flowed about the high-backed chair, the shadowy form shifting and shrinking and expanding. The face faded and solidified, again taking on recognizable human features. The eyes looked askance to Asher; the Adversary spoke to the whole group.

"And so... you are here," he said coolly. The form took on the motion of slowly sitting, arms resting on the arms of the chair.

Sgt. Costa entered the room. She quickly took in the scene, recognized that they had finally reached the Great Hall. She scanned the group, noted where each stood, noted their frames of mind by their stances.

Susan wasn't with them, but for the moment Costa held her silence. She moved to stand beside Church.

Church acknowledged the sergeant's arrival with a quick glance, kept his focus on their host.

"You are a most... *persistent*... species," said the Adversary. The shifting form appeared to shudder. "Your determination has been disquieting."

"We came at your invitation," said Asher. "Such as it was."

"The request was not mine, Professor Asher."

"Right. The one who sleeps. I got that."

The form grew darker, the words more bitter. "I do not want you here."

"That has been made obvious."

"You have nothing to fear from us," said Church.

"I am not afraid."

"We will help. Nothing more," said Church. "Please believe that."

The one who walks appeared to look down at his hand; the fingers appeared to grasp the arm of the chair. His words held a conceding tone. "It is possible the one who sleeps can be repaired."

Costa took another step forward. "But the ship cannot."

Inky tendrils stretched away from the shadowy form in the chair, drifted about and slowly drew back in. The face grew all the more opaque. The expression was grim.

"I do not think so."

"Oh my," said Church. "It is not us that you fear."

"You're afraid of dying," said Costa. "You're afraid of the end."

The one who walks continued to stare down at his hand. His fingertips brushed at the wood of the chair arm. He said nothing.

"This ship is already gone?" Asher wondered aloud. He moved now to stand just before the platform, the chair in the Great Hall. He looked into the eyes of the shadowy being as the Adversary looked down.

"The one who walks and the one who sleeps are one," said the being.

"You exist now only until he wakes."

The Adversary laid the palm of his hand flat on the arm of the chair, rubbed at the arm as he studied the movement, as he took in the sensation of flesh on wood. He looked hesitantly down to Asher.

"Professor Asher... what will happen to me?"

The morning sun faded. The shell of sky above the amphitheatre began to turn a dull flat gray. A heavy silence drifted across the landscape and over the ancient theatre.

Banister sensed something. He looked up toward the landing behind the back row.

A woman stood there, unmoving.

"Susan?" Banister moved tentatively across the stage.

Susan managed a smile. She stepped off the landing and began to work her way down the rows. Banister met her midway, wiping his eyes as he reached her.

"Hello, my dear. It is so very good to see you."

The others on the stage below gave them a few moments as the two wept and hugged. It had been a very, very long time.

"How's that old fart Nate holding up without me?" asked Banister, once they finally pulled apart.

"Doctor Church is holding up as well as you might expect. He is, after all, almost as cantankerous as you."

"So glad to hear it." Banister looked up past Susan. "And where is he? And the others?"

"We got separated." Susan looked at the stage. The canister looked very much like the one in the white room.

She realized then that it was in fact the same as the one in the white room; that the stage below *was* the white room; or at least a representation of the center of the white room.

"I was there," she said. "In the sleep chamber."

Those who had been milling about on the stage started up the seat rows to welcome her, leaving just the two figures standing next to the canister. One appeared to be the one who sleeps. The other was a woman in uniform with insignia showing her to be a major.

A third figure appeared at the back of the stage and started toward the canister. It was the Acolyte, dressed in his monk robe just as Susan had seen him only minutes before.

He ignored those scattered about on the amphitheatre rows. His attention was on the other two on the stage. He acknowledged the one who sleeps with a respectful nod before turning to Major Connelly. The two fell into hushed, intense conversation.

"Something is certainly happening," said Banister.

With the recent revelations by the Acolyte, Susan agreed that something was about to happen, and she was anxious about the course it might take.

Elizabeth Owen and General Wong stood nearby, the others on the rows above and below; all were now watching the scene play out on the stage below. They were more than familiar with the Acolyte, and most had some relationship with Major Connelly, as she had been a well-liked member of the command team for months, whatever her origin.

The general sensed something. He looked up behind them.

"Yes, I would call this a clear indication that something is indeed happening," said General Wong.

Susan and Owen turned and looked up to where the general indicated. Four figures stood along the back row: Costa, Ramos, Church and Lisa Powell.

"Well, hello there, kiddies," mumbled Owen.

"I see, I see," said Banister, a broad smile forming on his face.

"Where's Peter?" asked Susan, more to herself than to anyone else.

"Hey, Nate!" Owen called up to Church. "What'd you do with Peter?"

Church lifted an arm and pointed. Everyone turned to look down to the stage.

The canister was gone, and with it the one who sleeps. Asher was there, speaking with the Acolyte and Major Connelly. After a brief back-and-forth exchange, he continued across the stage. Quinn met him as he stepped up onto the first seat row.

"Hello, Professor. So what's the word?"

"Hey, Lieutenant. You look good. Well, on the bright side, I don't think we're gonna die today."

"Always a good start. There's a dark side, then."

"It kinda looks that way."

Asher smiled at seeing Susan coming down to meet him. Without saying a word he held out his arms and she stepped into them. They held each other until Owen let out a growling 'ahem'.

Asher pulled back, though he kept one hand on Susan's arm as he looked about at the others. "Good to see everyone."

"Yeah, yeah, gang's all here," droned Owen. "Are we going home, or what?"

"The Traveler is waking," Asher said, a bit of misdirection.

"Traveler?" asked Lake. Dr. Lake had been very quiet since their arrival in the amphitheatre.

Asher nodded in the direction of those still on the stage. "They much prefer it over the 'Adversary'."

"Oh, crap," sighed Owen. "We're not going home."

"Now, he didn't say that," said Ramos. He looked pleading to Asher. "You didn't say that, right?"

"He didn't answer the question," said Owen.

"Well?" General Wong folded his arms across his chest. "Professor Asher?"

The two teams waited. Asher hesitated. He looked around him. Some of the faces from the command team were new to him.

"Spill it, Peter," Owen growled.

Asher sighed. "I don't know the details, but there is a problem. It has to do with all those portals we travelled through."

"Oh dear," said Banister.

"Oh my," said Church.

"Each floor we went to was its own reality created by the Adversary. The one who walks. The ship."

"Yeah, we got that," Owen said impatiently.

"So... so the path from one of these bubbles to the next was through something they call a folded space layer."

"Yes," said Banister. "Folded space is how the Traveler traverses the vast distances between stars. He crosses from normal space into folded space, travels along the folds and then crosses back into normal space."

"That is also how we traversed floors. It was the only technology available to generate the portals between each reality bubble."

"What are you saying, Professor?" asked Lisa. "We're not on Earth?"

"We're on Earth all right," said Church. "That's where the ship is. That's where the sleep chamber is. And the Great Hall. And, I assume, this amphitheatre."

"Yes," said Asher. "Reaching the eightieth floor brought us back home."

"So... we're home. Good," Owen stated sharply. "Where's the door outta here?"

She knew, of course, that it wasn't going to be that simple.

"I'm sorry," said Asher. "Home isn't really home anymore."

"I don't get it," said Ramos.

"Crap, crap, crap," grumbled Owen.

"Of course," said Church. "Crossing into and out of folded space, and travelling the folds, traverses not just space, but time."

"Such is my understanding," said Asher.

"And we've done it eighty times," said Banister. "Reality bubble to folded space, travel the folds, and to the next reality bubble."

Owen was rubbing at her temple. "Again and again and again."

"How much time?" asked Lisa. "Years? Hundreds of years?"

"Thousands," said Asher. "So I'm told."

Everyone was stunned into silence. Several sat down, several wandered aimlessly along the stone rows. Each tried to sort out what this meant.

Family and friends were long gone of course, but more than that the world was now a very, very different place, if it was there at all. It wasn't just that it was no longer home; it was undoubtedly unrecognizable to them. Earth and the human race had gone on without them.

There was no going home.

The Traveler walked across the stage. He appeared very human, so was no doubt a persona created by the entity for their benefit. He held a hand out to Major Connelly, who took it and held tight. He spoke to her, looked to be comforting her.

He turned then to the Acolyte. After a few soft words, the Traveler reached out, pulled the Acolyte into his arms. He held him close for a long time.

He stepped back then and walked to the edge of the stage. He looked warmly up at those gathered in the amphitheatre.

"There are no words adequate to express my gratitude for all that you have done."

"Done? What the hell have we done?" snarled Owen.

The Traveler looked genuinely surprised. "Despite all the obstacles set before you, you persevered in your long journey here. Once in the Great Hall, you quelled the fears of the one sufficient so that I might awaken. You... saved me."

While he doubted that they had done much to actually quell any fears, Asher had to admit they had at least been there for the one who walks as he struggled to overcome those fears on his own. In all likelihood, it never would have happened without them.

"What now?" he asked.

Asher left his house an hour after dawn, walked down the street of the quiet neighborhood and turned up the main thoroughfare. He passed a once-empty lot that now held a large vegetable garden. A wire fenced enclosure at the back of the lot contained a chicken coup.

He knocked on the window of the café as he passed it. Elizabeth Owen, sitting at her favorite booth, held a coffee cup up in greeting.

There was a small meeting hall several doors down from the café that had been converted into a base of operations. There were several tables and desks about the room. A row of wall lockers on one wall held everyone's gear, and there was a changing room in the back.

There was a large map on the wall opposite the lockers. It was actually a collage of dozens of smaller maps and was growing larger most every day. Lt. Quinn was pinning the most recent addition to the wall as Asher came in. Asher glanced at it only briefly before heading over to his locker.

The neighborhood was detailed in the center of the map. To the north was the ghost town and beyond that the jungle floor and then the alien sea. To the west of the neighborhood was the office building. That one was odd. The elevator still only opened to the seventh floor.

There was a cemetery to the east, and a train station to the northeast. A train had yet to make an appearance.

They had only begun exploring, but they fully expected to find that every floor was here in this one reality; existed here on this single floor. There were still inherent dangers in many of these landscapes, but the more overt obstacles and threats of the Adversary were gone.

They had only seen the Traveler once since that day he first brought them here. He spent most of his time on his ship, hoped to one day repair it well enough to once again travel the stars.

As there was only the one reality bubble, the one they were in, that meant the ship was here too, somewhere. They suspected it was to the north of the alien sea, though that was really just a guess. It could be anywhere. But Church, Banister and Sgt. Costa had crossed paths with the Traveler during an excursion through a previously unexplored world that bordered the eastern shore of the sea. The Acolyte and Major Connelly had been with him.

So he had managed to maintain their existence here in the bubble. Until that chance meeting, they hadn't known the fate of either of them. It was welcome news. Owen in particular had grown fond of Connelly, though she would never admit it.

Susan came into the meeting hall and headed toward the wall of lockers. Quinn took a moment to wish her a good morning and good luck on their upcoming trip as he returned to his desk. She and Asher were part of the team that Captain Adamson was leading, that was starting out today. Along with Ramos and Lisa Powell, they would be traveling south beyond the desert island world, expected to be out for at least two weeks. They had already discovered a number of previously unexplored landscapes beyond the eighty floors they were familiar with, and hoped to find more.

They had no way of knowing how long they might be here. For now this was home, and it might be home for a very long time. They might never return to normal space.

They would make the best of it while they were here.

~ end of episode eleven

www.ingramcontent.com/pod-product-compliance
Lightning Source LLC
Chambersburg PA
CBHW021307250626
47155CB00002B/425